Moonstruck Madness

Laurie McBain

sourcebooks
casablanca

Published by Sourcebooks Casablanca, an imprint of Sourcebooks, Inc.
P.O. Box 4410, Naperville, Illinois 60567-4410
(630) 961-3900
FAX: (630) 961-2168

Originally published in 1977 by Avon Books, a division of the Hearst
Corporation

ISBN 978-1-61129-322-7

For my readers,
with affection and gratitude

The boast of heraldry, the pomp of power,
And all that beauty, all that wealth e'er gave,
Awaits alike the inevitable hour.
The paths of glory lead but to the grave.

—*Thomas Gray*

Prelude

Culloden Moor, Scotland, 1746

A NORTHEAST WIND BLOWING RAIN AND SLEET WELCOMED THE early morning watchers on the hill, their cloaked figures cowering together in vain for protection from the cold, penetrating wetness that seeped through to the skin. Some distance away, and farther down the slope of the moor, a lone figure crouched low in the heather.

Sabrina Verrick hugged her cape more tightly around her as she stared in horrified fascination at the scene before her. The battlefield was the only patch of color across the wide expanse of gray moor. Colorful blue, yellow, and green standards waved above the scarlet-coated battalions of the English king's army, its Union flag boldly flying in Scottish skies.

Sabrina raised her head and felt the icy rain fall on her face. In the distance she could hear the monotonous beating of the drums. Drums beating in time for marching English feet, bringing them closer to the bright tartan plaid of the clans. Below her Sabrina could see her clan with her grandfather stalwartly leading them. His bonnet, trimmed with eagles' feathers, was cocked jauntily over his weathered brow, the blues and reds of his tartan jacket and kilt now darkened by the rain; but on his left shoulder the silver and cairngorm brooch that pinned his plaid still gleamed richly. He'd drawn his broadsword and was swinging its double-edged blade threateningly before him. He stood tall and magnificent before his men as they awaited the signal to attack. A burnt wooden cross, tied together by a piece of bloodstained linen, leaned crookedly in the ground—silent now that the call to arms had been answered.

The haunting notes of the bagpipes echoed through the air as the fierce Highlanders surged forward to meet the enemy, their heavy broadswords singing as they sliced through the air in defiance of the shining bayonets of the English.

But few reached the English ranks before they were cut down by the roaring cannon ripping through the clans, dismembering and leaving only parts of bodies where once bold men had stood.

Sabrina screamed in terror as she saw half her clan wiped out by a single volley of cannon. Those who managed to escape the barrage of cannon fire were left to be cut down by the continuous, evenly timed musket fire that never stopped coming in waves of death and destruction. Sabrina felt the bile rise in her throat as she stared down at the massacre. Red was the only color that penetrated her numbed mind. Scarlet coats, bloodied swords and red-stained heather jumped before her eyes as English and Scot lay dying alike. It was impossible to separate the two enemies now. They were one surging mass of violence.

Sabrina narrowed her eyes, straining them as she searched for her grandfather among the men below her, praying that she wouldn't see him crumpled to the ground with the countless others. Where was he? Where was her clan? She stayed low, sinking down into the heather as she sought desperately for a sight of their tartan. She turned suddenly at screams behind her and watched in disbelief as English soldiers, gradually making their way up the slope, bayoneted the small group of watchers on the hill. They began to scatter in panic, running for their lives as the soldiers bore down upon them, ruthlessly cutting down everything in their path. Sabrina remained still, afraid to move at all lest she meet the same fate. As she silently stared at the battlefield she caught a flickering movement as a small band of men made their retreat through the mangled bodies of their comrades and the enemy, escaping the field of their devastating defeat. Three carried her grandfather, and what was left of the clan limped along behind, their broadswords still raised to ward off any attack from the rear.

They were not the only ones fleeing the moor. The battle had been lost. The clans were now trying to gather together what remained of their members and escape to safety in the hidden glens and lochs, losing themselves forever up in the craggy hills and unapproachable valleys that cut in deep chasms through the barren countryside.

Sabrina carefully fled her hiding place and followed. She ran as though the devil were at her heels, running until her breath came painfully and her legs felt leaden. She followed them up into a narrow opening that twisted and climbed until the slaughter across the moor was hidden from view, and made her way through the passage, her mind a blank until she saw a small sod-and-stone cottage, little more than a hut, some distance ahead.

"Let me pass," she told the guard blocking the door, his bloodied broadsword held defiantly before her, barring her way.

"Nay, lass, I couldna' dae that," he answered slowly, his blue eyes still dazed from shock. His face was darkened by streaks of blood from a deep wound beside his ear that was now clotted with dried blood the color of his hair.

"I'm the laird's granddaughter. I must be with him!" Sabrina cried, pushing past the beaten sentinel who gave easily and moved wearily aside.

Sabrina stopped abruptly as she entered the one-room hut. A peat fire was burning weakly in the middle of the room while an old woman squatted nearby, a worn shawl wrapped about her thin shoulders as she steadily stirred a rusted iron pot that hung over the fire. A sickening sweet odor of stewed mutton floated to Sabrina as she moved into the room.

It was quiet, deathly quiet, as if all the men had died. They watched silently as Sabrina walked to the far end of the room and knelt down beside her grandfather. She choked back the sob that rose from her throat as she stared at his broken body.

He was breathing heavily, an odd rasping sound that shook his chest in deep, painful shudders.

"Oh, Grandfather, what have they done to you?" Sabrina sobbed as she wiped the blood trickling from the corner of his lips with the edge of her cape.

"Grape. Tha' did it." A voice spoke sharply beside Sabrina.

Sabrina looked up into the blazing eyes of the man bending over the other side of her grandfather. His eyes were the only spot of color in his pale face. They glowed fanatically as they stared into hers, hatred pouring out of his soul.

"It wae like a thousand knives bein' thrown at us. They couldna' just shoot us doon, nay, they had tae cripple us with tha'," he said bitterly, indicating the rusty iron nails and leaden balls that littered the ground, shreds of tartan still clinging to some.

"Ripping us apart, aul tae pieces, nae knowin' wha' hit us." He looked down at Sabrina's grandfather, a frown between his eyes. "They even got the auld laird," he mumbled as if he couldn't believe it yet. He looked at his own bloodied hands, rubbing his fingers convulsively. "But they did nae get me pipes. I'll play for ye ever' nicht," he promised the laird. "They'll nae stop Ewan MacElden."

Sabrina was staring in alarm at the half-crazed man when she felt her hand grasped by shaking fingers and looked down to see her grandfather's eyes opening. She closed her hands about his cold fingers, trying to warm them as she looked into his face. It was devoid of expression and feeling, and she knew she gazed into a death mask. His eyes seemed to be pleading with her and she bent lower as his lips parted.

"Shouldna' come doon from the hills. Waur fools tae fight in the open. Slaughtered like sheep," he whispered, his usually perfect English now thickened with an accent.

"Please, Grandfather, don't speak," Sabrina pleaded, "we'll get you back to the castle."

Sabrina looked to the others who stood silently about her. There were only five or six of them, and she wondered frantically why they just stood there.

"Do something!" she screamed. "Can't you see he's

dying?" Tears wet her cheeks as she watched a shudder shake his once proud body, now powerless as he lay in his own blood. She flinched as his fingers suddenly tightened painfully on her small hand.

"Must tell ye. Knew this wae tae happen, but haed tae ficht. Go awa', lass," he struggled to say as he coughed up blood that oozed from his mouth.

Sabrina bit her lip as she fought for control. "I won't leave you here."

"Ye can dae nothin' tae help me. I'm a deid mon. Sabrina, lass," he implored her, "ye must get awa' frae Scotland. A ship on the loch tae take you tae safety. Go awa' an' take my grandson. His richt—his inheritance. For the clan and—" He stopped as another cough shook him, leaving him gray-faced and shuddering.

"No, I'll not run," Sabrina declared in a small, tight voice that throbbed with tears.

"Lass, ye forg't," her grandfather whispered, "ye be half English yesel'. Ye can leave. Nae one need know tha' ye haed been here. I planned it this way—ye must. I'll nae hae my bloodkin aul die with me."

"Someone's comin'!" the sentinel warned from beyond the door, his cry jolting the silent men into life. They seemed to surge like a wave out of the door, their claymores lifted for the last time, prepared to wreak vengeance before they died.

"Nae time," the laird whispered almost inaudibly. "Tae late. Sabrina, listen, child. Buried it, near the—" He choked, his face turning purple as he was seized by a convulsion.

"Grandfather," Sabrina whispered pleadingly, willing him not to die.

"Must tell ye the secret... false... the kirk... threads... gold... golden threads."

Sabrina jerked her head up as the old woman began to wail, her body swaying back and forth. Through the door she could hear shots and yells as the combat was renewed.

"Grandfather," Sabrina began, only to stop as she looked into his gray eyes that stared past her into nothingness. He was dead. She crumpled over him, her body shielding his as she cried in despair.

"Oh, Grandfather, why? Why?" she asked aloud. She raised her head from his chest and with gentle fingers closed his eyes and pressed her soft lips to his cheek. She felt something hard and cold against her hand and looking down saw his claw-handled pistols still hanging from his belt. She quickly removed one of the Highland dags and then the richly wrought silver dirk from his hip. Its sharp blade pricked her skin as she secured it in her bodice.

Sabrina turned around quickly, startled as the door was swung open and MacElden fell in. He closed the door sharply and rushed over to her, looking down at her as she held the pistol pointed nervously in his direction.

"Deid?" he asked quietly.

"Aye," Sabrina answered automatically as she had heard her grandfather answer so many times. She got to her feet slowly. "You'll see that he's buried with his broadsword and dag? That he's not left to…" She paused, unable to finish her words and the image they conjured.

"Aye, he'll rest wheer he should. On his own land," MacElden promised grimly. "They'll nae strip him like scavengers, nor desecrate him—nae the laird."

Sabrina shivered uncontrollably as she heard the fighting outside, wondering who the victors were. The old woman's wailing droned in her ears like a warning—but where could she flee? She was trapped with no avenue of escape.

She felt the pistol in her hand and wondered whether she would be able to kill any of them before they killed her. Or would they take her prisoner and torture her as they had so many others? Suddenly MacElden pulled her to the corner of the hut. Shoving aside a rough-hewn table and shabby wool rug, he knelt and removed several large stones, disclosing a small opening in the side of the hut.

"Quick with ye, through here an' oop tae the pines. Follow them tae the castle," he said, pushing her through the small space he'd made.

Sabrina glanced back over her shoulder at the dead body

of her grandfather and murmured a last farewell. "Aren't you coming?" she asked MacElden.

He drew himself up, straightening his shoulders. "I canna' run oot on the laird. He would nae ken wheer I be," he answered incredulously.

Sabrina nodded, then wiggled through the narrow space which opened into the back of a large wall of peat, stacked and drying for fuel in the winter months. Sabrina crawled along its length, then cautiously looked around the edge. She could see the pines standing tall against the barren line of hill in the distance.

Suddenly the ground seemed to shake as the loud, mournful wailing of MacElden's pipes began. All other sounds were drowned by the shrill, uneven notes of the bagpipe. Sabrina quickly fled the neat stack of peat and hurried into the protection of the pine trees, the pipe's lament still reaching her ears as she struggled up the hillside. She glanced back over her shoulder and began to cry as she saw the red and white coats of the English soldiers surrounding the little hut while other soldiers followed the few men of the clan who'd managed to escape yet again into the cover of the hillside.

Sabrina missed her footing and fell heavily, feeling her breath knocked out of her as she hit the ground. Struggling to rise she leaned against a rock as she pulled herself up, closing her eyes as she breathed deeply of the frigid air, feeling it burn her lungs as she tried to catch her breath.

Suddenly she stilled, a cold sweat breaking out over her body as she sensed that she was not alone, and slowly opened her eyes to stare at a pair of shiny, black jackboots. Her gaze traveled on up past the white breeches and scarlet coat, lingering on the drawn sword before coming to a halt at the face.

Sabrina's wide eyes stared in fascination into those of her captor, her lips trembling with fear.

The soldier sheathed his sword and then shook his head with its cocked hat perched high above his brow. "A child. Just a little girl," he spoke softly, almost to himself. His voice was very cultured and smooth, and some of the fear Sabrina had felt shaking her began to recede.

"I won't hurt you, child. What are you doing here?" he asked in a voice used to command, his eyes narrowing as he noticed for the first time the pistol she carried in her hands.

Sabrina swallowed nervously. "M-my grandfather, the laird. He lies dead in the hut," she answered, her fingers wrapping themselves around the trigger.

"I see," the officer replied casually, his body seemingly relaxed. "Why don't you put down the pistol. It's much too heavy for such little hands."

"I'd like to put a hole in you," Sabrina said shakily as she raised the barrel to the center of his scarlet-breasted chest.

"I know you would, little one, but that won't bring your grandfather back. I saw him fight. He was a brave man, but he was badly wounded, and he's better off to have died quickly."

He frowned as he stared at her upturned face, taking in the delicate features. What an unbelievably beautiful creature, he thought as he stared into the heart-shaped face with its huge violet eyes, and how ironic to discover such a perfect being in the midst of battle. He shook his head and raised his hand to touch her to make sure that she really existed.

Sabrina took a panicked step backwards as the English officer started to reach out. She stared at him, feeling hatred coursing through her veins. This tall, red-coated man represented all that she despised and feared. The memory of her grandfather's torn body suddenly surged before her, and with a small, anguished cry she pulled the trigger.

A deafening roar cut through the air, surprising Sabrina by its shattering effect and the violent jumping of the pistol in her hands. But the officer had read the hatred in her face and deflected the barrel of the pistol before she had even fired it, sending the bullet harmlessly through the branches of the pines.

"Run along, little girl. Run back to your family where you belong. God only knows who let you loose this morn. Hurry, be off!" he yelled at her astonished face, pushing her suddenly into action as she turned and ran, her cape flicking her ankles as she fled.

He stood silently under the pines watching her disappearing figure, a tightness about his mouth as he turned back to the clearing.

"See any more Highlanders, sir?" a soldier called out as he came running up the hill with an excited gleam in his eyes, his bayonet dripping blood.

"No, Sergeant, I saw no one up there," he replied coldly as he led the way back down to the hut.

Colonel the Honorable Terence Fletcher stared at the slaughter around him. The dead and dying were beyond his help, but he promised there would be neither looting nor massacre of innocents by his command and called to a stop the torching of the hut by several soldiers as the mournful notes of the piper still sounded from within.

"Follow those into the hills," he ordered, waving them away from the hut.

The sergeant beside him spat as he eyed the colonel speculatively. "What of the chief? They always dress real fine. Pity to let someone else lay claim to his finery, sir."

"You'll find plenty of others to strip, Sergeant. This one will be buried as is his right. Do I make myself understood?"

"Yes, sir," he answered surlily, "but what of the castle? Must be up here in the hills somewhere. Got orders saying we're to destroy any strongholds, don't we?"

"Yes, those are our orders, and we will do what is necessary to secure our position, even if it means destroying the castle," the colonel answered to the sergeant's satisfaction.

Terence Fletcher shook his head as the sergeant hurried off. What did he really expect from these men? Most were riffraff: poor, uneducated hirelings here to obey commands, treated like dirt and paid little more than that. He shouldn't be surprised that they wanted to get what they could when they saw riches within their grasp and while their bellies ached with hunger.

He glanced about him at the inhospitable hills and gray skies above and wished he were back in England. He'd rather be anywhere than here in these desolate Scottish Highlands where time seemed to have stood still and men still fought as their ancestors did three centuries past. Now their way of life faced destruction because of their foolhardy support of the Young Pretender, Charles Stuart, or as they fondly called him, Bonnie Prince Charlie. As successor to the long line of Stuart kings who had been driven from power in the seventeenth century, he now had the support of these Jacobite Scots in his vain attempt to overthrow the Hanoverian Georges ruling Great Britain.

As he stood staring at the tall pines, hearing the eerie notes of the bagpipe still coming from the hut, he saw again the face of that beautiful child and wondered what would become of her. Her face had, in an instant of time, etched itself in his memory. It was a face he would never forget.

❧

"Hurry, hurry for God's sake," Sabrina urged her aunt. "We've got to leave here now."

"But where is Angus? He really should be here," her aunt replied calmly as she carefully folded a delicate, lace-edged handkerchief. "I do so dislike hurrying," she complained softly.

"Please, Aunt Margaret. Just this once try to hurry," Sabrina pleaded with the older woman, who continued to carefully pack a few personal articles with unhurried ease. Her black hair was sprinkled with silver and neatly covered by a small, white lace cap, the puffed-out crown stiffly starched and high on the back of her head.

Sabrina shrugged in exasperation as Aunt Margaret smiled at her, blue eyes vague and dreamy in her soft, sweet-expressioned face.

"I never allow Hobbs to touch my sewing. She is quite incapable of packing it correctly—besides, I always have it with me. A lady never just sits and fiddles her fingers, my dear," she explained as she collected the rest of her items and put them in a tapestried bag.

"Sabrina!" a voice called, followed shortly by a young boy who ran into the room breathlessly. "We're ready. Mary is already belowstairs."

"Help Aunt Margaret down, I'll see to the rest," Sabrina said, quickly running from the room despite Aunt Margaret's disapproving stare.

Sabrina hurried down the worn stone steps of the large banqueting hall. The shields and arms of the past glory of the clan hung solemnly on the stone walls. There was neither fire in the large, stone hearth, nor food laid upon the long trestle table. The servants, those who had not fought in the battle, had fled to their families' crofts up in the hills. Hobbs, her aunt's English maid, would be the only one accompanying them on the fishing boat that would carry them to the coast and then to a French ship, waiting to sail with them to safety.

Behind her Sabrina could hear her brother Richard cajoling Aunt Margaret down the steps. Below in the hall Mary waited, nervously pacing with tears still wet on her pale face.

"Oh, here you are at last, Sabrina," she cried thankfully, her light gray eyes showing relief as she saw her aunt and Richard just behind. "I thought you'd never come. We must hurry before the English come. Oh, do hurry, Aunt Margaret, please," she begged her aunt as the woman stopped to check her bag for a second time.

"It's all right, Mary, we'll make it safely," Sabrina reassured her older sister calmly.

"Grandfather thought so too," Mary reminded Sabrina worriedly, a look of fear on her pretty face.

"I know. I was there." Sabrina looked around them regretfully. What would happen to the castle? Would the English burn it down, destroying it as they had so many other Highlanders' homes since the fighting had begun? The numbness that had paralyzed her feelings was beginning to fade as she took a last look at the ancient hall. Her grandfather's face would only be a memory now, along with so many other memories of this day and their life in the Highlands.

"Sabrina!" Mary called from beyond the doors. They had climbed into a small cart pulled by two shelties and were waiting impatiently. Their trunks had already been sent on before them, and now they would follow the narrow, rocky road winding through the glen to the loch. From there they would travel through the night on the river that would let them slip into the North Sea and onto the ship waiting for their signal.

Beware, as long as you live,
of judging people by appearances.

—Jean de La Fontaine

Chapter 1

England, 1751

A SHAFT OF YELLOW LIGHT REACHED ITS THIN FINGER OF brightness into the black night, a night otherwise devoid of habitation. The parting between the thick velvet hangings through which the recalcitrant beam had escaped revealed within a warmly lit tableau, isolated in apparent unconcern from the bleakness of the world existing beyond the exclusive and impenetrable barriers of those four gilt walls.

Exotic birds, flowers and cherubs gazed down from the high, plaster ceiling on the gentlemen below who sat laughing and drinking about the cluttered dining table, their glasses well filled with port and rum, and their appetites well satisfied from the meal they'd heartily eaten earlier.

"It's treason, I say," Lord Malton blustered loudly. "No respect for tradition. Bunch of bantam-cocks, the whole lot of them."

"What's treason? Not those Jacobite Scots again? Lud, I thought we'd finished off those heathens once and for all?"

"No, no, not the Scots. Wigs! Wigs, man, wigs. Those young jackanapes have the effrontery to forswear wigs. Going about bareheaded." Lord Malton choked, his face flushed pink under the mass of powdered curls that fell to his shoulders.

"Not wearing wigs? I say, how barbaric. Do give me their names so I don't mistakenly invite them to dine," sniffed another bewigged diner.

"I'd ask the duke to have a word with 'em, but look at that wig he's wearing. Hardly one at all, it's so simple. No, don't think he'd do it. Doesn't even shave his head," Lord Malton confided in a loud whisper to half his end of the table. "Personally, I do. Get a much snugger fit, and not half as much trouble with fleas.

"Wish he'd take them in hand. I've seen the duke deal with loose fish before." He glanced slyly at the object of his words before adding quietly behind his hand, "How do you think he got that scar, eh?"

They chuckled at the thought of a confrontation between the parties concerned and went on to discuss in detail the possible fate of the upstarts at the hands of the duke.

"This is an absolute honor, you know," Malton added to his neighbor, "to have the duke visit. He's never down this way much, but I've some land I'm selling and he wanted to see it first. Handles all these things himself. Bit odd, that." Lord Malton smiled indulgently as he looked at the duke.

The Duke of Camareigh was oblivious to the speculations of his powers of persuasion as he stared in boredom into the dregs of his glass, wondering why he had accepted Malton's invitation rather than putting up at an inn. How quickly he'd forgotten how outrageously dull these rustic supper parties were. He smiled cynically as he remembered that Malton was, after all, his host.

"What is so amusing, your grace?" Lord Newley demanded, a sour look on his dissipated face.

"A mere thought at my own expense, Newley, nothing more," the duke commented, the smile momentarily widening over his aquiline features, touching just briefly the thin scar that etched its way across the left side of his face, from the edge of his high cheekbone to the corner of his mouth. It added an almost sinister cast to his features, his expression masked in heavy-lidded, thickly lashed eyes that gave nothing away in a mocking glance.

"I hope you remember about our engagement for Friday? I intend to win back that pair of dueling pistols I lost to you. Finest pair I had, too. German-made by Kolbe. Shouldn't play against you, you're too damned good, or maybe lucky," Lord Newley grumbled, putting up a thin hand to straighten his wig, which was slightly askew above his sunken cheeks.

"It's not luck, but expertise. What else is a gentleman of leisure to do but refine his talents at gambling?" the duke replied lazily.

"And with *les jeunes filles*, eh?" Lord Newley snickered, giving a broad wink at the others.

"Wish you'd put me wise to that refinement, your grace," someone guffawed loudly.

"Ah, *donnez-moi l'amour*," another added dramatically, kissing his fingers to his lips for effect.

"Better not let your wife in the next room hear that," Lord Malton bellowed from the other end of the table, "or she'll teach you how to play the game."

No one noticed the velvet hangings move imperceptibly as if a draught had disturbed them, and none thought anything amiss until a masked figure emerged silently from behind their concealment.

"Please, gentlemen, no sudden moves. If you will just keep your hands upon the table like good lads, I'll not be forced to kill you," the masked figure warned as he motioned with the barrel of a pistol in one hand and a thin sword held deftly in the other. He stood brazenly before them, dressed in a black frock coat trimmed with silver braid, a silver brocade waistcoat and black velvet breeches. A tartan sash in vivid reds and blues stretched across his chest and was pinned by a cairngorm brooch to his pure white stock. Heavy jackboots reached above his knees, with spurs that jingled above the square, massive heels. On his head he wore a cocked hat with an eagle's feather stuck into its high brim. The upper half of his face was covered by a black crepe mask, the thin silk gauze covering his features except for the two holes where his eyes stared malevolently at the assembled guests.

Lord Malton jerked upright in his chair, an incredulous look of surprise spreading across his broad features. A murmur of shock passed through the room as the other gentlemen reacted similarly, dismay mixed with outrage showing in their expressions, except for one who remained casually at ease in his chair, the only visible sign of his anger the scar whitening along his cheek.

"Very wise of you gentlemen," the highwayman commented as they remained motionless as ordered. He laughed softly. "Now who was it who said that aristocratic gentlemen were shallow-brained half-wits? My apologies, gentlemen, for you are certainly showing a degree of intelligence tonight."

"Why you—" Lord Malton began speaking, rising in outraged dignity from his seat, only to be silenced as a giant of a man slipped from behind another curtained window, two cocked pistols held firmly in his fists, while another equally large man stepped out from behind the first highwayman, dwarfing him in contrast. They were also masked, but dressed in leather breeches and waistcoats, covered by black frock coats while their legs were encased in enormous jackboots.

"Yes, my good lord, you were saying?" the masked man asked softly, then laughed with amusement as Lord Malton slumped back onto his seat.

"You'll pay for this, Bonnie Charlie, you'll hang from the gibbet for this deed," Lord Malton sputtered angrily, a gasp of surprise coming from the diners as their assailant was named.

"You have to catch me first, and the English are better with words than deeds."

"You swine. This is an outrage." Lord Newley snarled, his face turning a mottled color in his rage.

"No... this is a robbery, and I intend to relieve you gentlemen of some of your pretty trinkets. And unless you wish me to disturb your ladies, who are busily gossiping in the blue salon, I believe you call it, then you will keep quiet and allow me to get to my work." He grinned devilishly. "No comment? Excellent. Obviously you find no fault with my reasoning."

The large bandit standing behind Bonnie Charlie stepped forward and held out a leather bag.

"The small gold ring, I think, and possibly the watch,"

Bonnie Charlie directed. "Ummm, yes, definitely the watch. A bit too ostentatious, I should think, Lord Newley. Try an enameled one next time. These rubies and diamonds are much too large."

Lord Newley clenched his hands as if he held the highwayman's neck between his fingers, and glared impotently up at the robbers as they made their way down the table, selectively picking only one or two items from each gentleman, leaving the rest untouched. As Bonnie Charlie came abreast of the long side table still laid with food he sampled a pastry off one of the china plates.

"A bit too sweet for my tastes," he commented as he dusted the fine sugar from his coat sleeve, picking up his sword where he had carelessly placed it on the buffet. "Now, what have we here? No jewels or pretties for the poor?" Bonnie Charlie demanded as they halted beside the duke.

"Come now, don't be shy," Bonnie Charlie requested genially. The duke's eyes stared like burning coals in his face as he shrugged and handed over a gold snuffbox and gold watch from his fob pocket.

"Our scar-faced gentleman is very wise," Bonnie Charlie said tauntingly, "for he fears having his other cheek marred as well."

The duke's jaw visibly hardened as he looked up into the highwayman's eyes, shadowed by the mask, and drawled, "I look forward to meeting you again, Bonnie Charlie, when my sword shall feel more than your cheek beneath its point." His voice was low and quiet, yet held a definite threat in it to all who heard it

But the highwayman only laughed in the same husky whisper as his voice. "Indeed?" he replied doubtfully. "Most of you exquisites wouldn't know which end of a sword to pick up, much less how to wield it."

"Of all the impudence. I'll have your head for this," Lord Newley threatened.

"Will you really, my lord? So bloodthirsty over a few trinkets that you can well afford? Be glad I don't take it all and leave you impaled against the back of that satin chair. But now I think I must give you more reason for desiring my head. I rather fancy that diamond stock buckle," he jeered as he snipped it from Lord Newley's chest with the point of his sword.

"And, Lord Malton, as my host, I'll relieve you of that charming silver saltcellar."

The silver saltcellar was added to the bag of loot by the duke, whose lips twitched slightly as he also added Lord Newley's stock buckle.

"You smile, my scar-faced friend," the highwayman observed dryly, "but I think I like yours as well... if you'd be so generous?"

"By all means." The duke's grin widened. "I compliment you on your good taste. But you have it on loan, for I shall redeem it in due time."

"I look forward to the transaction with pleasure," the highwayman grinned, revealing straight, white teeth, not in the least cowed by the obvious challenge of the scar-faced gentleman's words.

With a slight bow Bonnie Charlie backed toward the window, his henchmen's pistols still trained on the captive audience. "I bid you *adieu*, gentlemen, and my compliments to your ladies."

With that final insult he disappeared from sight through the windows, followed quickly by the other two robbers. For an instant all was still, then Lord Newley cursed violently and made to rise, Lord Malton following, when a flash of silver sped past their startled faces and a knife embedded itself with a thud in the middle of the table.

"Good God," Malton mumbled, searching for his pocket handkerchief carefully, lest another knife should find its way into his chest.

"I wonder what the fellow does for an encore," the duke commented as he slowly stood up and stretched lazily, feeling oddly refreshed by the strange incident.

The others stared at the duke, mesmerized for a moment, and then in relief broke into confused conversation with no one voice being heard.

The duke stood silently looking out of the window, a meditative look in his eyes and a slight smile on his lips.

"An outrage. The insolence of that blackguard. I'd have run him through if I'd my sword," Lord Malton muttered, pouring himself a drink with shaking hands.

"The Jacobite cur. Flaunting his plaid before us. He's an agent of that rogue Stuart, I'll wager. I say call out the militia on him. They'll run him to earth soon enough."

"Haven't caught him yet," someone commented, "nor would I care to cross swords with those two great hulking henchmen of his, either."

The duke turned from his contemplation of the night, listening with interest to the gossip. "What was that name again of this highwayman who seems to elude capture so effortlessly?"

"Bonnie Charlie they call him, because of the blasted plaid sash he wears across his chest and the eagle's feather in his hat. Mocks us all, damn his eyes if he doesn't, the Highland savage."

The duke smiled thoughtfully. "And yet he talks and acts like the perfect gentleman. Quite a puzzle, wouldn't you say? How long has he been about?"

"Three, maybe four years, I suppose," Lord Newley answered. "Cursed nuisance. Third watch he's had off me."

"And yet no one has any idea who he really is? Never seen his face, or even tracked him down? How obliging of him," the duke murmured, "that he only takes a few items at a time. Certainly not greedy, is he?"

"That's just it. Damned impertinence. Makes me feel overdressed half the time."

"Has he murdered anyone?"

"Wouldn't be surprised to hear he had, although I couldn't say for certain," Lord Malton answered grudgingly.

The duke straightened the lace of his cuff, then automatically reached for his snuffbox only to remember it had been taken. Shrugging off his irritation he said, "I would advise we join the ladies. They must be wondering by now what is amiss."

"The ladies! Good God, forgotten all about them," Malton gasped, rapidly rising to his feet. "Shouldn't tell them, but don't know how I'll keep it from my wife. Knows everything, that woman, yes she does. Come along, mustn't keep them waiting, eh?"

The duke watched as they filed out, still talking amongst themselves in excited undertones. Then, walking over to the table, he removed the knife from the center. He examined the hilt, touching his finger gingerly on the sharp tip, and with a reluctant smile dropped it back on the table and followed his host from the room.

❧

"Lud, but did you see ol' Malton's plump face when we interrupted his party?" Bonnie Charlie chuckled in amusement. "And Lord Newley's look when I relieved him of his watch. What is it, the third or fourth one now that we've taken?"

"Third, I think, Charlie," one of the big men answered seriously.

"Yes, well, I'll have a sixth and a seventh from him before I'm through, eh, John?"

"That's the truth, Charlie. Really showed them gentlemen tonight. Thought Will was going to have to shoot the fat one."

"No shooting, remember," Bonnie Charlie warned. "We'll not have murder charged against us as well. Once we've killed, especially a gentleman, this whole country will be swarming with militia. It's bad enough as it is."

They urged their horses along the hillside, avoiding the road below where there would be patrols. The scent of sweet, wild strawberries and honeysuckle was strong in the night air as they traveled through the woodlands and pushed their way through the bramble bushes and thick shrubs. Suddenly the horses shied nervously, frightened by the shadowy figure seen dimly ahead. Bonnie Charlie narrowed his eyes, the mask he wore obstructing his view. The figure seemed to be coming nearer, and yet it remained where it was.

"What is it?" Will whispered nervously, holding tight to the reins of his reluctant mount.

An owl hooted softly as they approached cautiously and viewed the suspended object.

"Lord, but it's Nate Fisher," John said, recognizing the figure that hung from a gnarled branch of an oak, a rope drawn tight about his neck.

"Dead."

"He was poaching again, but this time they caught him," Bonnie Charlie spoke softly as he saw the rabbit tied to the dead man's neck.

"What else was he to do? His family's starving. Five little ones to feed and a sick wife." Will spoke angrily.

"That be true, and this once being the common land until Lord Newley and Lord Malton took it over and closed it off. What's a fellow to do? Watch his family starve?"

"I know, Will, it's unjust. There they sat stuffing their faces while poor Nate swung here in the night, just because he was trying to feed his family. I wish now I'd taken everything from them instead of leaving them with their pockets still half-full. I swear I'll make up for it next time," Bonnie Charlie promised. "Cut him down. He'll not be a carcass for the crows to pick clean. You know the Fishers well, John, take him home. Half of our profit tonight goes to them," he added, then urged his horse ahead and slowly disappeared into the trees, leaving John to see to the body.

Bonnie Charlie and Will cautiously threaded their way down into a small, wooded valley, hearing the murmur of several creeks, the bubbling sound of the water cascading through the trees muffling the noise of their horses. Crossing into the soft bottom of one of the creek beds they hurried their horses, the muddied water from the horses' hooves quickly clearing as fresh water fed into it. The horses splashed through the water as the highwaymen followed the stream for a short distance, past several bends and overhanging banks until it widened, becoming sedentary and stagnant, overflowing into an expanse of inaccessible marshland.

In the center of the marsh was a firm rise of ground where a small stone hut stood sheltered under the camouflaging limbs of a large willow. Tying their horses to the dangling branches they entered the hut, standing still in the darkness until Will, fumbling with his tinderbox, managed to strike a spark with a piece of flint against steel and as the tinder flamed, lit the short candle that he'd drawn from his pocket.

The sparse, shabby furnishings of the hut were thrown into shadowy light by the flickering flame. Dark hangings of shag hung over the open windows, shielding the revealing light from any prying eyes in the night.

"Quite a booty, Charlie," Will chuckled as he emptied the bag of jewelry onto the rough wooden table. His smile thinned, however, as his thick fingers came in contact with the emerald stock buckle of the Duke of Camareigh. "Wish you'd not baited the scar-faced gent. Don't like the looks of him. He's no lily-livered fool, that one. Didn't recognize him either," Will puzzled, rubbing a hand over his stubbled chin.

"Some fancy coxcomb from town, out for a little country air, no doubt." Bonnie Charlie dismissed him with a contemptuous shrug.

"I don't know, Charlie. I didn't like his eyes, nor that mean grin on his face." Will shook his massive shoulders. "Mark my words—he means trouble."

"A carpet-knight, no more than that, Will. What can one of those town toffs do to me?" the highwayman laughed derisively. "Slap my face with a scented hankie and call me out? No, I think not. They hold no threat to us. After all, what have those fine gentlemen accomplished these past years? I still roam freely, no shackles or hangman's noose for me."

He bent suddenly and scooped up the emerald buckle in his gloved hand. Tossing it in the air, he amusedly said, "It's a beauty and will fetch us a fair price. I must admit the previous owner did indeed have good taste."

"Maybe, but I still don't like it," Will said stubbornly.

"Oh, come now, Will. You're not superstitious about this little shiny thing?" he teased.

Will remained silent, a brooding look on his usually cheerful features. "It bodes no good for us, I say."

"I'll remember your dire predictions when I pocket the handsome profit, and you needn't take your share of it if you're still superstitious about it." Bonnie Charlie laughed as he watched the sudden change on the big man's face.

"Well, now, I didn't say I was that worried about it,

Charlie. I'm not letting some city swell cost me my fair share," he rallied, stiffening his spine as he stretched to his full six-foot-five frame.

"That's the spirit, Will. Now you know what to do. Take these to London and our Mr. Biggs. He'll sell them and get a good price, and I think we might manage a little higher price than last time, eh, Will? Biggs isn't above trying to hoodwink us," he warned.

"He won't try anything on me and John. He knows better. Values his serpent skin too much to double-cross us."

"Good, and let me know if you hear any other news. You know what I'm waiting to hear about."

"Sure, Charlie, I'll let you know."

"All right then; a good night's work, I'd say. Let's be off."

Charlie bundled up the jewelry, stuffed the bag into an old sack, then handed it over to Will, who wedged it behind a loose stone in the wall. Snuffing out the flame between a large thumb and forefinger, Will followed Bonnie Charlie from the hut, his premonitions of disaster left behind with the loot. They traced their way back through the marshy ground with difficulty, and then up into the trees and away from the wooded valley, riding fast through the countryside.

Silently they entered an apple and cherry orchard, coming quickly to the walled end, beyond which lay a garden. The sweet fragrance of climbing roses hung heavy in the still night air and invaded Bonnie Charlie's senses as he climbed from his mount's back to the top of the stone wall. He waved, waiting as Will led the horses off, then jumped down on the garden side with a slight thud. He made his way easily through the rows of daffodils and roses to a large rhododendron hedge hugging the house. Slipping past it he moved behind to a recessed area beside the brick chimney. Sliding back a false, half-timbered section of brick he entered the house unobtrusively. Making his way through a short, dark passage well-swept of dust and cobwebs, he came to a panel and locating the latch slid it open and entered a dimly lit room. The embers of a fire glowed faintly from the large fireplace and did little to lessen the chill that rose from the parquet-tiled floor. He slid the panel securely back into place. The false wall of the fireplace looked undisturbed before the massive oak table that sat squarely in the middle of the hall. Climbing swiftly up the oak staircase, he silently made his way through a small gallery and then quietly entered a sleeping chamber, closing the doors behind him. A fire burning in the grate lighted the room, revealing a carved oak bedstead with dark blue velvet curtains partly drawn to keep out the draughts.

Charlie glanced longingly at the embroidered silk quilt that covered the bed and the plump pillows covered in matching embroidered silk. He ignored the invitingly turned down bedclothes and went to stand before a small mirror hanging on the wall.

"You're later than usual." A soft voice spoke from the bed, and then two slimly arched feet appeared, followed by a white, nightclad figure.

Bonnie Charlie turned with a smile on his face. "Late, but we had a very profitable evening."

The woman slid from the warmth of the bed and hurried over to the fireplace, where several kettles were steaming. "Even in summer these floors pick up a chill." She removed a large kettle and poured the steaming water into a tub, adding another, followed by a can of cold water. She placed a warm towel close to the tub, then sat down on a tapestried chair, curling her legs beneath her as she stifled a sleepy yawn.

"I wish you wouldn't wait up for me," Bonnie Charlie told her as he began to pull his black chamois gloves from his hands, tossing them carelessly into an oak chest. He carefully placed his weapons on the floor of the chest, and with amusement flickering in his eyes he removed the concealing mask from his face.

"You know I can't sleep until you've returned safely," the woman replied.

"I thought you'd know that without having to see me," the highwayman answered with a laugh, his eyes no longer shadowed by the mask lightened now to their true violet-blue color.

The black cocked hat followed the gloves and mask into the chest. With slender fingers the highwayman carefully removed the powdered wig he had worn beneath his hat and placed it into the chest. Straightening up, he shook his head, loosening the thick mass of blue-black hair that curled down below the fitted waist of the full-skirted coat.

The mirror on the wall reflected the creamy smoothness of the highwayman's face with delicately molded features; the nose short and slightly tip-tilted above curved lips and a dimpled cheek.

Shrugging from the loose-fitting frock coat and waistcoat, he folded them into the chest and stretched indolently, the fine, white lawn shirt tautening over the smooth outline of firm, rounded breasts.

Where before a masked highwayman had stood, the mirror now reflected an incredibly beautiful woman standing before it. Her cheeks were flushed rosily and her lips parted in remembrance of the night's excitement as she turned to face the nightgowned figure.

"You constantly amaze me, Sabrina," Mary said from her curled-up position on the chair. Her red hair hung in a thick braid over her shoulder and her gray eyes were bright with mischief. "I sometimes have the sneaking suspicion that you really enjoy masquerading as Bonnie Charlie."

Sabrina laughed gaily. "Not always, especially when I have to pull off these heavy boots." She sat down tiredly on a chair and struggled to free one of her legs.

Mary jumped up and helped her pull, laughing as she fell backwards carrying the boot with her. After the other boot had finally been removed, Sabrina rolled down the thickly knitted, worsted stockings that protected her soft skin from the chafing leather, revealing slim legs and small feet. She quickly removed the tight black breeches and full-sleeved shirt, then twisted her thick black hair into two braids and pinned them on top of her head.

Closing the carved lid of the chest, Mary glanced about

the room, reassuring herself that nothing remained of the highwayman, Bonnie Charlie.

Sabrina gratefully slipped into the warm water of the tub and relaxed, letting the sweet-scented bath oil Mary had added soak into her body. With her hair pinned up she looked like a small child as she yawned widely.

"I'm glad we don't have to do this every night, or I'd be swooning over the breakfast table," Mary said, curling back up in her chair as she waited for Sabrina to bathe.

"I do really appreciate your waiting up for me. It's good to know that you're here and I can talk to you."

"Have you ever thought what an odd life we're leading?" Mary asked. "I do wish sometimes that we could just live normally like everyone else."

"Because of our odd life, Mary, we are able to live normally," Sabrina contradicted. "We live very simply compared to others, and even that takes money."

"Oh, I know, Rina, and I'm not complaining, truly I'm not," Mary reassured her, "It's just this gnawing fear and worry that you'll be shot or captured. I suppose it's my own guilty conscience but I'm constantly in fear of letting something slip."

"I know how you feel. I'm tired too," Sabrina confessed. "But what can we do? This is our only means of support. Do you imagine I'd do it otherwise?"

Mary looked at Sabrina's set face, hesitating for an instant before she replied reluctantly, "Well, maybe. You are a bit of a devil, Rina."

"Mary!" Sabrina cried with an indignant laugh, splashing water on her playfully. "Of course I must admit I do so enjoy seeing my lords Malton and Newley's faces when I have them at sword point." Her eyes darkened at the thought of them and she angrily wrung the soapy cloth free of water.

"What is it?" Mary asked in concern, seeing the look on her sister's face.

"We found Nate Fisher in the woods tonight. He'd been caught poaching, and for his punishment he was hanged by the neck."

"Oh, no," Mary breathed.

"Oh, yes," Sabrina assured her in a hard voice. "Do you remember how we hated all of these people when we first came here? They were all the same to me, and I hated the lot of them. But gradually that changed as I came to know them, and I discovered that people were pretty much the same no matter where you were. The poor and underprivileged still going hungry and the rich that bully them still getting away with it."

"Do you know, Rina," Mary confided, "I've come to love it here. I want to stay here always. We won't go back to Scotland, will we?"

Sabrina shook her head regretfully. "There's nothing to go back to. This is our home now, Mary."

Mary smiled with relief. "I never thought I'd hear you say that. I've always loved this house, especially when Mother was alive and we were just little girls. Remember playing in the orchard and stealing apples?"

Sabrina laughed. "Yes, very well. And I haven't mended my ways, have I? I didn't want to think of those days when we first returned to Verrick House. I was so full of hate and revenge that I didn't want to remember the nice things about it. But now that I'm seventeen I can look at life differently, more objectively than when I was a little girl, and I can accept both my memories and the present."

"It's taken you a while," Mary said.

"Ah, but then we were hardly made welcome, were we? I don't think the marquis' solicitor could really believe his eyes when we stormed into his offices. Do you know, I think for the first time in his life he was actually speechless. The marquis probably had neglected to inform him that he had children."

"You'll never call him Father, will you?" Mary asked curiously.

Sabrina looked at her steadily. "And why should I? He's no father to us. Why, he's never seen his only son and heir. No, he can stay in Italy with his rich contessa as far as I'm concerned. In fact, I would say we've been exceptionally lucky that he's been living abroad. Do you think he would've taken us in with welcoming arms? He's hardly proven himself to be paternal."

Sabrina laughed harshly. "He would have sold Verrick House by now if he had to pay the upkeep and taxes. If it weren't for my unlawful activities, we would most likely be in debtors' prison. I haven't forgotten how things were that first year we came here and tried to survive without outside help."

No, Sabrina thought to herself, she hadn't forgotten their first year in England. Five years had now passed since her grandfather had died, so long ago that she sometimes wondered if they'd ever lived in Scotland. And then she would have one of the nightmares. She would see again the blood-soaked heather and tartan, smell the death and fear on the moors, the scene haunting her nighttime dreams. She would waken, feeling that choking, horror-filled fear that left her sweating and gasping for breath, her body shaking uncontrollably.

So long ago, yet still so vivid. They had sailed away from the destruction in the Highlands. The slaughter of men, women and innocent children. The burning and sacking of their homes. Sometimes she wondered what had been the fate of the castle.

They had arrived safely in England, Aunt Margaret and Mary ghastly ill with seasickness from the turbulent crossing, Richard fretful and confused, and herself so full of hate she could scarcely conceal it from the English coachmen and innkeepers they'd dealt with on their journey to Verrick House.

The ancient family home had been uninhabited and inhospitable. The marquis, their father, whom they had not seen in the ten years since his Scots wife had died, had long ago abandoned it for the more refined atmosphere of London life and countless other diversions.

But their hard work and determination had made a home out of the small Elizabethan manor house that had changed little over the past two hundred years. The high gables, mellow brick and mullioned windows gazed down on a garden and orchard overgrown with weeds and fields that had lain fallow year after year. But the richly carved oak paneling and strapwork ceiling of the entrance hall still welcomed the visitor. The finely worked tapestries that hung from the walls were still in good condition, and with a little beeswax the old oak furniture glowed into new life.

They had managed to live comfortably through that first summer, their money stretching through the warm months, but with the advent of winter their hardships began. Aunt Margaret had caught a cold that lingered and kept her in bed with a fever and cough. The doctor's bills had mounted daily, despite Hobbs's efficient care of her mistress, and food bills had risen each month until they were forced to ration their meals.

The marquis had already sold years before any valuable object that might have brought a good price, leaving only the bare essentials of the house that would bring very little if sold.

Her resentment had grown as their neighbors had called, partly out of good manners, but mostly out of curiosity, to see the family of the long-absent marquis. In their finery they had rolled up to Verrick House in elegant coaches, displaying their wealth to their impoverished neighbors. Graciously accepting tea as they laughed behind their fans at vague Aunt Margaret busily sewing her tapestry, patronizing their awkwardly young hostess as she tried to serve them. Sabrina had seethed as she'd watched Mary reduced to tears.

Sabrina had seen the poverty of the villagers, the maimed limbs of many unsuccessful poachers who'd only been trying to feed their families. The unfairness of it all had finally goaded and angered her into action.

It was a problem not easily solved by a young girl, but once she discovered the solution she set about making plans and strategies that would have complimented any general.

It was indeed ironic that the solution should come from Lord Malton himself. He'd been complaining of the unsafeness of the roads and apparent ease with which travelers were held up and robbed.

"Like taking candy from a child," he said angrily after

church one Sunday morning while Sabrina listened, "the way these ruffians and footpads steal a person's property. No fit place to live anymore."

How easy, indeed, Sabrina had speculated, to act the highwayman.

The first attempt had been a terrifying failure, nearly costing her her life and limbs when the coach she'd tried to waylay had not stopped and had nearly run her down.

Her second attempt had been more successful and netted her a ruby brooch and a gold watch, relieved from her first victims, Lord and Lady Malton. She had sold the jewelry, then retired the old mare for a speedier mount and with what was left, a cow for the barn.

Fortunately, misfortune had turned into good fortune when she'd inadvertently stumbled across the path of Will and John Taylor. Rabbits poached from forbidden land were slung across their shoulders when she interrupted them, a company of dragoons on her heels at the time, and time being of the essence, they had saved introductions until later.

Sheltering under the trees, they had watched the soldiers thundering by, turning to inspect each other suspiciously when the immediate danger had passed.

She remembered now with amusement how the two big men had towered over her as she'd stood bravely before them in her jackboots, her paling face hidden by her mask.

John had looked down at her from his great height, his thatch of straw-colored hair gleaming like silver under the bright moonlight

"Well, what have we here?" he'd asked with interest.

"Looks like a little Scots gentleman to me, John," Will laughed deeply.

"Aye, tha' I be, lads," she had answered huskily, her hands placed arrogantly on her hips.

"Well, little man, you're a bit south of the mark, then. Don't you think you oughta head north a bit? Wouldn't want you stumbling into us again," John had threatened.

"Yeah, looks as though you'd been busy, too, little Scot. What'd you get for yourself? Maybe you oughta share it with us for our trouble," Will had suggested with a smile splitting wide his mouth.

Sabrina remembered reaching for her pistol, unwilling to share her first profits with those two country bumpkins, but before she could find it she'd found herself wrapped in a fierce bear hug. Her little bag of loot was searched to their disappointment and then her mask had been tugged loose. Their surprise had been very satisfying to her ruffled feelings.

"Lord, but it's little Lady Sabrina Verrick," John had said, shaken.

Sabrina had enjoyed their discomfiture for a few brief moments, then had made them her startling proposal, having been suitably impressed by their strength and also preferring to have them a part of her secret rather than just knowing about it.

Never once had she regretted her decision, as Will and John made themselves indispensable to her and her family, finding servants and gardeners from the village to work at Verrick House and somehow managing to get them credit with all the local shopkeepers until they had built up their income enough to pay.

It had worked out beautifully, almost too well, she sometimes worried.

"Are you going to soak until dawn?" Mary demanded sleepily. "You're going to be as wrinkled as a prune."

Sabrina climbed from the tub, wrapping her slender body in a warm towel as she dried herself before the fire and then slipped into her nightgown, smoothing the soft material over her hips.

Mary gave her a hug and disappeared into her own room. Sabrina walked over to the chest, opening the lid and looking down at her sword and pistol lying on top. She glanced at the claw-handled pistol and then dug down deeper, coming up with her grandfather's dirk, the haft richly wrought with silver. She cradled it to her breast for comfort, trying to visualize her grandfather's face, the glint in her violet eyes and the half-smile on her lips very reminiscent of the old man's, had she but known it.

"I promised I'd take care of Richard, didn't I? But I don't think you'd planned it quite this way, did you, Grandfather?"

She replaced the knife in the chest and climbed into bed, her eyes closing with sleep as soon as her head touched the pillow.

Alas, regardless of their doom
The little victims play!
No sense have they of ills to come,
Nor care beyond today.

—*Thomas Gray*

Chapter 2

SABRINA HAPPILY DESCENDED THE STAIRS, HER THOUGHTS centered solely on the lovely summer morning. Birds were chirping melodiously from boughs near the open casement windows, and the scent of roses was carried in with the slight breeze.

She barely resembled the armed highwayman of the night before in her light blue silk damask gown with a creamy yellow, quilted satin petticoat showing in front. Her long black hair had been waved back from her face and secured in a simple knot atop her head, the thick coil looking too heavy for her slender neck that rose like a fragile stem from the bodice of her gown. Golden rings pierced her ears and gleamed on her fingers, and as she checked the gold watch slung from a chain around her neck she looked up sheepishly.

"I've overslept horridly, haven't I?" she called to Mary, who was arranging a vase of fragrant lilies in the center of the oak table in the hall. "And it's such a beautiful day, I hate to waste a minute of it."

"I know, but I've the accounts to settle and the linen to check before we can go on the picnic you're planning," Mary smiled.

"Always practical, Mary. And I have yet to keep a secret from you. Is there nothing you don't know?" she asked as she lifted a lily from the woven basket and held it to her nose.

Mary's smile faded. "You know how I wish I didn't have

the Sight, Sabrina. I don't want to see the future. It frightens
me. I have this feeling, this dread"—Mary paused thoughtfully—"this awful fear that something is about to happen to
cause everything to fall in upon us."

"You've seen something since last night, haven't you? You
weren't this nervous then," Sabrina said.

Mary shook her head. "No, it's just that feeling again—
nothing more. It's making me edgy." She smiled apologetically.

"Something usually does happen, though, when you get
these feelings."

Mary looked into Sabrina's clear violet eyes, tears clouding
her strangely light gray ones and whispered, "Oh, Sabrina, I
don't want anything to happen to you."

Mary dropped the lilies she held and hugged Sabrina to her.
"You're so small and sweet, and yet so brave to risk your life
for us. I just couldn't bear it if they should catch you."

Sabrina shook her head admonishingly, returning her hug.
"Silly goose. Nothing will happen to me. I have Will and
John, and your gift to guide me. What can happen?" she
scoffed, full of confidence.

"Now, shush." She held a finger to her lips. "We promised
never to discuss this during the day in case we might be overheard by the servants. Anyway," Sabrina added, holding her
arms out as if embracing the morning, "it's far too glorious to
be worrying about what isn't about to happen."

Mary shook her red head in defeat. "I give up. No one
can resist you when you turn on the charm." She finished
arranging the last lily and stood back to admire the effect, and
obviously satisfied, turned to Sabrina.

"Come along, you must be famished."

"I'm absolutely starved. I can't understand how I manage
to work up such an enormous appetite," Sabrina puzzled. "It
must have something to do with the company I keep," she
added innocently, a twinkle in her eyes.

"Really, Sabrina, you're an incorrigible little minx," Mary
laughed as they entered the dining room and she helped to fill
her sister's plate from the sideboard laid with covered dishes.

"Proper society ladies would look with horror upon what

you're eating this early in the morning," Mary stated as she added sausage to the eggs and buttered toast on Sabrina's plate, taking a small plate with only bread and butter for herself.

"I'd like to see them riding about at midnight and then be satisfied with a little piece of bread and butter," Sabrina replied as she swallowed a piece of sausage and took a sip of hot tea. "Will you be out this morning?"

"Later, after I've seen to the household duties. I've prepared a basket for Mrs. Fisher. Some eggs and cheese and beef pies."

"Mrs. Taylor will probably have gone over after Will told her last night," Sabrina said. "You might take an extra blanket or two. Mrs. Fisher has been ill."

"All right, I'll see what I can do," Mary replied, her mind going over the contents of the linen cupboard.

"My dears, how lovely to find you here," Aunt Margaret commented as she drifted into the room. "Pour me a cup like a dear, Mary."

She sat down opposite, glancing at Sabrina's plate curiously, then looked away politely.

"Thank you, dear. You know, I don't know where it goes?" she said looking out of the window distractedly.

"Where what goes, Aunt Margaret?" Mary inquired as she buttered a small wedge of bread and placed it before her aunt. She followed Aunt Margaret's stare, but could only see flowers abounding in the garden. "Everything is blooming beautifully. The Sweet Williams are especially lovely this year."

"Oh, are they dear, well, that is nice," she smiled and then directing a look at Sabrina added, "Blue suits you admirably, dear, but where are you putting that vulgar display of food? One should really just nibble delicately at a morsel. A lady, no matter how hungry, must never show that she is hungry. One really should leave the table quite famished. Which reminds me, dear, I really must have some more scent. Aqua Mellis, if you please, nothing else will really do, and another bar of that lovely Genoa soap. Do you think I should use the indigo blue or the violet, dear?" she asked worriedly.

Sabrina and Mary exchanged tolerant glances, well used to Aunt Margaret's vagaries by now.

"The violet, Aunt," Sabrina answered automatically.

"Do you think so? Well, I suppose so," she murmured, wrinkling her smooth brow, "but I really should think about it, dear. We mustn't be too hasty."

She rose gracefully and patting Sabrina on the top of her head affectionately wandered from the room, her tea untouched.

"Dear, sweet Aunt Margaret," Mary sighed. "I do wonder where she is half the time. She wasn't always this scatterbrained."

"I thought she'd always been a bit dreamy and abstracted," Sabrina commented as she wiped the corner of her mouth delicately, having cleaned her plate of its contents.

"No, something to do with unrequited love," Mary explained sadly.

"Unrequited love? Rot."

"Sabrina!" Mary looked astonished.

"Well?" Sabrina demanded. "No man's worth losing your wits about. I'd sign his death warrant first, and then launch him into eternity riding my sword," Sabrina vowed with a laugh.

"The way you do chatter at times. I don't know whether to laugh or pray for salvation? Grandfather often said he'd thought you'd been left by the merfolk from the loch as retribution for some offense," Mary replied. She sometimes worried; Sabrina could be so elusive, like quicksilver in her moods. She was much too passionate, so easy to provoke into a rage and so stubborn when she'd set her mind to something.

"You'd better pray to the ancient god Mercury that my feet remain fleet, for I've no desire to join them on Mt. Olympus yet."

"More likely into Hades, Rina," a boyish voice predicted. "It's the fate of all fallen angels."

Sabrina sent Richard a warning glance while Mary only shook her head.

"Not before I see you there, Robin Goodfellow," Sabrina retorted with a smile.

"I never do get in the last word with you," Richard complained, taking a slice of bread and spreading it liberally with butter. "Men don't care for sharp-tongued females, Rina."

"Yes, I'm well aware of that, Dickie."

Richard smiled, seeming far too adult for his ten years of

age. His red hair looked as though he'd just run an impatient hand through it, and there were faint shadows beneath his blue eyes. "Rather that than a fathead. I couldn't stomach that."

"Were you up reading late again last night?" Sabrina asked.

Richard's mouth turned sulky as he concentrated on a small crumb next to his plate. "I can't sleep when you're out, Rina."

Mary choked on her tea, glancing up at Sabrina with wide, startled eyes full of consternation, but Sabrina continued to stare calmly at Richard's bent head.

"Out where, Richard?" she asked quietly.

Richard looked up then, a brightness in his eyes as he said impatiently, "You know where—Bonnie Charlie."

Mary gasped, opening her mouth to speak, but Sabrina shook her head.

"Well," Richard continued obstinately, "aren't you going to deny it?"

"No, that would be foolish, wouldn't it?" Sabrina answered.

"Yes, it would. I'm not a fool. Don't you think I know what's been going on all these years?" He looked over his shoulder and then continued more quietly, "Do you think I like to have my sister ride about the countryside at night as a highwayman? Don't you think I ever wondered where the money came from that paid for my tutors, or put food on the table."

He smote his fist on the table causing the dishes to rattle. "Well, I did. I never believed the tales you made up about getting it from the solicitor as a special allowance from the marquis. He doesn't give a damn about us. Don't you think I ever wished I could help in some way? I've always been too young, or too much of a coward. A poor-spirited milksop, afraid to even ride a horse, much less shoot a pistol. What good am I to you?" Richard demanded angrily, and jumping up, overturned his chair and ran from the room.

Mary and Sabrina remained seated, silently staring at each other.

"What a coil. I had no idea he even knew, much less felt this way. It's hard to believe, Mary, but Richard's grown up on us. He's always been a serious fellow, so we've just never noticed how mature he's become."

"I'll go to him," Mary said worriedly. "I hate to have him so full of self-doubts. He's still just a little boy, despite how mature he tries to act, and he shouldn't be ashamed because he doesn't ride," Mary said in his defense.

"No, I think he should be left alone—for now, at least," Sabrina advised her. "We'll just have to start taking him into our confidence. But I'll not have him involved in anything that will endanger him."

Mary nodded her red head in agreement. "I don't fancy seeing us all hanging from the gallows, either."

Sabrina watched as Mary withdrew a piece of paper from her apron pocket and began to go over her list of household details, her face absorbed as she mentally calculated her figures. Sabrina smiled fondly at her sister's bright red head. Nothing must happen to Mary. Not Mary. She was far too good and virtuous to end up on the gallows. Sabrina bit her lip nervously as she allowed her doubts to overwhelm her. What had she led them into? If anyone deserved hanging, it was she.

❧

It had been a lovely afternoon, Sabrina thought, as she glanced about the colorful garden. In scattered disorder Sweet Williams, carnations. and gillyflowers blended with the fragrance of violets, sweetbrier, and wild thyme. Sweet pea, honeysuckle, and jasmine clung to the arbors, while the yellow and gold of daffodils and marigolds marched steadily through the pinks and reds of tulips and columbines. Sabrina closed her eyes and listened to the quiet. She could hear the busy hum of the bees from their hive in the herb garden where they flavored their honey from rosemary, lavender, sage, and marjoram planted nearby. It was so restful, so peaceful, so removed from the world beyond the high stone walls.

"Are you finished, Rina?" Mary asked as she began to gather up the empty dishes and return them to the large woven basket. Richard tossed the remains of roast chicken, ham, and pickled salmon to the floppy-eared, black-and-white spaniels waiting patiently for their share of the picnic. The gooseberry tart and custard pudding had long since been eaten, but the leftover fruit and cheese was repacked, and the empty container of lemonade as well.

Sabrina finished hers thirstily and added it to the pile. "I enjoyed that so much. It is so pleasant to just relax and daydream for once," she commented lazily, stretching her arms above her head, then laughed and covered her face as one of the spaniels began licking it with a soft, moist tongue. He rolled over as Sabrina rubbed his long silky hair playfully, laughing as he held up his paws begging for more.

"I wish every single day could be as nice, but," Mary added regretfully, "it must end, and I've still the accounts to see to." She glanced at the lengthening shadows on the lawn and sighed. "Aunt Margaret, shall we go in now?"

"Yes, dear, quite right," Aunt Margaret answered. "Do remind me to embroider this garden. I must capture these glorious colors, and really, the pickled salmon was just a wee bit too salty." She smiled, gathering up scattered threads with quick, nimble fingers and tucking them into the large tapestried bag that was her constant companion, along with the two spaniels.

"When are you going to finish that tapestry you've been working on for the past few years, Aunt?" Sabrina asked, looping her arm through her aunt's as they walked towards the house, the spaniels underfoot. "You've never shown it to us."

"In time, dear, in time," she answered vaguely.

They entered the hall through the side door that opened onto the garden and were stopped by the butler who'd just closed the doors to the drawing room.

"Visitors, Lady Margaret," he announced deferentially, but looked to Mary for his orders.

"Who has called, Sims?" she asked curiously, checking her gown for grass stains and straightening the lacy, flounced sleeves at her elbows.

"Lords Malton and Newley, your ladyship," he replied stiffly, ill-contained dislike of the two visitors barely concealed in his well-trained manner.

Mary cast an inquiring glance at Sabrina, who shrugged and merely tipped the wide, floppy brim of the pale blue silk slouch hat she wore to a more rakish angle over an amusedly arched eyebrow.

"I suppose we must find out what they want. Come along Mary, Aunt—" she began, but Lady Margaret had disappeared up the staircase with the dogs in tow, a thin strand of scarlet thread the only indication she'd been present.

Sabrina turned to Richard. "Would you care to be present?" she asked the solemn-eyed boy. His eyes brightened visibly, and he nodded his head in agreement.

"Please, Rina," he spoke eagerly.

"Mary, Richard." She clasped their hands and they moved forward as one into the drawing room, past the doors held open by a footman, to greet their unexpected guests.

"Ah, Lady Mary," Lord Malton greeted her loudly, nodding to Sabrina and Richard, as he bent over Mary's outstretched hand. "A pleasure."

"Our pleasure, surely," Sabrina spoke softly, smiling sweetly as she caught his eye.

"I must say, Lady Mary, your sister grows more beautiful with each day that passes, as indeed do you yourself."

"If I might be allowed to add my compliments also," Lord Newley added suavely, looking directly into Sabrina's violet eyes. "We must see more of you ladies, eh Malton?"

"Certainly. Of course we understand that without a man to act as escort, and only your aunt to chaperone you, it is most difficult for you to get about. Ah, how is the dear woman?" he asked hesitantly, looking around the room nervously in expectation of being surprised by her sudden appearance. "I knew the dear lady when she lived here with your father. They were, of course, a bit older than me," he added quickly.

"Aunt Margaret has never been better and hardly seems a day older than my sister and I," Mary smiled. "Please do be seated, and may we offer you a refreshment?" Mary invited, her good manners overcoming her reluctance to issue such an invitation.

She avoided Sabrina's grimace and seated herself demurely on a winged settee. "Richard, ring for the footman. We've a very fine elderberry wine?"

"Or lemonade and ginger beer?" Sabrina added helpfully, knowing full well that the gentlemen would much rather have had a brandy.

"Really, we mustn't put you to any trouble, dear ladies," Lord Malton said quickly with a beaming smile, which faded as he broached the subject of his visit. He leaned forward from the chair he was seated in and confided, "We have paid this call on a most serious note, I'm sorry to say."

"Oh, dear me, how dreadful."

"You may well say that, Lady Mary," Lord Malton expostulated, settling his bulk more comfortably in his chair, his sword and gold-headed cane complicating matters as he tried to cross his legs.

"We come to warn you, dear ladies," Lord Newley began carefully. "We certainly do not wish to frighten you, but we are all in the gravest danger."

"Oh, dear. Whatever from?" Sabrina exclaimed.

"Last night, in my own dining room, a few friends and myself were held up at pistol point and robbed!" Lord Malton told them vehemently, his face turning red.

"Robbed. How scandalous. Surely you jest. Who would dare?" Mary asked faintly.

"Bonnie Charlie, that's who," Lord Newley spat, his thin lips drawn back from his teeth in almost a snarl.

Richard gasped, his blue eyes widening in admiration as he stared at Sabrina's elegant figure as she sat quietly on the settee, appropriately frightened by the news.

"An outrage. Why I should think you'd have his head," she whispered.

"Exactly my words, Lady Sabrina. The impertinence of it all. Well, that is why we've come. You ladies must be warned, and prepared to defend yourselves. Have you good, strong footmen to protect your home?"

"Why, yes, we've several big country boys footing for us," Mary reassured them.

"Not sure even that'll do it. Monsters they were. Stood seven feet tall, those henchmen of his. And him, let me tell you, he was six feet if an inch, and a meaner ruffian I've yet to meet."

"Tch, tch. Six feet if an inch, you say? How distressing," Sabrina breathed. "I do fear, Mary, that I shan't be able to sleep a wink for fear of my life."

"Dear lady," Lord Newley exclaimed contritely, leaning closer, "you've no need to fear. I don't believe he's killed anyone yet, and besides, we're calling in more dragoons to patrol. I shall personally guarantee your safety. I promise you we shall hang that scoundrel before the week is out. He has gone too far this time. Coming into a man's home, it's uncivilized."

"You're too kind to be concerned on our behalf, and I am sure we shall be quite safe. We do live a very simple life," Mary reassured them, and then added ingenuously, "Why, I'm sure we have nothing here that he doesn't already own."

"You're too modest, my dear," Lord Malton contradicted. "Well, we really mustn't detain you any further. We just wanted you to know the truth, should you have heard any exaggerated rumors, that there are going to be reinforcements coming."

"Thank you, I'm quite reassured now," Mary thanked them. "We appreciate your solicitude, my lords, don't we Sabrina?"

"Indeed we do, and although your description of the high-waymen quite terrified me, I am most interested and reassured to know about the dragoons."

"As good neighbors it was our duty, and of course it's always a pleasure to visit such lovely ladies," Lord Malton complimented as they heartily made their good-byes.

After the doors had been closed behind them, they remained silent for a moment until Richard couldn't control his giggle and started to laugh, his slight body shaking with mirth.

"It is just too priceless. I should've asked Lord Newley for the time," Sabrina laughed as she untied the ribbons beneath her chin and flung aside her hat.

"Yes, it is rather," Mary agreed, wiping her eyes with a lace-edged handkerchief. "But I hope we aren't underestimating them. Foolish though they are, they're not completely blunt-witted."

"No, but they're windbags. They couldn't keep a secret if their lives depended upon it. With their chatter, Will and John can pick up any news at the tavern from their servants, who love to gossip, and we can gather what we may direct from the horse's mouth, for I'm sure the dragoons will not be able to make a move without Malton's advice."

Richard stared at Sabrina in open admiration, his face flushed with excitement. "When are you going out again, Rina? Can I ride with you? I promise I won't be frightened," he pleaded hopefully.

Sabrina shook her head. "You know I told you we would never discuss that. Besides, you're needed here. Should anything happen to me, what would Mary and Aunt Margaret do? They'll need you, Dickie."

"Nothing will happen to you," Richard vowed, flinging himself at her feet and wrapping his arms about her waist "Nothing, ever!"

Sabrina looked over his head into Mary's eyes and wondered what she saw, but Mary shook her head despairingly, unable to answer the question in her eyes. Nothing must go wrong now, nothing must happen to interfere with their plans. Sabrina intended to make sure that nothing did, and vowed to herself that she would not allow anything, nor anybody, to upset their lives.

A bold bad man.

—Edmund Spenser

Chapter 3

THE DUKE OF CAMAREIGH LEANED INDOLENTLY AGAINST THE portal of the double doors and watched as the carefree dancers glided past. First they slowly danced the minuet with its bowing and crossing, the partners flirting provocatively as they drew together, and then a more lively bouree, followed by a courante to keep them breathless with its quick, running steps.

"Aren't you going to join in, Lucien?" Sir Jeremy Winters inquired, as he took two glasses of champagne from a tray offered by a liveried footman and handed one of the brimming goblets to the duke.

"And have my feet trod upon? No, thank you," Lucien declined wryly as a red-faced, perspiring gentleman stumbled past.

Sir Jeremy laughed. "Even if you shun my more lively entertainments, I'm glad you accepted my invitation. Only sorry I'd already planned such a cursed large party. Don't get you down this way much."

"I thought I might as well look up an old friend, as long as I was here looking over some property I've acquired," replied the duke.

"Heard you'd won Davern's estate. Not much, I'm afraid," Sir Jeremy informed him. "He'd let it go for years."

"Yes, I'd thought as much, but I like to know what I possess. It may be worth saving," he paused, taking a sip of champagne. "If not, I'll sell or lose it in a game of hazard next week."

Sir Jeremy shook his head. "Lavenbrook lost everything last week in one hand. Shot himself dead in his host's dining room."

"If you can't afford to lose, you shouldn't play the game," Lucien commented unsympathetically. "We're all bound to lose sometime and should be prepared to pay."

"But for God's sake, man," Sir Jeremy replied fervently, "sometimes you just can't help it. I've often found myself in too deep and just luckily managed to extricate myself in time."

"When I play a game, whatever it may be, whether at the tables or elsewhere, I expect to pay my debts, and," he added, his eyes cold, "I expect to collect what is due me. I make no allowances, and I always collect."

"Well, I like to collect too," Sir Jeremy began, "but I give a friend a chance to regain his losses and time to pay."

"I never gamble with friends who can't afford to lose—it's the best way to lose your friends," the duke replied lazily.

"I'd have thought you'd be, of all people, the most understanding, Lucien. After all, you were in tight spots many times before you managed to break even and eventually make your fortune."

Lucien smiled thoughtfully as he answered seriously, "That is precisely why I feel as I do. I had to make my fortune at cards, a professional gambler you might say, and therefore it was a business, and charity and compassion played no part in it. I couldn't afford to feel either. That is why I didn't and prefer not to play with friends."

Sir Jeremy shook his head regretfully, his friendly features mirroring dissatisfaction. "Cursed nuisance having your inheritance tied up the way it is."

The duke's jaw hardened as he ran his thumb along his scar. "More than that, Jeremy. Up until a couple of months ago I thought I'd managed to circumvent my grandmother's ploys, but as usual she refuses to concede defeat and continues to dictate and meddle in my affairs. This time she has outmaneuvered me and I must swallow my pride and give in gracefully. I have no other choice if I wish to own my ancestral home, and I have vowed that no one but I shall inherit it. So, I find myself in the position of being engaged to the Lady Blanche

Delande, my grandmother's choice as a perfect wife for me, despite my feelings to the contrary. However," he shrugged in resignation, "there is little I can do to remedy the situation except marry the chit—as ordered—for I'll be damned if I'll let my cousin Percy inherit."

Sir Jeremy felt a twinge of unease as he stared at his friend's haughty profile, the sherry-colored eyes narrowed reflectively and the finely chiseled lips curved in an unpleasant smile. In an untrimmed cream silk, full-skirted coat with matching waistcoat and breeches, the duke was an elegant foil to the brightly dressed dancers in their gaudy pinks and puces, oranges and reds, lavishly embroidered and trimmed in gold and silver.

"Well, shall we see how the play is going in the gold salon," Sir Jeremy broke into the duke's thoughtful silence.

They drifted from the room to the gold salon, where tables had been set up for games of chance, and stood watching the engrossed card players. As they continued to stand there another man moved closer and stood nearby, his face flushed with drink as he glared at the duke's arrogant profile.

Lucien turned his gaze slightly and glanced dispassionately at the man staring so rudely at him until the man shifted uneasily and turned his eyes elsewhere.

"Who is the malcontent who's trying to put me to the blush?" Lucien inquired casually.

Sir Jeremy glanced around the room in surprise as he looked over his guests, who were busily absorbed with their cards, until his eyes alighted on a stocky gentleman in salmon colored velvet, his brow thunderous as he stared at Lucien in a definitely unfriendly manner.

"What the devil?" Sir Jeremy demanded, looking at Lucien questioningly.

The duke returned his look steadily. "I've not the slightest notion why this fellow should bear me malice. I haven't even had the pleasure of making his acquaintance."

"He's Sir Frederick Jensen. A real hothead, always in a sulk about some imagined slight."

"Really," the duke drawled in boredom. "How tiresome."

"A real hot-air merchant. His mouth has gotten him into countless duels," Sir Jeremy confided distastefully.

"Then how is it he's a guest of yours, Jeremy?"

"Someone else's guest, not mine. There's always some parasite worming his way in. But short of throwing the braggart out, what can I do but cold-shoulder him?"

"Well, you shall have to do better than that because the fellow is coming this way," Lucien stated dryly, "and unless I'm mistaken, with the express purpose of engaging us in conversation."

Sir Frederick Jensen swaggered up to the Duke of Camareigh, ignoring Sir Jeremy, and cast a baleful eye at Lucien's amused expression.

"Laughing in your sleeve at me, are you, your grace?" he sneered loudly, causing the nearby card players to glance up in interest.

"Hardly that, since I know nothing about you to laugh at," Lucien replied indifferently.

Sir Frederick's mouth curled into a sneer as he leaned forward, and jabbing a finger on the duke's wide chest said, "No, you do yours behind a fellow's back. Maligning my character, holding me up to ridicule."

"It would be a waste of my time since you seem to be doing that yourself," Lucien replied coldly.

"Why, I'll—" Sir Frederick began heatedly, his face a dull red.

"Now, now," Sir Jeremy interrupted, a placating note in his voice. "Don't get in a stew, Jensen. You've had a few too many. You're fuddled, man."

"Fuddled! Me? I can drink any man here under the table, even his grace, the all-powerful Duke of Camareigh. Too good for the likes of me, are you?" he accused.

The gentlemen in the room had now stopped their gaming and were giving their full attention to the little contretemps being enacted before them. In the silence Sir Frederick's heavy breathing could be heard loudly, and all eyes were focused on the two men who stood facing each other.

"You owe me an apology," Sir Frederick demanded aggressively, his chin jutting forward pugnaciously.

"Indeed?" the duke asked disdainfully.

"Indeed, yes, your grace. You called me a yokel, a slow-coach, and said I was only fit to inhabit a dunghill. I demand satisfaction," he spat, throwing his gloves in the duke's face.

A gasp of surprise and a few whispered comments went around the room as they waited nervously for the duke's reaction. The scar on his cheek had whitened visibly as he insolently took a pinch of snuff from a small gold box and putting a dab in each nostril sniffed disdainfully.

"It would be obvious from your actions this evening that had I indeed made such remarks about you, they could only have been the rather unpleasant truth," the duke drawled, and looking at Sir Jeremy as he held a handkerchief delicately to his nose added, "Do open a window, there is the most loathsome and offensive odor in here—enough to turn one's stomach."

The duke had begun to walk away from the red-faced and humiliated Sir Frederick when he turned and spoke to him, a bored tone in his voice. "Do have your seconds with you, say dawn tomorrow morning under the oaks, and don't keep me waiting, for I must make an early start if I'm to reach my destination by afternoon."

Sir Frederick Jensen's mouth dropped open and sweat broke out on his brow as he watched the duke and Sir Jeremy stroll nonchalantly from the room. And then as excited conversation broke out amongst the astonished guests, Sir Frederick hurriedly fled from the room with several of his friends.

Sir Jeremy poured himself a glass of port after handing Lucien one, and took a deep swallow. "What the devil got into Jensen? Never seen anyone act so bellicose. He purposely forced you into defending your honor, and yet you say you've never even met the fellow?" Sir Jeremy shook his head, clearly unable to understand the situation.

"Never set eyes on the fool before tonight," Lucien answered. "Yet it would seem someone insinuated that I offended and insulted him." He gazed ruminatively into the fire burning in the grate. "Now I wonder why anyone should want to do that."

Sir Jeremy stopped his pacing abruptly. "What? A trick?"

"Well, it doesn't all ring quite true," Lucien replied. "Here is a fellow I've never met accusing me of lampooning him and, being something of a hothead, will not be satisfied until he's called me out and hopefully killed me."

Sir Jeremy frowned. "Jensen may be a fool—but he's a damned good swordsman. Prides himself on being a successful duelist. The fact that he's still alive proves that."

"I always prefer a fair fight myself, but any man who allows himself to become someone's cat's paw, and be led into conflict at another's direction, is easy prey for any schemer off the streets. No." Lucien continued grimly, "I'm afraid our friend Jensen is ruled by his passions and not his head. There can be only one outcome to this affair."

"Which is?" Sir Jeremy asked hesitantly.

Lucien glanced up, shrugging his shoulders fatalistically. "Sir Frederick Jensen will come to grief. It is inevitable and unfortunately it must be by my hand, but eventually he would have met this end. His unavoidable destiny, I fear."

"You're mighty cool about it, Lucien," Sir Jeremy observed, a look of admiration on his face.

"Am I?" Lucien shook his head. "I'm just resigned, that is all. But I am curious as to the identity of the schemer behind this little scenario. I would hazard a guess that I've an enemy who plots my early demise."

"It's scandalous. The effrontery of some people," Sir Jeremy complained. "Have you any notion who this villain is?"

The duke drained his glass and smiled. "You have a certain way of dramatizing situations, Jeremy, but to answer your question, no, not for a certainty. I've my fair share of enemies, so it could be any number of people, but most of them I know. This rascal would prefer to remain anonymous, and I can't effectively deal with a phantom."

He stood up and smiled at Sir Jeremy's worried expression. "Don't fret, Jeremy. I'm an obstinate fellow and insist upon having the last word. My only regret is having to rise so cursed early, so I'll bid you good night," he said, stifling a yawn as he left the room.

Sir Jeremy shook his head in bemused exasperation and

pouring himself another drink sat down for further contemplation of the situation, grateful that it was not he who was meeting the duke tomorrow morning at dawn.

❧

It was quiet under the avenue of oaks as the first light of daybreak summoned the crow of a rooster and the answering chirpings of awakening birds. Crystal-like dew still clung to the leaves of the trees and the tall grasses in the fields. Sir Jeremy stood silent, Lucien's coat, waistcoat and stock across his arm as he waited along with those of the other guests who'd managed to rise so early. Most were still slumbering back in their rooms after the late night's revelry. Lucien's throat was bare and vulnerable, his shirt opened halfway to his waist, revealing the dark golden hair on his chest. He'd shunned a wig and thick golden hair curled back from his temples and ears, gleaming richly under the sunlight.

Lucien flexed his sword experimentally, then turned to face his opponent, his face expressionless.

"On guard!"

Sir Frederick Jensen lunged wildly and the duke parried the thrust of Sir Frederick's rapier expertly as he sidestepped. His wrist was firm, his hand steady, his feet agile as he lunged, meeting Sir Frederick's sword point at each thrust.

Sir Frederick was fighting offensively, constantly on the attack, using brute strength to beat down his foe, but Lucien's quickness and finesse withstood the assault and gradually reversed the positions and began to tire the stockier Sir Frederick, who was by now breathing heavily, his face red and perspiring from his exertions. Summoning what little reserves he had left, he charged the duke like a mad bull, his sword swinging wildly as he tried to penetrate Lucien's guard and pierce the smooth column of his throat, just tantalizingly out of reach of sword point. But Lucien easily parried Sir Frederick's lunge and drove the point of his sword into the exposed shoulder of his aggressive opponent. Sir Frederick grunted in pain and fell back, his sword dropping from his hand as he clutched at the profusely bleeding wound.

Lucien stood back as the surgeon who'd stood readily available on the edge of the crowd ran forward and knelt down beside the fallen swordsman.

"Why didn't you kill him?" Sir Jeremy asked, as he held Lucien's waistcoat for him as he shrugged into it.

"No sense in it," the duke answered matter-of-factly, his breathing coming quickly as he wiped his sword clean of Sir Frederick's blood with a white handkerchief. "He'll suffer enough with that shoulder wound. I don't want a fool's death on my conscience."

The duke walked over to his coach and handed his valet his crumpled stock and accepted a freshly starched one in its stead, carelessly knotting it about his neck.

"I regret taking my leave of you so hastily, Jeremy, but I've business to see to, and"—he paused, casting an amused glance at Sir Frederick who was being led away, surrounded by a group of commiserating friends—"Sir Frederick should be allowed to enjoy his convalescence to the fullest without my presence to distress him."

"He's lucky to be alive," Sir Jeremy replied disgustedly. "Not many are given a second chance as he has been. Now look at him. Lud, but I think he's fainted."

The duke laughed. "I'll keep in touch, Jeremy." He disappeared into his carriage. A footman closed the door with a flourish and then jumped aboard quickly as the coachman whipped up the team of horses and they pulled out with a splashing of mud beneath the hooves and heavy wheels.

❦

They had traveled for several hours, stopping for luncheon at a small inn and then continuing as a thunderstorm broke above and poured down upon the quickly moving team, slowing them down as the rain muddied the roads and created a quagmire out of the potted surface.

Lucien shifted lazily. Pulling back the hangings over the window he looked out in disgust at the muddy road and dismal countryside. The carriage wheel hit a deep hole and, lurching through it, threw the duke against the side of the coach.

"Damn," he mumbled, cursing the coachman atop, and was about to send some select phrases to him when the carriage slowed and he heard the coachman commanding the horses to a halt.

"What the devil?" Lucien demanded as he opened the carriage door and leaned out, the rain falling lightly on his face.

Ahead, halfway in a ditch on the other side of the road, lay an overturned carriage. The horses had been unharnessed and were being quieted by a couple of outriders. The coachman was rubbing his shoulder while he and another servant struggled to open the carriage door, behind which came a wailing moan that rose hysterically until a resounding slap was heard, then muffled sobbing.

"*Dio mio!*" someone spoke in exasperation.

The duke's lips twitched with a grin as he heard the feminine voice. "See what you can do for them," he commanded his coachman, who was surveying the scene of chaos with contempt.

"Aye, Sandy, Davey, hop to it," he called to the young grooms who'd run to the duke's lead horses to hold them and were standing gawking at the commotion.

The duke reluctantly climbed down from his coach and walked through the mud to the overturned carriage. He could have sent his coachman, but he was curious about the inhabitants of the coach, especially if there was an Italian beauty to match the voice he'd heard. He was not disappointed, for as he approached the carriage a dark head adorned with a red silk hat appeared from the confines of the coach. Lucien's eyes traveled slowly, and appreciatively, over her well-rounded figure. The décolletage of her dress was low and wide, the scarlet damask a perfect contrast for the four rows of pearls clasped about her smooth, white neck. His eyes returned to her face and the reddened lips that were parted in a wide smile as she stared at her gentlemanly rescuer, her dark brown eyes full of surprised pleasure.

"*Buon giorno.*"

"Good afternoon," the duke replied. "You seem to be in some difficulty. May I be of some service?"

"Oh, *grazie*, we would be so grateful," she sighed with relief.

"We?" Lucien inquired politely.

"*Si, aspetti un momento, per favore.*" She disappeared into the carriage while the duke waited as she'd requested, until another figure appeared through the window. Lucien hid his disappointment as a well-dressed man stared down at him from his perch on the side of the carriage.

"Can't you get your men to move any faster and turn us upright?" the man demanded peevishly as he took in the scene. Then as his eyes saw the ducal crest emblazoned on the side of Lucien's coach, his demeanor swiftly underwent a change and he looked closer at their rescuer.

"I say, don't I know you?"

"I seriously doubt that," the duke answered coldly, regretting his impulse to stop.

"Of course. You're the Duke of Camareigh," the man spoke triumphantly. "We met in Vienna. I'm James Verrick, the Marquis of Wrainton. I've been out of the country for quite a few years now." He looked into the dark interior of the coach, saying something in Italian, then glanced at the duke gratefully. "We were on our way to London when this disaster happened and nearly cost us our lives. We've just arrived from France, the seat of civilization, I'm beginning to believe. I'd forgotten how surly these English servants can be," he complained spitefully.

"*Per favore*, but I grow much fatigued sitting here upside down while you make conversation, James," a fretful voice echoed from the coach.

"My dear, of course, I beg your pardon," Lord Wrainton answered quickly as though afraid of possible hysterics. "Will you be able to help us, your grace?"

Lucien nodded reluctantly. "Naturally, I couldn't leave you and the lady—?" He paused delicately, waiting to be enlightened.

"Lady Wrainton, my wife; but living in Italy as we have, she is used to being addressed as the contessa."

"Of course," the duke sighed, "I'll escort you to the

nearest inn, where you may hire conveyance to London. I am afraid that we are traveling in opposite directions after that."

"We shall be most grateful just to get out of this cursed ditch."

Lord Wrainton jumped down from the side of the coach, splattering his pumps as he did so and nearly slipping in the slick mud as he regained his balance. He was a middle-aged man in his forties, slight of build, and almost too handsome to be masculine, with his thickly lashed, violet eyes.

"Luciana," Lord Wrainton called to his wife. The contessa looked down from the carriage doubtfully as Lord Wrainton told her, "Jump and I'll catch you, my dear."

"If you will allow me?" the duke interrupted. "I would be pleased to assist the contessa."

Lord Wrainton frowned, then nodded his head. "Yes, I am rather shaken up from the accident, otherwise I could easily carry my wife."

The duke hid his smile, not wanting to offend Lord Wrainton's pride, but as he stepped forward and lifted the contessa from the carriage he doubted seriously if the older man could have managed. He followed Lord Wrainton to the carriage, the contessa's scarlet silk stockings and white silk shoes with their high, slender heels revealed to the gaping grooms as Lucien swung her into a firmer grip in his arms.

He carefully traversed the muddy road, his foot slipping once in the slime, causing the contessa to grasp his neck tightly with her arms. Her heady perfume drifted to Lucien and he grinned as she allowed herself to press closer.

"*Grazie*," she murmured, her breath warm against his throat.

"My pleasure."

He lifted her into the coach, tucking her fur-trimmed pelisse snugly about her and then placing a sable rug over her lap. Lucien was about to follow when a frightened wail drifted to them from the overturned coach, followed by a scream and a flow of excited Italian.

"*Dio mio*, I'm afraid I forgot poor Maria, my maid," the contessa confessed. "And I really can't leave her stranded here; she speaks no English," she explained apologetically, her big brown eyes full of wishful pleading.

Lucien shrugged. "By all means, you must have your maid, contessa." He looked around and seeing one of the grooms standing idle ordered him to see to the other occupant of the overturned coach. At the sound of an outraged scream, the duke glanced back and laughed as Sandy staggered across the road carrying a large, struggling woman, her face red and puffed from crying and issuing a tirade on the flushed Sandy's blond head. As they neared the carriage Sandy's foot disappeared in a large hole filled with water, and, losing his balance, he fell backwards and disappeared beneath the bulky figure of the contessa's maid.

Stoically, Lucien assisted the flustered woman to her feet and hefted her into the carriage from which she called forth a volley of abuses on the unfortunate Sandy, who'd quickly struggled to his feet and was hastily making his way some distance from the carriage, his face as red as a beet and his backside covered with clinging mud.

"Maria, *silenzio!*" the contessa ordered, a quiver of laughter still in her voice.

After a moment's consultation with his coachman, Lucien climbed into the coach, the door closing behind him as he settled himself comfortably beside Lord Wrainton.

"You've a broken axle, so there is no question of using your coach."

"It's just as well. I didn't trust those coachmen anyway. Wouldn't be surprised to find them in league with highwaymen waiting to rob us."

"*Dio mio*, that is all that I need now," the contessa swore beneath her breath.

"I don't think we need fear that occurrence," the duke replied calmly. "My men are well trained to act in our defense."

"This country is most inhospitable, I don't know why I let you talk me into visiting it," the contessa spoke tiredly.

"Now, now, Luciana, I promise you that you'll find London much more to your liking," Lord Wrainton placated her.

"I gather this is your first visit to England, contessa?" the duke asked.

"*Si*, and I hope my last. It is not a country I have a liking for. *L'Italia è molto bella*, but this country, aah," she said in disgust, throwing her hands up in the air.

Lucien laughed. "It takes the Englishman to love England. As when a man is in love with a woman, he often doesn't see her faults."

"So you admit this England has faults." The contessa smiled thoughtfully. "Me, I wish to be back in Venice in the smooth swaying of a gondola," she sighed as she was thrown sideways when the wheels of the coach bumped through a hole. "These carriages were made for fools."

"I didn't think you had holdings in these parts, your grace?" Lord Wrainton inquired curiously. "Isn't your estate farther north?"

"Yes, I'm just looking over some recently purchased property," Lucien replied. "You seem to know this area. Have you lived hereabouts?"

"Born and raised around here," Lord Wrainton confided. "In fact, I have an estate in the next valley, Verrick House. Not much to look at I'm afraid. It's just a small Elizabethan manor house, and I haven't even seen it in Lord knows how many years, come to think of it. Wonder what it's like now." he speculated idly.

"*Caro*, we should pay a visit to this little house," the contessa suggested, then turning to the duke explained, "You see, I am the marquis' third wife, and as yet I have not met his family. How many *bambini* do you have, *caro*?" she demanded with a frown. "Two or three, *n'é vero?*'

Lord Wrainton shrugged carelessly. "Three, I think."

"You obviously haven't seen your children in some time," the duke commented sardonically.

"This one has not been the proud papa, but soon," she smiled knowingly, glancing slyly down at her waistline, "he shall be, and he will not run off and leave this one as he has these other poor *bambini*."

The marquis turned a dull red under the lash of her tongue, shifting uncomfortably at the truth.

"And you, your grace?" she asked Lucien, gaining his wandering attention. "You are married and have a family?"

Lucien smiled derisively. "No, not yet, contessa," he replied shortly.

"Ah, you suffer from the broken heart, *si*? This is too bad, but I think you have many *amores* just the same." She glanced at the duke provocatively, her gaze lingering on his face. "You seem the cool one, but I think you are like Lucifer the fallen angel with your scarred face—a warning, perhaps, for one to beware?"

The marquis looked nervously at the duke. "Please excuse Luciana, your grace, she is Italian and inclined to speak her mind without thought," he apologized, sending a quelling look to the contessa who merely smiled teasingly at him.

The duke laughed. "I think your wife keeps you very busy, Lord Wrainton, and I am too well used to sharp-tongued females to allow the contessa's words to trouble me."

They traveled throughout the afternoon, the rain continuing to fall lightly as the team of horses pulled the coach swaying and lurching down the road, becoming bogged down in numerous potholes and streams.

"We are to arrive soon, I trust? I never thought to find myself seasick in a coach," the contessa remarked impatiently and then gave her maid a shake. "Wake up, Maria! You begin to snore."

The coach began to slow down, and as it came to a complete halt the contessa leaned forward expectantly. "*Bene*, we are here at last."

The duke frowned and made to look out the curtained window when the door was thrown violently open and a breath of cold, damp air rushed in.

"What the—" Lucien began.

"Stand and deliver!" a voice called from outside and before Lucien could reach for the pistol strapped to the side of the coach, the other door was swung open and a large man holding two pistols pointed them at the occupants of the coach.

"*Dio mio!*" the contessa cried, cringing backward as Maria screamed in terror and fell across her lap in a dead faint.

"Ah, we've ladies present, have we now?" the voice commented with amusement. "If the gentlemen will remove themselves from the carriage for just a moment, we won't keep them longer than it takes to relieve them of their purses," the highwayman invited politely.

The duke looked at the pistols pointed at his heart, and shrugging at the contessa's frightened face and Lord Wrainton's outraged one, he climbed from the carriage, pausing briefly as he saw the tartan sash of the highwayman before stepping carefully into the muddy roadway.

"Well, well, if it isn't my scar-faced friend from the party. You do have the misfortune of being in the wrong place at the right time for me," Bonnie Charlie laughed.

The coachman and grooms were standing nervously on the other side of the road, their weapons in a pile in the middle of the road and under guard of the highwayman's other large companion. In the growing twilight it was becoming difficult to distinguish details, everything turning palely indistinct in the fading light.

"Would our other fine gentleman care to join us?" Bonnie Charlie requested.

Lord Wrainton climbed slowly from the coach, the collar of his greatcoat turned up to protect him against the light drizzle that fell and his cocked hat shadowing his features as he stood nervously beside the duke.

"Now, what will we be donating to the cause today? A few golden guineas would not come amiss. After all, no gentleman of means travels without a full purse. Hand it over," Bonnie Charlie demanded, hardly glancing at the man who stood beside the tall duke.

Lucien reached into his coat, his hand disappearing beneath the thick material.

"Carefully, lad. I'd hate to ruin your finery," the highwayman cautioned as he watched Lucien remove his purse and toss it over to him. "And your friend?"

The marquis handed over his purse with ill grace, cursing under his breath as he did so.

"Now, if we might have a look at the ladies and see if they would care to share their wealth with those not as fortunate?"

Bonnie Charlie waved Lucien aside, staying out of the aim

of Will's pistol, which was trained on the two gentlemen, and glanced inside the coach.

The contessa was fanning Maria frantically, trying to revive her, when she looked up into the face of the masked bandit.

"*Dio!*" she squeaked, beginning to fan herself instead.

"You're not English," Bonnie Charlie commented regretfully as he eyed the milky pearls around her neck, "so I'll leave you your lovely pearls and take only your earrings. As the other lady is insensible and obviously unadorned, I shan't trouble her."

The highwayman bowed, a grin on his lips as the contessa stared in bemused silence at this gentleman of the road. "*Arrivederci.*"

Backing from the opened door of the coach, Bonnie Charlie turned to confront the duke, whose coat was dampened from the misty rain that was beginning to fall more heavily.

"My apologies for keeping you standing in the rain," Bonnie Charlie mocked, his own clothes covered by a black greatcoat that enveloped his figure warmly. "You may both get aboard, and I trust I haven't inconvenienced you too greatly, although it is a pity that you must look the fool in front of so lovely a lady. Better that, however, than a foolish attempt to fight me and find oneself dead. Yes, far wiser to play the fine gentlemen and return to the lady in one piece."

The duke grinned, the scar on his cheek whitening as he said deliberately, "So brave, my small foe, with your giants behind you. I've yet to see you prove your worth. You do a lot of fine talking, but I'll wager you're no more than a bluffing puppy giving himself airs." Lucien laughed scornfully, adding softly, "You swine, you're not fit to lick the boots of a guttersnipe."

Bonnie Charlie's violet eyes blazed with anger at the duke's sneering contempt, and losing control at his baiting, lifted a hand and struck the duke full across the face.

Lord Wrainton gave a gasp of astonishment and remained deadly still. Lucien smiled. "Not much strength for a renowned and supposedly vicious highwayman, but as much as I'd expected from a braggart."

"Get back in the coach if you value your mongrel skin," Bonnie Charlie ordered hoarsely, his gloved hand shaking as he leveled his pistol even with Lucien's heart.

"My pleasure. I begin to grow chilled," Lucien acquiesced in a condescending tone and followed the marquis into the coach.

Bonnie Charlie backed up to his horse and agilely mounted, and for just a second glanced away from the coach as he grasped the reins. In that instant the duke withdrew a pistol from his coat and fired it at the giant guarding his coachmen from the back of his horse. John grunted in pain and momentarily dropped his guard, but before the astonished coachmen could react Will had fired a shot into the ground before them, halting any movement they might have made, and Bonnie Charlie had fired his pistol into the door of the coach causing the contessa to scream in alarm and Lucien to draw back for protection.

Signaling to Will and John, Bonnie Charlie urged his mount through the prisoners, scattering them in alarm, and disappeared into the trees, Will and John doing likewise, but in different directions.

The footmen ran to their weapons, but by the time they'd reached them and turned to aim, the highwaymen had disappeared into the darkness of the forest.

Lucien stared grimly after them, his lips thinned in anger, then climbed from the coach to confront his coachmen who were standing sheepishly in the road.

"Well, how did this happen? I had assumed you were all armed for the likes of these highwaymen?" Lucien demanded, a dangerous glint in his eyes.

"Was a tree, your grace, fallen across the road and causin' us to stop. In this weather we never thought 'twas highwaymen. And then from nowheres these giants appears and aims them pistols at us before we could even draw ours. Would've laid us low if we had," the head coachman explained ruefully, seeking confirmation from the other abashed faces around him. "Got to move the damned tree besides," he added, looking balefully at the fallen tree across the road that had caused all their trouble and was now still blocking their way.

"I trust this will never happen again? I only allow one mistake of this nature while you're in my service, so don't disappoint me again," the duke replied coldly. "Now get this cleared as quick as you can," he directed. "We've been delayed long enough as it is." Turning, he walked back to the carriage, his broad back looking uncompromising and stern to the chastened servants.

"Well, don't just stand there gawking. Get to it. You're not in a funeral procession yet," the head coachman yelled, giving the closest boy a cuff on the ear that sent him scurrying.

"We shall be on our way presently," the duke informed Lord Wrainton, who was leaning weakly against the soft cushions of the seat. "Are you quite all right, contessa?"

"*Si,*" she replied faintly, her fingers nervously clasping and unclasping her pearls.

Lucien settled himself in the coach and stared silently out of the window. The scar on his cheek still throbbed with anger.

"Why the hell did you do it?" Lord Wrainton finally found the courage to ask the duke's aloof profile.

Lucien glanced over at him indifferently. "Do what?" he asked haughtily.

"Risk all of our lives by baiting that highwayman? I could scarce believe my ears when I heard you insult him." Lord Wrainton took out his handkerchief and mopped his brow. "He might have shot me as I stood there next to you."

Lucien shrugged unrepentantly. "You were in little danger. I merely was curious how far I could push the fellow, and now I know his weaknesses."

The duke's eyes were narrowed in thought and gradually a cruel smile curved his lips and he suddenly laughed, a satisfied expression settling on his features as he slapped his leather gloves carelessly against the palm of his hand.

"And so you put us all into danger for that?" Lord Wrainton demanded incredulously, feeling a shiver of apprehension as he saw the duke's expression.

"*Per favore,*" the contessa broke in before the duke could make his scathing remark. "We are safe, *si?* There is no cause for further alarm? So, we will forget the incident. Of course, I must admit it was quite exciting," she added mischievously.

"Luciana!" Lord Wrainton said in exasperation.

"It was the first time I have been held at pistol point," she excused herself. "*Si*, I was most excited, and this *bandito*, he was quite the gentleman, too," she murmured, touching her pearls reassuringly.

"I personally found him to be impertinent," the duke answered softly, "and in need of being taught a lesson."

"Well, I found the whole thing distasteful," Lord Wrainton said irritably. "Why, we came close to being murdered, and you two think it was exciting. Lud, but I must be the one half-crazed." He held his handkerchief to his lips, dabbing at the beads of perspiration.

The contessa stared at him, then said in an uncertain voice, "This *bandito*, there is something strange about him, something not quite right." She shook her head in self-derision. "Ah, I am silly. It is nothing really, and quite ridiculous."

"What is ridiculous?" Lucien asked curiously.

"No, we will not discuss this notion of mine. I will look the complete fool then," the contessa laughed and snuggled down into the fur of her pelisse, then issued an abrupt "*Silenzio!*" to the sniveling Maria.

They arrived at the King's Carriage Inn early in the evening, the duke dining with Lord and Lady Wrainton, and then bidding them farewell as he planned to make an early start the following morning. But he did not go to bed immediately. He sat in the darkness of his bedchamber for over an hour, his mind preoccupied with a certain scheme he'd been devising all evening, until, finally satisfied, he slipped between the sheets of his bed and slept contentedly.

※

"Here, give me the bandage," Sabrina told Will as she held a piece of cloth against the wound in John's shoulder.

"And give me the bottle," John said between clenched teeth as he grimaced at Sabrina's ministrations. "Don't worry, Charlie, Mam'll see to it," he said confidently.

"I just want to stop the bleeding or you'll never make it to her," Sabrina answered shortly, nervous perspiration threading down from her temples.

"He'll be all right, Charlie, John's as strong as an ox. Take more'n a bullet to kill him off."

"Yeah," John agreed, taking a deep swallow from the bottle of rum Will had handed him. "More like a cannon-ball, eh, Will?"

"More'n one," Will chuckled.

"I wish you'd stop joking," Sabrina spoke worriedly.

"Like I said, Charlie. Mam'll take care of him, all we got to worry about is spending these guineas."

Sabrina wasn't listening. "This is the first time anyone has dared to shoot back at us. John could've been killed," she cried.

Will rubbed his big thumb against the side of his nose. "Told you I didn't like that scar-faced gent. Would be his carriage we'd have to hold up. Looking daggers at us, he was."

"Gave me the shivers," John contributed thickly, the rum he'd drunk beginning to take effect.

"Revenge is what he's gonna want, Charlie. And once you're at his mercy, he'll want blood for blood," Will warned. "You shouldn't of hit him."

"Speaking of accounts to be settled," Sabrina promised, looking at John's shoulder wound, "I've one to settle with our scarred friend."

"Go easy, Charlie," Will entreated her. "He's different. If he ever gets his hands on us, well, I'm a big man but that look of his sent a chill up my spine."

"Do you think I'm frightened of that town fop?" Sabrina demanded incredulously.

"You should be, Charlie," Will told her quietly.

Sabrina's lower lip jutted out, and with her hands on her hips and the light of battle still in her violet eyes she vowed rashly, "I don't know who he is, or why he's here, but he'll soon wish he'd never set eyes upon me, and I'll give him time to lament the fact before I send him to his grave."

Will gazed at this little firebrand who was the brains behind their misadventures and shook his head sadly. They'd come to love her these past years, admiring her courage; but she was a tough, determined little lady who would have her own way, and he had an awful feeling in the pit of his stomach that it would lead to ruin. He felt like they were sitting on a barrel of gunpowder with Charlie going around striking sparks off everything, fearing nothing and no one. He shook his mop of corn-colored hair in resignation. They'd end up on the gallows yet.

It is a double pleasure to deceive the deceiver.

—*Jean de La Fontaine*

Chapter 4

SABRINA CLIMBED DOWN DAINTILY FROM THE HORSE-DRAWN GIG. To any observers she was playing Lady Bountiful to her less fortunate neighbors, bearing a basket of homemade goods, perhaps bread and soup, to the ailing Taylor son who'd hurt his shoulder chopping wood.

Sabrina knocked once, then twice rapidly and waited, the scent of lavender and herbs heavy in the warm afternoon air. Sad-faced pansies stared back at her from the flower beds and the loud notes of a storm thrush called from a chestnut tree.

"Ah, Lady Sabrina, come along in," Mrs. Taylor welcomed as she escorted Sabrina inside the cottage. "You don't mind going into the kitchen? I've bread in the oven and it's likely to burn if I'm not there to watch it."

"Of course not. You know I like that room above all; it's always so warm and smells so good in there."

Mrs. Taylor smiled. "You and the boys'll never grow up. Hoping for a piece of freshly buttered bread, are you?" She chuckled happily as she pulled out a cane chair for Sabrina to sit on.

The large farm kitchen was full of the aroma of baking bread from the brick oven built into the fireplace, where a great kettle hung over the open fire.

"How is John?" Sabrina asked.

"Well, a bit feverish, but that's to be expected. I'm not worried, though, I've applied a salve and he's gettin' plenty of rest. Be himself in no time," Mrs. Taylor answered assuredly. "Now, how about a cup of coffee? I've just brewed some over the fire."

"I was hoping you'd ask me to have some," Sabrina admitted. "I've been tantalized by it since I came in, and with the coffee mill still fragrant, it must be freshly ground."

"Not much misses your eye, Lady Sabrina," Mrs. Taylor beamed. "Just finished grinding it shortly before you knocked."

Mrs. Taylor took down two pewter mugs and placed them on the table, then removed two loaves of crisp, golden bread from the oven. Holding one of the loaves with the edge of her voluminous apron, she placed it on the table in front of Sabrina. Going back to the fire with the mugs, she tipped a small kettle from its adjustable hanger and filled the two mugs with the steaming brew.

"Now, some butter." She reached for a large wooden bowl with freshly churned butter that hadn't yet been patted into shape and a small pot of honey.

"This should do us," she sighed, dropping down in a chair at the table. "I've been on my feet all day, about worn them off."

Sabrina took a dab of fluffy butter and spread it across the piece of warm bread, licking her fingertip as the melting butter dripped over the edge. "No wonder John and Will grew so big, with this good food inside of them."

"Well, no one can say I didn't feed 'em proper," Mrs. Taylor agreed proudly, spreading honey liberally across her slice of bread.

Sabrina sipped her coffee thoughtfully. "I can't tell you how awful I feel about John. It's my fault. I sometimes regret ever having started this charade," she spoke passionately, deeply troubled by the incident.

Mrs. Taylor patted Sabrina's hand comfortingly. "It's not you I blame. The boys were poaching long before they met you, and could've come to grief by that, sure enough,"

"Poaching is not highway robbery," Sabrina said despondently.

"No, but it would've led to it soon. Things are bad hereabouts, people out of work, starving and nothing to be done for it. Not until you came, at least. Now you've leased your land cheap to them, and given food, money, and jobs to those who can't farm. You've saved half the village. What did them other fancy gentlemen care? None, that's what," she spoke angrily.

"You make me sound like another Robin Hood, and I'm not. I can't claim that I began this so charitably, or from a divinely guided altruism. I did it selfishly and out of hate and revenge. I was motivated by self-interest," she contradicted Mrs. Taylor stubbornly.

Mrs. Taylor shook her head, not to be swayed from her opinion. "You might have started it for the reasons you say, although it be for your family more than yourself, I say. But you don't now, do you? Why do you help us and the villagers if you hate them? No, you're an angel, Lady Sabrina, and I'll hear no different even from your own lips." She closed her lips firmly together, refusing to hear any more on the subject.

"I don't suppose we'll know the truth of that until the final accounting, but I don't think I'll need my cloak," Sabrina predicted. "Where is Will?"

"Gone into the village for a spot of ale at the tavern, and to pick up on the latest gossip. More coffee, Lady Sabrina? And you've hardly touched your bread."

"Yes, I have. You're just used to the giant-sized helpings of John and Will. This is plenty," Sabrina reassured her, taking a bite to placate her motherly instincts.

Sabrina glanced around the room, feeling relaxed. It was such a peaceful cottage. Sitting here eating bread and butter, sipping coffee like any other well-bred lady of the neighborhood paying a duty call. But at the back of her mind there was always that constant fear. That niggling doubt that plagued her conscience. She was a highwayman, a thief and a liar. And yet, was she so very bad? She helped people less fortunate, and only stole what was needed. She wasn't greedy, she hadn't really hurt anyone, although her temper had driven her closer than ever before to wanting to kill someone. She still intended to even the score with the scar-faced gentleman at some future date.

Sabrina suddenly felt something strike her foot and giving a startled cry looked down to see a small, furry face peeping up at her from the folds of her gown. Laughing, Sabrina leaned down and scooped up the playful kitten in her hands, rolling it into her lap in a fluffy ball.

"Where did you come from?" she asked the kitten as it licked her fingers with a rough pink tongue. "You like butter, don't you?"

Tickling the little gray and white cat's tummy she watched Mrs. Taylor, who was busy gathering ingredients from her shelves. "I thought you were tired? What are you making now?" she asked in puzzlement as Mrs. Taylor placed a large pot on the table and a pile of dried flowers beside it.

"Mead. I'll mix honey and ginger and a couple of handfuls of elder flowers in this pot of water and let it boil for an hour. Then after it's cooled and been skimmed, I'll pour it into a tub and let it cool off so I can add the yeast. Then I'll let it sit overnight so it gets that good mellow taste and then into the barrel over there. Best thing around on a warm afternoon when you're bone weary and parched with thirst," she chuckled. "Put away my fair share, that I do." She patted her thickening middle regretfully.

"Next time I come, I'd like to sample your brew," Sabrina told her, snuggling the kitten under her chin.

Mrs. Taylor made a mock frown. "Now what is that cat up to?" she demanded, flicking the kitten playfully under the chin. "She's a sweet-talking little rascal. Loves butter, and when I'm making it, tries to lick up all the cream before I can get it into the churn. Nearly split her sides the other day, the little pig. Waddled out of here so full of cream her little tummy was fair to bursting." She threw back her head and laughed heartily.

"What's her name?" Sabrina asked with a smile.

"Well, now, I don't rightly know, never got around to naming her," Mrs. Taylor admitted. "Would you like to name her?"

"Oh, yes, I think I'll call her Smudge because she has a little smudge of butter on her cheek," Sabrina proclaimed, rubbing the velvety black nose of the purring kitten who was asleep in her lap.

"Charlie!" Will exclaimed from the doorway.

"Hello, Will," Sabrina greeted him, casting him an interested look. "I hear you've been sampling some of the village ale and gathering a little gossip."

The big man shifted uncomfortably, a reluctant look crossing his face. He nodded his head and, avoiding Sabrina's eyes, stuffed a large hunk of bread into his mouth and was unable to answer her query.

Sabrina smiled. "You know that as soon as you've swallowed that mass you'll have to answer me and tell me what you've heard."

Will swallowed with a gulp and stared out of the window, an obstinate look on his broad features.

"Come now, Will," Sabrina appealed. "You know I'll find out eventually. You might as well tell me and save me the time."

"Will! You do as the Lady Sabrina asks. What's wrong with you?" Mrs. Taylor scolded.

Will turned, and facing Sabrina with dogged resolution answered, "All I heard was that some gent was throwing a private party tonight."

Sabrina's violet eyes brightened with interest as she looked expectantly at Will for further information. "Well?"

'That's all," Will said perversely.

Sabrina's eyes narrowed. "Since when have you bridled your tongue?" she demanded. "You usually talk yourself out of breath. Why are we so tongue-tied now?"

"I didn't think we would be interested in this. It's not in our vicinity. You know we like to stay close to home where we know the countryside," Will explained reasonably. "Besides, with John sick we're short a man."

"I know, but that doesn't explain your reluctance to tell me about this party. Who is the host and where is it?" Sabrina asked curiously.

"If you'll excuse me, Lady Sabrina, I'll take some of this coffee and warm bread up to John."

Mrs. Taylor bustled out as she always did when they began to talk privately.

Will shrugged his massive shoulders. "It's the Davern estate. It's been empty for a long time, and it's just got a new owner, and he's giving a party for some of his friends at it. Supposedly brought in an army of servants to clean it up and now he's planning to do some entertaining."

Sabrina watched Will's flushed face curiously. "I still don't see why you were so reluctant to tell me this news? It is beyond where we usually work, but it does sound too good to pass up. However, I don't know. We've plenty of work hereabouts," she concluded.

Will heaved a grateful sigh of relief. "Thought you'd feel that way," he grinned widely.

"But why were you worried?" Sabrina asked in confusion.

"Well, 'twas the scar-faced gent's man who told me. He's the new owner of that estate, and his man was in the tavern getting good and primed, and he tells me about this party his master's giving tonight. Ordering bottles of rum and wine, and—" He stopped abruptly as he saw the surprised, then determined expression on Sabrina's face. "Charlie, you ain't going to go, are you?" he asked worriedly. "That's why I didn't want to tell you. I don't like it. The scar-faced gent's bad news."

"I would've thought you'd be the first to want to get revenge on the man who shot your brother?" Sabrina accused him.

Will doubled up his fists. "I'd like to draw and quarter him, but John's going to be all right, and I got this feeling about the scar-faced one. I don't think it'd be worth the price we'd have to pay."

"I know you're not a coward, Will, but if you'd feel better not going tonight, then so be it. I'll not blame you, but I intend to go," Sabrina told him firmly.

Will shook his head. "You know I won't let you go alone. You need me. Only wish we'd John, too."

"Listen, Will, we're always in danger. Every time we ride out we risk capture and death. This is no different—except that we already know where we're going and who we're up against. The odds are in our favor more than if we stopped a coach on the open road. Don't worry, this will be one of our easiest and most rewarding jobs," Sabrina promised with growing confidence. "To see our scar-faced friend's surprised face when we arrive unannounced at his private party. He'll pay for his misplaced courage of the other evening."

Will nodded agreement, worried indecision still evident on his face.

"I must go, but I'd like to see John first," Sabrina told Mrs. Taylor who'd just returned to the kitchen. Sabrina put the fat kitten on the floor where it scampered off quickly to a basket near the fire and curled up again to fall immediately to sleep.

John was propped up in a large feather bed, dwarfing the four posts that surrounded him. A quilted coverlet was pulled up over his nightshirt and he was staring moodily out of the casement window, his mug of coffee in one hand, when Sabrina and Mrs. Taylor, followed by Will, entered.

"Charlie!" John exclaimed happily, then turned a bright red and sunk deeper beneath the quilt in embarrassment. "This is no place for a lady. Mam, you shouldn't have brought her in here," he complained.

"Now when has anyone been able to tell the Lady Sabrina what to do? She does as she pleases, as it should be," she berated the flustered John. "Be glad she even thought of a big turnip-head like you."

"How are you feeling, John?" Sabrina inquired sincerely, perching on the edge of the bed.

"Oh, fine, Charlie, just fine. Be up now if Mam would let me," he reassured her.

"I brought you some playing cards, and Mary made you some gooseberry tarts, knowing you've a sweet tooth." Sabrina dug into the basket she'd brought into the bedroom with her and placed next to her on the bed.

John grinned, his hazel eyes full of pleasure. "Well now, that's real kind of you, Charlie. And you thank the Lady Mary for her kindness, too," he added shyly, confirming Sabrina's suspicion that he secretly admired Mary.

"I will, John, and I know she'll be pleased to hear you're doing so much better. Now, I must be off." Sabrina gave Will a beckoning glance and left the room with him behind her.

"Meet me in the orchard about nine. We don't want to arrive too early. We'll let the play get underway so the gentlemen will be well into their spirits and less inclined to heroics," Sabrina directed, then added with a glint in her eyes, "although I almost wish our scar-faced friend would try something. With little or no provocation I would run him through."

Will shook his curly head in defeat. "I'll be there, but it seems a warning to me, with John laid up with a wound, and there being a full moon tonight and that gent that shot John being the one we're going to rob again. It adds up to trouble, if you asks me."

Sabrina's mouth tightened ominously as she stood before the large man, her head only reaching the middle of his chest, her hands placed firmly on her hips. "I didn't know Will Taylor was a coward and frightened of his own shadow."

Will's face burned red and his hands automatically doubled into fists as he controlled his temper.

"Listen, Will," Sabrina cajoled, placing her small hand on Will's big, muscular forearm. "Mary would've said something if there was danger. You know she has the gift. She'd have felt something, and yet she's said nothing so far. Now, don't worry." She patted the still rigid muscles of his arm and added truthfully, "You know I'd not have another with me. I've complete trust and faith in you and your courage, Will. Forgive me?"

Sabrina smiled up into his broad face that still mirrored the hurt she'd inflicted to his pride. He suddenly grinned sheepishly.

"Sure, Charlie. I can't be mad at you, even though I know I shouldn't listen to you."

Sabrina's smile deepened as she turned away, waving to Mrs. Taylor, who stood watching from the bedroom window. Climbing back into the gaily painted cart, she urged the horse down the path and onto the road that cut through the small village. The horse trotted along pulling the yellow-wheeled cart across the stone bridge that spanned the river as it meandered through the village. The brick and oak walls of the old mill towered over the bridge while the huge mill wheel turned noisily. Entering the village with its cobbled streets Sabrina drove slowly past the high-roofed, half-timbered houses and flower gardens, cheerful sunflowers standing tall above the rest as they nodded somnolently in the afternoon heat. She left the main road of the village before entering the busy marketplace and the tavern opposite that would be busily serving thirsty customers. She could see the tall tower of the church rising into the blue sky above the town until it was blocked out by the shade from the overhanging boughs of chestnuts and elms bordering the road. In the distance, red bullocks grazed peacefully in green meadows of yellow cowslips and droopy-headed bluebells.

A lazy afternoon, Sabrina thought idly as the cart jogged along the dusty road, the horse automatically turning up the narrow, twisting road that led to Verrick House. But before leaving the main road, Sabrina's breath caught sharply as she recognized a troop of patrolling dragoons farther down the road. Her gloved hands tightened unconsciously on the reins as she controlled the impulse to whip the horse into a gallop and send him out of reach of the King's men. She forced herself to loosen her grip and keep the horse trotting at a steady, even pace. Glancing curiously from beneath the wide brim of her hat, Sabrina watched the troop gallop past on the road, not recognizing the officer who rode ahead, one of the new ones brought in to capture her, she thought in amusement. He wouldn't be riding so proudly in the saddle after the many fruitless chases she would lead him on, she thought, and breathed a sigh of relief as they rounded a bend and were hidden from sight.

Nearing Verrick House the road narrowed and was bordered by oleanders and cherry laurel hedges. Guiding the cart along the drive she slowed as she entered the stable yard and an ostler came running forward to assist her. She entered the hall, and removing her bonnet climbed the stairs, her thoughts centered on this evening's activities. She would talk with Mary first, just to reassure herself; not that she herself was really worried about this evening.

She found Mary in her room, sitting on the edge of her bed, a faraway look in her light gray eyes. Sabrina sat down beside her, taking one of her cold hands between her own and squeezing it softly.

"Mary," she whispered. "Mary, it's me, Sabrina." She looked into Mary's eyes, trying to see what she was gazing at, but they stared through her, seeing something beyond the room. "Mary?"

Mary's fingers gripped Sabrina's hands and she shivered, her eyes closing as she breathed a deep sigh. Sabrina waited patiently, knowing it would be a moment before Mary regained her composure.

Mary's eyes opened slowly and she turned her head and smiled at Sabrina.

"You knew, didn't you?" Sabrina asked.

"Yes, I felt your questions and your doubts before I think even you did," she replied softly, the trance still holding her in its spell. "I have never felt quite this strange before."

"What did you see?" Sabrina asked anxiously.

"I saw a strange house, and a stranger."

Sabrina gripped her hands together as she asked, "What did this stranger look like?"

Mary frowned. "At first he frightened me, you see; he had a scar across his cheek, and I felt very nervous and uneasy."

Sabrina stared down at her hands in her lap, nervously chewing her lower lip as she listened to Mary's startling information—for she had never spoken of the scar-faced man before.

"I'm worried about this man, and yet I don't feel the same cold, desolate ache that I did when Grandfather died." Mary laughed nervously. "I know it sounds insane and doesn't really make much sense, but what is going to happen, I feel, is inevitable." She looked to Sabrina for understanding.

Sabrina returned her stare gravely, nodding her head in acceptance. "Well, as long as you don't see me hanging from the gibbet, then all is well, because I shall be facing that scar-faced man this evening," she confessed reluctantly, "and unless he's armed to the teeth, then you can look for me around dawn."

"So there really is a scar-faced man," Mary breathed in awe.

"It's not really a disfiguring scar," Sabrina explained, "it just makes him look rakish, and he has a disposition to match. He's the one who fired at John."

The worried look returned to Mary's face. "I wish I felt certain about this. How can I allow you to go riding off into danger, danger I know exists, and yet I can't really warn you against anything specific," she cried in disgust. "Everything is so vague. I always see just enough to tantalize me, but never enough to do any good."

"Yes, you do, Mary," Sabrina replied. "Remember when you warned us of the dragoons waiting on the hillside to ambush us? And the time Richard was lost and you knew exactly where to find him? Oh, Mary, you've been right so many times, don't despair now, just because you can't tell me everything."

"But why do I see this scar-faced man? Who is he? And why is he important to us? He's always there, Sabrina. I hadn't told you earlier, but I've seen him before—in other dreams," Mary confessed. "But it doesn't make sense. Is he an enemy, or not?"

"Of course he is. What else could he be?" Sabrina demanded. "But he won't be troubling us further after tonight."

Mary clasped her hands together tightly. "I hate it. I hate having the gift," she said tearfully. "I'm cursed. I want to be normal, Rina. I don't want to be different," Mary sobbed. "I think sometimes I'm a witch. Why do you love me? Why do you care about me? I only see evil."

"Don't, Mary. You're not evil. What you have is God-given. It has to be," Sabrina said persuasively, putting her arm around Mary's shaking shoulders.

"Don't you remember the English ship you warned us of? The French captain still must say prayers to you for saving his skin. And remember the night you warned Will and John and me not to go on the highroad, and the next day two highwaymen who'd been caught by a patrol of dragoons that night were seen hanging from the gibbet. Your gift is good, Mary," Sabrina coaxed. "Now dry your tears and give me a smile. I'm tired of long faces about me. What with Will's woebegone faces, I'm out of all patience with the lot of you."

Mary gave her a watery smile and got to her feet, smoothing down her skirts. "You're right, Rina. I've been acting like a wretch these past few days, but everything will be all right. It has to be."

Sabrina smiled in satisfaction. "I know it will. Have I failed yet? We've many more profitable years yet to come, you wait and see."

∽✧∾

Sabrina shook off her uneasiness as she and Will left their familiar countryside of valleys and woodlands, and through the dark of night under a full, yellow moon riding high in the sky they traveled across a desolate expanse of wild heath, then a forest of dense, black fir trees. Gradually the whole atmosphere of the land began to change into a nightmarish quality. The stone villages surrounded by their high, thick, medieval walls had a fortressed look to them. The fields and lanes were a mazework of stone walls and fences that would impede a quick and facile escape. In the distance they could see dim silhouettes of the massive chimneys of isolated houses and groves of twisted elder and crab trees, blown grotesquely out of shape by the winds, dotting the hillsides.

"I don't like it at all," Will spoke softly, his voice sounding like a clap of thunder in Sabrina's ears.

She looked at his big bulk in the dark, its familiarity comforting her nervousness as her horse shied at a scuffling noise from the hidden underbrush.

"It's too late now," Sabrina answered as she saw the triple chimneys of the house ahead. The gossiping servant had mentioned its unique appearance and the avenue of sycamores lining the drive when he'd been drinking in the tavern.

"It seems too quiet." Will frowned as he tried to see into the darkness enveloping the grounds.

"It appears normal to me. See, there are lights coming from those windows, and anyway it's not a full household. It's just a small party, and they're still in the process of moving in," Sabrina reasoned aloud. "It's in our favor, Will. He and his friends, and a couple of servants. Mere child's play, eh, Will?"

They made their way closer to the house, moving silently into the shadows, and, tethering their horses, crept close. Sabrina examined the house before whispering to Will, "You go to the window and stand ready to step in when I call. I'll slip around the side. I saw a window above, partially open, and I'll climb up the trellis and come down from upstairs. This way we'll have them between us. This window is locked, so you'll have to break it."

"I don't like it. We shouldn't separate. I'll come up with you. We don't know the plans of the house, Charlie, or who's upstairs. No, I'll come with you," Will said adamantly.

Sabrina shook her head. "And have the whole lot of them alerted as you crash down from the side of the house? You don't think that flimsy trellis will carry your weight? I'm light as a feather, but you're as big as an ox, Will, and about as noisy as one. No, this is our best plan. From the stairs I'll get an idea of the situation and be able to act."

Leaving Will stationed at the lighted window, Sabrina crept silently to the side and climbed swiftly and noiselessly up the clinging trellis. Entering the darkened room through the open window she cast a quick glance about her, taking in her surroundings. It was an unused bedchamber. She could make out the cumbersome shape of a four-poster and chest of drawers. Moving across the room where a small ribbon of light seeped beneath the closed door, Sabrina opened it and carefully peered out into the wide gallery that was lighted by several wall sconces.

Walking down its length, her footsteps echoing faintly, Sabrina suddenly shivered. It was so quiet. Like a tomb. Certainly too quiet for a rollicking midnight card party. But then gambling was the only thing these dandies and fops took seriously—and indeed, showed any competence at, Sabrina thought scornfully, unless it was in their own elaborate appearances; prancing peacocks, the whole lot of them.

Sabrina grinned beneath the concealment of her mask as she thought of her own finely cut velvet breeches and coat and the strip of bright tartan. She had a part to play, a reputation to live up to, and these popinjays would be sorely disappointed if her appearance fell short of their rather fanciful expectations of what the infamous Bonnie Charlie, the impudent, gentlemanly Scots highwayman, should look like.

Sabrina felt the hilt of her sword riding comfortably at her hip—a necessary tool of the trade. She drew her pistol, primed and ready to answer, just in case one of the gentlemen had a sudden urge to play the hero.

Most of the furnishings of the upstairs were still shrouded in protective dust covers. That army of servants Will had spoken of hadn't been too busy, Sabrina thought as she swiped at a cobweb in front of her face.

The large hall below was quiet and shadowy, the light from a few candelabras barely lighting it as Sabrina quietly made her way down the staircase, pausing cautiously as she heard scuffling and voices from the servants' door beneath the staircase. Descending the last few steps quickly, she pushed an oak chair in front of the door and tipped it so the back was wedged beneath the doorknob. That would detain the servants, should they become curious. From beyond a closed door Sabrina suddenly heard laughter and the clink of glasses.

Smiling in anticipation, Sabrina moved forward, her gloved hand reaching out for the doorknob. Turning it slowly with her left hand, her right firmly holding her pistol, she opened the door suddenly and rushed in to take her victims by surprise—only the room was empty!

"Looking for someone?" a satisfied voice asked.

Sabrina turned quickly, her heart beating in her throat as the scar-faced man stepped from behind an oak screen, a pistol held casually in each hand and pointed at her head, a mocking smile on his face.

"You seem surprised, Bonnie Charlie," he laughed. "Did you get the wrong information? One of your spies must've heard wrongly if you thought there was to be a card party here this evening—for there is only I," he informed her with a widening grin. "And you, of course."

Sabrina's fingers tightened on the trigger as her hand shook imperceptibly and she looked over at the curtained window expectantly.

"Oh, if you're hoping to see your large friend, you'll wait in vain, for I fear he has met with a slight accident," the Duke of Camareigh explained carelessly, a gleam in his sherry-brown eyes.

"A trap," Sabrina said beneath her breath, her eyes darkened by fear.

"Yes, a trap. But I should introduce myself to you. A captive should have the pleasure of knowing who entrapped him. I am the Duke of Camareigh. You may address me as 'your grace'."

Sabrina felt suffocated. She had to keep a clear head. This was no time to panic, and drawing on some deep reserve of courage, she found her voice.

"You seem to have overlooked the fact, your grace, that I also have a pistol pointed at your head."

"I had noticed," the duke replied evenly. "But I seem to remember you threatening me with your sword point." He glanced at Bonnie Charlie insultingly. "Of course you were surrounded by your armed friends at the time. By the way, did I kill your big friend the other night? I'm afraid I aimed hastily and might have been a bit off the mark."

Sabrina's temper flared at his offhand and callous inquiry. He was a swine, and she'd like to knock that mocking smile off his face. "No, you only winged him, your grace," she answered smoothly. "Which leads me to wonder how good a shot you are if you can't hit as big a target as my friend," Sabrina taunted in return.

The duke laughed in genuine amusement. "You are a cool one, Bonnie Charlie. So how do you prefer to die? I'll let you choose. I could put a hole in you now, but I think I prefer to play with you a bit before I run you through and send you to your grave."

A deafening roar cut through the silence, and Sabrina took an involuntary step backwards as she gasped and saw the eagle's feather from her hat float to the floor and land in front of her boots. Behind her mask, her face paled and cold perspiration broke out on her forehead. Carefully she placed her pistol on the floor as he directed with the barrel of his other pistol.

"I yield to your superior treachery, your grace," she spoke softly, a blaze of fury beginning to glow in her eyes. Very well, if she was to die at his hands then she would, but only after she'd done an injury to this meddlesome duke, she thought in anticipation of drawing his blood.

He smiled coldly and moving forward kicked the surrendered pistol from out of Bonnie Charlie's reach and placed his own on the mantel shelf.

"I do dislike fighting in an obviously unequal match," he commented as he drew his sword from his hip, "but you have asked for it." He shrugged his shoulders regretfully. "No one slaps me and goes unpunished. You may not be much to look at, but you're a vicious little fellow and I think it's about time that you learned a few lessons in manners."

Sabrina drew her sword, raising her chin arrogantly. "As I promised once before, I shall give your grace a matching scar for his other cheek."

The duke stood facing her, his buckskin breeches molded to his muscular thighs and his fine lawn shirt and stock covering a wide expanse of chest and shoulder. His blond head gleamed like newly minted gold under the flickering candlelight as he pushed back a chair with the heel of his boot, sending it sliding across the floor.

"On guard, my soon-to-be-dead friend," he challenged with a laugh.

Sabrina sidestepped agilely, her smallness to her advantage as she thrust at the duke's chest with her sword. He parried it effortlessly and lunged, pushing Sabrina back as she struggled to parry the driving force of his thrust. The clashing of steel against steel rang in her ears as she danced about the larger man.

Sabrina began to gain confidence as she kept the duke busy defending himself, until she saw the wide smile on his face and knew that he was merely amusing himself while he played with her. He knew he had her outmatched and was only prolonging the moment until he would cut through her guard and pierce her heart with the point of his sword. A black rage rose in Sabrina and in a fit of uncontrollable passion, lending her renewed strength, she lunged suddenly and caught the Duke off guard, pricking his shoulder slightly before he ducked out of reach and turned on her fiercely, the amused light gone from his eyes as he viciously attacked, his sword seeming to flash fire as she fought him off. In her frightened eyes he looked like a madman with his scarred face and blazing eyes. Sabrina couldn't hold him off any longer. Her arm ached from the effort and felt like lead as she struggled to keep up her guard and protect herself from each mighty thrust of his sword.

With a suddenness of movement the duke twisted adroitly and slipped his sword point in beneath Sabrina's wavering sword, driving his point deep into her shoulder. Sabrina felt a searing pain like red-hot coals and giving a muffled cry dropped her sword as she staggered against a chair for support, momentarily stunned. She felt a wave of blackness engulf her as she fell to her knees, feeling an ache not of the body, but of the soul as she realized she was near death and in her mind's eye saw her family for the last time.

The duke stared down at the fallen highwayman, a disgusted look on his face. "Not much of a fight in you, eh?" He flicked the tartan sash contemptuously, cutting it in two and drawing a small spurt of blood. A dark patch was beginning to stain the highwayman's coat as his blood from the wounded shoulder seeped through the velvet.

"Let's have a look at that roguish face of yours, Bonnie Charlie. It's about time we unveiled the mysterious high-wayman, and I'm curious about who I'm delivering to the soldiers to be hanged," the duke said with a tigerish smile curving his lips as he carelessly slashed the highwayman's hand that had been reaching for a knife at his waist, leaving a long red scratch across the back of his gloved hand.

"Still have a little fight left in you?" He sneered as he reached out and ruthlessly tore the concealing mask from the highwayman's face. "What have we here? You're certainly a pretty little fellow, what—" He stopped abruptly.

The duke's smile faded as he stared more closely at the highwayman's revealed face. A look of amazement spread across his features as he took in the heart-shaped face, the large violet eyes made brilliant by tears of fear and pain, the cupid's-bow mouth that trembled slightly and the creamy smooth skin of her cheeks.

"My God!" the duke ejaculated as he dropped his sword and reached for the crumpled figure that now fell forward in unconsciousness.

He lifted the highwayman easily in his arms and kicking open the partially closed door made his way to the staircase, noting the jammed servants' door as he climbed the stairs with the unconscious girl high in his arms, a grim tightness about his mouth.

Entering the bedchamber that had been cleaned and aired for his use, he carefully lay the highwayman down on the big bed. He stared bemusedly down at the small face for an instant, then removed the cocked hat and tossed it across the room. He lifted the powdered wig from the highwayman's head and revealed long black hair. It tumbled about the pillow as he uncoiled it and it sprung up softly beneath his fingers, soft as a child's, he thought suddenly, as he smoothed a thick curl back from a vulnerable temple.

Carefully he removed the heavy coat from the highwayman, frowning as he saw the blood-stained shoulder and scratch he'd made beneath the tartan sash. Then taking the highwayman's knife he cut the shirt from the unconscious form, his face pale as he stared down at the body before him, his worst doubts confirmed.

"A woman," he whispered, still unable to believe the positive proof before his astonished eyes.

Small breasts rose and fell rapidly beneath his hand as he dabbed at the blood with a clean handkerchief, leaving it on the wound to stanch the flow. He pulled off her boots and, covering her, left the room. Belowstairs he sent his servants hurriedly about boiling water and making bandages, his grim face stalling any curious questions they might have had.

"Where's the other highwayman?" the duke demanded.

"Safely locked up in the cellar and nursing quite a head-ache and sore jaw I should imagine," his valet answered calmly, a smug look on his face as he thought of the surprised grunt from the giant as they'd sneaked up behind him and walloped him good before he could swing those ham fists of his—although even then he'd taken a right to the jaw before finally toppling over. Sanders glanced curiously at the duke, wondering about the order for bandages. "Is there anything I can do, your grace?" he asked. "I assume you dealt with the other bandit successfully."

The duke hesitated a moment, then drew Sanders aside as he confided, "I'm afraid we've a small difficulty. Our high-wayman happens to be female."

Sanders's eyes grew enormous and he choked back an exclamation as the duke shook his head for silence.

"I want no one to know of this, do you understand?" the duke told him. "You bring the medicine and bandages when ready, I'll be up with our guest."

Sanders returned to the business at hand as the duke left, but half of his thoughts were following the duke upstairs.

Sabrina opened her eyes through a haze of pain. Her body felt like it was on fire and she gasped as a sharp, searing pain went through her shoulder as she tried to sit up. She lay back panting, her thoughts confused as she tried to remember what had happened. The vagueness began to sharpen in her mind and suddenly in a flash she knew. The scar-faced gentleman. He had tried to kill her, and nearly succeeded, she grimaced, as she struggled to sit up, a faint feeling spreading through her at the effort.

She glanced about the room fearfully for her attacker, but it was empty. Sabrina shivered, feeling a draught of cool air caress her bare shoulders, and pulled the coverlet closer about her.

A strained look entered her eyes as she realized the implica-tions of that. The person who had removed her mask and wig, and bared her shoulders, must have had a surprising discovery. She put her trembling fingers to her temples and tried to think. She couldn't seem to gather her wits and act. First, she must escape. She must get away from this scar-faced man who had caught her. What had he thought, she wondered, when he'd found out he'd dueled with a woman.

Pulling the coverlet over her shoulder, wincing with pain as she moved her arm, Sabrina struggled from the bed, biting her lip to keep from crying out. She felt the warm blood from her shoulder trickle down her arm, feeling sticky between her fingers. Stumbling to the window she pressed her hot face against the cool pane and rubbed a spot clean of grime to peer out, but only darkness met her eyes. The simple task of opening the window became a tiring struggle in her weakened condition until she finally succeeded, and cool air rushed in to bathe her flushed face.

She saw her coat crumpled on the floor across the room and slowly made her way to it. She was standing dumbly in front of it when the door was opened and the duke entered, coming to an astonished halt midstride as he saw his wounded prisoner swaying before the coat.

Two dark, violet pools of pain stared up into his eyes as he came to stand before her. His mouth tightened ominously as he noticed the blood dripping from her fingers.

"Are you trying to kill yourself?" he demanded angrily.

Sabrina continued to stare mutely up at him. The scar on his cheek fascinated her. She lifted a bloody finger to touch it, unaware of the glazed, feverish look in her eyes raised to his.

The duke felt the chill from the opened window and looked over at it; the truth dawned on him, his eyes narrowing as he returned his stare to the blanketed form before him.

"Trying to escape, are you?" He laughed harshly, the sound ringing in Sabrina's ears like a death knell as she fell into his outstretched arms, his face swimming demoniacally in her eyes.

Let those love now who never loved before;
Let those who always loved, now love the more.

—Thomas Parnell

Chapter 5

MARY WIPED AWAY HER TEARS WITH THE BACK OF HER HAND, her small lace handkerchief already soaked from her crying. Where was Sabrina? What had she allowed Sabrina to walk into with her damned premonitions? Oh, how she cursed the day she was blessed with second sight. If only she hadn't reassured Sabrina that all would be fine. She had given her a false sense of security because of it. How could it have happened? She hadn't seen anything terrible happening to her. Although she had foreseen some trouble, she hadn't believed it to be serious—and yet, Sabrina was missing. She'd been gone now for over six days. Not a sign of her, or Will Taylor.

Mary threw back her head and gave a watery, near-hysterical laugh with no amusement in it. What could she do? Go to the authorities and tell them that her sister, Lady Sabrina Verrick, who was actually the notorious Bonnie Charlie who had robbed them all at one time or another, was missing? That she had disappeared on one of her midnight forays with one of her armed associates in crime?

A week now. Mary's nails bit into her palms. She had to do something. She couldn't stand this fearful uncertainty much longer. Something deep within told her that Sabrina wasn't dead—but that didn't set her mind at rest. John Taylor had scoured the countryside, but had found nothing. They seemed to have been swallowed up from the face of the earth.

Mary walked over to the window and stared hopelessly out at the trees and hills in the distance. They were shrouded by a fine mist from the rain shower and looked ghostly to her worried eyes. How many times had she stood at the window staring out? And yet she saw nothing. Each time it was the same never-ending question—where was Sabrina?

"A gentleman to see you, Lady Mary," the butler announced from the doorway.

Mary composed her face and tried to erase any trace of tears as she turned from the window. "Who is it?"

"A Colonel Terence Fletcher, your ladyship."

"Show him in, Sims," Mary told him, her voice shaking. A colonel? What could he possibly want with her—unless they had captured Sabrina?

She twisted her damp handkerchief nervously between her fingers as the colonel was shown in. Mary stared up into his penetrating gray eyes as if magnetized. His stern face and military bearing intimidated her and she took an instinctive step away from his impressive figure. His jackboots shone spotlessly and his scarlet coat was impeccably cut. A long sword hung from his waist and as he came forward his silver spurs jingled a warning.

"Colonel Fletcher," Mary greeted him weakly.

"My pleasure, your ladyship." He spoke quietly, his voice oddly soothing to Mary's frayed nerves. "I hope you will forgive me this intrusion upon your privacy, but I am just recently arrived from London, and acquainting myself with the neighborhood," he said, explaining his uninvited presence.

"Please sit down, Colonel," Mary invited him, her gray eyes showing a distressed look, "And what brings you to our county, Colonel Fletcher?"

"I have been assigned the task of tracking down and bringing to justice the highwayman who calls himself Bonnie Charlie."

Mary let her eyes slide away from his direct gaze as she studied a floral arrangement. "I see."

Colonel Fletcher watched her curiously as she continued to twist her handkerchief unconsciously. Something was worrying the lady, but it was no concern of his, unless what he'd said had alarmed her; however, she'd seemed distracted before he'd been introduced.

"I hope what I've said hasn't caused you distress? The fact that you live with your sister and young brother, and only an aunt to chaperone you, led me to make this call and make myself known to you. Lord Malton, upon whom I've recently called, told me of your circumstances, and I must admit I am quite concerned lest you and your family be molested by this outlaw. Going unprotected invites danger. I thought of posting a few sentries about your property to insure your safety, if it meets with your approval?"

"Oh, please, you mustn't!" Mary protested. "I mean, it would be too much bother and upset my aunt terribly, what with the constant reminder of our immediate danger." Mary quickly recovered, smiling frozenly into the colonel's interested stare.

"I really can't allow it. We are perfectly safe. Just knowing you are here in the neighborhood sets my mind at rest. Lord Malton exaggerates on our behalf, truly. After all, we have not been robbed. Surely that proves that we are safe? We are not excessively rich."

Mary averted her eyes, praying the colonel would agree. If he posted his men around their property, Sabrina might stumble into them trying to get into the house.

The colonel controlled his expression as he answered carefully, "It will, of course, be as you wish, although I have doubled the patrols and I'm confident of catching this highwayman. I doubt whether you are completely safe, even though you've not been robbed." He pondered that fact silently. Odd that the Verrick family had not been harassed by the highwayman. But then as the lady had said, they were not rich.

He accepted Lady Mary's offer to tea, unwilling to take his leave of this rather unusual woman's company for a few minutes yet. For there was a puzzle here. Most women enjoyed his company, he had found, although he hadn't had much time for prolonged affairs, but he would have sworn there had been a look of terror in Lady Mary's eyes when she'd seen him and a sense of revulsion when she'd held out her hand.

He watched her carefully while she poured the tea from a silver teapot, her hands slim and steady now that she'd seemed to regain some of her composure.

Her hair glowed red beneath the wisp of starched lace that served as a cap, and her features were delicately molded, although there was a sprinkling of freckles like gold dust across her nose. But her most unusual feature was her eyes; light gray with the translucence of crystal.

She was holding out his teacup and saucer, a quizzical look in those eyes now as she patiently waited to gain his attention.

"I beg your pardon for staring," he apologized, "but you've most unusual eyes."

Mary flushed and took a sip of tea in embarrassment, her lashes sweeping low and masking her expression.

"Have I embarrassed you? I didn't intend my compliment to do that," he said with a challenging light entering his eyes as he watched her shy away from him like a startled fawn. He smiled slightly, getting to his feet.

"I'll take my leave of you, Lady Mary," he addressed her, startling her by his use of her first name. "It has been a pleasure. I am only sorry I didn't get the opportunity to meet the rest of your family."

Mary responded volubly, relief evident on her face. "Oh, Aunt Margaret seldom comes down when we've visitors, and Richard is at his lessons and my sister Sabrina," Mary stuttered in nervousness, "s-she isn't feeling too well, a c-cold."

"I'm sorry to hear that. I hope she'll feel better soon," Colonel Fletcher commiserated, a thoughtful look on his face as he sensed Mary's unease. "I will keep you informed on my progress, Lady Mary, concerning the highwayman. I shouldn't want you to worry needlessly. Good afternoon."

Mary sank back against the cushions of the settee, feeling drained of emotion. There was something about that man that worried her, a certain singleness of purpose that meant he seldom gave up or accepted failure. The colonel had frightened her. If only Sabrina were here—she would have known what to do, and how to have handled the colonel. She was never at a loss for words. It would have been very interesting, Mary thought, to have seen the colonel and Sabrina meet and exchange barbs.

⤞✦⤝

Sabrina opened her eyes sleepily and yawned. She began to stretch, but her shoulder felt stiff and sore and was restricted by a firm bandage. She frowned and put a curious hand to it and noticed the fine white fabric of the shirt she wore. It was too long for her arms and flopped over her fingertips. She rolled back the lace-edged cuffs and sat up in the big bed. A fire was burning softly and casting a glow about the room, while rain tapped against the window outside. She was weak, but somehow refreshed, and the burning heat she'd been consumed by was gone. She put a tentative hand to her forehead and felt the dry coolness of it beneath her fingertips.

"I see you have rejoined the living," a deep voice commented from a corner of the room, and as Sabrina's startled glance sought it out, a large form rose from a winged-back chair in the shadows.

Sabrina felt her pulses quicken as the scar-faced man came close to the bed and stood staring down at her. She pulled the neck of the large shirt together protectively and cowered beneath the coverlet.

A grin appeared on his face as he commented dryly, "Your modesty is misplaced, I fear, for I have cared for you since your illness, and…" He spread his hands dispassionately, letting her draw her own conclusions.

Sabrina glared up at him impotently, unaware of the lovely picture she presented to him wearing his shirt, her midnight-black hair tumbling over it in startling dark waves and her eyes a wild violet color in a face flushed pink with embarrassment.

The duke pulled up a chair and straddled it, his arms resting on its back as he directed an interrogating look at Sabrina's bent head as she toyed with the edge of lace that had fallen over her wrist.

"Now, I think it is time we had a few answers, but first allow me to reintroduce myself. I am Lucien Dominick, Duke of Camareigh. You might have forgotten in the excitement."

Sabrina stared up at him insolently. "Certainly not, your grace," she contradicted smoothly. "I'll never forget your name."

"Good. Now what is yours? Ah," he interrupted before she could open her lips, "not your professional name, if you please," he warned softly. "I don't imagine Bonnie Charlie is your Christian name."

Sabrina looked away, a mutinous expression on her face. She jumped as hard fingers closed around the point of her small chin and turned her face back to his. She stared up into his sherry-brown eyes unflinchingly.

"Why all the fuss, your grace?" Sabrina demanded flippantly. "I'll be hanged soon enough when the soldiers arrive, now won't I?"

The duke grinned unpleasantly. "Who said anything about soldiers?"

Sabrina put up her hand and tried to pry his fingers from her chin, only to have her hand grasped instead.

"Such a small, bloodthirsty little hand," he murmured and then put back his head and laughed. "And to think this has been terrorizing the countryside, a slip of a girl." He continued to laugh deeply, his muscular throat arched back and vibrating with sound, his body relaxed.

When he stopped laughing he stared down at Sabrina, his eyes narrowed and piercing, his body tense as he rapped out, "Who are you? Where do you come from?"

He continued to stare at her, taking in the delicate contours of her face, and asked suddenly, "Is that big fellow your husband?"

"Of course not," Sabrina answered unthinkingly.

The duke smiled. "I thought not, but I wasn't sure. I've not seen many husbands take orders so meekly from their wives, and it is evident that you are the leader of this little band of ruffians."

"Did you kill him?" Sabrina asked faintly.

"The giant? No, he had a mighty headache for a day or two, but he is safely locked up belowstairs."

Sabrina sighed in relief. If anything had happened to Will...

"You haven't answered my question," the duke continued. "Who are you?"

"Just a poor country lass having to live by her wits, your grace," she answered demurely.

"A very rich country lass, I would say, and one who has led us all on a wild-goose chase," he corrected her, his humor forgotten as he realized what a fool he'd looked to her. Challenging a woman to a duel, he thought in disgust. What if he'd killed her? He watched her as she sat smugly before him, feeling no remorse at what she'd done. He was in a quandary and he suspected she knew it. She wasn't the ordinary highwayman—nor was she low-bred. Her features disproved that—unless she was the illegitimate offspring of some nobleman? And yet she was well-educated and cultured. Her speech evidenced that.

No, this little bit of fluff was quite an enigma—and had caught his interest. She was too arrogant. She needed to be taught her place.

"You're a thief and a liar, and"—he paused, looking her over contemptuously, then added purposefully—"no telling what else."

Sabrina flushed. "I'm not a thief. At least not an ordinary one," she defended herself. "I never take more than I need, and even then I give half to people who need it. And," she finished haughtily, drawing herself up, "you insult me grossly with your other disparaging remarks."

The duke smiled cynically. "You are quite an actress, but your contrite little excuses won't change the verdict when a rope is tightened about that slim neck of yours." He spoke softly and, reaching out, encircled her throat with his warm hand, his fingers rhythmically smoothing the downy-soft hairs at her nape as he continued, "It would be a pity for such a beautiful woman to choke and gasp as the rope tightened, taking away her breath, her eyes bulging in terror, the blood pounding in her head as she felt her little feet swing in the air, that petal-smooth skin mottled and purple. Not a very pretty sight." His fingers gradually stopped and began to tighten around Sabrina's neck. Her pulse was beating rapidly beneath his big thumb and as it continued to press she began to hear thundering in her ears, and, reaching up, grabbed frantically at his fingers, trying to prise them loose from around her neck.

She stared into his eyes, which had turned almost black with his anger, disbelief on her face when he suddenly loosened his grip and allowed her to breathe. Sabrina took deep breaths of air, her chest moving rapidly as the room stopped swimming.

A smile curved the duke's mouth. "It wasn't very nice was it? Were you frightened?" He laughed heartlessly. "No, you wouldn't admit to feeling fear, would you, Bonnie Charlie? Defiant to the end, are you? We'll see," he told her enigmatically.

Sabrina controlled the shiver that threatened to shake her and spat back, "I'll never cower at your feet. Do you think you, a white-livered Judas, can dictate to me? You deceive yourself, your grace."

Sabrina raised her chin, the sparkle back in her violet eyes as she continued to ridicule him in her anger and fright.

"Do you really want your friends to know that the brave Duke of Camareigh dueled with a mere woman? That he nearly killed her? Do you really think that they would appreciate learning that the infamous and bloodthirsty Bonnie Charlie, who had been terrorizing them for so long, was in actual fact a woman? No, I don't think they would thank you on that score, your grace. They would never be able to hold up their perfumed heads in public again," Sabrina jeered laughingly, feeling the master of the situation.

She returned the duke's proud stare. "You're in a quandary, for your own self-esteem is at stake, and a gentleman's honor and name is everything, isn't it? No, I think you will not turn Bonnie Charlie over to the authorities."

"You speak very persuasively in your defense. However, who said I planned to turn a highwayman over to the authorities?" He smiled at the puzzlement on Sabrina's face. "On the other hand, I might turn over to them a thieving wench who broke into my home intent upon mischief. And along with her, a certain large friend. Ah, you had forgotten your giant protector, I see," he reminded her with a smile of satisfaction. "Yes, he will undoubtedly be hanged, or possibly after a prolonged stay in prison, you will both be deported. Not very pleasant, I assure you. Yes, you should really be quite frightened by the predicament you find yourself in. Either that or you're a fool, which for some reason I don't think you are."

Sabrina's face had whitened at his threatening words and her eyes had grown wide, darkening with fear.

The duke seemed satisfied with the calculated effect of his words, and sauntering to the door added, "You might think on that, and when you are a bit more communicative and forthcoming with the information I seek, we will have more to say to one another."

Sabrina stared in impotent fury at the closed door, his words sinking into her like quicksand. She fell back against the soft pillows and dragged the bedcovers over her shaking shoulders as a hesitant tear found its way from her eye onto her cheek.

What was she going to do? She couldn't seem to think clearly since this had happened. Always in the past she'd had her way. She'd never come up against someone like the duke before. He was ruthless, mean, vengeful—and intelligent. And, he had caught her.

Sabrina sniffed and wiped away her tears with the back of her hand like a small child, then sat up in dismay as a sudden thought struck her.

Mary! What must she be thinking? She'd been missing countless days now. Poor Mary, she must think she was dead, or captured. And John would be storming about the countryside looking for them, and he would find nothing because they weren't there. They'd left the area and no one knew where they'd gone. How could he possibly find them? And even then, there would be little he could do except get caught himself. This place was like a fortress, and the duke wasn't one to be caught off guard. No, if they were to escape it was up to her. But how?

Sabrina rubbed the back of her neck thoughtfully, the movement bringing back the memory of other fingers. Gradually a look of cunning entered her eyes as she remembered further.

The duke had not been unaware of her as a woman. She instinctively knew this. There had been something about the way his hand had caressed her waist when he'd held her to him and threatened to strangle her. It had been at variance to the violence of his actions. He had been trying to frighten her, yet he couldn't control the automatic gentleness of his hand at her waist.

His eyes had given him away also. They had softened, just for a moment, maybe with pity, but soften they had, and that surely meant that he felt something besides anger. Sabrina had seen other men's eyes widen when they'd gazed at her face and body, but she'd always disdained it and never encouraged a man—but now—now she would play the game.

Sabrina straightened her slim shoulders resolutely. She would attract this arrogant duke. She would bring him to his knees before her, and when he was at her mercy, deceived by her honeyed words, she would escape him. She would manage to free Will and they would flee this prison, leaving the beguiled duke looking the fool.

Sabrina climbed from the bed, feeling a momentary faintness as she stood and walked on wobbly legs to the porcelain bowl placed on the bedside table. Rolling the sleeves of the duke's shirt above her elbows, she poured icy water into the bowl from a matching pitcher, and splashed the refreshing water on her face. She toweled it dry with a large handkerchief folded next to it, and then began to brush her hair free of tangles, smoothing it back from her face in long waves. It was dull and lifeless from her fever. Sabrina frowned at her reflection in the mirror hanging on the wall. She would demand a bath, wash her hair and get clean linen. She felt her shoulder experimentally; it was stiff and when she moved it she felt a twinge of pain, but it was healing. At least she had been given careful treatment at his hands when she'd been ill; apparently his velvet gloves were off now that she'd recovered.

A frown of uncertainty settled on her face as she realized what she was about to do. She stared at the pale scratch across the back of her hand, remembering vaguely how she had received it. The sense of the danger she had placed herself in intruded realistically into her plans. That scratch could be a minor wound compared to what could happen to her along this course of action. But what else could she do? She had to escape and rescue Will, and they had to get out of the duke's way before he discovered her true identity—at all costs that must remain a secret. Besides, she would call a halt to the game before it progressed too far. She would play the seductress, take the duke by surprise, then when he was least suspecting it, attack and the game was hers.

⌒

The duke insolently tapped the giant's cheek with the tip of his sword. "Do be a good fellow and tell me about your escapades. I'm much kinder than my servants, one or two of whom are nursing sore jaws and the thought of revenge against you, my big friend," the duke said in a friendly tone.

Will glared back, one eye black and blue, his lip swollen, and remained silent.

The duke shrugged. "You will talk eventually. I'm merely trying to make it easier for you." He paused reflectively, then added significantly, "And of course it won't be easy for your small female friend. A pity, she is rather pretty, don't you think?"

Will strained ineffectively at the bonds that bound him to the chair. "You touch her and I'll cut you into a thousand pieces," he snarled in rage.

"My, my," the duke declared. "You've found your tongue at last. I seem to have touched a sore point with you."

The duke walked the small confines of the storage room and, turning abruptly, demanded sharply, "Who is she?"

But the giant remained mute, a venomous look in his clear blue eyes as he met the duke's stare.

"I'll find out sooner or later, then… well, it will be too late to ask mercy of me."

"You ain't going to do nothing," Will muttered, challenging the surprised look on the duke's face, "or you'd have done it by now. The soldiers would've been here and taken me and Charlie away by now. But I don't see no redcoats, Duke—so I call your bluff."

The duke gave a reluctant smile, which didn't reach his eyes, at the giant's reasoning. "Ah, but you're wrong. Why should I spare you and that hotheaded female friend of yours?" he demanded coldly. "I have a few debts to collect with interest, my big friend, and if that means amusing myself with you two for a while before I kill you—then that is my privilege. Who cares what happens to two vicious criminals who attacked me in my home?"

Will's face reddened with his anger and fear for Sabrina at this man's hands. "What have you done to Charlie?" he demanded, straining against the rope that held him firm. "If you've hurt her—?"

"She's in good health, for the moment at least, but who can predict the future good fortunes of people in the precarious business you're in? Anything could befall her. Such a pity too, for you seem quite fond of the little vixen." The duke smiled knowingly. "Of course she is quite a beauty in a wild, untamed fashion. You may have far warmer feelings towards her, eh? It might be interesting to form a closer friendship with her myself," he speculated aloud.

Will's face turned purple with his struggles to free himself. "She's not that kind! She's innocent, and if you lay your fine gentleman's hands on her, I'll cut your heart out and feed it to the crows," Will threatened, following it with further bloodthirsty epithets directed at the duke's head.

"My, my," the duke murmured with a thin smile. He moved to the heavy wooden door, but before opening it turned and added softly, "I'll let you think upon my words a bit, and should you decide to break your silence, call out for one of my servants who will be on guard outside of this door, but don't dally too long, my big friend, for I'm not a patient man." With that he left Will alone in the room to ponder his fate.

Lucien poured himself a brandy and stared out into the

bleak afternoon light. He hadn't planned to stay here this long, but then he hadn't foreseen this whole, incredible series of events, either.

A woman. Who would have imagined that troublesome highwayman was in actuality a young girl? It was beyond belief. He still felt chagrined at what he'd nearly succeeded in doing. To kill a woman—he'd never thought he'd come to that. But why should he blame himself? How was he to know that Bonnie Charlie was some common female masquerading in men's breeches? She had no right to be doing what she was. He shook his head. The problem was just that—she was no common female. She looked and talked like a well-bred lady. And even if she were not that, how could he turn a woman over to the authorities? Her fate would be doomed and he would have her death on his conscience. No, he must do something, for he couldn't just let the vixen loose.

He would learn her name, find out all there was about her, and that giant friend of hers, and then threaten exposure should she ever ride again as Bonnie Charlie. Yes, that was the thing to do. But how would he get this precious information from that defiant female?

Threaten? He could still remember the feel of her soft neck beneath his fingers. She'd been frightened, but he could not follow that course. Bullying women was not to his taste. He preferred a more subtle approach.

He saw again her small, heart-shaped face with those beautiful violet eyes and ivory-smooth skin, and had to admit that she was an unusual beauty.

It was odd, though. He had never seen her before, yet there was something tantalizingly familiar about her. He couldn't quite place it, but he must have seen her someplace before, that was the only answer to it.

He could threaten them with the demise of the other to get the information he desired, but there was another and far more pleasant way of going about it. He smiled. No woman who'd led the life she had could be as modest and innocent as she would have him believe—especially one as beautiful as she was. Some man would've caught her by now; besides, her type never had been innocent, they knew what a man wanted before he did, and she would welcome the chance to buy her way out of the predicament she found herself in. Right now she was too angry and frightened to realize this. But soon, the seduction would begin. Only he would be the seducer and not she. He would get the information from her soft lips without her being aware of it—or being able to help herself. She would not be able to call her soul her own when he had finished with the little firebrand.

He smiled in anticipation, for he was beginning to look forward to this little game as he remembered the feel of her beneath his hands. Yes, this should prove quite a diversion before he was forced to return to London.

Sabrina sat before the crackling fire, her freshly washed hair drying quickly from its warmth. It came to life beneath the brush and shone with mysterious highlights in its midnight depths, falling below her hips as Sabrina rose and stretched and it swayed sinuously.

The door opened as Sabrina stood before the fire. Her instinctive reaction was to abruptly crouch down, but remembering her desperate plan for escape she forced herself to breathe deeply and slowly, continuing the even strokes of the hairbrush, well aware that her body was outlined by the light from the fire behind her, the duke's nightshirt doing little to mask the shape beneath.

Lucien stopped momentarily, his eyes widening in surprise at the scene before him, then quickly recovered his usually calm mien. But a small muscle twitched at the corner of his scar as his eyes took in the beauty of the woman before him. Through the thin material of his nightshirt he could see the smooth line of hip and thigh, her small breasts high above a slender waist that he knew he could span with his hands if he wanted. He followed the tapering slimness of her legs to the small toes that peeped out beneath the edge of his shirt. If he hadn't seen the slow smile and the soft look in her eyes, he would have thought she was nervous.

He placed the tray with the decanter and glasses down on a table and moved closer until the light from the fire played upon the scar on his cheek. Reaching out a hand he captured a stray lock of her hair, his fingers brushing softly against Sabrina's breast. Threading the long strand through his fingers he was amazed by its vibrancy. It seemed to have a life of its own as it curled into his palm. He stared down into the upturned face that looked up into his and began to wind the long, soft strand of blue-black hair around his hand, pulling her closer to him as it tightened.

Sabrina's eyes widened slightly as she was forced to step closer to the duke. Her small bare feet moved between the glossy, black shine of his boots as his arm enclosed her lightly clad body, pulling her the remaining distance. She was pressed firmly against his broad chest and thighs, her heart pounding frantically against the hand that now covered her breast.

Lucien lowered his head and found her soft mouth with his. The fresh scent of jessamine engulfed him from her hair and body and he tightened his arms around her as he folded her closer into him, his senses beginning to swim alarmingly from her nearness as he felt her first response to his kiss.

Sabrina wrapped her arms around his neck, pulling his head closer to hers as she stretched up against him. His hard mouth seared hers in what was her first kiss and taste of a man's mouth.

His mouth moved against her lips, pressing and teasing and opening them. His breath was hot against her fiery cheeks as he left kisses on her eyes and ears, fondling them with his tongue, causing her to shiver uncontrollably when she felt the nibbling of his teeth against her shoulders.

His roaming lips caught at her mouth again and seemed satisfied to remain as the kiss deepened, taking the breath from her body. His hands moved against her back, down her spine slowly until they curved over her buttocks and held her intimately against the hardness of his thighs.

Sabrina's lips clung to his as he lifted her up into his arms and carried her to the big four-poster, laying her gently down on the feather mattress, his lips still holding hers as he leaned over her, his fingers separating the wrapped front of the nightshirt and revealing to his darkened eyes the smooth curve of her breasts. His lips left a burning trail across her throat and shoulders, their hardness softening slightly as his mouth touched the soft roundness of her breasts. Sabrina ran her fingers through his thick golden hair, her small hands delicately tracing his temples and ears and the back of the strong column of his neck where it was bent over her.

He drew back, snatching a kiss from her parted mouth, his eyes dark and passionate as they took in the pale loveliness of her nude body. Sabrina blushed and automatically pulled the gown together across her breasts and thighs. Her eyes were wide and darkened by passion and fear of the unknown.

Lucien and Sabrina stared at each other for a moment before he reached down to tug off his heavy boots, his shirt hanging loose where Sabrina's fingers had opened it, revealing the curly golden hair glinting with sweat on his muscular chest.

Sabrina sat up and stretched out a tentative finger to touch the jagged scar on his cheek. Lucien drew back, startled as she ran the tip of her finger down its length.

"How did you get this?" she asked softly, her voice husky.

Lucien smiled reflectively. "I didn't move fast enough." He laughed grimly and caught her hand, pressing a lingering kiss into her soft palm, then suddenly bit the tip of a tapered finger sharply.

Sabrina cried out in surprise.

"You once threatened to mar my other cheek, if I recollect correctly."

Sabrina grinned impishly and, leaning closer until her breasts pressed against his chest, moved her lips along the scar, her tongue feeling the roughness. Lucien turned his head until her lips touched his mouth and their tongues met. He pressed her back into the covers of the bed, his body covering hers. He felt as if he would crush her beneath him, but when she locked her arms about his neck he relaxed and returned her kisses with experience, teaching her how to respond and please him.

Sabrina felt his heaviness against her like a comforting

cover. His lips and hands were sending shivers through her and leaving her weak and malleable in his persuasive hands. She felt like drifting along wherever he guided her, her hips moving when his hands rubbed over them, her legs entangling with his. His sweat dampened her body and his breathing was shallow and rapid as he moved over her.

Then he wasn't the gentle lover any longer and Sabrina felt a sudden fear and repulsion of him. Sabrina pulled her mouth from his drinking lips and struggled frantically with him. Her eyes locked with his and she saw the surprise in their dark depths that gradually turned to anger as his scar throbbed and his nostrils flared above the beads of perspiration on his lip.

Sabrina pressed her hands against his chest futilely. Her strength was sapped and she had little fight left in her as she fought him. Her bandaged shoulder was beginning to ache with the effort and she finally gave up.

"Leave me alone! Please stop. I can't. I can't!" Sabrina cried incoherently.

Lucien's eyes narrowed and his mouth thinned ominously as he released her shoulders and sat up, letting her roll sideways and bury her head in her arm. Her sobs shook her slender body as she cried. Lucien watched, a puzzled and angry look on his face. He couldn't see her tears, masked by the heavy mass of black hair that had fallen across her face, but he knew they were real.

Lucien shook his head and climbed from the bed, pulling on the shirt he'd tossed aside and gathered up his boots and breeches from the floor. He glanced back at the shaking form huddled on the bed and with a scowl stalked from the room, feeling completely unsure of himself for the first time in his life. Nothing had gone as he'd planned. He had thought to sweet-talk and woo the little vixen, and yet she'd been waiting, her smile sweet and welcoming when he'd come to her, her lips soft and eager against his. He had forgotten his plan to seduce her and learn her secrets. He could only think of her clinging arms and small round breasts pressed to his chest. Damnation, what had happened? If he didn't know better, he would have thought he'd been seduced.

Sabrina looked surreptitiously over her shoulder at the empty room. He'd gone. She wiped at her tears with the long sleeve of his nightshirt and dried her eyes. Her fear was beginning to recede, leaving an emptiness in its stead. She took a deep, shuddering breath and pressed shaking fingers to her temples.

What had happened to her in his arms? How could she have forgotten everything as he'd held her so intimately, learning her body with his. Sabrina bit her lip, drawing blood. She knew what she had intended. She was going to seduce him. It had been so easy, so natural a thing to do, that she had been surprised by his immediate reaction to it. She had never tried to entice a man before and had acted blindly, receiving a response from him she had never expected. But she had not been in control of the seduction at all. Her mind had become blank, a void except for the image of him. Never had she imagined the uncontrollable feelings that built up between a man and a woman.

Sabrina squeezed her eyes shut, and for good measure placed her hands over them. If only she could forget it all. Nothing was the same now. New feelings had been aroused in her and she didn't know how to cope with them.

She felt chilled and glanced at the smoldering fire, the ashes glowing dully as the flame went out. The tall decanter of brandy still stood where the duke had placed it. Sabrina reached out and taking one of the glasses poured herself half a glass of the fiery liquid and taking a deep breath swallowed over half in one gulp. She gagged and her eyes watered, but she could feel its warmth spreading through her body. She covered herself and fell into a troubled sleep beset by the nightmares that haunted her.

Her grandfather's face was cold and lifeless beneath her fingers as it turned into a stone death mask. The pipe's mournful notes calling her back as she tried to escape from death. Soldiers surrounded her. Everywhere she turned they were there in their scarlet coats, calling out to her. She couldn't breathe. Her feet swung in the air and she felt the breath strangled from her body. They all stared. Mary,

Richard and Aunt Margaret sewing a tapestry of the gallows. Why wouldn't they help her? She stretched her hands out to them, but they turned away.

"No! Come back, I'm not dead! Don't leave me here, please—don't go!" she cried.

But they were deaf to her pleas. They were leaving her alone with the hangman and the soldiers. They were abandoning her, turning their backs on her. She screamed and screamed, the sound echoing in her startled ears as it broke the silence of the bedchamber.

Hands grabbed at her and shook her and she fought them. They mustn't be allowed to touch her neck. "Please don't hang me. No! Please, I beg of you!"

"Hang! Hang! Hang!" the crowd of faces chanted excitedly.

"It's all right. You're just dreaming, wake up."

Sabrina reluctantly opened her tightly closed eyes that still reflected the horror of her nightmare, letting the friendly voice coax her back to consciousness.

Lucien was sitting on the edge of the bed, a worried look on his face. His hands were still holding her shoulders in a viselike grip, forgetful of her bandaged shoulder, but she felt comfort rather than pain, and his arrogant features looked dear to her frightened eyes. Sabrina moved her arms up and around his neck, hugging him tightly to her shaking body.

Lucien stiffened in astonishment at her sudden move, remaining motionless as she whispered pleadingly, "Please don't leave me. I can't be alone anymore. I know they're still waiting out there for me. They'll hang me if they can catch me," Sabrina said hoarsely, raising her tear-drenched face from the warmth of his neck, her eyes, full of anguish, looking deeply into his.

Lucien stared back at her. No one had ever pleaded for comforting from him before. He wasn't sure that he even knew how to give comfort. Her eyes continued to hold his, reminding him of a trusting child's.

He slid his arms around her and lifted her into the middle of the bed. Her arms refused to loosen their frantic hold around his neck as he slid into the bed beside her. Pulling the disturbed bedclothes back over them, he enclosed them in a cocoon of warmth, the only light coming from the candle he'd carried into the room to guide him when he'd heard the anguished screams.

He could feel her tense body begin to relax against his as she snuggled closer to him. He could feel her need of him and it felt strange. He comforted her, smoothing back her tangled hair with gentle fingers, liking the feel of it in his hands. Their warmth spread between them and he heard Sabrina give a contented sigh, but she still clasped him tightly around the neck as though afraid that if she let him go he would disappear.

Sabrina felt safer than she ever had before. It was as if all of her defenses had suddenly crumbled around her, leaving her vulnerable and lost. She suddenly knew that she never wanted to leave the safety of the duke's arms. They held her so securely. No one could touch her while she was held by him. She had lost count of the times she had wished to be held and comforted by someone. Her father had never held her to his breast, and her grandfather had loved her, but he'd been strict and not one to show his feelings. But now she had arms around her, comforting her and keeping her safe. She was tired of making all of the decisions, of looking over her shoulder in fear. If only for a short while she could forget...

Sabrina shivered as she fought back the images of her nightmare. Lucien tightened his arms, pulling her against his chest and placing a comforting, light kiss on the pulse beating in her temple. He could feel her soft breasts touching his chest and her bare legs were warm on his, bringing her hip close to his.

They lay quietly together, not speaking, drawing from each other's presence. Lucien felt her fingers caress the hair at the back of his neck and wondered if she was even aware of what she did.

He waited a moment and then allowed his lips to move along her soft cheek, so smooth to his touch, until they reached her mouth. Her fingers stilled at the back of his neck as his mouth closed over hers, and then as she felt the gentleness of the kiss they curved up through his hair.

Lucien felt a thrill go through him and teased her lips with his mouth until they parted hungrily and licked at his. His hands moved over her body slowly and confidently, feeling the alluring curves he'd longed to fondle.

Sabrina moved against him, curving her body into his until she found a closer intimacy. She nibbled at his lips, pulling back from his when he tried to capture them and hold them beneath his. Her fingers played lightly along his back and down boldly to his hips. Lucien groaned and captured her small chin with his hard fingers until his mouth took hers in a deep and stirring kiss, leaving them breathless.

His parted lips left hers and he passionately kissed her face and throat, his hands cupping her breasts as he lowered his mouth to kiss them. He felt the bandage against his face, and looking up murmured, "To think I drove my sword through this small, perfect body of yours." He shook his head in disbelief. "Forgive me for hurting you."

He lifted her hand with the scratch across its back and pressed his mouth to the wound, then held its scarred back against his scarred cheek, binding them through pain suffered.

Their lips met and they kissed, Sabrina's heart racing under his hand. His face was hard and cruel-looking with the scar jagged across it as he gazed into her passion-dark violet eyes, his voice deep as he whispered into her delicate, shell-like ear.

"You puzzle me, little one. I am holding you close to my heart and yet I don't even know your name. Tell me," he commanded, biting playfully at her ear.

"Is it Elizabeth? Jane? No? How about Anne, or Kathleen?" he teased. "More unusual, eh? Well, then, how about Ariadne or Cressida?"

"No, it's Sabrina," she laughed.

"Sabrina," he whispered against her lips, liking the sound of it on his tongue. "I should have known. You're the nymph of the river Severn, and a princess of old England. Have you taken a fancy to a mere mortal and taken me as your lover, Sabrina? Will you be kind to me, or will you lead me through the woodlands and into the fens where I'd be helpless and at your mercy?" he asked mockingly before kissing her passionately and almost punishingly.

"I would never do that to your grace," Sabrina replied, the flickering light in the room casting mysterious shadows on her face.

"Ah, but you already are being cruel to me. 'your grace.' How dare you address me in that manner, as though we were strangers. Lucien is my name, Sabrina," he told her before his mouth found hers.

He held her to him intimately, and sensing a change in him, Sabrina tried to draw back, but he held her firmly locked in his embrace. "Don't turn from me now, not when you hold me in those small hands of yours. I'm wild for you, Sabrina, and I intend to make you mine."

Sabrina gave a gasp of surprise as he rolled over her, covering her bare flesh with his, gentleness turning to strength as he boldly pressed against her and let her know a man's body. She arched her back, moving her hips sinuously as she tried to get even closer, while his hands and lips urged her building desire to a heightened pitch. Delight was shattered by pain as he became part of her body and they moved together as one, his muscular and controlled strength overwhelming and frightening her until she felt the first stirrings of passion in her loins, and responded ardently to his every move as he tutored her in the art of making love.

Afterwards he lay beside her holding her close and kissed the tears from her face, then very gently tilted her face up to his.

"Why?" he whispered, feeling an unaccustomed tenderness for this young girl he held so closely in his arms. "Why did you let me take you? I had no idea you could possibly be a virgin." He shook his head in disbelief, but felt a certain possessive satisfaction at having been the first man to make love to her and know the delight of her charms.

Sabrina shrugged philosophically. "It was bound to have happened someday. Why shouldn't I seek fulfillment before the hangman stretches my neck?" she laughed, the sound coming out harsh and hollow.

Lucien's arms tightened around her, his mouth grim. "You'll not masquerade again. I'll see to it, Sabrina, that you never have the chance to." He forced her chin up roughly and stared into her still-passionate eyes.

"God, I can't even look at you without wanting you again." He kissed her reddened lips deeply, drawing the sweetness from them into his. Sabrina's arm curled around his neck as she answered his desire with a new-found confidence of her own.

"You learn quickly, little one," Lucien smiled, his hands straying over her taut stomach and up to cup her breasts.

"I've had a good tutor," she teased, a dimple peeping out as she smiled and added mischievously, "and imagine how I'll be after several lessons."

"Just as long as I'm the only one giving them," Lucien remarked with a smile that didn't reach his eyes. "I'll not share you with anyone."

"Jealous? Lucien," she experimented using his name, pronouncing it lovingly. "It suits you with your golden curls and arrogant stare."

"Arrogant?" Lucien retorted. "I'd never met arrogance before I met you. Strutting around in breeches and jackboots. Terrorizing the countryside."

He laughed deeply as he thought of the first night he'd met her and the chagrined faces around that banqueting table. If they knew? He laughed again at the thought.

"What is so amusing that you would shake me from my dreams?" Sabrina demanded, rising on an elbow across his chest, her breasts resting snugly against him.

Lucien looked up at her, amusement still brimming in his eyes. "You, my funny little princess. Now," he said with an imperious note in his voice, "we've a few details to straighten out. I want to know everything about you, and why an apparently well-bred young woman resorts to highway robbery?"

Sabrina pulled away from the warmth of his arms, feeling at once lost and bereft without them around her. She turned a dainty shoulder to him and stared into the shadowy room, the candle having guttered long ago and just a small, flickering flame remaining of the fire he had re-lit.

"Why must you know? Why must you meddle and interfere in what does not concern you? None of this would ever have happened if you hadn't entrapped me," she cried desperately as the memory of their passion was replaced with all of her old fears and the realization that she was still his prisoner.

Lucien pulled her back to him, angered by that little shoulder turned to him and the stiff, slender back she presented against him. He was not accustomed to resistance from a woman, or from anyone for that matter, and he did not like it—nor would he accept it.

"I am very much involved, as you have held me up at pistol point numerous times, stolen from me, and dueled with me. And, damnation, doesn't that give me the right to know the truth? By God, you'll tell me, Sabrina. I'll not let you leave this bed until you do," he threatened. "What harm can it do? If you implicate others, what can it matter, for I can't prosecute them without bringing you into it, and I'll be damned if I'll do that. What kind of man do you take me for? I make love to you tonight and then let the soldiers take you away to be hanged? Besides," he added arrogantly, "no one would dare threaten what is mine—and you are mine. I'll not give you up," he added in a hard, possessive voice.

His lips found hers and he kissed her hungrily, moving her onto his chest where she lay beneath the caress of his hands.

"What do you mean, Lucien?" Sabrina asked uncertainly, a sudden fear in her heart from the possessive note in his voice.

His answer was muffled by his kisses on her throat and shoulders as he explained reasonably, "I shall set you up as my mistress. How would you like a house in London, and a small country house? I've a nice one near Bath that has been recently refurbished. I can be with you most of the time, and when in London I shall visit you at your house."

His hands slid over her buttocks and pressed her gently against his hips, making her aware of his desire for her. He rolled her under him and made love to her again, guiding her to please and satisfy him, unsatisfied himself until she felt the ecstasy he could bring to her.

Sabrina sighed, listening to his deep and steady breathing as he slept beside her. She bit her lip and blinked to keep the tears from overflowing her eyes. She only had herself to blame. Why should he think to offer her anything more? How could she tell him she was the daughter of a marquis, and even then would he really believe her? But what could their future be? As far as she knew he might be married. He probably was. After all, he was a duke, and handsome and rich as well. He was in his thirties, she guessed, and probably had children as old as Richard by now. But she couldn't become his mistress. She looked down at him sleeping so soundly and peacefully, not knowing that this would be the one night for their love. Never would she see him again. Because she would not take the chance of meeting him, she would never again masquerade as Bonnie Charlie. The charade would end, and Bonnie Charlie would be retired. They had enough money now. She was tired, her nerves were frayed from constant fear and worry, and this latest fiasco had broken her confidence. She knew if they played the game too long they would get caught, as indeed they had this time. They had become careless, and her cockiness had led to entrapment and near-disaster.

No, she must never risk meeting Lucien again. He would be furious to lose her, and knowing his iron determination, she knew he would seek her out. She must be so careful. She must hide for a while and he would soon forget a night of wonderful love, tire of his futile quest and seek diversion elsewhere. She swallowed painfully as she admitted to herself that a diversion was all she was to him. He didn't love her, he wanted her merely to fulfill his lustful desires.

Sabrina gazed lovingly at his face. Why should she be any different for him? How many lovers had he had since he'd reached manhood? She was just another in a long succession of women he'd desired. But for her, he was special. Lucien was her first love, a young girl's idealistic dream of what a man should be, awakening her desires and changing her from an innocent girl into a woman. Lucien would always be special for her, not only because he'd been her first lover, but because he was the man she loved.

She had fallen in love with the scar-faced gentleman. No, never again would she call him that. She gazed down at his sleeping face, her violet eyes reflecting the love in her heart. She traced the cruel scar with a fingertip light as a butterfly, then the beautifully chiseled mouth that was slightly curved with a dream. His lashes were long and dark, and she ran her fingertip across their fineness. His ears narrowed at the top like a satyr's and Sabrina smiled as she thought of his passionate lovemaking.

A desolate feeling of her accepted fate swept over her suddenly, and carried along by this wave of inevitable destiny, Sabrina ran her fingers through the wiry hair on Lucien's chest, placing nibbling kisses in a frenzy across his face.

Lucien's startled eyes opened, then grew full of warmth as he stared up into the heart-shaped face above him. He gathered her to him, finding her soft mouth with his and sucking its sweetness as a bee sucks nectar from a flower.

"Ah, little one, how you do please me," he murmured as he felt her small hand fondling him boldly. He looked into her darkened eyes with pleased surprise. She was different. She had taken over the play and was on fire for him, guiding him now with her mounting passion. Her fiery responses and uncontrolled desire ignited a flame in him and he took her fiercely again and again, until they clung together unable to tell where they were not one.

❧

Sabrina looked down on Lucien as he slept deeply, her eyes capturing and memorizing each strong feature of his face. She turned slowly and tiptoed to the door, carefully pulled it open and passed through it soundlessly, then closed it silently behind her without a backward glance at the sleeping man in the four-poster bed. Quickly surveying the corridor she hurried across to a partially opened door and looked inside. The tumbled bedclothes and personal articles around the room showed her that it was the room Lucien had moved to while she convalesced in his. He would have brought her clothes and weapons here for safekeeping. Sabrina moved instinctively to a chest at the foot of the bed and opening the lid smiled with relief to see her coat and breeches. Beneath them were her pistol, rapier, and dagger. She quickly pulled the breeches on over the nightshirt. Her shirt and waistcoat were missing, too badly stained and torn to be mended, she thought, as she stood on one foot then the other and slipped her stockings on, rolling them up above her knees and over the tops of her breeches. Stepping into her boots she tugged them on and grabbed up her weapons. With a look of triumph she spied her mask in the dim corner of the chest and quickly donned it. Then braiding her hair with deft fingers she tucked it up and covered it with the wig and cocked hat that completed her disguise.

Checking her pistol, which was still primed, she made her way from the room and quietly down the hall, leaving undisturbed the sleeping occupant of the other bedchamber.

The house was quiet. It must be near to dawn, she reckoned, although it was still pitch-black outside the windows. Sabrina quietly made her way down the stairs, then through the door beneath the stairs and down a corridor to the kitchen area. Lucien had mentioned absently a storage room being strong enough to hold Will. Silently she entered the kitchen and carefully stood in the darkness.

From the corner came the unmistakable sounds of snoring. Sabrina steadied herself and then followed the sounds of their source. Pressing the cold barrel of her pistol against the sleeping guard's throat, she nudged him lightly and said softly, "I'd not make any abrupt moves, mate, or I'll blow a hole through your head."

The now-awake guard's snoring stopped with a choke and he nearly fell from the chair precariously tipped on its hind legs against the wall. He looked up as much as the steel against his neck would allow and gulped audibly as he focused on a black mask and two glowing eyes staring down at him.

"Now, unlock the door and let's see if our big friend wants to join us," Sabrina ordered softly.

The guard slowly stood up and fumbled at the lock, the

key scraping noisily as he turned it. As the door swung open, Sabrina gave the fellow a push into the room with the pistol and followed close behind.

"Who is it?" Will demanded belligerently.

"Who else but Bonnie Charlie," Sabrina replied jauntily, sighing with relief at the sound of his rough voice.

"Charlie!" Will cried joyously. "Is it really you?"

"In the flesh, no ghost haunting you, Will," she answered, drawing her dagger as her eyes found Will's trussed-up form before her in the darkness, her pistol still hard in the servant's back.

In a flash she'd cut his bonds and he was stretching his arms and legs painfully after first knocking out the guard with one effortless swing of his big fist.

"Been wantin' to do that since first I laid eyes on the fool's grinning face," he declared with satisfaction.

"Quick, it's near dawn and we must get far from here, Will, before the household awakens," Sabrina warned him nervously.

"Aye, we're away," Will agreed easily, his familiar voice like a soothing balm to Sabrina's highly wrought emotions.

Beware the fury of a patient man.

—John Dryden

Chapter 6

"DEAR LORD, SABRINA, I THOUGHT I'D NEVER SEE YOU ALIVE again. I've been so worried," Mary cried, her eyes red-rimmed and puffy from weeping.

She'd been arranging flowers in the hall when Sabrina had stumbled in, her face drawn and white, looking like death against the blackness of her coat. Hurriedly she had swept her upstairs and out of sight of the servants. She had gasped in horror when she'd seen the healing wound on Sabrina's shoulder and heard about the duel.

But something else was wrong. It hadn't only been the fear of death that had caused the pain in Sabrina's eyes, there was anguish as well. Her face had thinned and her cheekbones stood out visibly. The cockiness was missing from Sabrina's answers, and the swagger from her walk. Of course she was tired and weary from her ordeal—but there was something different about her. Poor little Rina, what had happened to her, Mary agonized silently as she saw the trembling of her sister's mouth.

"Couldn't you see my destiny in your visions, Mary? You did predict danger. But you said all would be for the best, remember?" Sabrina said softly. "But you were wrong... so very wrong."

"I thought I was wrong when you didn't return. John didn't know where you and Will were. We were frantic, but what could we do?" Mary wrung her hands helplessly.

"When I think that you might have been murdered by that evil man—I could die. Oh, why did I ever agree to this horrid plan?"

"You had little choice, Mary. How could you stop me? Or, how could we have survived without it? But you needn't worry any longer. Bonnie Charlie is dead. He will no longer roam the highroad after midnight."

"Thank God! I feel so relieved. After this, I don't think I could bear waiting for you night after night, wondering if this time you would be killed."

Mary pushed Bonnie Charlie's clothes distastefully into the chest and thankfully closed the lid on them. Then, perched on the edge of Sabrina's bed, she watched as Sabrina sipped her tea and halfheartedly pecked at her breakfast.

"I can't take the chance of running into the duke," Sabrina explained. "He knows I'm a woman."

"I imagine he was quite stunned when he discovered you weren't a man?" Mary said with satisfaction, hoping the duke felt terrible about what he'd done. "I don't like the idea of his caring for you, Sabrina. I mean he was a stranger." She blushed in embarrassment, reluctant to say more.

Sabrina smiled. The less Mary knew, the better. How could she explain what had happened? She knew it would stun and embarrass Mary if she tried to. She hardly understood her emotions herself. They'd been so primitive that she blushed herself to remember—but she was not ashamed. It was her memory to cherish.

"I told Aunt Margaret you were helping a sick family, although I'm surprised that she even noticed your absence. We also have a new difficulty."

Sabrina frowned slightly, giving Mary her full attention.

"There is a Colonel Fletcher in the area, sent from London expressly to apprehend Bonnie Charlie."

Sabrina sipped her tea thoughtfully. "I see, well, that needn't concern us. As I shall no longer masquerade as a highwayman, he has no one to catch. He is here on a fool's errand."

Mary shook her head worriedly. "I don't know, Sabrina, there is something about him. He is a very confident man, and I wouldn't underestimate him. When he looks at you with that penetrating gaze," Mary said with a shiver, "I feel as though he knows everything."

Sabrina laughed, looking like the old Sabrina. "That's your guilty conscience speaking. Besides, can you actually imagine suspecting us of being criminals? It's absurd, which is exactly what this colonel will be thinking, should such an unlikely thought enter his head. No, I see no problems with this Colonel—what was his name?"

"Colonel Terence Fletcher," Mary informed her, a blush spreading across her cheeks.

"Yes, I don't think we'll have any problems with this Fletcher fellow," Sabrina repeated contemptuously, not noticing Mary's flushed face.

"Then of course Lord and Lady Malton called, along with Lord Newley, who was quite distressed not to find you at home. You've made a conquest there."

"Anything in skirts makes a conquest with him," Sabrina commented dryly.

Mary sighed, shaking her head in regret. "I'm so worried about Richard. He's been so upset since you disappeared. He actually became surly and rude to me."

Sabrina looked up and showed the first signs of real interest in Mary's conversation.

"He would disappear for hours or lock himself up in his room, not answering my summons, missing meals. I can't do anything with him. He's always been closer to you, Sabrina," she added without jealousy or rancor. "Speak to him when he comes to see you. He doesn't know you're back. He went out so early this morning. Find out what's bothering him. He will probably be back to normal now that you're back. I've this feeling that something is wrong, but when I try to see it, it's just a blur, everything is indistinct."

"Don't worry, I'll have a word with him," Sabrina reassured her.

Mary leaned forward earnestly. "You are all right, aren't you, Rina? You have told me everything? Oh, my dear, if only I could have spared you this. I can't stand the thought of you hurt and suffering. I feel as though I've aged a lifetime since you disappeared."

Sabrina reached out and clasped Mary's hands with hers, tightly holding them. "I think we all have, Mary. It's time we changed our lives. We've been so lucky until now. I knew sooner or later our good fortune would run out—but we've stopped in time," she added fervently, trying to convince herself as much as Mary that they were safe. "What can happen? Who would ever believe that Bonnie Charlie was a woman? And the only one, outside of the Taylors, who knows the truth, wouldn't dare tell—he couldn't," Sabrina whispered to herself.

"No, I suppose his vanity and good name would be at stake. Being beaten by a woman," Mary scoffed, and patted Sabrina's clenched hands. "Don't fret, Rina. I suddenly feel wonderful, clearheaded and free of worry. We're safe. Safe—nothing can hurt us anymore." She collected the tray and smilingly left the room humming a little tune.

Sabrina lay back against the fluffy pillows and stared out the window. The sky was a deep, vivid blue with puffy white clouds floating past. A small robin with a yellowish-red breast landed on the sill and chirped importantly to the world, and then cocking its feathery head, it swooped from the sill, gliding over the trees to disappear.

"Rina?" a small voice asked hesitantly from the doorway.

Sabrina looked over and held out her arms. Richard cannoned into them, burying his head against her breast and holding on to her frantically, his sobs muffled against her nightgown. Sabrina soothed his brow, rocking him like a baby.

"I thought you were dead. I thought I'd never see you again. Oh, Rina, don't ever leave me again. Never!" His deep cry of anguish tore at Sabrina's heart.

"I won't, love. I'm through with all of that foolishness. We've got everything we need right here. A roof over our heads, good farmland, food on the table and a fire in the hearth. We have all we need, Dickie," she comforted him. "This is our home, and someday you'll be master here, and then you can look after me. How does that sound?" Sabrina asked him curiously.

Richard gulped and sniffed a couple of times before raising his head. He looked up into Sabrina's soft violet eyes, a smile beginning to show in his watery blue ones.

"We'll always be together? You'll never go off again, Rina? And I'll be able to care for you and Mary and Aunt Margaret? I'm real strong, see? Feel." And he held out a small arm, flexing the muscle manfully.

Sabrina squeezed it lightly. "You're quite right. Every day you seem to grow bigger."

"I know, soon I'll be taller than you, Rina, although you're pretty small to begin with, so it doesn't really count."

Sabrina laughed for the first time with real amusement, hugging Richard close. "Listen, mate, I can still box your ears in a set-to."

Richard grinned, and stretching out his legs in their blue knee breeches and buckled, black leather shoes, said complacently, "I finished six books while you were gone. Mr. Teesdale says I'm far advanced for my age." He looked up at Sabrina proudly.

"Indeed you are. I'm sure you know far more than me."

"Probably," he agreed casually, causing Sabrina to raise her eyebrows until she saw the imp of mischief sparkling in his eyes.

"Rat," she laughed and started tickling him in the ribs. He giggled and squirmed quickly off the bed, the harassed look gone from his eyes as he skipped from the room in childish abandon.

Sabrina curled into a ball and hid her face in the crook of her arm, closing her eyes and mind against all the thoughts that plagued her. She would forget for awhile. She would sleep, and everything would be better when she awoke.

❧

Lucien dismounted and walked his horse along the narrow woodland path. His face was set in angry lines and the scar still throbbed in his cheek as his thoughts swirled through his mind.

His steps were firm and confident as he callously trod through overhanging ferns and grasses. In the shade of a mossy bank he saw a small clump of late-blooming violets and ruth-lessly pulled them up, the soft moist loam still clinging to their roots. He stared down at the delicate purple flowers, his hard fingers breaking the fragile stems as he saw two dark violet eyes staring back at him. His eyes narrowed dangerously as he threw the violets to the path and viciously crushed them beneath the heel of his boot.

He continued on, his mind occupied with plans. He would find her—by God, he would! And heaven help her when he did. He could still feel the hot rage rise in him when he thought of waking this morning and finding her gone. She had escaped from him—along with that giant friend. He smiled in anticipation of getting his hands on her once again. She'd pay for making him look the fool. He had fallen for that innocent act of hers, the little schemer.

When he remembered her soft body and eager responses to his caresses, her lips kissing his hungrily and asking for more, all he wanted was to have her back in bed with him and wrapped close in his arms. Fool that he was to let the fire in his loins control him. He should've locked her in a dungeon and thrown away the key.

He admitted that his vanity and masculinity had been wounded by her disappearance. She had tricked him, had played the passionate lover, her soft lips deceiving him while she plotted. He laughed harshly, the sudden sound startling his horse. He was dwelling like some love-sotted, callow youth over his first love. He must be getting senile if that little black-haired vixen and her arrogant ways could disturb him. Well, he would find her, and then teach her a lesson she'd not soon forget.

His servants were at this very moment making inquiries in the villages and hamlets about two large men and a small, black-haired girl. They would soon have news of that roguish trio—and then he would exact his revenge. He'd ordered his men to be especially observant in the taverns, where gossip was rampant. Dropping that false information in a couple of taverns had led to his capture of Sabrina before—it just might again.

The news should follow him to London very shortly. He eagerly anticipated this—in fact, he felt elated at the thought of meeting her again. It should prove quite interesting. He climbed back into the saddle and urged his horse into a trot as he left the woods and joined the road, his mood lighter as his horse's strides lengthened down the road.

❧

"Richard! Watch out!" Sabrina called out a warning too late as Richard tripped over the handle of a sickle that had carelessly been left on the ground, the curved blade barely missing his knee as it swung up.

Sabrina ran toward him, her face pale. "Are you all right? Didn't you see the sickle? Really, Richard, do watch where you're going sometimes. You're always bumping into things," Sabrina admonished him, her voice harsh from the fright he'd given her.

Richard grinned sheepishly. "At least I didn't spill any of the milk," he beamed as he held up a wooden bowl triumphantly. "Sarah let me help her milk the cows."

"I can see that for myself," Sabrina commented as she noticed the white moustache above his mouth.

"Here, have some."

Sabrina accepted the bowl and drank deeply, the warm, fresh milk tasting sweet on her tongue. She handed the bowl back to Richard, only to have him start laughing.

"What is so funny?"

"You, Rina. You've got a moustache too."

Sabrina grinned and wiped the milk from her mouth. "Better?"

"Like a cat in pattens," he replied after a critical inspection of her upper lip.

"You'd better go in and clean up, you've lessons with Mr. Teesdale in less than an hour, Richard," Sabrina advised as she in turn inspected his breeches, soiled and stuck with straw, and his face smudged with dirt. In the distance she could see a rider coming up the narrow lane and recognized John's bulky shape. "Better hurry," she urged Richard.

Richard heard the horse's hooves and stared towards the sound, his eyes squinted. "Who is it?"

Sabrina stared at Richard's straining expression, a thoughtful look in her eyes. "It's John Taylor. Couldn't you tell?" she asked curiously.

Richard's face flushed. "Sure I could. I just thought it might be Will," he explained casually and then turned and hurried off, his thin shoulders hunched dejectedly.

Sabrina turned back as John rode up, a welcoming smile on her face. "Hello, John. What brings you calling?"

John dismounted, and taking off his hat greeted Sabrina politely. "Morning, Lady Sabrina. Mam thought you'd like this herb salve for yer skin." He looked about the stable yard and finding no one close enough to overhear added worriedly, "Some strangers been asking folks hereabouts if they knew of me and Will and a young black-haired girl, calling her Sabrina. Real nosey they are, too."

Sabrina glanced up at him apprehensively. "What did they learn?"

John smiled smugly. "No more than they knew when they came. Folks don't care to be telling strangers their business. Especially seein' how you been so good to them around here. Besides, anyone blabbering around here about something that don't concern them answers to Will and me. Anyway, there be a lot of black-haired females living around here. Heard tell there was a real pretty one near Tunbridge Wells, nice little ride on a warm afternoon." He grinned widely.

Sabrina smiled with relief. "I take it they won't have any luck?"

"Could be. And of course there're a lot of big men hereabouts too. Why, look at Ben Sampson at the smithy, or Roberts the brewer? Lot of big men. Pity if the wrong person was to go asking questions of them. No telling what might happen." He rocked back and forth on his heels, smiling with satisfaction.

Sabrina felt relief, but not the joyous relief she once would have at such news.

"Will and me bought the Faire Maiden, Charlie," John confided proudly. "Goin' to fix it up real nice."

"That's wonderful, John. I sometimes wondered if we'd ever be able to live normal lives."

"Well, since we ain't goin' to be out at night so much, and we got the last bit of money we needed, we figured we better buy it before old Jack changed his mind about selling, or sold it to an outsider."

"I can't tell you how happy I am for you and Will. You've helped me so much, I can't ever repay you," Sabrina told the discomfited giant, his face burning with an embarrassed blush.

"You know, Charlie, we'll still look after you—and if you need us for anything you can count on us anytime," he promised, then clearing his throat nervously added, "You sure you and your family have enough money, Charlie? I mean, well, if you was needing any, me and Will could give you some."

Sabrina was touched by his offer of support, and regardless of any curious eyes she stood on tiptoe and kissed his cheek. "Thank you, John, I'll never forget your kind offer, but we're fine. We've saved a lot of our money, and living simply we manage nicely."

John's face was still a bright red when he climbed back on his horse and rode off, waving as he rounded the hedgerows and disappeared front view.

Sabrina went back indoors, her light step purposeful as she made her way into the big kitchen with its large table covered with cooking utensils. Drying bunches of herbs hung from the rafters, lending a spicy scent to the blend of odors rising from bubbling plum tarts fresh from the oven and a cut of beef roasting over the fire. The cook was nodding in a chair near the hearth, her apron half full of peas to be shelled.

The young scullery maid rotating the turnspit with the roast on it nudged the cook when she saw Sabrina, a shy smile in her round eyes as she gazed in adoration at her young mistress. The cook woke up with a grumbled snort, ready to swing at the disturbance until she saw Sabrina standing nearby.

"Lady Sabrina," she exclaimed, straightening her mobcap off her forehead and heaving her bulk from her easy chair, the peas encompassed safely in her apron she held together firmly.

"I just want to rob you of some of that gingerbread. A couple of pieces, and one for Lottie," she added as the little girl's eyes widened and her lips smacked at the sight of the rich gingerbread.

The cook tied her apron together, then cut several big squares from the fragrant cake, shaking her head repressively. "Lottie'll never learn her place, Lady Sabrina, if you keep spoiling her. Already she's got airs above her station. Next she'll be wantin' to wear velvet and lace."

Sabrina smiled at the little girl. "It can't hurt her to have one piece of gingerbread, can it?" she cajoled, smiling as she accepted the gingerbread, her dimple peeping irrepressibly. The cook's disapproving expression relaxed a bit, a reluctant smile tugging at the corner of her tight mouth as she grudgingly had to admit that the Lady Sabrina had a taking way with her. Still, she'd always thought this one of the Verricks a wild one, not at all like the Lady Mary who was a proper lady.

Sabrina hurried upstairs to find Richard, the generous chunks of gingerbread crowding together on a parchment-thin china plate. She found him sitting in the schoolroom, an opened book before him as he awaited the arrival of Mr. Teesdale.

"Surprise!" Sabrina called as she held out the gingerbread enticingly before him.

Richard took a deep, appreciative breath and reached out an eager hand that unerringly guided the pieces into his mouth. Licking a crumb delicately from the corner of her mouth, Sabrina watched in amusement as he hungrily finished off his piece and then eyed hers covertly. Her smile widened and she broke off the rest of hers and handed it to him.

"Thanks, Rina," he mumbled through a mouthful.

Sabrina strolled over to the window and stood silently staring out when she suddenly called excitedly over her shoulder, "Oh, Richard, do look! Here's that little robin that serenaded me the other day."

Sitting demurely on a branch of the big elm tree outside the window was a plain-looking little sparrow. Richard came up beside Sabrina and peered out the window. "Oh, yes, quite a colorful little fellow with his red breast."

Sabrina stared at Richard's little profile, resisting the urge to hug him to her protectively. Instead she told him calmly, "It's a sparrow, Richard."

Richard's face paled and he turned an accusing face to her. "You tricked me. It's not fair." His thin shoulders shook and his voice was thick with tears.

Sabrina wrapped her arms around him and hugged him to her, comforting him the best she could. His sobs lessened and he gave a watery hiccup.

"Why didn't you ever tell us, Dickie?" Sabrina asked, her fingers combing his thick red hair back from his face. "I've been such a fool. Too busy to even notice my own brother's needs. How long have you had trouble seeing?"

Richard sniffed and shrugged, but kept his head pressed against Sabrina's breast. "Don't know. Long time, I guess. I can read, though. It's just things in the distance that are all blurred," he confessed.

Sabrina drew in her breath sharply as a thought struck her. "Is that why you don't like to ride, Dickie?"

She raised his tear-stained face and looked into his big, myopic blue eyes, a smile tugging at her mouth. "Dickie, I wish you'd told me. I'd have helped you. You don't need to worry anymore, nor be ashamed of it," she reproved him gently.

"I wanted to help you so much, Rina, but I was afraid to ride. It's awful not to be able to see where you're going, afraid you're going to bump into a branch you don't see, or fall into a bog. And when I tried to shoot, what was I going to aim at?"

Sabrina let Richard talk, all his childish fears and bottled-up emotions flooding out as he unburdened himself.

"How would you like to go to London, Dickie?" Sabrina asked him seriously.

Richard wiped at his face with a ruffled sleeve, rubbing his eyes dry as he looked at Sabrina in surprise. "Go to London?" he repeated in awe. "You mean I would go?"

"It would be especially for you. It will be your special treat. And when we're there we'll see about getting you a pair of eyeglasses. Do you like that idea?"

Richard lowered his head, but not before Sabrina saw his eyes light up with excitement. He gave a relieved sigh unconsciously. "You don't think I'll be a, well—" he began, struggling to find the words, "a sissy for wearing eyeglasses?" He looked up at Sabrina hopefully, his eyes pleading for reassurance.

Sabrina made a contemptuous sound. "Of course not. You will look quite the intellectual, and be able to see where you're going, too. It's most important not to fall into the gutter when we're trying to impress the prime minister."

Richard was laughing and jumping up and down when the stern-faced Mr. Teesdale entered the schoolroom, a look of disapproval on his severe features at this riotous display of abandon.

"I'm going to London, Mr. Teesdale!" Richard called out, his tutor's raised eyebrow for once not having the desired effect of silencing him.

"Are we indeed?" Mr. Teesdale murmured politely, his face inscrutable beneath his gray periwig. He greeted Sabrina, and placing his books and papers in a neat stack on the table inquired, "When will this projected visit to London occur, so I may adjust my student's schedule accordingly?"

Sabrina hid her smile and answered most seriously, "At the beginning of next week, for we've preparations to make and we shall probably be gone a fortnight or less. You see, Richard is to be fitted with a pair of eyeglasses."

Mr. Teesdale showed a moment's surprise across his usually impassive features, but quickly recovered his poise. "Quite," was all he murmured. "I shall suitably adjust our lessons so his schoolwork will not suffer."

Sabrina left them with Mr. Teesdale monotonously drilling Richard in mathematics, the sound droning after her as she made her way down the corridor.

She found Mary comfortably reading a book and Aunt Margaret sewing in the drawing room. They both glanced up as Sabrina entered, their faces mirroring surprise at her first words.

"We're going to London next week." Mary closed her book and watched Sabrina curiously. Aunt Margaret smiled vaguely and bent once more to her needlework, the spaniels at her feet snoring contentedly.

"Richard needs eyeglasses," Sabrina stated baldly, explaining her discovery to a surprised and dismayed Mary. "I feel rotten about the whole affair. We're the ones who need the eyeglasses for not having noticed Richard's problem before now. Poor dear, all these years existing in a blurred world. No wonder he turned to his books. Well, that will all end now. We'll get him proper eyeglasses so he will be able to ride and play like other young boys."

Mary shook her head guiltily. "Some elder sister I am. When do you want to leave?"

"Monday, I should imagine," Sabrina spoke thoughtfully, pausing for a moment before she added, "We shall have to use the town house. I suppose the marquis has a staff in residence, so there shouldn't be any difficulty. Besides, I don't plan on a lengthy visit. Aunt Margaret? You'll come too?"

Aunt Margaret looked up dreamily and nodded. "Of course, dears, anything you say."

"I'm going to see Mrs. Taylor. She has a brother in London who makes eyeglasses and she says he is very good at it, although not very rich or well-known."

Sabrina stood up, pacing restlessly. "I think it will be good to get away for awhile, better to be away from this area for a bit."

She was nervous and jumpy, even short-tempered at times. Mary watched her pacing with worried eyes. She was becoming quite concerned with this whole state of affairs. And now, she thought wisely, was not the time to tell Sabrina that she'd had another vision.

"Yes, I think you are right, Sabrina. It will do us all good to visit London for a bit. Do try and get back for tea, dear."

❧

Sabrina walked softly under the trees in the greenwood. The spinney was secretive and cool with only the sounds of pigeons fluttering through the branches to disturb her thoughts. In the middle of the thicket was a small, sun-dappled pool, deep and cool, reflecting the greens and blues of the sky overhead.

Quickly she removed her dress and undergarments, and slipped silently into the cool depths of the forest pool. She floated on her back, staring up into the endless blue of the sky, feeling the gentle caress of the water against her skin like a lover's touch.

If she could only forget—but she couldn't. Her body was a constant reminder of her lover. Her mind's traitorous thoughts betrayed her whenever she relaxed, even though she'd worked like a demon at every little chore until she was too tired to think and would fall into bed too tired to dream.

But now, now she remembered Lucien, wanted him near her. If she could gaze into his dark eyes for just an instant, touch his firm lips with hers for just a second.

Sabrina turned over with a splash and swam back across the pool, disturbing its serenity. Climbing onto the soft grassy bank she shivered, welcoming the cool air against her body. She held her arms up to the sun in almost a worshipful fashion, her head held high as she absorbed the strength and energy from its fiery body.

She stood silently, like a forest creature, her breasts full, the nipples taut from the chill of the water that dripped in rivulets across her slim hips, and down her legs, slightly apart with her feet planted firmly, rooting her to the earth. The raucous cry of a blackbird broke her spell and, shivering, Sabrina struggled into her clothes. The magic of the forest pool had left her. She wandered back through the trees to her cart and the horse lazily cropping grass. She led him through the brambles and wild flowers back onto the path that led to the road. She had gotten the name of Mrs. Taylor's brother in London, along with a letter of introduction from her, and now there was little to be done except to make the journey to London.

Returning to Verrick House, Sabrina entered the drawing room, anxious for tea, only to find Mary serving a scarlet-coated figure a plate full of cakes.

Sabrina stopped abruptly, then, recovering herself, continued into the room, a look of polite welcome on her features, but the accompanying smile froze on her lips as the officer stood up and turned around at Mary's greeting.

Colonel Fletcher's casually polite look faded as he stared at the raven-haired girl approaching him with the heart-shaped face and violet eyes as familiar to him as his own. There was no mistake in his mind who she was—and there was little doubt that she also recognized him. He could see it clearly in the wide eyes full of stunned fear frantically searching his face in disbelief.

"Sabrina, this is Colonel Terence Fletcher. My sister, Lady Sabrina Verrick." Mary made the introduction, unaware of the undercurrents between the two people supposedly meeting for the first time.

"A pleasure, Lady Sabrina," Colonel Fletcher spoke quietly, "and I must say I prefer our meeting today rather than the one almost five years ago. You must agree the peaceful surroundings of a drawing room are much more conducive to polite conversation than a battlefield."

Sabrina hesitated as she tried to gather her wits, and drawing a deep breath said, "I beg your pardon, Colonel?" She gave him a quizzical look as she sat down gracefully on the settee beside a puzzled Mary. Pouring herself a cup of tea she glanced up at the silent colonel.

"I seriously doubt that we've had the pleasure of meeting before—and hardly under the adverse circumstances you seem to think." She gave a disbelieving laugh. "My word, what on earth could I've been doing on a battlefield?"

Sabrina's attention was caught by the rattling of Mary's cup in its saucer as she quickly set it on the table. The colonel had heard it too, for as he took his seat, he commented idly, "Did not your sister tell you of our first meeting so many years ago?"

He selected a cake after a prolonged inspection of the assortment and settled back in his chair, his shiny black boots outstretched carelessly.

"She was little more than a child then, eleven or twelve at the most, I should imagine, and yet armed with a loaded pistol she aimed directly at my heart."

"That is absolutely preposterous." Sabrina spoke contemptuously.

"Is it?" The colonel shook his head. "I must admit I never expected to see you again. I even wondered if you had survived. Your grandfather's castle was deserted when my men finally reached it, and to their immense disappointment, little remained of any value."

He looked curiously between the two silent sisters. "Are you interested in what became of the castle, or what happened to your grandfather?"

Mary lowered her head and fidgeted nervously with a fold of her gown while Sabrina stared at the colonel angrily.

"Since you seem to have forgotten, allow me to refresh your memory, Lady Sabrina. I've forgotten very little of that day. The death and destruction on the battlefield. Your grandfather's bloodied body. That little hut where he breathed his last breath. You do realize that it isn't always possible to bury the dead, especially the enemy's dead. A pity, but—"

"Stop it!" Sabrina said, her eyes blazing furiously. "I wish I'd killed you that day. Who would've believed you'd one day walk into the drawing room of Verrick House?"

Colonel Fletcher did not feel triumphant at her confession. In fact, he felt rather disgusted at himself, but he wanted to know why she denied being in Scotland.

"Why not admit that you were in Scotland? There is no crime in that."

Sabrina shrugged. "Why bring up the past? Although we are English, we were raised by my Scots grandfather. We loved him dearly, so why should I want to remember that day, Colonel?" Sabrina explained. "We came to England after that and began to set up a new life here at Verrick House. When we arrived in London it was far wiser, and safer, not to admit to having Scots blood in our veins. The crowds weren't too friendly to their northern neighbors at that time. It was convenient for us to forget and we have, so you will forgive me if I don't greet you with open arms and affection," Sabrina told him bitterly. She stood up and facing him unflinchingly added, "As far as I am concerned, you and your men murdered my grandfather. I don't need your accounting of that day to remember his death. The blood of my grandfather stained my hands, Colonel. Do you really think I could forget that?"

Sabrina looked down at her hands, seeing it all again, and then up into the gray eyes she'd stared into only once before. "Was he decently buried?" she whispered.

"Yes," Colonel Fletcher answered abruptly, disturbed by the look on her face.

"I suppose you are responsible for that, and were I civilized I would thank you, but I just can't quite bring myself to do it. If you'll excuse me now," Sabrina said, and without a glance at either person left the room.

Mary sat as though turned to stone and stared into her cup at her tepid tea.

"It is tragic that some of the scars we receive in war are inside of us and not visible. You can seldom treat them, so they fester and don't heal," Colonel Fletcher said, looking at Mary's closed face.

"Your sister was just a little girl when she experienced what even hard-bitten soldiers like myself are sickened by. Because of the hurt she felt then, she has prejudiced herself against any other viewpoint, especially that of an English soldier who was there as well."

Mary stood up, her head lifted proudly as she turned to Colonel Fletcher. "If you will excuse me, Colonel, I must see to my family now. I truly think it wisest if you do not visit Verrick House again."

Colonel Fletcher's mouth tightened, but he bowed his head in agreement. "As you wish, Lady Mary. I do not wish to intrude where I am not wanted. Good afternoon to you."

He picked up his hat and gloves and walked swiftly from the room, his back military-straight. Mary sank back down on the edge of the settee, her lips trembling. What more could happen? She had foolishly thought their troubles were over, but were they? Then, squaring her shoulders, she went in search of her sister, finding Sabrina in her room nervously pacing as she chewed her lower lip. She looked up expectantly as Mary entered. "Has he gone?" she asked. "God, I never thought to see his face again."

"You never told me you'd met an English officer, Rina."

"Why? Nothing happened, and besides, we were rather in a hurry that day. And later, I forgot him. At least until a few minutes ago when it all came back. Odd how just a face can recall so much."

Mary nodded, then said in puzzlement, "Why didn't you want to tell Colonel Fletcher we were in Scotland?"

"The less that man knows the better. He is here to catch Bonnie Charlie. Don't you think he'll find it peculiar that a Scots family is living in the same area where an obviously Scots bandit is at work? I wonder how long it will take him to become suspicious of that coincidence."

"Oh, dear, I didn't think of that," Mary admitted.

Sabrina smiled. "It does him little good now. Bonnie Charlie no longer exists, so what evidence can the good colonel gather, and who'd believe him anyway?"

Mary breathed a sigh of relief. "You've always got an answer, Rina. I really don't know what we'd do without you."

Sabrina laughed. "You'd be leading very correct lives, without the cares and worry I've caused you."

Mary shook her head regretfully. "I'm afraid I'd find that far too dull after the life we've had these past years."

The fat is in the fire.

—*John Heywood*

Chapter 7

A CUMBERSOME COACH CARRYING THE VERRICK FAMILY BEGAN its journey to London, making its way along the dusty, hard-packed dirt roads, twisting up through ancient hamlets and down through quaint villages that hugged slumberous rivers. Signposts were few and far between as they passed through these nameless, centuries-old habitats of a people little changed since they had bowed down to Queen Elizabeth I.

Richard fidgeted nervously while Aunt Margaret sewed and Hobbs dozed in her corner. Mary was quiet as she stared out of the window, a slight frown marring her forehead.

"Is something troubling you, Mary?" Sabrina asked as she watched Mary's restless hands.

Mary jumped guiltily. "Wrong? Of course not, I'm just nervous about seeing London, and buying these eyeglasses for Richard," she explained lamely, knowing by Sabrina's penetrating look that she didn't believe her, but she had nothing else to say and turned back to the view.

Sabrina continued to watch her a moment longer, then looked out of the window herself. They were driving through a crossroads, and knowing what she would see, Sabrina averted her gaze as they passed the gibbet where some unfortunate highwayman was often seen hanging—a warning to all who passed to beware.

Sabrina swallowed painfully, the fear of capture still

haunting her in her dreams and thoughts. The gibbet had been close enough to the coach for even Richard to see and he tucked his hand into Sabrina's, giving it a comforting squeeze. Sabrina returned it with a smile, breathing easier as they climbed out of the small valley and disappeared over the crest of the hill.

After midday they stopped for luncheon at an inn, the coach pulling into the bustling courtyard of the King's Carriage Inn while ostlers rushed out to take charge of the horses. They hired a private room for their meal, the coffee room being noisy and full with every type of traveler off the public coaches that traveled the main highways, including the flying coaches that sometimes traveled as far as sixty miles in one day.

They dined on roast duck, turbot and fresh oysters and vegetables, followed by berry tarts and cheese carried in by a friendly serving girl, and spent an enjoyable couple of hours relaxing and recovering from their bone-jarring journey. They sipped tea before a cheerful fireplace, laughing at the confused and angry voices of a troupe of strolling players rehearsing their evening's play, *As You Like It*.

Continuing their journey they reached the outskirts of London in the early evening, twilight lingering and blending with the smoky haze that hung low over the city. They traveled through the open fields and small villages surrounding London, seeing ships flying the flags of countless foreign countries docked on the busy river Thames unloading their cargoes from far-distant lands.

London was a maze of twisting, cobbled streets far too narrow for the hubbub of traffic that surged through them. Coaches-and-six, oxcarts, sedan chairs, horsemen and pedestrians all jockeyed for position on the narrow streets. Gradually the congestion eased as their carriage made its way from the river front and business section of the city into the large squares and the straighter, wider streets surrounding them.

The Marquis of Wrainton's small Queen Anne town house was situated in a quiet square off Hyde Park, where the king still hunted deer with his royal party. The house's broad brick front with its double tiering of sash windows and steeply rising roof was accented by wrought-iron railings across the cornice, and massive chimney stacks.

"Richard, we're here." Sabrina nudged her sleeping brother. Mary alighted first after helping Hobbs collect Aunt Margaret's odds and ends that had become scattered about the inside of the coach. One of the grooms had alerted the household of their arrival and as Sabrina, followed by the others, made her way up the walk to the entrance she was watched by the majordomo, neatly attired in blue livery with a disapproving look on his disciplined features.

"I'm Lady Sabrina Verrick; my sister, Lady Mary Verrick; my aunt, Lady Margaret Verrick; and my brother, Richard Verrick, the Earl of Faver." Sabrina made the introductions as she stepped past the astounded majordomo who stood in front of the stately mahogany door that guarded the oak-paneled entrance hall.

"I'm absolutely fatigued to death," Aunt Margaret declared as she stumbled into the hall on the arm of the ever-helpful Hobbs. "Where are the lads?" she fretted, realizing the spaniels were missing.

"We left them at Verrick House where they can run around and play," Sabrina said, relieved when Aunt Margaret smiled distractedly. "Show Lady Margaret to a room, please," Sabrina requested as she swept into the salon, the majordomo close behind, "and send her up a bath and some tea. We'll have ours down here." She turned and gave the speechless servant, who was still floundering at this invasion of his master's home, a stunning smile that captured his loyalty as soon as it shone upon him.

"Immediately, your ladyship, and I'll prepare rooms for you and your family at once. Should there be anything at all you should need, we are at your complete disposal."

Sabrina beamed. "Thank you so much, and what are you called?"

"Why, I am Cooper."

"Very good, Cooper, we shall retire as soon as we've refreshed ourselves."

Cooper coughed, clearing his throat uncomfortably. "Will your ladyship mind sharing a bedchamber with the Lady Mary?" he asked. "You see, we are a bit pressed for space, what with the marquis and the contessa in residence."

Sabrina stood absolutely still, his words chilling her body. Her face had paled so suddenly at the majordomo's words that he took a concerned step forward in case she fainted.

"Are you ill, Lady Sabrina?" he inquired anxiously. "Shall I fetch the salts?"

"No, I'll be quite all right, it is just that you surprised me with your information concerning the marquis," Sabrina explained.

Cooper looked confused. "Yes, well, I had wondered myself, Lady Sabrina, because Lord and Lady Wrainton are visiting friends in the country, and had planned to stop off at Verrick House to see his family, but as they are expected back Saturday, you will of course still be here..." He trailed off as he noticed the look on Sabrina's face.

"They are at Verrick House?" she demanded in disbelief. "It cannot be true."

"Richard is too tired to have tea, I've tucked him up in a bed in one of the dressing rooms," Mary announced as she entered the salon. She stopped abruptly as she became aware of the strained silence and glanced between the two people nervously. "What has happened?" she asked in resignation.

"The marquis was here," Sabrina informed her, then added after Mary's gasp of surprise, "and now is on his way to Verrick House, or maybe already there."

Mary sat down weakly on the sofa, her hands shaking. Sending the majordomo for tea, Sabrina walked over to stand in front of her sister, looking down at her compassionately.

"You knew, didn't you?"

"Yes," Mary whispered, then looking at Sabrina with anguished eyes explained chokingly, "I knew something strange was happening, but when you disappeared, I attributed what I saw to that—only now I know I was wrong. You see, I could see your face. The violet eyes, the dimple, everything so familiar, and yet, different. It wasn't quite right, not quite you, and yet who else could it have been? Now I know—the marquis. You look like him, Sabrina, that's why I couldn't separate the two of you. I'm sorry. If only I'd told you."

"Damn him," Sabrina cursed the marquis, her face stormy. "What are we going to do? How dare he go to our home after all these years."

Sabrina stood fuming as the tea tray was set up, waiting until they were alone again before continuing angrily, "I hate the thought of him at Verrick House. We're the ones who made it livable, made it our home. He has no right to go there."

Mary poured the steaming tea into wafer-thin cups and held one out enticingly to Sabrina. Sabrina accepted it and sipped at it gratefully.

"No sense in ranting and raving," she spoke calmly, "for it will do us little good. What we must do, however, is take care of Richard's eyeglasses, and then as soon as possible leave the marquis' house. I do not care to be here when he returns, which will not be for some time, hopefully.

"In fact, I think it would be wise if we sought other lodgings until we've finished our business here." She shook her head in exasperation. "We certainly can't go back home, not with the marquis possibly at Verrick House, but at least we have until Thursday or Friday until we need leave here. You can't tell me how long it will take with Richard, can you?" Sabrina asked.

Mary shook her head apologetically. "I'm afraid not, Rina."

"Then we had better get some sleep, for we shall be busy in the next few days. I just hope that all goes well for Richard, it means so much to him, and to us."

When they reached their bedchamber several maids were waiting to help them undress and prepare for bed. Brass warming pans had been placed in the cavernous bed, warming the cold pockets beneath the sheets. Sabrina stretched out tiredly next to Mary.

"I prefer wood fires to this messy black coal," Sabrina said sleepily as she watched the smoldering coals behind the fire grate.

Mary smiled in the darkness. "You're a rustic, Rina. You

like apple logs scenting the hearth, dogs sleeping before it, and you supping on homemade mead and pigeon pie."

Sabrina snorted indignantly. "Pigeon pie, indeed. I'll sup on lobster and champagne, and almond cheesecake any day. And I'd wear satin and lace rather than linsey-woolsey, and perfume my body and wear diamonds in my hair, and—"

"—and ride through Berkeley Square in a golden coach-and-six, wearing a powdered wig and black velvet petticoat as you are presented to the king," Mary added ridiculously.

Sabrina couldn't help but laugh at her absurdities, and as she laughed she felt some of the tension leave her body as she relaxed against the soft mattress.

"Thanks, Mary," she whispered.

The next morning she and Richard left early for their appointment with Mr. Smithson. Richard had nervously sat through breakfast, fiddling with his eggs and chocolate. He was dressed in a gray cloth suit with gold buttons and a silver brocaded waistcoat, his neckcloth and stockings snowy white. He looked like a small, well-dressed gentleman until he rubbed the round toes of his buckled shoes nervously on the back of his calves, leaving a black smudge across their white surface.

"Are we going now, Rina?" he demanded time and time again.

"Yes, now we are going," she was finally able to answer him as they finished breakfast.

With one of the marquis' coachmen to guide them, they set off. Sabrina pulled her pelisse closer about her throat, the morning air still cool and fresh as they traveled along the London streets. Leaving the big squares and stately homes they made their way along the cobbled streets with their small, sash-windowed shops and swinging signs proclaiming their trade. Booksellers, tea dealers, goldsmiths and silk mercers competed for dominance down the narrow alleys and courts with perfumers, wig makers, chandlers, drapers and undertakers.

This early in the morning the streets were clogged with farmers herding their cattle to market, grocers heading to Covent Garden to buy fruit and vegetables, and street vendors hawking food. Pie-men and muffin-men, oysters sold from wheelbarrows; fishmongers and butchers, their shops open-fronted to display their products—all crying their pitch to the passersby.

Sabrina held a delicately scented handkerchief to her nose at the strong odors that wafted in through the coach windows. The stench of the open sewers and gutters blended with the smell of fish and garbage was almost overpowering.

Richard wrinkled his nose distastefully. "Phew! What a stink."

"Richard, really," Sabrina laughed uncomfortably, her breakfast sitting queasily in her stomach.

The coach left the busy thoroughfare and came to a rest before a small neat shop in a quiet court. The liveried groom hopped down, and opening the door helped Sabrina to descend, Richard crowding close behind her. She looked about interestedly at the shop front, the blue sky blocked from view by their overhanging eaves and crowding rooftops. A chemist's shop and a printseller's were wedged close against the little shop whose address Sabrina had given the coachman.

Above the door in small lettering was printed SMITHSON'S OPTICAL INSTRUMENT MAKERS. Grasping Richard's hand with her gloved fingers, Sabrina entered the shop, a tinkling bell over the door announcing their arrival. It was clean and cool within, a display case with various oddities in it against one wall, while a long counter with assorted paraphernalia stretched along another. There was a small fireplace, and before it a rug and several chairs. Somewhere in the shop a clock chimed the hour and from a flight of stairs a stooped man in a black silk coat and breeches with matching stockings descended slowly. He wore the old-fashioned full-bottomed wig and was checking the time on a heavy gold pocket watch.

"Good morning to you, Mistress, may I be of some small service to you?" he inquired courteously, with an old-world charm.

Sabrina pulled the shy Richard forward. "Good morning. I'm Lady Sabrina Verrick, and this is my brother, Lord Faver. Are you Mr. Smithson?"

At his nod, she reached into her purse for the note from Mrs. Taylor and handed it across to him. He looked curiously at it, then withdrawing a pair of eyeglasses from his waistcoat pocket and perching them on his high-bridged nose, read the note. A smile curved his thin lips and brightened his austere features as he carefully folded it up and put it in his pocket.

He looked at them both intently for a brief moment, the young boy with bright red hair hanging shyly back behind the beautiful girl with jet-black hair under a small, sky-blue silk hat, a matching blue ribbon tied around the small column of her neck and matching the blue satin of her gown.

"So, you are the young lady who has befriended my sister? It is a pleasure to make your acquaintance, your ladyship," he told her sincerely, nothing servile in his manner to indicate they were on different social levels. "And how are those two large nephews of mine?"

Sabrina's smile widened and warmed her eyes. "As big as ever," she replied, relaxing as she told him all about Mrs. Taylor and Will and John, answering his questions patiently until finally coming to the reason for their visit.

"Mrs. Taylor recommended you to me. You see, my brother, Richard, has difficulty seeing things in the distance, and we were hoping you might be able to help him."

Mr. Smithson narrowed his eyes as he looked at Richard's pale, upturned face. "Well, Lord Faver, let us see what we can do for you." He motioned to the chairs and invited Sabrina to take a seat when he examined Richard. He held up a variety of lenses, directing Richard to look through them into the street. Mr. Smithson made copious notations, murmuring and mumbling beneath his breath, until finally with a sigh of satisfaction he replaced his instruments in their velvet-padded wooden box and led Richard over to take a seat next to Sabrina. Before he sat down Mr. Smithson pulled a bellpull hanging nearby.

"I hope you will give me the honor of sharing tea with me? My housekeeper will bring it down shortly."

"Thank you, that would be welcomed," Sabrina accepted his invitation graciously. "Do you live above your shop?"

Mr. Smithson nodded serenely, his gentle hands spread and encompassing his surroundings. "This is my home, where I was born, and where I shall die. Today, the modern merchant or professional man leaves his shop to live in a villa outside of town. It is no longer fashionable to live above your shop. But me..." he paused as his housekeeper entered carrying a heavy tray and placed it on a small table beside Sabrina. "If you would be so kind to pour?" he asked. And as Sabrina complied, he continued, "but me, I am old-fashioned and too set in my ways to change this late in the day." He thanked Sabrina for his tea, and sat sipping it ruminatively.

"I am quite pleased with my examination of young Lord Faver," he finally told them. "If you will return in a week, I think I can promise you that your brother, with a little practice, of course," he warned, smiling at Richard's eager blue eyes, "will be able to shoot the center out of a half-crown like the best of marksmen."

Richard jumped to his feet and hopped around the room ecstatically, his tea forgotten. Sabrina leaned forward and touched Mr. Smithson's hand lightly. "How can I ever thank you enough? I feel criminal as it is, by not having noticed his infirmity before this," she told him remorsefully, "but I never knew until a few days ago. He kept it from us, and of course one is always too busy to really look at the people closest to them," Sabrina berated herself.

"My dear child, don't be so harsh on yourself. The young gentleman will now be able to see normally, and from his conversation I would allow that he is far better off than his contemporaries, for his years of enforced confinement and devotion to his studies have matured him and given him a mind of his own. You can be very proud of him." Mr. Smithson patted her hand reassuringly.

Sabrina placed a light kiss on his cheek. "Thank you," she said fervently, tears glistening in her eyes, much to Mr. Smithson's dismay.

"Come along, Richard, we must be off," Sabrina called as the bell above the door tinkled and another customer entered the shop.

"Friday," Mr. Smithson called after their departing figures and received two smiling waves in answer.

They arrived back at the house a little before two, flushed and excited and loaded down with packages. Richard ran into the salon with a laughing face, twirling a new amber-headed cane in one hand and a package of brand-new books, securely tied together, tucked under his other arm. A dab of dark chocolate still smeared the corner of his mouth as he threw himself down on the rug and eagerly opened his books.

Sabrina flopped into a chair and gave a tired smile. "Richard shall have his new eyeglasses on Friday, and will see as well as you or I," she told Mary, who'd been watching Richard in amazement, her face mirroring her hopes.

"That's wonderful. I can scarcely believe the change in him already, Rina," Mary sighed in relief, then chuckled, "of course, it could be those new books he is poring over."

Sabrina smiled in satisfaction and sorted through the packages in her lap, giving Mary, Aunt Margaret and Hobbs each a gaily wrapped parcel.

Hobbs's cheeks flushed red as she undid the wrapping to find several delicate lace handkerchiefs and matching gauze mobcaps. She fingered the frilly caps lovingly with shaking hands, tears in her eyes as she looked up at the faces around her.

"Oh, Lady Sabrina," she gulped, her thin face puckered with emotion, "these are the nicest pretties I've ever seen, or ever had. Are they really for me?" she asked hesitantly, afraid someone might snatch them from her as she tightened her bony fingers over the box.

"They are yours to wear to church on Sundays, or whenever you feel like dressing up," Sabrina declared stoutly.

"Oh, thank you," she crooned, her eyes devouring the little bits of lace.

"Aunt Margaret, see what we bought you," Sabrina told her aunt who was for once watching everything around her with interest. She moved her ever-present sewing aside as Sabrina put a large package on her lap. Mary crowded close to watch as Aunt Margaret excitedly opened her present.

She gave a gasp of sheer pleasure as her eyes feasted on the beautiful black japanned box. Opening it, she gave a squeal of delight as she saw the piles of colorful silk threads: three shades of green, four of blue, five of purple, countless shades of every hue available in the shops.

"Oh, my dears, thank you! So precious," she murmured as she excitedly fingered through all of the colors, inspecting them carefully.

"Mary, for you." Sabrina gave her a small package.

"I wonder what it is," she asked excitedly, as she carefully unwrapped the gift while Sabrina watched impatiently. Mary drew out an ornate gold box with colorful pictures enameled on its surface, and opening it found a gold heart-shaped locket attached to a thin gold chain. "It's beautiful, Rina," Mary breathed, a soft smile curving her mouth. "I won't say thank you, because it isn't enough, but you know what this means to me. Mother had one very similar." She reached up and hugged Sabrina, then asked, "What did you get for yourself? You did buy something?"

Sabrina laughed. "Of course, I'm not that unselfish."

She unwrapped a large package and lifted from its folds a lavender-blue velvet, fur-trimmed pelisse. She slipped her arms into the arm slits and rubbed the fur with the tip of her chin.

"How lovely, Sabrina," Mary cried out in admiration. "Turn around and let me see the back."

Sabrina paraded around the room, spinning and whirling to their delight. "We are going to relax and enjoy ourselves, and not worry about anything for the rest of our stay in London. Everything is working out perfectly," Sabrina stated confidently as she hugged the fur pelisse around her.

From then on the days passed quickly. They toured the city, watching the big ships dock on the Thames, and they shopped and explored the parks, feeding the ducks and watching the swans regally glide past on the placid lake.

By the end of the week Aunt Margaret had stocked up on Bohea tea and her favorite snuff and scent and accompanied Sabrina and Mary on their trips to the milliner, dressmaker and bootmaker, where they placed orders to be sent to Verrick

House and added to their wardrobes several hats and gloves purchased on the spot.

By Friday they were packed and ready to leave London. It had dawned stormy, and the cobbled streets were slippery and dangerous as Sabrina, snug in her fur-trimmed pelisse, and Richard left for Mr. Smithson's. With a warming fire burning behind the fire grate in his shop, Mr. Smithson fitted Richard's eyeglasses.

Richard stood silent as he gazed out on a sharply defined scene, the cobbles and windows across the court clearly visible. Sabrina held her breath as she watched the back of Richard's head as he stood so still. When he turned and looked at her a solitary tear was clinging to his cheek.

"I can see everything, Rina. I can see as good as you, now." He hugged Sabrina fiercely, then held out a small hand to the very quiet Mr. Smithson. "Thank you, sir, you've given me something I can never repay," he told the old gentleman seriously, his young face very adult behind the gold-rimmed eyeglasses now sitting snugly on the bridge of his small nose.

Mr. Smithson took the extended hand and shook it heartily. "It was my pleasure, Lord Faver, my pleasure indeed."

Sabrina paid Mr. Smithson, and with messages for Mrs. Taylor and his nephews, they left him standing in the doorway waving as their coach rumbled down the street.

Richard craned his head out of the window constantly, pointing to this building or that monument, jumping around the coach like a small monkey in a tree. "It's so wonderful, Rina. I can see the river and the ships going down it, and the docks, and look at that!" he called to Sabrina as they turned off before reaching an overturned carriage that had collided with a farm wagon loaded with poultry, feathers floating down on the crowd that had gathered around the mishap, the road blocked as traffic clogged the intersection.

"I wonder if anyone was hurt?" Richard asked, still straining to catch sight of the accident. "I can hardly wait to get back to Verrick House and go riding," Richard confided, his excitement bubbling over.

As they entered the town house Richard's hand found

Sabrina's and he asked diffidently, "Will you help me learn how to ride properly?"

"Of course, and I'll be a hard taskmaster," Sabrina warned, thankful to see his eyes shining behind the small, round eyeglasses. "And if you learn quickly I'll take you to a special place and we can have a picnic," Sabrina promised him, noticing for the first time the nervous tension of the footmen standing in the hall, and the harassed look on Cooper's face as he greeted them and held open the door to the salon, his back very stiff and his manners at their most formal.

Sabrina frowned as she walked into the room. Richard bounced in, unaware of the tensions within as Mary sat quietly, a frozen expression on her face, and Aunt Margaret was huddled over her needlepoint, the top of a white, starched cap bobbing every so often as her fingers busily moved.

"Mary?" Sabrina asked. "What is the—"

"Well, well, if it isn't little Sabrina," a voice spoke softly from the corner of the room.

Sabrina stopped walking abruptly, Richard bumping into her from behind. She reached out automatically to catch him as she turned to face the voice. Richard stood silently beside her, Sabrina's arm protectively across his shoulders.

A medium-sized man in a rose-colored silk coat with matching waistcoat and breeches, white silk stockings and elegant pumps, his powdered wig tied back with a black ribbon and a black silk patch on one cheek, bowed mockingly to them as they stood there like ghosts.

Sabrina's face paled as she stared hypnotically into eyes the same shade of violet as her own, black eyebrows that arched in the same curve. But there the similarity ended, for the man's face was tired and lined with cynicism. His mouth curved into an unpleasant smile at the stunned expressions on the faces about him.

"What, no glad cries of greeting from my daughter?" the marquis asked amusedly, then his eyes narrowed as they focused on the silent Richard. "So, you are my son? Don't take much after me, do you? Look like a real little Scotsman with that red hair," he sneered, casually taking a pinch of snuff.

"Your seed did little to mark him, my lord. He has his character and intelligence from his Scottish ancestors. I, as you can plainly see," Sabrina mocked him back, "am the only one who bears the Verrick looks—and the cursed temper and tongue that go with them. So beware, my lord, should you decide to exercise your wit at my family's expense."

The marquis sucked in his breath in a gasp of surprise, sneezing violently several times. He recovered quickly and a reluctant smile of admiration crossed his dissipated features.

"I stand warned, but my friends also say that I can charm the devil, too. I wonder if your forte extends to that also."

"Friends?" Sabrina questioned doubtfully, a dark, silky brow arched delicately in disbelief. "I didn't think you had any, my lord?"

The marquis was silent for a moment before laughing loudly with genuine amusement, his face for once innocent of its contemptuous expression. He was still smiling as the salon door opened and the contessa entered, a surprised expression on her face as she saw the marquis' smiling face.

"Luciana, my love, she is priceless, and a chip off the old block. By God, it is too much to be hoist on my own petard. Imagine being bested by my own daughter." He wiped at his eyes with a jessamine-scented handkerchief. "How fortunate that the contessa and I decided to return a day early, or I would have missed this loving little exchange with my family."

"A pity we are leaving this afternoon, but then it is always wiser to take one's medicine in small doses," Sabrina said sweetly. "If you'll excuse us, my lord, we've things to see to before we depart."

"Now where are your manners, my dear? You haven't met my wife, Luciana, yet."

The contessa had been standing silently in the doorway and now she swept forward in a wave of perfume and rustling silk, her fingers weighed down with jeweled rings as she stretched out her welcoming hands.

"Oh, *caro*, this one *è molto bella*," she cried, and cupping Sabrina's small chin in her hand stared down into her face in amazement. "It is unbelievable that she would look such as you, *caro*. And this one, oh, so dear," she said, and gave the speechless Richard a big hug. "Such hair!" She chuckled good-naturedly, then turned her attention again to Sabrina, whose eyes had widened in realization as she'd watched the contessa, remembering where she'd seen her before. Her lips quivered with amusement as she thought of the incident and the contessa's pearl earrings, her dimple appearing briefly in her cheek.

"Ah, she even has the dimple, *caro*," the contessa said shaking her head.

"Yes, it would seem that she is a great deal like me, my love," the marquis admitted proudly, with a touch of vanity as he saw himself in Sabrina.

The contessa made herself comfortable on the settee beside Mary, and taking one of Mary's cold hands she commented, "This one is like the Madonna, she is very quiet, but she sees and knows, eh, child?" she asked, looking into Mary's surprised eyes. "I have ordered tea, a disgusting custom, for your family, but for me a little sherry," the contessa told them as she stared at Mary and Sabrina with a penetrating gaze, then said something to the marquis in Italian, her words seeming to have a startling effect on him, for his eyes narrowed speculatively and an amused smile softened his mouth. "I have always believed you to be an astute and very clever woman, Luciana, but now I must congratulate you."

Sabrina stared at them uneasily, not liking the assessing look they were giving Mary and herself. Richard's arm sneaked around Sabrina's waist and he moved closer as he silently watched the man who was his father, and whom he had seen for the first time today. Aunt Margaret had closed herself off completely from the unpleasantness, seldom looking up at her brother or the contessa.

Sabrina came to a decision. "Come along, Mary, Richard, Aunt Margaret." She motioned to them to follow her. "We will take our leave of you, my lord, and trust that we will not meet again."

"Oh, but we shall," the marquis answered conversationally as he poured both himself and the contessa a sherry from the decanter a footman had brought in on a tray, along with a silver teapot and plate of sweets which the contessa was choosing from. "I've a notion to become reacquainted with my dear family. It has been such a long time. A pity I didn't visit you at Verrick House sooner, you've made it quite comfortable, although a bit rustic for my tastes. Yes, I think I really must get to know you all much better," he taunted, watching Sabrina with detached interest as her eyes flashed with anger. She walked over to him, looking unbelievably beautiful. He sat down with his sherry, prepared to enjoy himself.

"Family?" she repeated. "Since when have you, the irresistible marquis, admitted to having a family? You've always been too busy traveling through Europe on your Grand Tours to inquire about the health and happiness of your family. Oh, no, why you even were too busy to come to see your wife buried. Before she was even cold you were off to London, your son only a few days old and not even seen by his father, the mighty marquis. And what has it been now? Ten years since we last saw your fatherly face? Are you sure you even remember our names, or how many children you sired?"

Sabrina's angry eyes flashed as she stared down at the marquis whose face had become a pale and rigid mask, his knuckles white as his hand gripped the fragile crystal stem of his glass.

"You're no father to us. The only father we ever knew was our grandfather. The only affection we ever received was from him."

Sabrina turned on her heel and stalked to the door where she turned around, Mary and Richard on each side of her, and Aunt Margaret nervously hovering nearby. "We don't need you, or want you, my lord," she told him, bitterness shaking her voice.

The marquis stood up slowly, a disagreeable expression on his face. "My, my, no love lost between us, is there? Quite a little family you've become. So loyal and clannish, it must be the Scots blood in you. The old man did a thorough job on all of you, didn't he? I should never have allowed him to snatch you off to the Highlands with him. Even my own sister as well, who hasn't a drop of Scots blood in her, has turned against me." He looked at the contessa, who'd sat in silent dismay through the scene, and gave a wry smile. "You see, they have turned against me, Luciana."

He picked up his gold-headed cane from the floor beside his chair and began tapping it thoughtfully as he pondered his words, then looking up he spoke in a hard voice directed at the four people standing before the door.

"Now let me tell you a few truths. I am still your legal guardian. I have full and complete authority over the lot of you. Should I decide, I could throw dear Margaret out of the house and leave her to manage on her own. You wouldn't like that, would you?"

Aunt Margaret gave a wounded cry, tears crowding into her eyes, and with a sniff slumped down into the nearest chair. Mary rushed over to her and put a comforting arm about her shaking shoulders, and glared back at her father.

"Of course, I haven't decided to do that yet. And, of course, there's the rest of you. I could easily separate you. Take Richard on my next trip to Europe. Educate him properly."

"*Caro*," the contessa pleaded softly, "you upset the *bambino*."

"I'll handle my family," he answered in a bored tone, taking a pinch of snuff carelessly. "You see, Sabrina, I still hold that winning hand. I always have and always will. No, you will stay here in London—at least, you and Mary will. The house is too small to accommodate all of us comfortably, and besides, there isn't much to amuse a small boy, or Margaret, here in town. They will proceed back to Verrick House as planned." He met Sabrina's angry look, daring her to contradict him, unmoved by Richard's unhappy face and trembling mouth.

Sabrina glared at him for a moment, feeling impotent and furious, then with an angry stamp of a small foot, turned and ran from the room. At that, as if they were all released from immobility, Mary, Richard, and Aunt Margaret followed her in a quick exodus, leaving the marquis and contessa sipping their sherry in the salon.

Mary and Richard found Sabrina stretched out on the bed in their room, her face buried in her pillow. They climbed onto the bed and sat beside her. Sabrina rolled over onto her back, shaking her head in disbelief.

"What is happening? Why, Mary? Why is everything falling apart? Nothing is the same—nothing. Why is everything changing? We were so happy at Verrick House. We should never have left there."

At Richard's sob Sabrina turned a grief-stricken face to him. "Oh, honey, I'm sorry. You know I would give anything to have gotten your glasses. You know that. I don't regret one single thing because of it." She hugged him close and felt his trembling body.

"It would have happened anyway. They would've come to Verrick House and found us there. It was out of our hands; it was inevitable."

"Damn his eyes," Sabrina swore. "He thinks he can come back and play the father to us, ordering us about. Well, he has a surprise coming if he thinks to get away with that." Sabrina sighed despite her show of bravado. "I wonder what his game is. He doesn't do something unless there is some gain in it for him."

"I don't like him," Richard said sullenly, sniffing at his tears. "And I won't go with him, either."

"He'll leave soon, he must. He'll get tired of playing with us."

"You won't let him take me, will you, Rina?" Richard tugged at her arm, a pleading look in his eyes.

Sabrina smiled. "He'll never take you from us—or separate us." She smiled with anticipation. "Should he decide to play rough, then so can we."

Richard visibly relaxed against Sabrina as she and Mary exchanged worried glances, Mary's tinged with apprehension at the determined look on Sabrina's face.

Mary suddenly gasped, giving Richard an encompassing stare. "In all of the excitement I nearly forgot about your eyeglasses, Richard," she exclaimed.

Richard's face cleared, and with a beaming smile held his face up for her inspection. "I can see ever so good, Mary. I'm going to learn how to shoot as good as anybody, too."

Mary smiled happily. "That's wonderful. The only bright spot in this day. It makes everything worthwhile."

Sabrina looked at Richard's happy face and knew that what Mary said was true—it had all been worth it. After a quiet luncheon by themselves, Mary and Sabrina bid a tearful farewell to Richard and Aunt Margaret, Hobbs muttering under her breath while she gathered up Aunt Margaret's scattered sewing. They watched from the door, waving until the coach disappeared from sight, and then went back inside to wait anxiously in the salon for the marquis' next move.

It came at teatime while Mary was pouring the dark brew into, wafer-thin cups. The door was opened and the marquis entered, relaxed and fresh from a rest.

"Ah, just what I need, a cup of tea. Pour your father a cup, Mary," he ordered pleasantly. He watched her for a moment as she capably fixed him a cup, her movements smooth and sure. "I really had no idea that I had two such attractive daughters. Of course, Sabrina's looks are extraordinary, but you, Mary, with your red hair and gray eyes, are quite lovely, a quiet, serene type of beauty. Yes, yes, I'm really quite pleased. It was the contessa who brought it to my attention. You see," he confided, "we are in a bit of a financial difficulty at the moment. That is why we came to England, partly to escape our creditors and to see if I could raise some money by selling some land I own." He looked at Sabrina slyly. "And maybe even Verrick House, since I don't believe it's still entailed."

"You'd sell Verrick House? But that is Richard's inheritance, and our home," Sabrina said in disbelief.

"Well, it may not be necessary, now. Marvelous tea, my dear," he complimented Mary, nodding his head complacently, a smile of smug satisfaction on his lips.

Sabrina sipped her tea, a mistrustful look on her face as she watched him covertly, still smarting under his threat to sell Verrick House. He was definitely up to something.

"I've been looking over my correspondence and see quite a few suitable invitations to balls and assemblies which will be perfect for launching my two lovelies into society," he said archly, watching for the effect of his words on their faces.

Sabrina and Mary sat in stunned silence as the meaning of his words sunk in, their faces stony as they stared at their father.

"I think we might do quite well. There are quite a few eligible, and rich, dukes around. Nothing less than a marquis, I should think though," he declared, a calculating look in his violet eyes.

"So, you're going to sell us to the highest bidder?" Sabrina jeered, the numbness leaving her as she felt the heat of anger flush her face. "We're to find you and the contessa a pair of rich sons-in-law, are we? Well, you will have to face a disappointment, for I have no intention of falling in with your schemes."

The marquis shrugged amicably. "You have no say in the matter, my dear. You should be pleased that I intend to make such suitable matches for you. What sort of prospects would you have stuck in that backwater village?" he laughed derisively. "Some rustic? A country squire? Hunting, fishing, riding all day, only to have him fall into a drunken stupor before the hearth each evening and snore you to death?"

He laughed at his witticism. "I can see that doesn't amuse you. No, you leave the matrimony stakes to your dear father, and I shall have us all living the life of ease."

He stood up, gathering his cane and gloves. "I've checked your wardrobes, and although you've plenty of clothes, you've not any ball gowns or fancy dress outfits. I've made appointments for you two and the contessa to get you fitted out proper. There's a masked ball tomorrow, so we'll have to hurry if you're to be presentable. Oh, and don't be difficult, my dears, I really do so hate having to play the villain—but I will, you know, I will."

He left the room with a jaunty step, humming a cheerful tune under his breath. Mary gave a sigh of despair and poured herself another cup of tea. "More?" she asked Sabrina wearily.

Sabrina shook her head. "I'd rather a brandy, I need it. We must have been born under an evil star."

"What are we going to do, Rina?"

Sabrina shook her black curls. "I don't know. All we can

do is play along with him. There's nothing else we can do, at least for now, but he won't have his way for long," Sabrina promised. "Let's just hope nothing else happens to complicate our lives."

Chapter 8

THE DUKE OF CAMAREIGH TURNED AS THE DOORS OF THE SALON were opened and his fiancée, Lady Blanche Delande, entered with two small, yapping dogs at her feet. Lucien stared at her dispassionately, noting the flushed cheeks and windblown auburn curls that had strayed across her temples, bright blue eyes sparkling beneath the brim of her peacock-blue bonnet.

"Oh, Lucien," she said breathlessly as she saw him rise from the settee. "I had no idea it was you."

"Why should that surprise you? A man does on occasion visit with his fiancée," Lucien said without much interest. "I've been out of town, and thought I would see what you've been up to while I've been away."

"Up to?" Blanche laughed nervously. "Why ever should you imagine I had been up to anything?" She dropped her scarf, gloves and purse in a chair, and pulling off her bonnet, smoothed her curls with agitated fingers.

Lucien glanced at her curiously. Blanche was always in a fidgety, excitable mood, reminding him of her two lapdogs that danced around and were constantly underfoot. After the first few minutes of her company he was bored senseless, her conversation running to little more than the latest fashion and most scandalous gossip. She was a silly little creature, but harmless, and although he felt little affection for her, he couldn't really dislike her, either.

"What have you purchased now?" he asked.

Blanche looked blank for an instant. "Bought?"

"Yes, you've been out shopping again, haven't you?"

"Oh, yes, of course," she replied quickly, her cheeks pinkening in confusion. "I've bought a few gowns."

"I trust by now that you've about completed your trousseau? We do get married next week."

Blanche perched on the edge of the settee, one of the dogs panting in her lap as she rubbed its head. "Of course, I have. And, I took you at your word and charged everything to your credit."

She peeped at him. "I have been horribly extravagant, Lucien."

Lucien shrugged. "If you are to become my duchess, then you must be dressed accordingly."

"What do you mean, 'if I am to become your duchess'? I have every intention of marrying you, Lucien."

"I've no doubts on that score, Blanche. It was just a manner of speech, although one would think you had a guilty conscience," Lucien remarked casually.

Blanche gave an incredulous laugh, its shrillness grating on Lucien's nerves. "Me? Don't be ridiculous, Lucien. Just because I've become engaged to you, doesn't mean I shall forgo my pleasures, nor shall I retire to the country as soon as I am wed," she informed him, and with a challenging look added, "Besides, a married woman has far more license to enjoy herself than an unwed girl."

Lucien smiled. "And you intend to participate fully, if I understand you correctly?"

"Yes," Blanche answered adamantly, "as indeed you do."

"Well, at least we shall have no misunderstandings in our relationship, nor tiresome theatrics of jealousy and wounded pride."

Blanche preened herself, feeling very pleased. "When do I get the family jewels?"

"In due time. My grandmother, since she is still the duchess, has them in her keeping, and will turn them over only to my wife, so I would imagine you will receive them on our wedding day."

"Oh," Blanche murmured in disappointment. "I so wished to wear them with my new gown tomorrow night. I've already told Lettie I would. Oh, please, Lucien, talk her into giving them to me. Please, Lucien," she pouted prettily, glancing at the duke under her eyelashes expectantly.

"I'm hardly on favorable terms with the duchess, Blanche," he replied crushingly. "Of course, if you tempted me with a few kisses I might intercede on your behalf," he added sarcastically, expecting the look of revulsion that she could not hide as her big blue eyes were drawn irresistibly to his scar.

As she shuddered delicately, Lucien was suddenly reminded of another woman's eyes that had looked at him unflinchingly, even going so far as to rub her cheek against his scarred one.

"What are you going to do when we wed, Blanche, and I demand my rights as a husband and lover?" he asked, a smile of contempt on his lips.

Blanche turned her delicate profile to him and replied steadily, "I shall submit to you, of course."

"Of course."

Blanche turned to him in puzzlement. "What do you want, Lucien? I know that you do not love me. You are only marrying to gain your inheritance. I want to be a duchess. It is all very simple, isn't it?"

Lucien stared at her moodily. "Is it?" he answered enigmatically.

Blanche looked away from the duke's scarred cheek, feeling uncomfortable as he stared at her, and looked out of the window instead. She could hear the carriages passing by, and a gleam of anticipation entered her eyes as she remembered the thrill of lips against hers and the promise of more to come.

❦

Lucien sat back against the cushions of his coach and contemplated the rabble beyond the coach window, his farewell to Blanche having been brief and desired by both. Taking out his pocket watch he checked the time impatiently and was putting it back in his waistcoat pocket when his coachman poked his head into the coach, and he knew he would be late visiting his grandmother.

"Bit of a snarl-up, your grace. Damned riffraff clogging the streets; don't know how to handle the ribbons, the bog-trotters," he said with disgust at his fellow travelers.

"Very well, but do try and hurry us along before I need another shave," Lucien answered dryly.

"Right, your grace," the coachman chuckled as he hopped off, flinging curses at the wagon blocking the way ahead. The wagon directly in front of them had lost a wheel and another wagon had closed behind, wedging them between the two. Directly to the right a narrow street joined the busier one and it was on this one, opening directly onto the place where Lucien's coach now sat immobile, that a runaway farm wagon careened out of control, heading straight toward the big black coach with ducal crests boldly emblazoned on the doors for all to see.

Lucien heard the cries of terror and warning blending with a rumbling sound and glancing up curiously, looked out of the coach window to see a wagon, heavily laden with supplies and gaining tremendous speed, rolling down the narrow side street toward his coach.

He reacted on a surge of adrenaline and dove through the coach window, hitting the cobbled street in a hard, tumbling fall, rolling over and over until he was clear of the wheels of the coach. Faces and feet flew past him and he heard the loud crash of splintering wood as the two vehicles met. His team of horses panicked and pawed the air in fear, their neighing screams piercing the moment of stunned silence before the crowd reacted.

Lucien felt rough hands help him to his feet as he staggeringly tried to rise. The cloth of his coat and breeches was torn and muddied from his fall, and somewhere beneath the shuffling feet of the crowd were his wig and hat. The cobbles were slick from the light rain that was falling, but people still came running to see the destruction of his coach, and any injuries he might have suffered.

"Cooee! But that was a grand bit 'o tumbling, guv'nor," an awed voice congratulated him. "Never seen anyone fly like ye did. Eh, but it was a sight to see. Yer wig and shoe going one way, and the rest o' ye going the other," the man chuckled in remembrance.

Lucien looked at the speaker, whose shirtsleeves were rolled above his big hairy forearms and had a leather apron tied about his wide girth. For the first time, Lucien felt the wetness seeping through his stocking, his shoe having gone in another direction as the butcher had said.

"Boy, did you give us a show! Better'n the cockfights, for sure. Would've bet, though, you'da been squashed flatter'n a flounder. Thought ye was a real goner."

"Your grace!" called the coachman, a look of relief on his face when he saw the duke standing in the center of a gawking crowd. "Are ye all right? My God, I've never seen anything like it in all my born days. Thought you'd been finished off, your grace."

Lucien grimaced and shook his foot free of mud. "I thought so too."

He made his way with his coachman toward the remains of what had once been a very comfortable coach. His team of horses had been released and were being quieted by his grooms. The farm wagon had split in two and practically upended over his coach. As they stood there, one of the cages full of frightened, squawking poultry that had been precariously off-balanced by the crash, fell from its perch, sending chickens and feathers in all directions. Lucien looked down at his brown velvet coat, now covered in downy feathers and then at his coachman, who was fighting a feather from the tip of his nose, and a reluctant grin curved his mouth at the picture they must present.

"Whose wagon is this?" he demanded, his humor fading as he realized how close he'd come to being trapped underneath the twisted wreckage.

"Odd, ain't a soul to say it was his, your grace," the coachman responded. "Though don't guess anyone would want to claim it, seein' how it was a runaway and nearly killed a duke."

The coachman stood gazing at the wreckage, then added worriedly as he looked at the duke who stood tall and dignified despite his dishevelment, "Don't see how the wagon could'a been goin' so fast though? That street ain't that steep. Seems a mite strange, your grace."

One of the grooms came running up at that moment, his face mirroring disbelieving excitement. "Bloke over there says he saw two rowdies pushing the wagon down the street and just standin' and watchin' as it gathered speed, then took to their heels and disappeared."

"It would seem as though someone has gone to a great deal of trouble to insure my death," Lucien commented in a hard voice as he exchanged looks with his coachman, who spat contemptuously on the cobblestones and began to curse volubly at the unknown assailants.

"I suggest that you find me some other mode of transportation," Lucien ordered as he became aware of the coaches slowly traveling past as they skirted the accident. "I feel quite conspicuous and not exactly at my best standing here in one shoe."

When Lucien finally knocked on the large mahogany door of the grand mansion in Berkeley Square that was the residence of his grandmother, he was two hours late. When recognized, the majordomo's arrogant demeanor changed to obsequious cordiality as he showed the duke through the hall that was crowded with liveried footmen, to wait in the salon while he was announced.

Lucien glanced at the clock ticking away the minutes and smiled in grim amusement as he realized he was to be kept waiting for his audience in retaliation for being late. He was too well aware by now of the stratagems being played out in his grandmother's Berkeley Square home to be surprised by her next move, but it never failed to amuse him and slightly irritate him, which he knew was the purpose. Only this time he would checkmate.

Making himself comfortable, Lucien pulled from a pocket the deck of cards he'd brought along for just such an occasion and shuffling them, dealt them out on the tapestried seat of a chair he'd pulled up close to the settee. Half an hour later he was still amusing himself with his cards when the majordomo entered and announced that he would now be received.

Lucien looked up in boredom and casually played another card. "In good time. You may tell her grace that I shall be up shortly," he said lazily, and turned his attention once more to the cards before him, a smile tugging at the corner of his mouth at the majordomo's look of affronted dignity as he nodded his head and stiffly left the room, closing the door firmly on Lucien's deep laugh.

Fifteen minutes later Lucien presented himself before the door of the upstairs salon, and in answer to his knock he entered the room and approached the large winged-back chair situated like a throne before the window, the revealing light falling on the visitor as he sat in a small chair facing it.

"*Bonjour*, Grandmère," Lucien greeted the duchess, a smile on his lips as he kissed the hand held regally out to him.

The duchess snorted. "A good morning, indeed. Keeping me waiting two and a half hours. It's outrageous, but then you always have been."

"Thirty minutes of those two hours were of your own making, if I remember correctly?" Lucien advised her audaciously.

The duchess laughed grudgingly. "Trying to best me at my own game?"

Lucien sat down, laughing softly. "No one has been able to do that yet, Grandmère."

The duchess smiled and leaned forward on her cane, her blue-veined hands thin and shaking slightly as she tapped Lucien's booted leg. "You insult me by coming to my house like a lackey from the stables. You young blades don't give a damn how you appear. No wonder Blanche is scared half out of her wits by you. I sometimes think I made a mistake in selecting her for you."

Lucien stared expressionlessly into the same sherry-colored eyes as his own. "I think perhaps it is the scar, Grandmère, that makes the fair damsel ill at ease. She fears that my buccaneerish visage is more than skin deep," Lucien commented dryly.

"In my day—well, that's past, but the fancy pieces strutting about today have no spirit. A lot of lace and pretty bows are all they are made of. No sense of adventure in them," she complained contemptuously, then catching Lucien's smile demanded, "Well, what are you grinning about?"

"Oh, just that I wish you and a certain person could've had the opportunity of meeting."

"A woman, eh?" the duchess guessed.

"Very much so; however, I've seen her wield a rapier, sit a horse, and scare the wits from twelve men so well that you might be doubtful of her sex."

The duchess chuckled. "Sounds like quite a woman. Must not know her, though," she pried.

Lucien smiled grimly. "No, and if you did meet her I doubt whether it would be under circumstances you'd enjoy," he told her obliquely.

The duchess banged her cane. "You've piqued my curiosity. Tell me, who is she?" She raised her eyebrows in sudden thought. "Oh, I see. If she has that much spirit, she must be one of your opera singers or a little dancer, eh? Well, you'd better concern yourself for now with getting Blanche to the altar. Time enough for your other type of friend later."

Lucien smiled without humor. "You remind me very much of this other woman. Both of you are willful, obstinate, and a thorn in my side. You and your pack of solicitors must have sat up all night figuring out that damned condition you added to your will."

"Bitter, Lucien?" she baited him.

"I dislike having my life interfered in, and I dislike being given an ultimatum," he said angrily.

"You always were headstrong and difficult, even as a baby. In and out of trouble, always answering me back. Impertinent brat, that's what you were, but I must admit I preferred your insolence to little Percy's sniveling virtue."

"Then why are you giving dear Percy the chance to inherit my estate?" Lucien asked coldly.

The duchess laughed with delight. "Only thing that would finally bring you around. Thought at first all I had to do was keep a tight rein on the purse strings, but no, you have to go out and win yourself a fortune and create quite a reputation for yourself at the same time," she spoke coolly. "I'm still not certain I have forgiven you for ignoring me for two years. You didn't come to see me once, Lucien," she told him, remembered hurt in her voice.

But Lucien remained unmoved. "Obviously it didn't affect you too deeply, or you would not be threatening me now. You resented the fact that I didn't have to depend on you for my every need. I proved that I could support myself, and managed to acquire a fortune three times as large as that which I should have inherited, but you still have to try and rule my life. Well, this time you have succeeded. My freedom, or my heritage? An interesting choice, but I am no longer quite the hothead that I once was when I stormed off the first time, denouncing you and my heritage. I find that I can swallow my pride, because Camareigh means more to me than your machinations. It is mine, and I intend to have it."

"So, you've learned your lesson," the duchess smiled. "I'm surprised it took you this long to realize that I intended to have my way. You don't like the idea of your cousins spending your money and living in your home? Odd to think that Percy would have been master of Camareigh and Kate its mistress, for you know that she would be there. Percy's wife has little to say when Kate is around—which is all of the time. Kate the beautiful, the heartless, the aspiring, and so jealous of you, Lucien. Wasn't it over some toy of yours that she scarred your cheek, my boy? She can be a vicious creature when she can't have her way. I wonder how Percy's wife feels about having his sister living with them now that Kate is a widow. The poor-spirited little mouse, Kate will walk all over her."

"Would you really have turned Camareigh over to Percy and Kate, Grandmère?" Lucien demanded, his voice frigid.

The duchess looked sad for a moment, then straightening her shoulders, replied regretfully, "You are still angry with me, resentful. I fear I have lost your love, my boy, but I intend to see future Dukes of Camareigh inherit all that your ancestors built. I'll not have our line die out. I do not want a

Rathbourne to walk the halls of Camareigh, but at least Percy has children, our blood will continue through them," she said obstinately, then her eyes softened slightly as she gazed on Lucien's face. "But I would prefer that they were your children, Lucien. If it were left up to you, you would never marry, and I despaired of your death before you could insure that our name and title would live on."

"Well, you will have your cherished wish, Grandmère," Lucien answered quietly, "and I will have Camareigh—but don't ask me to forgive you."

The duchess' lips trembled as she spoke in little more than a whisper, "I never expected to have a complete victory over you, Lucien. I knew I would lose something as well."

Lucien looked away from his grandmother's face, tired and lined with age, but still alive with emotions. He felt guilty, but he resisted his feelings, knowing that this was probably one more of her stratagems to bring him under her influence. He knew her too well to fall for her act of suffering a broken heart. He looked back quickly and caught the duchess watching him, a smile curving her mouth which quickly disappeared as he turned to her.

"I think we both know one another by now. After all, Grandmère, I am your grandson."

There was a knock on the door, and the majordomo announced visitors below. The duchess smiled tartly. "Show them up."

Lucien walked over to the mantelshelf and stared at his reflection in the large mirror overhanging it.

"Were I a young, pretty thing, I'd find that scar of yours most intriguing, Lucien," the duchess commented as she saw him run a finger down it.

Lucien smiled at her in the mirror. "Ah, but you, ma'am, were and are a woman of spirit and adventure, and as you yourself have said, there are few of that caliber of female left today."

The duchess was laughing when the majordomo showed Percy Rathbourne, Lord Feltham, and his sister, Katherine, Lady Morpeth, into the room, their smiles of greeting fading abruptly as they saw the casually dressed figure of their cousin standing before the fireplace, completely at home.

"Lucien," Percy greeted him shortly, a petulant look on his face before he turned to accept the duchess's hand, a smile of delight now lighting up his features. "Dear, Grandmama, how lovely you look today."

"Nonsense! I'm old and wrinkled, but I'm not a fool yet, so you can stop humoring me."

Percy flushed and then, shrugging, turned to Lucien in puzzlement. "I'm surprised to see you here. I thought you and the duchess were not speaking."

"Oh, we manage to call a truce every once in a while, much to your disappointment, eh, Percy?" Lucien inquired dryly.

"Why should we care?" Kate commented as she sat down, her perfect profile turned for Lucien's admiration.

"As always, you are looking lovely, Kate," Lucien told her to her satisfaction. "A pity it goes only skin deep," he added, wiping the smile from her lips.

Lucien watched as the pale blue eyes narrowed with malice. Her features were unbelievably perfect, like those of an angel. Her silver-gold hair and translucent skin created an almost ethereal quality about her that contradicted the diamond hardness of her eyes. Percy came to stand behind her, his face as delicately molded as hers, his silver-gold hair hidden by a wig. The only difference was Percy's sherry-colored eyes. Twins, with Kate being older by a few minutes. They seemed to think and breathe as one as they faced him. It had always been like this when they were children. Kate and Percy against him, banding together to gang up on him. He had been lucky that he'd always been bigger than they, and could usually manage to fight them off. Only once had they caught him off guard, and in that instant Kate had scarred his cheek—branding him for life. He still remembered the triumphant smile on her angelic face as the blood had dripped from his face.

"You should know about things going only skin deep," Kate retaliated, caressing the smoothness of her cheek with the back of her hand as she stared at his scarred cheek.

"Odd, isn't it," Lucien said conversationally, "how some of the worst-looking apples on the outside are the sweetest to the taste, and yet how often, I wonder, does one find that shiny, red apple to be rotten to the core."

Percy's face paled and he clenched his fists as he heard Kate's gasp of rage. "I'd like to cut you open to see how rotten you are, Lucien," Percy threatened.

The duchess banged her cane on the table, attracting their attention. "Enough! You carry on like brawlers in the street. While under my roof, you will act civilized."

"I apologize, Grandmère, for offending you," Lucien said, "and now I must bid you adieu, I've appointments to keep." His bow was just short of being insulting by its briefness.

"Lucien," the duchess called out in a shaky voice, but he had gone.

When Lucien reached his home he was not in the mood for further irritations, and so it was with anger in his eyes that he stared down at the papers on his desk impatiently. Nothing. Not one word, not one clue to the whereabouts or identity of Bonnie Charlie or her two cohorts. This report his servants had sent up from the country was useless. How could someone just vanish into thin air as she had? No, he realized, it wasn't magic—it was just not knowing where to look or whom to ask. These villagers were notoriously close mouthed when it came to discussing their own with outsiders. They'd probably spun a pretty tale for his servants, sending them on a wild-goose chase to God knows where, and laughing all the while.

He should be able to forget the little wretch, but here he was, still mooning over her like Lysander, who, with love juice clouding his vision, fell madly in love with Helena. But his life was not a Shakespearean play with fairies causing mischief and mayhem.

Enough is enough, he thought in disgust. He would join the social whirl and enjoy himself. There were several balls and routs he should take Blanche to, and he would renew certain acquaintances he had neglected recently.

Reaching out, he poured himself a brandy from the

decanter on his desk, and raising the glass in a toast said beneath his breath, "That black-haired, violet-eyed vixen be damned."

❧

"Thought I must be seeing a ghost when I walked in and saw that damned scarred face of his," Percy cursed as he threw down his cane and gloves onto a satin chair, and began to pace nervously up and down.

Kate tossed her burgundy velvet cloak onto the bed, her cheeks still flushed with anger as she turned on her brother. "I thought he would be dead this morning. Instead, one more failure to add to the list. I don't know why I believed that this time he would be finished off. You haven't had the best of luck in your past attempts. How you imagined that bungler Jensen could kill Lucien in a duel is quite beyond my comprehension. I've come to suspect that our dear cousin, Lucien, leads a charmed life. What is it now, the third accident we have rigged that he's managed to survive?"

"If I remember correctly, the first two were your ideas. Let me see, first we hired a couple of cutthroats from the docks to accost and murder Lucien in the street some evening after leaving Vauxhall, the unfortunate victim of a brutal robber— just one of many such incidents that happen all of the time. So what happens? Lucien drives his sword through one, and puts a bullet in the other."

"Fools," Kate commented in a bored tone.

"Fools?" Percy laughed nervously. "I think we're the fools to think we can get rid of Lucien. What was our other, oh so clever, plan? We paid that charming little actress from Drury Lane an exorbitant price to seduce Lucien, and then while he slept stick a knife in him."

He sent a speaking glance to his twin. "I believe she left town quite suddenly, suffering from a broken wrist, and doesn't plan on returning to England in the near future. Oh, yes, we've been absolutely brilliant, have we not?"

"Oh, do shut up, Percy, you're giving me a migraine," Kate told him sharply, tapping her fingers with their reddened nails on the dressing table.

"I tell you though, I am becoming quite peeved. One can't get away with anything anymore. Try to plan a simple murder, and you have countless busybodies hanging over your shoulder. And these absurdly ridiculous Bow Street Runners of the Fieldings. I don't know what London is coming to."

"Damned interference, but what are we to do, Kate?" Percy demanded in despair.

Kate fingered the golden cross around her neck unconsciously as she stared at her reflection in the mirror.

"If our side of the family hadn't been Catholic, and involved in so many damned plots against the Crown, we wouldn't be in this fix now," Percy said bitterly.

"If we weren't all spendthrifts we wouldn't find ourselves in this fix today, m'dear," Kate corrected him acidly. "The awful truth of the matter is that we spend money with an unsparing hand."

"Well, hang the expense, Kate," Percy complained. "What the blazes is money for if you can't spend it and enjoy yourself?"

"Yes, well, it's quite a shame that we should be the improvident branch of the family, rather than our dear cousin."

"Damned pinch-fist. Treats us pretty shabbily, making us go down on hands and knees so he can dole out a few pence," Percy said resentfully, a truculent look on his face.

Kate got to her feet and stared around her in despair. "Bills, bills, bills. Lud, but I grow fatigued of dodging the creditors, and I'd like to once answer the door without fear of it being some low-browed lout demanding to be paid. We must, at all costs, keep Lucien from inheriting his estate. Since he seems unwilling to die, I think we'd better put our other plan into action," she told Percy decisively, expectant smile curving her lips. "You should enjoy that."

Percy smirked. "I've been most discreet, m'dear, and have the little pigeon in the palm of my hand." He squeezed his hand together, his fingers curving into his palm like a vise.

"What a pity, and how embarrassing for poor Lucien, to be stood up at the altar, for I fear that is what is about to happen to him."

Percy gave a low laugh. "You'd love to see Lucien humiliated, wouldn't you? I've often thought, dear sister, that you
suffered from a case of unrequited love for our dear, arrogant
cousin. But he's never looked your way, has he? Not surprising,
considering what you did to his face."

"Careful, brother dear, or I'll have your wretched heart
carved on a platter for dinner," Kate replied tightly.

"I call truce," Percy laughed, holding up his hands placat-
ingly. "As a team we are invincible and shall see our fondest
desires. We shall have Lucien groveling in the mud at our feet."

"When do you plan on kidnapping Lucien's fiancée?"
Kate asked curiously. "Time is running out for us, so we
must act now."

"Oh, I think tomorrow evening at the ball being given by
Lord and Lady Harrier will be soon enough," Percy told her
complacently.

Kate smiled in anticipation. "It should prove to be an
interesting evening."

⚮

"Breathe in," Mary ordered as she pulled tight the laces of
Sabrina's corset and tied them behind snugly. The front was
low, with black, crisscross lacing down its length, and barely
covered the top of Sabrina's breasts.

Sabrina sat down on a chair, sighing deeply as she rolled
black silk stockings up over her knees and secured them with
two frilly garters tied with silver ribbons.

Mary glanced at her worriedly. "Too tight? I wish the
contessa would hurry up with her toilette so we could use the
maids. I'm afraid I'm not too good at this," Mary apologized.

"You're doing just fine, Mary. Now help me into this
hoop." Mary held the wide hoop while Sabrina stepped into
it. Next came a black petticoat, the fine silk shot through
with silver threads, and then the gown of white satin with
black and silver embroidery and frilly black lace flounces
falling from the elbows and opened down the front to reveal
her petticoat.

"It's exquisite, Sabrina," Mary said in awe as Sabrina slipped her feet into white silk shoes trimmed with silver, the heels high and slender.

"Rather startling," Sabrina answered in amusement, "but then that is what the marquis has in mind," she said as she fastened diamond drops in her ears and then clasped a diamond pendant around her neck.

"You first," she told Mary, indicating the velvet patches in the small box before her. Mary stuck a small black silk patch on her cheek, then looked into the mirror to see the effect.

"It isn't quite me, I think," she laughed as she removed it, leaving her cheeks smooth and pink, her gown of white silk damask, heavily embroidered with flowers and birds, rustling as she turned from the mirror.

Sabrina took a small heart-shaped black velvet patch and carefully placed it near the corner of her mouth; then taking a small pot of color, rouged her lips. She stared back at her reflection as if seeing a stranger. Her black hair had disappeared beneath its lavish powdering of white and sparkled with a spray of diamonds behind one ear when she moved her head.

"You look beautiful, Rina," Mary told her simply, her own red hair powdered white and held in place with gold hairpins. A small gold locket hung from her neck, matching the gold rings in her ears and a golden girdle buckle set with pearls around her waist. "It was kind of the contessa to lend you some of her diamonds," Mary said as she stared at the sparkling gems.

"Kind?" Sabrina repeated doubtfully, then standing up she pulled on her musk-scented, elbow-length gloves and picking up her fan and purse, turned to Mary. "Shall we go?"

The marquis and the contessa were waiting in the salon, the marquis finely attired in a cream silk suit embroidered in claret, while the contessa was resplendent in burgundy damask with blood-red rubies clasped around her neck.

"*Belle*," the contessa whispered beneath her breath as she stared in amazement at the two sisters, her eyes glowing with pleasure at the result.

"My God, I had no idea the contrast between you would be so startling," the marquis said, clapping his hands in excitement, the impatient expression that had been on his face immediately lifting as he stared in awe at his two beautiful daughters. "This is marvelous. I am so pleased, but now, to add a touch of mystery, put on these masks," he told them, handing them each a black velvet half-mask. "It's quite in vogue."

Sabrina tied hers on and stared at herself in the mirror, a grin widening her mouth as she started to laugh. She turned to face Mary, who after a startled gasp of dismay, started to laugh also.

The marquis frowned ominously. "What is so damned funny?" he demanded peevishly, looking from one masked daughter to the other in exasperation.

"I always wondered how it felt, Rina," Mary said with a nervous giggle.

"How ironic that I should attend my first ball in a mask," Sabrina chuckled as she straightened the mask over her small nose.

"Well, damned if I know what you two are talking about," the marquis grumbled. The contessa was silent, however, as she continued to stare in fascination at Sabrina's masked face.

"There is something so familiar..." she spoke softly, a puzzled look on her lovely face.

"Come, we must go, we're already much too late as it is," the marquis interrupted. "Here, these just arrived from the dressmaker's." He handed them each a scarf to cover their shoulders, Mary's white velvet, and Sabrina's a thin gauze that encircled her shoulders in a silver cloud.

They rode in silence along the London streets, the coach wheels on the cobbles the only sound as they moved towards Berkeley Square until the noise of other coaches, with yelling coachmen directing fellow coachmen to unsavory places, disturbed them.

"Damned traffic," the marquis cursed as he looked out at the long line of coaches waiting their turn to unload their passengers at the party.

They lurched forward, then stopped, then moved forward a little, time and time again, before finally coming to a halt before the well-lighted entrance of the great town house, the liveried footmen escorting the guests along the red carpet rolled across the walk and up to the doors.

Mary's fingers closed over Sabrina's as they followed the marquis and the contessa into the crowded entrance hall, chandeliers glowing with light above their heads as they moved through the throng, the marquis crying out greetings to acquaintances as they passed. He smiled superciliously at the curious and interested stares he was receiving as he ascended the grand staircase surrounded by his beautiful wife and daughters.

"Darling James," a bejeweled woman cried joyously at sight of the marquis. "I was hoping you would return to London in time for my little ball." She turned her avid gaze on the two masked figures standing silently beside the marquis. "I've already met your wife, the contessa," she said, giving the contessa a slight smile, "but did I hear correctly? These surely can't be your daughters, darling? Why, I had no idea you even had a family," she remarked with feigned surprise, and giving the contessa an arch look, added delicately, "Of course, they could be the contessa's daughters? You are old enough, I suppose, to be their mother?"

The contessa smiled thinly. "No, they are James's first wife's daughters, but soon I shall be the mother of his child," she informed Lady Harrier, and making a moue of her mouth, said regretfully, "A pity, is it not, when a woman becomes too old to bear the child, eh?" She looked at the older woman understandingly.

Lady Harrier drew in her breath sharply, her mouth tight. "Why haven't I seen these daughters of yours before? Keeping them hidden away, have you?"

The marquis smiled artlessly, his face the picture of innocence.

"How can you think such a thing, Lady Harrier? I've merely been waiting for the proper opportunity, shall we say, of introducing my lovely daughters to proper society." He turned a beaming face of fatherly pride on his daughters. "Allow me to introduce you to Lady Mary, my eldest, and little Lady Sabrina, who I am told takes after her father," he said modestly.

Lady Harrier was amused. "I can see that this evening will

be quite extraordinary, you devil. You shall have all of my guests, especially those in breeches, burning with curiosity to have a peek beneath those tantalizing masks."

"Do you really think so?" the marquis asked ingenuously.

Lady Harrier gave a disbelieving laugh. "The devil take you, James, now go and find some rich suitors for these daughters of yours."

As they moved on, joining the crowd milling about, the marquis seemed to be searching for certain faces, introducing Mary and Sabrina to select persons only, snubbing those he felt were beneath him. Sabrina couldn't help but become caught up in the excitement as the drifting sounds of musicians warming up rose above the din of conversing voices, her small foot beginning to tap in anticipation.

The marquis stopped abruptly before a plump young man in pale blue brocade, pulling Mary and Sabrina close beside him. "Your grace," he began audaciously, "you've not met my rustic beauties on their first visit to town. Mary, Sabrina, meet the Duke of Granston, my daughters, your grace."

They curtsied politely, the duke kissing their gloved hands, a spark of interest in his pale eyes. "M'pleasure, ladies," he slurred drunkenly. "Care t'dance?" And without waiting for an answer he swept Mary off into the dancing crowd.

"Devilish rich," the marquis whispered to the contessa, a satisfied smile on his lips. "See how easy it will be, Luciana? We'll be rich enough to buy half of Venice if we want."

The contessa laughed mockingly. "It would be wise, *caro*, not to anticipate too much, just yet," she cautioned gently.

"Yes, my lord," Sabrina added caustically, "one needs an acquiescent bride, and then, of course, a willing groom. Do you believe your good fortune will run to both?"

The marquis gave Sabrina a look of dislike. "I knew the first minute I saw you, you were a troublemaker," he said, "but just don't you forget what I told you, remember?" He looked at her meaningfully, then said to the contessa, "I'll be back shortly, I see someone I want to have a word with."

Sabrina's mouth was mutinous beneath her mask as she watched the marquis walk jauntily off into the crowd. She was so absorbed in her thoughts that she jumped when cool fingers touched her arm.

"Child, it does little good to fight him," the contessa said softly. "He will have his way, and I think there is little you can do about it."

"You think not?" Sabrina replied bitterly.

The contessa shrugged. "I know you do not have the feelings of love for James, and I admit that he has not been the good papa, but he is my husband now. I know his faults, but when I look into his violet eyes, so much like yours, then all is forgiven and forgotten.

"Someday a man will look into your eyes, little Sabrina, and he will forget your faults, as well. Oh, yes, you have the faults your papa does. You think not? You are obstinate, temperamental, willful, and very beautiful. You are used to getting your own way, and now your papa has come and upset your plans. I am sorry for this, but I must look after my own. We are in need of money, and if you were to marry a rich man, well..." she said, smiling apologetically, "it would be acceptable for us to receive a settlement."

"In other words," Sabrina said angrily, "a payment. I am to be bought by the richest customer."

"You do not put it so very nicely, but it is true. It is the way it has always been. A man either marries for beauty or money; unfortunately, they do not often come together. So, in your case, it will be for beauty. He will have to be very rich to get you, Sabrina."

Sabrina turned from her in disgust, the glitter of the ball suddenly looking tawdry and sickening her.

"You are too cynical for one so young," the contessa commented, giving Sabrina a penetrating look. "Of course, it has not been easy for you, this I understand. You have had to support your family, which puzzles me much. How is it that your family has managed to live? I know for a fact that James has sent no money."

Sabrina shrugged. "We have made the estate pay, and we had a little from my mother's father," she lied, giving the contessa a haughty stare.

"So, I mind my own business, Sabrina." The contessa laughed, not offended by her stepdaughter's aloofness. "You are the proud one, eh? I think your papa is going to have trouble with you."

Sabrina smiled, her eyes glinting behind their mask. "More than he could possibly believe. *Mi scusi*, contessa," Sabrina murmured before being led away by an overly eager partner.

The contessa's mouth dropped open momentarily as she remembered another masked face that had spoken in the same husky Italian. *Dio mio*, she thought in disbelief. It could not possibly be! But there had been something troubling her about that highwayman—and also about this little one. She had thought her suspicions ridiculous at the time, but now, she was not so sure. It is something only a woman would have sensed, a certain recognition despite the disguise.

"What are you giving such concentrated thought to?" the marquis asked as he came up beside the contessa, slipping his arm around her waist.

The contessa turned to him, startled, then relaxed her features into a caressing smile. "Nothing, *caro*, nothing to concern you. I'm just planning how to spend our money," she prevaricated. For now, this discovery would be her secret, and should the little one become too difficult—then she would use this startling information to their advantage.

"Well, in all modesty, Luciana, my daughters are causing quite a sensation," he boasted, a satisfied smile on his lips as he watched Mary and Sabrina dance past in the arms of two very eligible partners. "I do not foresee any difficulties in obtaining sons-in-law with the necessary requirements, my dear. No trouble at all."

Sabrina lost count of the names and faces of the rich suitors the marquis paraded before her. Her feet were tired and her head ached abominably. If only she could sit down for a brief moment.

"I do believe I cannot move another inch," she told the young man who was dancing with her. She gave him a dimpled smile, her violet eyes glowing behind the mask as she stared up at him.

"Of course, my dear Lady Sabrina, how thoughtless of

me not to see how fatigued you are," the young gentleman quickly apologized, masking his disappointment at losing such a delectable creature as a partner. He led her off the floor, reluctant to part with her, and spying a footman with a tray of champagne-filled goblets, suggested shyly, "If you would care for a breath of fresh air, allow me to escort you into the garden, and then I will fetch you some champagne?"

Sabrina smiled gratefully, her eyes lighting up with genuine warmth. "That would be marvelous, you are too kind."

The young gentleman beamed with pleasure as he stared in bemusement into Sabrina's beautiful eyes, then making a flustered departure disappeared back into the crowd as Sabrina relaxed on a stone seat beneath the balustrade of a balcony. She had only been sitting there a moment when she was startled from her relaxed state by the sound of voices practically beside her. She glanced about quickly but saw no one, then smiled as she realized the voices were coming from overhead. The couple had obviously sought a rendezvous in the seclusion of the balcony.

"You're late."

"I'm sorry, Percy, but I couldn't get away from him," Blanche complained sulkily. "You've hardly noticed me at all. I've seen you watching that creature in the mask."

"Come now, Blanche, you know it's you I love," Percy placated her. "I was merely curious about her, that is all."

There was a prolonged silence, and then Sabrina heard a muted giggle.

"Now, does that prove to you that I love you?" Percy demanded smoothly.

"Oh, Percy, I wish we could be together all of the time," Blanche pouted.

"As a matter of fact, Blanche, I've been thinking that we might find that time tonight," Percy suggested.

"Tonight? But how on earth can we?" Blanche asked, excitement quivering in her voice.

"You merely tell my dear cousin that you've the migraine and must leave the ball, then I'll slip away as well," he explained persuasively.

"Oh, I don't know." Blanche hesitated doubtfully.

"If you're worried about my dear cousin, then don't be. He'll never miss you. All he had eyes for was that bewitching creature in black and silver."

Sabrina smiled without amusement, wondering if she had danced with the poor fiancé, now being deceived by his cousin and fiancée?

"All right," Blanche decided suddenly. "I'll meet you, but where?"

"We must be most careful that no one suspects. If you tell my cousin directly, he'll insist upon you making use of his carriage, so just send him a message that you've left, then hire a coach to take you home, only stop around the corner and I'll be along to pick you up in mine."

Sabrina remained silent as she heard them depart, a cynical smile on her lips as she thought of their little deception. She sighed impatiently wondering where the young man was who'd gone to fetch her a glass of champagne. Sabrina heard the sound of approaching footsteps and looked up expectantly, a smile of welcome on her face.

"I thought you had forgotten me," she said softly.

"Forget you, Sabrina, never," a mocking voice answered as the approaching figure stopped in front of her.

Sabrina gave a small cry of fear as she stared up in dismay at the tall, silk-clad form of the Duke of Camareigh. "Lucien," she whispered faintly.

"I beg your pardon, it *is* Lady Sabrina Verrick, is it not?" Lucien corrected himself, his lips twisted into a faint smile of contempt. "I saw you leave with your admirer, and decided to substitute for him, much to his disappointment," he told her, and reaching out grasped her arms with hard fingers that closed about her in a punishing grip. "Now answer me, damn you."

"Yes." Sabrina confirmed her identity, wincing as he released one arm from his painful grip to jerk her mask from her face. Sabrina stared mutely up at him, as he pulled her to her feet.

"So, history repeats itself. I seem destined to be the one to unmask you, and each time I am surprised by the revelation." He stared down into her pale face, the light from the balcony above shining down on them. His mouth curved into a sneer as he accused her. "How you must have laughed, what a fool you must have thought me."

He laughed bitterly. "I could scarce believe my eyes when I first saw you dance past. I thought I must be seeing a ghost."

"You recognized me?" Sabrina asked in disbelief.

"You may now be wearing skirts, but the mask is the same. Ironic, isn't it? I must compliment you on your audaciousness. Or maybe you are so accustomed to wearing your mask that you feel naked without it? A pity for you that I happened to be here tonight to spoil your little game. Did you really imagine that you could deceive me? Your arrogant swagger gave you away."

Sabrina avoided his eyes and the smoldering rage she could see held in check. "I didn't think that I would see you," she said weakly.

Lucien gave her an abrupt shake, making her head jerk up. "What is your game, Sabrina? What is the daughter of a marquis doing dressed up as a highwayman? Is he in this with you?" he demanded. Then suddenly a thought struck him and he gave her a penetrating look. "He doesn't know, does he? Answer me. Does he?" Lucien's grip became unbearable and Sabrina cried out.

"Let me go. You're hurting me, Lucien."

"Tell me what I want to know first, then I will release you," he bargained.

"No, he doesn't know," Sabrina admitted in defeat.

Lucien's grip loosened, but he did not let her free completely. "No, I thought his performance the night you held up my coach far too realistic to be an act. Besides, he and the contessa had just arrived in England after years abroad, so he couldn't be aware of your activities. In fact, if I remember correctly, he commented that he had not seen his family in years. This is priceless. You held up your own father. Did you know it when you did it?"

Sabrina gave him a defiant glance from under her lashes, her initial fright at his sudden appearance fading as her resentment built. "No, I did not know who he was. It was only when I met the contessa that I realized what had happened. As the marquis told you, we haven't been an especially close family."

"I want a few answers, Sabrina," Lucien said quietly, "and you shall not escape me this time," he warned with a glint in his eyes.

"Who the devil do you think you are? You have no right to interfere in my life."

"I have every right," Lucien contradicted coolly, his grip tightening in anger. "I think you owe me a few explanations, Sabrina."

"I owe you nothing. What can you do? You certainly can't reveal the truth about me. It would be far too embarrassing for you as well. Besides, I am no longer playing the highwayman. That should satisfy you," she told him.

"I will not be satisfied until I know everything about you, Sabrina," he retorted. "You are an enigma, and a challenge I cannot resist. When I think of the wild chase you've led me on, damned if you aren't the most exasperating female," he swore beneath his breath.

"No one asked you to follow. No one asked you to interfere, and it is obvious that we only anger one another, so I would appreciate it, no, I demand that you do not concern yourself with my affairs," Sabrina told him.

Lucien's jaw hardened and he cursed her beneath his breath before pulling her against him roughly. "I swore I'd find you and make you pay for playing me the fool, and by God I shall. Regardless of whether you're the daughter of a marquis or a footman, you'll pay, Sabrina," he promised before his mouth found hers and he began to kiss the angry defiance from her as his lips moved hungrily against hers. Sabrina struggled against him, unwilling to have her lips betray her true feelings for this arrogant Duke, but he would not be denied and kept kissing her until her lips began to soften beneath his.

"Sabrina!" a voice called from the path.

Lucien raised his head reluctantly, listening as he heard the voice call out again. Sabrina was breathing heavily as she struggled from Lucien's arms, managing to free herself except for her wrist, which Lucien wrapped his fingers around.

The marquis found them standing side by side as he marched forward angrily, not recognizing the duke at first. "Where the devil have you been, Sabrina? Sir, I demand that—" the marquis began curtly, only to stop as he recognized the man standing beside Sabrina. "Why, your grace, is anything amiss?" He looked sharply at Sabrina's flushed cheeks and bright eyes, and then nervously at the duke. "If you'll excuse us, your grace, I would like my daughter to meet a few people. This is her first introduction to society and as she is new, she isn't aware that it is bad for her reputation to walk alone in the gardens with a gentleman. Sabrina," he said in a tight voice, taking her arm in a firm grip as he eased her away from the duke. "We'll see you later, perhaps, your grace?"

"My apologies for detaining your daughter," Lucien replied casually, before walking away.

"What the devil do you think you were up to?" the marquis accused Sabrina, turning on her as soon as the duke was out of sight. "He'll ruin your reputation, and then we can't get anyone to wed you."

"I had little choice in the matter," Sabrina answered shortly, her nerves still taut from her meeting with Lucien. "I can hardly snub a duke, can I?"

The marquis sighed irritably. "No, but it won't do you any good, my girl, to be setting your sights on him, for he is practically wed. He and his fiancée are set to be married next week," the marquis informed her, not seeing the anguish that entered her eyes at his news. "A pity, for he's damned rich."

The rest of the evening seemed to pass in a haze of unfamiliar voices and faces. Every time Sabrina glanced up she was aware of the duke's presence; he was always there staring with sherry-colored eyes, a cynical twist to his lips as he watched the marquis maneuvering his daughters into the upper circle of eligible bachelors, especially that of the Duke of Granston.

Sabrina was pale and wan-looking when the marquis finally decided to end the evening, his unconcealed smile of triumph at the success of the evening sickening her. Sabrina glanced uncomfortably at the contessa, whose complacent smile and knowing eyes that studied her every move seemed to hint at a shared secret. But what could she have possibly found out, Sabrina wondered. She twisted her fingers together nervously, feeling as though a rope were tightening around her neck. Sabrina glanced at the silent Mary, who had a hand pressed to her temple. She would have to find out what Mary was feeling—if she sensed anything.

But Sabrina didn't have to ask Mary, for she sought Sabrina out later that night as they undressed for bed, her gray eyes worried as she confronted Sabrina.

"I don't like this situation at all," she began as she threaded her hair into a thick braid over her shoulder. "I feel something is about to happen, Rina, and I don't know if we can stop it."

"Stop what?"

"It's a who," she corrected Sabrina. "It's the duke. I saw him tonight. Before it has only been in dreams, but tonight I actually saw him in the flesh, and, Sabrina, he frightens me. He is such a cruel-looking man," she said shuddering, "and he had eyes only for you, Rina. He recognized you, didn't he?"

Sabrina nodded. "Yes, and now he knows who I am, but I don't know what he can do. I really don't think anyone would believe his story; besides, it would only cause a scandal, and I know he would not desire that." Her violet eyes were clouded as she looked to Mary for answers. "But I don't trust him, Mary. He wants revenge against something he believes I did to him, and I don't think he'll rest until he has it—and that means ruining me in some way. I don't know what to do," Sabrina whispered shakily.

"I want to go back to Verrick House, Rina," Mary told her suddenly, a new firmness in her voice. "I feel it's dangerous for us to be here in London."

Sabrina raised her face from her hands. "Dangerous?" Sabrina asked incredulously. "Surely you don't think Lucien would try to harm me that way?"

"No, I don't feel physical danger from him, although I know he means to cause trouble, Rina," Mary explained.

"But I am disturbed by something, some feeling of evil I felt this evening. I felt so chilled, so deathly still, that I know someone has died, Rina, and in some way we are involved." Mary grasped Sabrina's hands, her hands so cold that Sabrina shivered as she touched her.

"We've got to leave here, Rina, and soon," Mary pleaded with her.

Sabrina bit her lip until it hurt. "How can we? You know what the marquis threatened about Richard and Aunt Margaret. He'll do it, too, unless we give in to him." Sabrina sniffed, her eyes filling with tears she tried to hold in check. "I don't know what we can do. I'll have to think of something to spoil the marquis' plans, and soon. At least there is nothing the duke can do. Besides," Sabrina added huskily, "we needn't worry about him much longer for he is to be married next week, and I doubt whether he will be giving a thought to me. He'll have other things to occupy his mind. I'm not going to worry about him, for I must devote all my energies to the marquis."

Mary nodded absently and crawled into bed still feeling chilled. She tried to sleep, but in the back of her mind she could still see the image of a coach on a lonely road, hear a scream of terror and then the silence that came from a grave. How this could possibly have anything to do with them still perplexed her as she dropped off into a restless sleep.

※

Percy Rathbourne stared down at the crumpled form of Lady Blanche Delande. He rubbed his bloodied hands distastefully on his breeches, mindless of the stain, just anxious to remove the stickiness from his hands. He continued to stare in fascination at Blanche's body. She was dead. He had stabbed her through the heart. He was surprised how easy it had been, but then she had been so trusting until she had seen the gleaming blade and felt its coldness against her skin. Then she had given that horrible scream. Percy shook his head. He could still hear it ringing in his ears.

He continued unconsciously to rub his hands against his

thighs as he pondered what to do next. He had led Blanche
some distance from the road into the woods, despite her
reluctance to enter them in the dark. If he just left her
here and quietly walked back to the coach where only his
coachman awaited, then how would the man know that she
wasn't already in the coach? Then he would have him stop at
some corner in town and pretend the lady had gotten out. He
would never realize she had never gotten back in the coach.

Percy smiled in satisfaction, looking down at Blanche's body
dispassionately. "You didn't really imagine that I would allow
you to cheat Kate and me out of our inheritance, did you,
Blanche?" he asked softly. "You were such a silly little fool to
imagine that you would become mistress of Camareigh. Poor,
foolish little Blanche," he mocked, his hands still rubbing
against his thighs as he tried to wipe them clean of her blood.
"Lucien is finished. By the time he discovers you are gone, it
will be too late for him to find another bride that the duchess
will approve of, and Camareigh will be mine."

He turned and without a backward glance at her body left
the small clearing where he had murdered Blanche Delande.
He made his way back to his coach waiting on the deserted
road, a smile of anticipation on his face. Kate would be so
proud of him. They had actually won against Lucien. He
could hardly wait to see Lucien's face when he found his
fiancée and fortune had escaped his grasp. Poor Lucien, he
chuckled, as he settled back against the cushions of the seat for
the long ride back to London.

There is no love lost, sir.

—*Miguel de Cervantes*

Chapter 9

SABRINA WAS FASTENING A PEARL EARRING INTO THE LOBE OF her ear when Mary entered her room, her dress rustling as she moved forward.

"Mary," Sabrina spoke to her reflection in the mirror. "Maybe the solution to our problem lies right here under this roof."

"What do you mean, Rina?" Mary demanded nervously as she came up behind Sabrina. At the Duke of Granston's invitation they were spending the weekend at his estate outside of London.

Sabrina turned around and stared up at Mary hopefully. "Why shouldn't I marry the duke? It would solve all of our problems. We would be free from debt and worries. The marquis could be paid off. It is obvious that the duke is interested in us. You've seen the way he leers."

"You can't, Rina," Mary answered. "Why, he's horrid. He's a drunken slob. Oh, Rina, please, don't even consider it," she begged.

Sabrina's mouth tightened. "I really don't think we've any other choice. I've tried to think of some way of getting enough money to satisfy the marquis, but it's hopeless. I could begin robbing again, but it's far too risky to do it at the rate I'd have to if I intended to get enough for the marquis. Besides, Will and John are out of it now, and I won't get them involved in a personal problem. No, this is our easiest solution. How could I be so selfish to put my personal distastes over the needs of my family? If it means sacrificing myself to the Duke of Granston, then I will."

Mary knew better than to argue when Sabrina had set her chin at that angle, so, shrugging, she told Sabrina the news she had heard.

"The Duke of Camareigh arrived a short while ago, Rina."

"Here?" Sabrina demanded, shaken.

Mary nodded her head. "I'm afraid so."

Sabrina felt her face grow flushed. Damn Lucien, she should have guessed that he would not leave her alone. What was he up to? He was here to cause trouble. When Mary had first said he was here her heart had leapt with anticipation at seeing him, yet she knew instinctively that he would try to destroy her. He was here to taunt her, to embarrass her, to be a constant reminder of their secret. He wanted revenge for having been duped by her. His pride was wounded, and that he could not forgive.

"I wonder what he'll do." Sabrina worried aloud.

"I don't like him," Mary said unhappily.

Like him? No, Sabrina thought, he wasn't an especially likeable person, but she couldn't seem to resist the attraction she felt for him, nor could she forget him. She despised herself for feeling such a weakness, but she just couldn't help herself. But she would be careful and not let Lucien know that he had the power to disturb her. She would show him that he meant little or nothing to her. She would have Granston eating out of the palm of her hand before this weekend was over. She didn't care if Lucien was getting married in a week. It was no concern of hers. She couldn't help but wonder, though, what kind of woman Lucien would pick to marry. He must love her if he was marrying her. Maybe she would be with him now? Sabrina squashed the sudden pang of jealousy she felt for this unknown woman who had Lucien's love, and jerked a satiny curl over her shoulder painfully. She didn't like Lucien, nor did he like her. He was merely a girl's first love and she would get over him soon enough.

Sabrina put her plans into action that evening as she sat next to the duke at the head of the table. She avoided Lucien's grim face across the table from her as she played the coquette for a responsive Duke of Granston.

"You are so clever, your grace," Sabrina flattered him, "do tell me that story again." She leaned forward eagerly, the low, wide bodice of her rose-colored gown revealing to his eyes the alluring roundness of her breasts, barely covered by the delicate wisp of lace tucked into the deep vee between them. She smiled up at Granston, her dimple attracting his bloodshot eyes to her soft mouth.

He reached out and caught her small hand in his fleshy one, his thumb tracing a pattern around her wrist. "How dare Wrainton keep you hidden in the country all of these years," he whispered hoarsely into her small pink ear, managing to touch his lips to a soft curl.

Sabrina pulled back, masking her repulsion at the touch of his lips with a pouting smile as she flirted with him. "Papa always said that the fruit was sweeter that had been left to ripen under the caress of the summer sun."

The Duke gave a roar of laughter and Sabrina glanced up and into the glinting eyes of Lucien, glaring at her across the table. As he continued to stare at her his mouth gradually curved into a smile that caused a shudder of apprehension to flicker along Sabrina's spine.

"Of course, one shouldn't allow the fruit to stay on the tree too long," Lucien commented, "or someone might be tempted to steal a piece and take a bite out of it."

The Duke of Granston laughed appreciatively. "Never at a loss for words, eh, Lucien? Wish you'd be my guest more often."

Sabrina looked down at her plate, the only one who realized the threat behind his casual words. She looked over at the marquis and contessa who were exchanging contented glances as they watched Sabrina charm their host. They were already counting their money, she thought in disgust. Sabrina tried to catch Mary's eye, but she was staring in fascination at Lucien, a small pulse beating visibly in her temple.

Following custom the women left the men to their port and smoking, while they retreated to the salon for gossip.

"I am glad to see you are the sensible one, Sabrina," the contessa remarked. "The Duke is enamored of you, it is plain to see," she paused, "however, it is this other one, the scarred one, who has me intrigued.. He has some interest in you, of course, he is attracted to you; but he seems to be angry, and there is hate in his eyes as he stares at you, little one. Why should this be?"

Sabrina's face whitened. "I hardly know the gentleman. Why he should dislike me I haven't the slightest idea."

"Ah, I did not say dislike. I said hate, which is far stronger, and involves the heart. It is said that you must hate a little in order to feel the strongest emotion of love."

"That's ridiculous," Sabrina denied faintly. "Besides, he is to wed next week. Surely he is in love with this woman?"

The contessa smiled cynically. "I doubt it. You see he must marry the woman his *nonna*, the duchess, has chosen if he is to inherit his estate. They have had the argument about this for many years, it is said, so he finally gives in."

Sabrina stared in amazement at the contessa. "So, he doesn't love this woman. He's being forced into marriage against his will." Sabrina couldn't resist a smile of satisfaction at Lucien's predicament. In her misery she welcomed company, glad that she was not the only one being forced against her wishes to do something.

Mary came into Sabrina's bedchamber as she was preparing for bed later that evening, her face mirroring her doubts. She took the brush from Sabrina's slim hand and began to brush the long black hair in even strokes down her back.

"I think you are asking for trouble, Rina," Mary said after a moment's silence. She saw Sabrina's shoulders stiffen, but continued to brush the fine hair. "I won't harangue you, Rina, because I know that you've all of our interests at heart, but I don't think it will work out. I don't want to see you disappointed, or," she hesitated, her voice breaking as she continued slowly, "involve yourself with someone that you despise. I know you can't bear to have the duke touch you. He may be our host, but I think he's despicable."

Sabrina stood up, looking touchingly young in her long white nightgown with her dark hair hanging loose to her hips.

"I saw you looking strangely at Lucien this evening, and I wondered if you'd seen something, Mary. Please tell me," Sabrina pleaded almost desperately. "I need so much help in what I'm doing. I have to know if he is going to interfere."

"Do you know what I saw? I saw you and Lucien together, laughing and," Mary gave a self-conscious laugh, "kissing under a big tree. How can that be, Rina?"

"It can't be," Sabrina answered angrily, her cheeks flushed. "You are completely wrong this time, Mary," she said scornfully. "I think your gift must have left you and you are merely dreaming now."

Mary bent her head, hurt by Sabrina's harsh words. Sabrina ran across to her, regretting her outburst, and put her arms around her. "I'm sorry, Mary, forgive me? I always speak before I think, and you know I wouldn't hurt you for anything. Please, forgive?"

Mary smiled half-heartedly. "I forgive you, but I want to go home, Rina. I don't want to be paraded around anymore. I long so much for the quiet of Verrick House and Aunt Margaret's vague comments, and I'm worrying about Richard, there by himself and feeling bold with his new glasses."

"I know, I do too. Soon, Mary, soon we'll have everything back to normal, you just wait and see," she promised.

Mary bid her good night and left for her own room, leaving Sabrina sitting on the edge of her bed, a candle burning softly on the table beside it. She had been sitting there for several minutes staring into the flickering flame when she heard a sound, and looking up saw Lucien standing just inside the door.

"Casting spells, Sabrina?" he asked as he came forward into the room, the door partially opened behind him.

Sabrina jumped to her feet and faced him. "I didn't invite you here, Lucien," she told him, despite the quickening of her heartbeats.

"No?" he questioned doubtfully. "It seemed to me that you were issuing an invitation to all comers at dinner. Many

men watched your little game of seduction this evening."
He spread his hands, drawing Sabrina's attention to his dark
red dressing gown tied at the waist. "I decided to accept the
invitation so you would not be disappointed."

Sabrina swallowed painfully. "Leave my room at once!" she
ordered his approaching figure in a quivering voice.

"No," he answered softly, coming to a halt not more than
a foot from her.

"Lucien, please," Sabrina told him in a soft voice, "don't
do this."

Lucien grinned, unmoved by her plea. "Why, are you
expecting some other nocturnal visitor? Our host, perchance?"
he guessed, then reaching out caught a long curl and wrapped
it around his hand as he had done once before. He pulled her
unresisting body into his arms, hugging her close to him. He
lowered his head and touched her lips with his, softly at first,
enticing her mouth to part beneath his as his hands slid slowly
over her body.

Sabrina breathed deeply of his scent, letting her fingers curl
around the back of his neck as she pressed closer to him. All
of her firm resolutions fled as she stood wrapped in his arms
and held close against his heart. He wasn't angry at her any
longer, she thought in triumph as his lips clung to hers. He
really must care for her. She would tell him that she loved
him, too. Sabrina struggled from his deep kiss reluctantly,
leaning away from him so she could look up into his eyes,
her violet eyes glowing with love as she opened her mouth
to speak.

"Lucien," she said. Then out of the corner of her eye she
saw a movement and turning her head stared in amazement at
the Duke of Granston, who stood watching the scene with a
regretful look on his florid face.

"My pardon," he said a trifle thickly, "I hadn't known the
lady was currently preoccupied with another."

Lucien glanced at him without surprise, as though he had
been expecting the duke to appear. He released Sabrina from
his arms without a glance and turned to face him casually.
"If you've a prior claim to the lady's favors, then I quite

understand and will take my leave," Lucien offered graciously, ignoring Sabrina's sudden indrawn breath.

"Certainly not, first come first served, I always say," the Duke of Granston laughed. "Sorry to have intruded," he apologized, making a wry face of regret. "Some other time, eh, Lady Sabrina?" he asked, winking broadly as he turned and left the room, closing the door firmly behind him.

Sabrina stared at the closed door in stunned silence, then looked up at Lucien who was watching her with a satisfied look on his face. Sabrina swallowed back her tears as the truth dawned on her.

"It was all a trick, wasn't it?" Sabrina whispered, her face a pale, frozen mask. "You knew the duke would come here this evening."

Lucien smiled hatefully. "He intimated that he might pay a visit to the lovely Lady Sabrina, who had flirted outrageously with him all evening."

Sabrina nodded her head numbly. "I see, so you thought you would play the lover first, and then allow the duke to discover you. Why?" Sabrina asked bluntly, her big violet eyes gazing at him directly, making him feel uncomfortable, but he shrugged it off contemptuously.

"I told you that you would pay for making me look the fool," he reminded her. "You thought to catch the duke in marriage, well, I seriously doubt that he will ask for your hand, now. Even he has a little pride, and to think that I had his bride in his own home before he did, well, that is too much for even him to overlook. Of course, he may wish to form an alliance with you, but it won't lead to his purse strings, my dear."

Sabrina took a deep breath, straightening her shoulders and lifting her chin proudly as she stared in contempt at Lucien. "Do you actually believe that I wanted to marry that drunken fool? Do you think that I would have gone into that marriage any more willingly than you are going into yours?" Sabrina asked him scornfully, her violet eyes searing him with her disgust.

"You may feel satisfied with your damned revenge, for you have succeeded far beyond your wildest expectations. Not only have you degraded me and ruined my reputation, you have also destroyed my family," Sabrina told him shakily, then laughed hysterically. "Do you believe the marquis will be pleased, your grace? It was he who planned my marriage to the duke. He is the one in desperate need of money. And how do you imagine he persuaded me to follow his plans? Do ask me how, your grace, for I want you to know how he threatened to evict my aunt from her home, and how he plans to take my little brother from us. Oh, yes, do let me give your regards to my family, for they should know the man who has destroyed us."

Lucien stared down at her ravaged face, his eyes narrowed, the expression masked by his heavy-lidded eyes as he listened to her. He put out his hand and placed it on her shoulder comfortingly and was startled by the strength of her hand as she knocked it away.

"Leave me alone," Sabrina told him in little more than a whisper. "I hope I never see that scarred face of yours again, Lucien. It's scarred your soul as well," she told him, and turning from him ran from the room and down the hall to Mary's room, bursting into her bedchamber and throwing herself into a startled Mary's arms.

Sabrina cried until she was drained of emotion and lay docile and silent in Mary's comforting arms. Finally she felt Sabrina's breathing become steady, although still ragged from her crying, as she fell into a troubled sleep. Mary had to comfort her several times in the night as her sleep was broken by terrible nightmares that left her trembling and sweating in fear. Sabrina hadn't told her anything, but she had the feeling that it concerned the Duke of Camareigh. He had some kind of hold over Sabrina that she couldn't seem to resist, for Mary had seen the look in her eyes as she stared at his scarred face. It was a warm and loving look that had never softened her eyes in that way before. Now, when she had mentioned his name to Sabrina, her eyes had filled with hate. When he had driven his sword into Sabrina's shoulder he had not hurt her more than he had now by whatever he had done. He might as well have driven it through her heart, for he had killed something in Sabrina this night.

The next morning Sabrina had gained control of herself and presented a normal, if subdued, face to the assembled guests. Lucien had left early, and with both Mary and Sabrina unusually quiet and reserved, and the Duke of Granston's attentions directed elsewhere and noticeably cool when speaking with Sabrina, the marquis became quite annoyed. The night before everything had seemed to be moving along nicely, but now it seemed as though the duke regretted having issued his invitation for the weekend. The last day seemed to drag on forever, until finally they made their departure the following morning. Sabrina huddled in her corner of the coach silently staring out of the window, oblivious to the smoldering looks the marquis sent her every few minutes. Mary sat next to her, her face calm but her hands nervously fiddling with her gloves as she prepared to act as a shield should the marquis decide to confront Sabrina with the disappointing outcome of their weekend. But the marquis maintained a brooding silence the whole journey, only occasionally saying something in Italian to the contessa, who wore a worried expression on her usually tranquil features as she glanced between the occupants of the coach.

When they arrived in London Sabrina and Mary quickly fled the coach and made for their bedchamber, but the marquis had other plans, for he followed after their retreating figures.

"Sabrina! I want a word with you, girl." He pushed his way into their bedchamber, his violet eyes flashing with anger that he could no longer control. He stood facing them, his hands clenched in frustration as he stared at the small, defiant face so like his own.

"I know now why the duke suddenly cooled towards you. What a fool you were to let him find you with Camareigh. You've ruined everything, even any other chances we might have had to wed you to some other rich suitor," he spat. "The contessa heard the gossip from everyone there. It is now common knowledge that you are Camareigh's mistress. Didn't I tell you not to look in his direction? Was his lovemaking worth it? You could've been a duchess, but no, you can't resist a night in bed with Camareigh, and that is all you'll get from him."

Mary's mouth dropped open in astonishment at the marquis' accusations, and turning to look at Sabrina, felt her heart stop as she saw her sister's anguished expression.

The marquis was breathing heavily, his face ruddy with anger. "Well, aren't you going to deny it? Claim your innocence? By God, I'm going to teach you a lesson I should have long ago," he threatened as he saw a riding crop on a nearby table and picking it up, raised the whip above his head and brought it down on Sabrina's unprotected shoulder.

ஒ௸

Lucien stared at the woman sitting nervously before him. Her auburn hair was sprinkled with gray, and there was a marked resemblance between Henrietta Delande and her daughter.

"What are you trying to tell me, Lady Staddon?" Lucien inquired softly, holding a tight rein on his growing anger. "Blanche has disappeared?"

Lady Staddon ran her tongue across her lips nervously, moistening their dryness while she tried to find the right words to tell the Duke of Camareigh that she didn't know where Blanche was. "She never came back from the Harriers' ball, your grace."

Lucien frowned. "But that was at least four days ago. Why in the world didn't you come to me sooner, madam?" he demanded impatiently.

Lady Staddon twisted her handkerchief until Lucien felt like grabbing it from her. She looked up finally, her cheeks pink with embarrassment. "I thought she might have been with you."

Lucien shook his head. "I received a note from her that evening informing me that she had the migraine and wished to leave early. By the time I received it she had already hired a conveyance to take her home. I certainly would have driven her home in my carriage had I known sooner," Lucien explained, his eyes narrowing as he stared at the distraught woman. "And you say she never reached home?"

Lady Delande nodded, pulling at her bonnet ribbons as though they were too tight.

"You must have known she wasn't with me. Why didn't you get in contact with me earlier?" Lucien demanded.

Lady Staddon coughed and looked around the room at the blue and gold satin-upholstered chairs and settee, the mahogany sofa table and bureau-bookcase. In a large, carved gilt mirror she saw her own reflection and was startled by her own face.

"Why?" Lucien repeated.

"When I realized that she was not with you, I had seen you the next day in the park, if you remember, and you inquired after her health. Well, I knew she must have lied to you, and was not with you," she admitted, then looking up at him bravely added, "and must be with someone else."

Lucien's mouth thinned. "You came to that conclusion quite fast. Had you reason to believe that she was involved with another man?"

Lady Staddon sighed despondently. "Yes, she was seeing someone else, your grace. And I also have found out since the ball, from one of Blanche's friends, that the man she was involved with was," she hesitated nervously, "your cousin Lord Feltham."

"Percy?" Lucien looked startled, his face taking on an alert expression. "So you think she must have left the ball with my cousin Percy Rathbourne?"''

Lady Staddon nodded reluctantly as she saw the blazing anger in the duke's eyes. "I'm worried, though, Blanche should've come home by now unless—"

"Unless what? I think she values my dukedom more than a casual dalliance with a married man." Lucien spoke contemptuously.

"But you see, all of her things are still in her room. She doesn't even have a change of clothes. Her perfumes, jewelry, and most of all, her laudanum. She can't sleep without it," Lady Staddon told Lucien unhappily.

A grim look settled on Lucien's face as he began to specu-late on possibilities. "You realize, of course, that I must marry by the end of this week, or I lose my estate?"

"Yes, I know," Lady Feltham answered faintly. "Oh,

please, your grace, I am sure there must be an explanation for Blanche's disappearance. There must be," she whispered desperately.

Lucien stood up, conflicting emotions of compassion for Lady Staddon and anger at Blanche and Percy warring within him. "I'll see what I can do, Lady Staddon, but you can appreciate the fact that I am in a predicament. I will get to the bottom of this, you may rest assured on that score," Lucien promised, stroking his scar absently.

An hour later Lucien was admitted into the home of Percy Rathbourne and was greeted timidly by Lady Feltham, her smile coming and going like a ray of sunshine on a cloudy day. She hovered around Lucien, trying to entertain him until Percy arrived. Lucien felt sorry for her as he stared at her drab appearance, her thin face worn and harassed beneath an untidy mop of blonde curls, the yellow gown she wore bringing out a sallowness in her skin.

"Would your grace care for tea?" she inquired nervously.

"No, thank you, Lady Feltham, I haven't a lot of time," Lucien answered shortly.

"No indeed, you do not, does he, Percy?" Kate commented upon hearing Lucien's words as she entered the room. She was dressed in a superbly cut riding habit of superfine, the masculine cut molding the cloth of the jacket and waistcoat to her body, and matching the same shade of blue as Percy's coat and breeches. With their wigs and matching three-cornered hats they looked identical except for the long skirt of Kate's habit.

"We really haven't much time, either, for we are going out riding," Kate informed Lucien casually as she walked over to the mirror above the mantelshelf and stared at her reflection in satisfaction, noting the creamy smoothness of her skin and her lovely profile.

"You really should try and do something with your looks, Anne," she criticized Lady Feltham. "Just because you are married and have a brood of brats doesn't mean you should let yourself go the way you have." Then with a cruel, baiting smile she added, "You'll have people believing that Percy married you only for your money, which of course we all know isn't true—is it?"

Anne Rathbourne's lips trembled under the vicious attack from her sister-in-law, especially when Percy smiled in appreciation.

"I think what I have to say had best be said in private, Percy," Lucien suggested.

Percy glanced at Kate in surprise and apprehension. Kate merely shrugged and taking a seat settled herself comfortably. "Run along, Anne dear, I'm sure you can find something to occupy your time." She ordered Lady Feltham from her own salon as though ridding herself of an irritating gnat.

Lady Feltham made her excuses, her face a tight mask of martyred suffering as she scuttled from the room under Kate's contemptuous eyes. "Percy and I have no secrets, cousin dear, so I don't think I need vacate the salon as well, do I, Percy?" Kate asked, staring up at Lucien with a quizzical smile.

"No, I suppose neither of you have any secrets from each other, do you?" Lucien commented. "But then you aren't really whole without the other one, are you?" he said quietly.

Percy bit his lip anxiously for he knew Lucien in one of these quiet, sarcastic moods, and it usually meant an uncomfortable time for the person it was directed at.

"How is it you managed to romance Blanche Delande by yourself?" Lucien asked suddenly, then sending a sharp glance at Kate, added, "or was dear Kate in the background whispering in your ear?"

Percy gave an involuntary gasp followed by a quick, incredulous laugh in an attempt to cover it up. "Me, romancing your fiancée? Really, Lucien, you go too far."

"No, you go too far, Percy. I want the truth, and now," Lucien told him, his voice icy with rage. "Where is Blanche?"

"You don't mean to tell me, dear Lucien, that you have misplaced your fiancée?" Kate asked with just the right note of disbelief in her smooth voice.

Lucien looked at her in disgust. "Beautifully done, Kate, but you haven't quite mastered the art of concealing the expression in your eyes. The cunning and greed glows brightly from within. A bit more practice and you may succeed."

Kate glared up at him. "I don't need to hide the hatred in them now, do I?"

"That would be the impossible, even for a woman of your accomplishments."

"What the hell are you getting at, Lucien?" Percy demanded belligerently, feeling brave in his own home.

"What I am getting at is a series of misadventures I seem to have been experiencing the last few months," Lucien informed them calmly. "A series of hard-to-explain accidents and incidents that have now culminated with the disappearance of my fiancée. At first, having my share of enemies, I foolishly attributed these close calls with death to one of them. But as they continued with annoying regularity, I began to suspect a well-thought-out, cold-blooded plan had been devised by someone to insure my death. It didn't take me long to figure out who would profit most handsomely by my death, eh, Percy?" Lucien asked, his sherry eyes glowing with deadly intent.

Percy swallowed and shifted uneasily before Lucien's hard stare, looking to Kate for help.

"And how will you prove these allegations, Lucien?" Kate asked idly, not even bothering to deny his claims. "Has anyone ever seen Percy and I lift a finger threateningly against you? You have merely had a few more accidents than most people experience, certainly not reason to suspect your dear, loving cousins of plotting your murder? It is ridiculous, and no one, Lucien, will believe you," she taunted him. "People will feel sorry for the poor duke, who lost not only his fiancée, but also his estate. Apparently Blanche Delande preferred running away with her lover rather than marry you," Kate speculated, then stared at Lucien analytically. "Possibly it was the scar that sent the little dove flying?"

Lucien smiled unpleasantly. "And is she still flying high, Percy? Or was she brought down by some hidden hunter, just waiting to flush her out and bring her to earth?"

Percy flushed, perspiration breaking out on his forehead as he rubbed his hands against the cloth of his suit as though wiping them clean. "I don't know what you are implying, Lucien, but I resent it. No one can connect me with your missing fiancée. Kate and I were together the whole evening of the Harriers' ball, and we left together," Percy blundered as he sought to clear himself.

Lucien walked over to him, his face devoid of expression. "I never told you when Blanche disappeared, Percy. Strange that you should know that she never returned home from the ball. Did she die easily, Percy?" Lucien asked softly as he reached out and grabbed Percy by the throat, pressing against his windpipe and cutting off his air. Percy's eyes bulged with horror and Kate screamed, running up beside Lucien and trying to pry his fingers from her twin's throat.

Lucien released his death grip reluctantly, staring down in contempt as Percy fell to his knees clutching his throat "You bastard, I ought to skin you alive, and hang you, Kate, by that lily-white neck of yours. You haven't won yet, dear cousins, for you shall never set foot in the halls of Camareigh. I swear by all that is holy that you shall pay for your sins, and by God, I'll exact punishment for them one of these days."

Kate looked up into Lucien's scarred face, flinching at the blazing fury in his eyes, his face looking like a devil's as he turned from them in disgust.

"You won't win, Lucien!" Kate screamed at his broad back as he made for the door. "You haven't time to find another bride before the duchess's deadline. And do you imagine any woman would want to risk marrying you?" she called out triumphantly.

Lucien turned at her words. "Yes, dear cousin," Kate raged on, "you might be suspected of murdering your fiancée in a fit of jealous rage. Everyone knows you've an uncontrollable temper when aroused. Blanche had decided not to marry you, perhaps, or maybe she left the ball with her lover and you caught them, and in a black rage murdered them both. Who knows what rumors might spread about your missing fiancée? And if you dare to tell the duchess about your suspicions then you will kill her. She's old and frail, and so very proud. You tell her, Lucien, and you sign her death warrant."

Lucien turned, feeling sickened at the sight of Percy and Kate. He felt dirtied and disgraced by them. His body felt as though turned to stone as he sat in his carriage, which jostled to join the mainstream of traffic. What in God's name was he to do? He would not lose Camareigh—he would see Percy and Kate dead before he allowed them to own Camareigh. But Kate had been right about one thing—if he told the duchess about their murderous actions it would kill her. She was a proud old woman to whom the family name meant everything. To know that her grandchildren were murderers, and had plotted to kill their cousin, would surely kill her. No, he could not, and would not, tell her. Kate had played a beautiful hand, he had to admit, and only he knew it. But he would not give up—never.

The duchess was resting when he arrived at her home seeking an audience with her. Refusing to be put off by the majordomo he vaulted up the grand staircase and forced his way into his grandmother's room. He stopped as he entered the darkened room and accustomed his eyes to the diminished light.

"Who is there?" a shaky voice asked from the depths of a canopied bed.

Lucien followed the sound of her voice until he was standing beside her bed. "It is I, Lucien, Grandmère," he spoke softly.

"Lucien?" she asked in puzzlement as she propped herself up on the mound of pillows behind her. "How dare you storm into my bedchamber when I do not wish to be disturbed," she demanded, her voice gaining strength as she woke from her sleep.

"I beg your pardon, most deeply, but I have to tell you something of the utmost urgency, Grandmère," Lucien explained, looking down at her in the shadowy darkness of her bed.

The duchess waved him away. "Nothing is that urgent; however, as long as you have already disturbed me, I shall allow you to remain," she conceded. "Now light that candle so I may see your face," she commanded.

When the light spread across a small area around her bed and lit Lucien's face she sighed deeply. "You are troubled. Never before have I seen quite that look of desperation on your face. What has happened?" She straightened her shoulders, her regal air seeming incongruous beneath her frilly lace cap and nightgown.

"I am afraid that my scarred face has frightened away my fiancée once and for all. She has fled me, Grandmère, and I am faced with a wedding ceremony without a bride."

The duchess drew in her breath sharply. "I do not believe it. How do you know this?"

"She has been missing since early this week, and today Lady Staddon came to me and told me. She had not wanted me to know sooner, should Blanche have returned."

"I do not believe the foolish child would run away from your title merely because she did not like your face. Did she have a lover?"

"It is thought that she might have," Lucien replied evenly.

"If you had paid the chit more attention then she would not have needed to seek romance elsewhere," the duchess accused Lucien angrily.

"If you recall, she was not of my choosing to begin with. However, that is not important now, since it may be possible that she has met with an accident."

"What leads you to suspect that?" the duchess demanded curiously.

"Lady Staddon tells me that her daughter's possessions have not been disturbed—nothing is missing. I doubt whether she would elope without a change of clothing. She did leave the ball early, complaining of a migraine and hired a coach to drive her home. She may have met with an accident," Lucien speculated, "but we may never know. That is why I have come to you. Will you hold me to your condition of my marrying to inherit my estate? It is impossible for me to meet the deadline now."

The duchess was silent. "You forced this upon yourself, Lucien. You need not have waited so long in coming to my terms. It was pure defiance by you, and now you are faced with the unforeseeable results. No, you must still marry to inherit," the duchess spoke adamantly. "However, I will grant you an extra couple of weeks in order to find yourself another bride. Fail this time and you lose Camareigh, my boy."

Lucien stepped back from the bed and bowed politely. "Thank you, Grandmère, my apologies again for disturbing you," he said sardonically, resentful and thankful to her at the same time.

"Don't disappoint me, Lucien." She spoke softly from the bed as he neared the door.

"I won't, Grandmère," Lucien promised as he opened the door and left.

When Lucien left the duchess he directed his coachman to drive towards Hyde Park, his destination a house in a small square off it. He settled himself back against the cushions, a plan forming in his mind as he remembered his weekend at the Duke of Granston's. He had been seeking only revenge at that time, little knowing that it would become part of a larger scheme, and what he had put into effect then would now reap him far greater rewards. By chance, or mischance, Sabrina Verrick would now be his salvation.

❧

Sabrina fell to her knees under the cruel punishment of the whip, her shoulders and back stinging from the blows the marquis rained on them. She heard Mary scream in protest as she felt the first flick of the whip, but failed to see Mary run forward and try to wrestle the whip from the marquis' hands, only to be pushed away and fall against the bed, her head striking one of the thick posts. Mary fought off the feeling of nausea and faintness that momentarily overwhelmed her and struggled to rise. She had to get help. Sabrina was curled in a ball on the floor, her face hidden in her arms as she tried to protect herself from the whip.

She groaned in pain as time and time again the sharp pain tore across her soft shoulders, ripping the thin material of her bodice and scoring the tender skin with angry welts.

Mary slid past the marquis, who was completely oblivious of anything except the blinding rage he felt as he beat the arrogance and defiance out of his daughter. Mary's red hair tumbled about her shoulders as she ran from the room and down the hall to the head of the staircase, a bluish bruise beginning to rise on her forehead, her gray eyes wide with fear. As she stumbled weakly down the stairs the front door was opened by the majordomo and the Duke of Camareigh entered, looking up curiously as he heard her gasp of relief.

"Oh, thank God, you have come," she cried, taking him completely by surprise. He quickly took in her distraught appearance and reached her as she collapsed down the last few steps, falling into his arms. The majordomo called for help, sending one of the footmen for smelling salts as he hovered over Lucien's shoulder.

"Please," Mary whispered, her hands clutching at the duke's arm, "you must stop him. He'll kill her if you don't."

"Kill whom?" Lucien demanded incredulously, staring down at her as if he thought her crazed.

"Sabrina. The marquis is beating her, and it is all your fault," she accused him, tears streaking her cheeks.

Lucien eased her into the majordomo's arms and sprinted up the stairs, heading toward the sound of a whip slashing through the air, his mouth set in a grim, determined line as he found the room. He grabbed the marquis' raised arm and twisted it painfully behind his back, forcing the marquis to drop the whip as he gave a grunt of surprise at the attack.

"What the devil?" he demanded and turned to see who dared to interfere, his face contorted, his gaze unseeing, until his rage faded as he stared up into Lucien's eyes and the scar whitening along his cheek. He felt a flicker of fear as Lucien's grip tightened painfully, then cried out as Lucien pushed him away in disgust.

"Get out! And if you ever lay another hand on her I'll take that whip and strip your coward's hide from you," Lucien warned the astounded Marquis, and turning his back on him knelt down beside the fallen figure crumpled on the floor.

Lucien carefully lifted Sabrina up into his arms and placed her gently on the bed, laying her on her stomach to avoid the raw strips of flesh exposed through the torn gown that was stained with drops of blood. His face was taut as he smoothed a deep wave of black hair out of her face and stared down at her pale face, lines of suffering still on it. He waited while her eyelids fluttered and gradually opened and she stared up at him with her great violet eyes.

"Lucien," she whispered. "Have you come to gloat over your victory?"

Lucien's mouth tightened at her words, for that was what he had come to do, and instead he had found her nearly unconscious with pain because of him. "I'm not gloating, Sabrina. I would never have you harmed like this," he told her truthfully.

But Sabrina's faith had been broken, and her young girl's love for him shattered, and all she felt now for him was hatred. "Liar," she told him, her lips curling with contempt as her thick lashes came down and closed over her eyes, blocking him from her mind.

Lucien continued to smooth the soft hair from her face despite her unresponsiveness to his touch. He looked over his shoulder as Mary entered the room with a bowl of water and cloth to bathe her wounds. She stood beside him staring down at Sabrina's bloodied back, tears starting afresh in her eyes at the sight of proud Sabrina humbled and humiliated this way.

"You will now leave us, your grace," she spoke imperiously, her eyes still on her sister.

Lucien got to his feet and without a word left the room and Sabrina to Mary's ministrations. He walked purposefully down the stairs, heading for the door where raised voices could be heard.

"How could you beat the little one?" the contessa demanded angrily. "That is not the way to handle such a one as she. You bring out the rebellion in her to do that. Besides, you might have ruined her beauty, and that is all that we have to offer her for," the contessa continued practically. Then her brown eyes softened for just an instant. "I am fond of the little one, oddly enough, and I do not like to see you crush the spirit out of her."

"Nor do I," Lucien spoke as he entered the room. "She was not to blame for the incident at Granston's. She was duped by me, and I am here to make amends, and come to an arrangement that should meet with your approval."

The marquis eyed the duke mistrustfully, keeping a good

distance from him. "I do not think that we've anything to discuss, your grace," the marquis replied, still feeling affronted by the rough handling he'd received from the duke.

"Oh, but I think that we do," Lucien contradicted him smoothly. "You see, I intend to marry your daughter, Sabrina."

The marquis choked at this sudden announcement and couldn't have been more startled had he been shot. "Marry!" he demanded, his eyes wide. "This is preposterous. You are already engaged, and are to—"

The haughty look on the duke's face silenced the rest of the marquis' sentence and he spluttered to an abrupt stop. "Due to some unfortunate circumstances, that engagement no longer exists, therefore I am free to select another bride," Lucien informed the marquis and contessa, who were listening in silent amazement, "and I choose your daughter, Sabrina."

"*Aspetti un momento, per favore*," the contessa murmured, "while I sit down, for this news is too much excitement, and order some wine for I am in need of it, *caro*."

"Certainly," the marquis beamed, his good humor restored, "after all, this is cause for celebration."

"You'll forgive me if I must decline," the duke said in a voice that left little doubt that he felt just the opposite, and with a cool nod turned to leave the room.

"But what of the arrangements? When will you marry? Do you not have to by a certain date if you are to inherit your estate…" The marquis trailed off uncomfortably under the duke's arrogant stare.

"*Per favore, caro*," the contessa intervened quickly, "we will leave it all up to the duke. Of course, we will have to come to some small financial arrangement, *si*?" she said meaningfully.

Lucien inclined his head. "It will be taken care of, contessa, I will have my solicitor draw up the papers. Now if you will excuse me?" He didn't wait for an answer and left the room, but not before he heard the marquis' gleeful chuckle.

Returning upstairs he entered Sabrina's room without knocking to find her stretched out on the bed, a blanket covering her hips while Mary bathed her bruised shoulders and back. Lucien's mouth tightened ominously as he saw the ugly weals across the smooth, previously flawless skin. Every so often she gave a small involuntary groan as Mary's gentle fingers caused her pain, but for most of the time she maintained a suffering silence.

Mary looked up quickly as she suddenly became aware of his presence in the room and stood up protectively before Sabrina. "Who do you think you are that you may enter our room unannounced?" The usually quiet Mary attacked him, her gray eyes stormy. "I will thank you, of course, for intervening and saving Sabrina, but if it hadn't been for you in the first place, this would never have happened."

A flicker of respect entered Lucien's eyes at this outburst from one he had mistakenly thought to be rather a nonentity, her quietness and serenity having surprised him at first considering she was Sabrina's sister. And now she had flared up like a firecracker. His eyes went to the red hair as if in explanation.

"As it so happens," he said quietly, "I do most certainly have a right to enter Sabrina's room—I shall be marrying her," he said bluntly.

Mary gasped in dismay, and then rushed to Sabrina who was struggling to sit up, the sheet held against her breasts as she stared up at Lucien, her violet eyes wide and darkened with both pain and confusion.

"Is this another of your games, Lucien?" she demanded in a small, choked voice.

Lucien moved forward until he stood next to the bed. "No, Sabrina, I have never been more serious than at this moment. You and I are to be wed, and despite the words you are about to fling at my head, we will be married," Lucien told her firmly, noticing the rebellious look enter her eyes as she stared up at him.

"Have you not forgotten your fiancée?" she asked icily, her round chin raised with dignity despite her dishabille.

"No, I have not forgotten her," Lucien answered quietly, his eyes clouded for a moment as he wondered about the fate of poor Blanche. "We are no longer engaged, so I have decided to marry you."

"*You* have decided?" Sabrina laughed shortly. "How

fortunate for me. However, it is a pity that I shall have to turn you down. Certainly a man of your noble bearing and experience will be able to find another poor fool to share your inheritance with you," Sabrina told him, feeling deep pleasure at being able to thwart his plans, "for that is why you've asked me, isn't it? You need a bride, and since you so ruthlessly destroyed my reputation you thought that I would jump at the chance of marrying you. Well, I do not need you, or your title, or your money. I can get all the money I need without having to resort to marriage with someone I find repulsive and offensive," Sabrina told him fiercely.

Lucien stared down at her angrily. Never had anyone defied him as much as this little slip of a thing. "You little fool. It's time you grew up and faced the realities of life. This isn't some game you are playing at. They hang men for doing less than you have. Do you even have the slightest idea what you'd face if you were captured and sent to prison?" he demanded, enraged by her devil-may-care attitude. "There are no separate quarters for the men and women during the day, and at night you sleep on straw infested with lice and fleas, living in little more than a pigsty, eating boiled bread and water. Of course, as a thief you are well versed in the ways of the criminal? You have heard of 'pay or strip,' where you are required by the other inmates to pay an entrance fee in order to keep your clothes. A pity if you don't have the necessary guineas, for they will strip the clothes from your back." Lucien described the scene in detail, well aware of Sabrina's shocked face and Mary's white one as she leaned against the bedpost feeling sick.

"And should you survive your confinement, you face hanging at Tyburn, or maybe you will be more fortunate and die from fever. I do believe that is what gets most of them. It's not a very pretty life, is it, Sabrina?" Lucien asked softly, satisfied with the effect of his words on both young girls. "I think life with me will not be quite so harrowing, nor dangerous, Sabrina."

He turned and walked unhurriedly to the door. "Ironic how things work out. Who would have thought that I would be marrying the highwayman who held me up at sword point?" His sherry eyes encompassed both figures lazily as he paused at the door. "And I trust that I needn't warn you not to put your heads together and make some foolhardy plans to try and hinder me? It is too late, your father has agreed, and all of the arrangements are being made, so accept your defeat, Sabrina, for I can promise you it won't be as bad as you think."

Sabrina stared at the door as it closed behind Lucien's tall figure, her eyes a dark, brooding violet. She put a hand to her trembling lips, unable to believe what had just taken place.

Mary stood up, an indecisive look on her face as she stared at Sabrina, who looked like a small child who had been unjustly and cruelly punished.

"Rina," she began hesitantly, "you're not going to defy them, are you?"

Sabrina looked up at her blankly, her face a frozen mask from which the hatred and despair had been wiped clean, but so had the gentleness and innocence, and Mary felt as though she were staring at a stranger.

"I'm going home to Verrick House, Mary," she said dully, her eyes glazed over. "I'm going to get the marquis all of the money he could want, but I'll not marry Lucien. He will have to find someone else to help him win his inheritance, but I hope he doesn't, I hope he loses it," she added, incensed by her predicament, then looked up at Mary's concerned face, a wildness in her eyes. "Don't ever let the marquis near me again, Mary, or I swear I will kill him and feel no regret."

A great flame follows a little spark.

—*Dante Alighieri*

Chapter 10

THE THREE HORSES PAWED THE SOFT EARTH IMPATIENTLY AS their masked riders sat awaiting the sound of coach wheels creaking and rumbling along the darkened road.

"Should be coming soon, Charlie," Will whispered as a beam of silvery moonlight bathed the three of them where they sat silently on their horses beside the road.

"They was talkin' and drinkin' their fill this afternoon in the Faire Maiden. Expectin' guests at Lord Newley's tonight."

"We will welcome them first," Sabrina replied with a grim smile. Her eyes glittered through the mask as she heard the first sounds of an approaching carriage. "Across the road, John," she directed quickly, then pulled her horse back under the overhanging branches as the coach-and-six appeared around the bend of the road. She could hear the coachman yelling to his team and the cracking of his whip until he saw the fallen tree across the roadway and began to slow the horses.

The two outriders were halted in front of the tree by now and as they looked around they were confronted by the muzzles of four pistols aimed at their heads. They quickly dropped their pistols and dismounted as Will directed them to the side of the road and then walking his horse around them, wrapped a piece of rope about their two figures, securing them to a tree.

The coach halted within feet of the fallen tree, the coachman calling out for assistance, but by then John had dealt similarly with the outriders following behind, and now the coachman sat with a bemused expression on his face as he looked into Sabrina's pistol barrel.

"Disarm yourself, coachman," she ordered as Will opened the coach door and accosted the frightened occupants of the coach.

Quickly jewels and loaded purses changed hands, and without bloodshed Bonnie Charlie disappeared into the night, leaving outrage on the victims' faces.

Time and time again they struck, gathering together one of the largest plunders they had yet seen. Bonnie Charlie's name was once again spoken of throughout the countryside, the suddenness and frequency of these holdups stunning people after the relative quiet of the past month when Bonnie Charlie had apparently disappeared.

Less than a week had passed since Sabrina and Mary had left London so abruptly. Nothing had happened so far, and that was worrying Sabrina. She knew that either the marquis or Lucien would follow and try to force her into marriage—but so far she had heard nothing. But she vowed she would get the money for the marquis and then they would be rid of him.

"Slow up, Charlie," Will called warningly as his big roan raced beside Sabrina's black stallion. They slowed their horses' pace as they neared the crest of the hill they had been steadily climbing. As they cantered over the top they pulled up abruptly as they saw a patrol of dragoons making their way up the other side.

"Thought I heard the cursed jingling of harness," Will spat as they swiftly turned and fled back down the hill, but not before the soldiers had caught a glimpse of them and were following in close pursuit.

They galloped across the fields, jumping fences and hedges, the determined yells of the soldiers urging them on. As they neared the first trees of a heavily wooded area bordering the fields, they split, each masked rider going in a different direction as they disappeared into the thick belt of woodland. Sabrina sent her mount through the brambles and thickets, heading deeper into the concealing trees, but still behind her she could hear the breaking of twigs and snapping of branches as the soldiers traced their way after her.

Breaking from the cover of trees, Sabrina headed over a rising mound, and with a casual wave of a gloved hand as she glanced over her shoulder at the three soldiers just leaving the forest, disappeared from their view over the other side.

Colonel Fletcher stared about him, dawning dismay spreading across his features. "Where the devil did he go?"

Below them, down the easily sloping rise, the countryside was empty. How could there be no sight of the highwayman? Colonel Fletcher's mouth tightened into a grim line as he realized that he had been outwitted.

"Sir?" the young lieutenant beside him questioned tentatively. "Which way?"

Colonel Fletcher shook his head in exasperation. "Which way? As far as I know he has disappeared underground, the cursed fellow. We're on his home turf. He knows every hiding place around here. But where he's disappeared to now, God only knows. We'd need an army to search the whole area," he said in disgust. "We might as well head back to the road, we'll not catch him tonight."

The two soldiers rode off, but before following them Colonel Fletcher spoke aloud to the empty darkness. "This time you've gotten away, Bonnie Charlie, but not always. Someday you'll make a mistake, and I'll be waiting."

Sabrina quieted her horse as she heard the colonel and his men leave the hill. So, he would be waiting, would he? Well, like the good man said, this was her turf and they played by her rules here, she thought with amusement. She sighed, shuddering in the darkness that smelled of decay as the richness of the damp soil permeated the air. The smooth stone slabs surrounding her were cool and hard against her palm. This ancient stone-chambered burial ground for some forgotten race made an excellent hiding place. Little did the colonel and his men realize that she stood hidden beneath their very feet in this barrow covered with smooth earth, the upright stones holding the man-made roof above her head and forming a perfect, man-sized rabbit hole. Will and John wouldn't enter it, superstitious of the ghosts of the dead, and Sabrina had to admit that she seldom cared to use it herself. She waited patiently until it was quiet, and then led her horse past the fallen piece of stone that shielded the entrance and through the shrubbery that had grown up densely in front of it.

Will and John should by now have safely eluded the soldiers and made their way into the marsh. Sabrina smiled as she mounted and made her way to the trees, her saddlebag full of money and jewels. Men were such fools at times, she thought contemptuously. Through their own masculine conceit they underestimated women, and fooled themselves.

They had begun to rob in the daylight, a dangerous practice, but she was racing against time, for soon someone would arrive and she wanted to be able to turn over as much money as she could. Will and John had not even hesitated when she had humbly asked for their help once more. She had hated having to involve them again, but she could not succeed without them, and it wouldn't last forever. They would soon be back to normal, she reassured herself, as she rode through the lonely darkness.

The following morning as Sabrina was standing in the hall, Richard called down to her. "There you are! I thought I had missed you." He hopped down the stairs, his whole demeanor having undergone a complete change since returning from London. "Mr. Teesdale says my mind's wandering, so he let me off early."

Sabrina caught the wistful look in his blue eyes and asked him what was troubling him, even though she suspected already what it was.

"Well," he began shyly, "the fair starts today, Rina, and I was kind of hoping to go, maybe?" He looked up hopefully, his eyes full of anticipation and excitement. "Of course, I know you've been extra busy and all, so if we can't go, well, I understand," he added unselfishly, but unable to hide the disappointment in his voice.

"Who said we were not going?" Sabrina demanded gaily. "Now go ask Mary if she wants to come, while I go fetch my bonnet."

"Oh, you really mean it, Rina?" Richard jumped up and down in joy.

"I most certainly do. Now, hop to it, we don't want to miss anything."

Richard skipped off, loudly calling for Mary as he went. Sabrina climbed the stairs, her shoulders drooping tiredly. She was having trouble sleeping and the restless nights had left their mark with the faint purplish shadows beneath her eyes. She stood before the mirror and put on a wide-brimmed straw hat, tying the leaf-green ribbons that matched her gown beneath her chin. She carelessly knotted the ends of a large, rose-colored silk handkerchief she had folded diagonally and draped over her shoulders, partially concealing the décolletage of her gown. It was the same shade as her quilted petticoat and the roses embroidered on the skirt of her gown. Sabrina smoothed the folds, liking the feel of it beneath her hands. With a purposeful sway of her hips she picked up her gloves and purse and left the room, enjoying dressing as herself for a change—men's breeches were a bit too revealing for comfort. She liked to hear the rustle of silk and feel the soft sway of her petticoats as she moved.

Mary and Richard were waiting in the hall as Sabrina descended the stairs.

"I've told Richard that we are going to keep a very vigilant eye over what he eats," Mary said. "You remember the stomachache he got last year after the fair."

"Oh, Mary, it's no fun if you can't eat what you want. Please," Richard pleaded. "I've saved lots of money, too!"

"We'll see," she answered as she winked at Sabrina who was openly grinning. Mary gave a sigh of relief. Sabrina had been so morose these past few days, and so brittle, Mary thought she would shatter soon. If only they did not have this awful fear and uncertainty hanging over their heads.

"We're going to the fair, Sims," Mary declared as the butler held open the door for them.

"Yes, Lady Mary," Sims agreed stoically as they filed past.

"I'll bring you back some cake, Sims," Richard promised over his shoulder as he climbed into the cart.

Sims nodded, a smile lurking in his eyes as he closed the door on the carefree trio.

They traveled quickly down the road, hearing the continuous bell-ringing calling the countryside to the fair. As their cart pulled off of the road and onto the bumpy ground of the field, they could see the little city of tents that had been set up for six days of merriment and trading. Farm wagons and coaches, carts and horses crowded together as their occupants tried to get closer to the loud sound of voices coming from the enclosed area.

Richard led them first to the baker, no sign of direction needed to find his tent, where the aromatic scent of freshly baked cakes and cookies drifted in all directions and guided the hungry unerringly to his door. Richard's eyes sparkled and he licked his lips in expectation as he stared at the display of treats before him.

"And what will the young master be wantin' this fine summer day?" a cheery-faced individual asked from behind the counter.

Richard frowned as he ran his gaze over the wide assortment of baked sweets. "I'll have some of those sugar-and-cinnamon sprinkled cakes, and the almond pastry shaped like the lion and the eagle," Richard decided firmly even as his eye lingered over a spicy confection filled with cream.

The baker grinned as he glanced for approval at the pretty ladies standing behind the young gentleman. At their nods he wrapped Richard's selection in paper and exchanged it for the coins Richard held out in his palm. "Pleasure doing business with ye, sir," he beamed as Richard took a hefty bite from one of the cakes.

They wandered through the crowd, bumping elbows with farmers' wives herding their unruly children from amusement to amusement, their scrubby faces full of excitement and adventure. Colorfully clad jugglers and minstrels strumming their tales sauntered through the milling crowd, enticing and guiding prospective customers up to various rows of stalls. The fires of hot coals smoldered as the braziers worked their malleable brass and displayed their wares behind them on loaded shelves. Pewter gleamed dully from Pewterers' Row and a cloth exchange brimming with colorful fabrics of every description filled several large stalls. Fine French cambric, Indian cotton, cherryderry, damask and denim; drab, Florentine silk and gauze; soft mohair, nankeen, and poplin all caught the eye. Silver ribbons and bright velvet bows waved in the breeze as young country maids gazed rapturously at the beautiful colors, their fingers clenching enough coin to buy a gay length of ribbon to thread through their curls, or a silk handkerchief for Sunday morning.

Mary smoothed a square of blue and green Indian silk. "I've been meaning to buy a handkerchief to match this dress. Do you think it does?" she asked Sabrina who was deciding between a striped yellow and purple handkerchief and a solid turquoise one, while Richard fidgeted beside them, his eyes watching a puppet show across the path.

"I think it's a shade too green. Try this."

Mary held the piece of sky-blue silk against her, the shade matching the blue of her gown perfectly. She wore a long decorative apron tied about her waist and embroidered with blue and green flowers that matched the strip of lace bordering her bodice, and a blue silk bonnet covering her red curls.

At Richard's urging they walked on with their purchases to stand and watch the puppeteer manipulate his puppets for the amusement of the gathering audience while his costumed helper made his way through them collecting any tribute they might care to make.

Laughing at their antics Sabrina and Mary moved on, tugging Richard by sticky hands behind them. A furry little monkey on a chain was dancing for bits of food, and before a large tent people were lining up to view the unfortunate freaks.

They paused as a pie-woman and a gingerbread woman blocked the way, fiercely arguing over customers, their faces hot and perspiring from hustling their goods. As they stood there waiting, Sabrina caught sight of two unmistakable straw-colored heads rising above the crowded path. A moment later a path was cleared for them and they made their way through

the crowd. Sabrina looked up at the broad shoulders blocking
out the sunlight.

"Now you see what we little people have to suffer, Will,"
Sabrina teased. "I thought you would be at the Faire Maiden
with all of these thirsty people about?"

Will shook his head. "Ain't going to get around to our
place until much later. Plenty of refreshments to keep 'em
happy here," he explained, "so John and me decided to have a
little fun, Charlie." His deep voice boomed as he watched the
growing excitement of the crowd, his breath smelling of ale.

"Hey, Charlie, they got some good horseflesh going down
at that end," John told her, his cheeks flushed with pleasure
and drink.

Sabrina flinched as he used their nickname for her, glancing
about apprehensively as she stood there dwarfed by their large
forms. She placed her hands on her hips, her chin lifted arrogantly as she stared up at the two laughing giants.

"Be sure that it is only ale you spill today and not your guts
to some interested listener," Sabrina warned, a twinkle in her
eye as she saw John puff out his chest in offended pride.

"You ain't got no cause to fret, Charlie. I'm just a wee bit
merry, I'm not blind to the world—yet," John reassured her
with a hearty laugh.

Sabrina laughingly waved them off and looked around for
Mary and Richard, spotting Richard's red head amongst small
heads of every shade gathered around the toy seller's stall.
Cries of delight and wistfulness could be heard as they listened
to a musical box with a singing bird, and Sabrina smiled at
Mary who had come up beside her as they watched Richard's
happy face. Suddenly Sabrina's smile faded, and Mary looked
at her in concern until she also heard the lyrics of the song
floating through the air from the balladeer singing gently
beneath a tree.

> "O good Lord Judge, and sweet Lord Judge,
> Peace for a little while!
> Methinks I see my own father,
> Coming riding by the stile.

"Oh father, oh father, a little of your gold,
And likewise of your fee!
To keep my body from yonder grave,
And my neck from the gallows tree.
"None of my gold now you shall have,
Nor likewise of my fee;
For I am come to see you hanged.
And hanged you shall be."

Sabrina closed her ears to the following verses that carried the heroine begging for salvation from her brother, sister and mother, all to no avail, until finally her sweetheart saves her from the hangman.

"Rather appropriate song for him to be singing—Charlie?" a deep voice spoke close to Sabrina's ear.

Sabrina looked up in surprise at the use of her nickname and stared into Colonel Fletcher's penetrating gray eyes that were locked on her face as though seeing her for the first time.

"Rather an odd name, this Charlie, that your very big friends call you," he puzzled. Then as the last notes of the song died out, he commented, "You don't care for his song, or is it that it brings painful images to mind?"

"It does not bother me, Colonel. Why indeed should it?" Sabrina responded casually, a pulse beating in her throat.

The colonel smiled thoughtfully. "It would me, if I were in your position."

"My position?" Sabrina questioned doubtfully, giving him a sympathetic look. "Are you sure the sun is not a bit too strong, Colonel? It has been known to cause hallucinations."

The colonel continued to stare at Sabrina's upturned face, shaking his head in disbelief. "I do feel dizzy from the startling discovery I have just made, and should I dare to make it known, I do believe I should be suspected of derangement," he admitted, then staring into Sabrina's violet eyes added very softly, "but we would know different, would we not, Bonnie Charlie?"

Mary gasped and stared in horror at the colonel's tall figure, seeing only his sword swinging at his side and representing disaster.

Sabrina gave an incredulous laugh that sounded convincing. "You are indeed crazed, Colonel, if you imagine anyone in their right senses would believe such a harebrained story as that. Why, one would think it had been concocted in a tavern when one had been in high spirits, but hardly believable, or indeed, amusing," Sabrina told him presenting him with a haughty profile.

"That act of affronted dignity may work on some, but not on me. This is not the time or place to discuss your affairs, but discuss them I shall. You may expect a visit from me this afternoon. Until then, ladies." He bowed and disappeared into the crowd, leaving Sabrina and Mary standing speechlessly beside each other.

"Oh, dear, what are we going to do, Rina?" Mary asked faintly, still staring into the crowd after the colonel.

"Nothing, absolutely nothing," Sabrina replied, her mouth twisting into a smile. "We shall call the good colonel's bluff, for that is all that it is. He has no proof against me, and he shall be able to find none. And should he pursue his suspicions," Sabrina shrugged complacently, "he will be laughed out of the county."

"You really aren't worried, are you?" Mary said in amazement as she saw Sabrina's calm expression.

"I've been up against far smarter men than the colonel and won. Besides, this charade is drawing to a close and then we need not worry at all about Colonel Fletcher," Sabrina said contemptuously, hiding the momentary fear she had felt under mocking laughter. "Come on, let's enjoy ourselves. I'll not have that redcoat spoil my day," Sabrina proclaimed, urging Mary along with her.

They moved on through the crowd with Richard in tow, passing groups of men whose voices were raised as they called for their favorites in a wrestling match or cockfight, the refreshments flowing generously as the heat parched their throats and spirits rose as the alcohol heated up their blood. They stood for a minute watching the auctioning off of colts and horses at the trader's stalls, but turned back before reaching the area set off for bull-baiting. The cruelty and viciousness of setting dogs at a chained bull for a shilling, and watching the dogs get tossed around and the bull bitten at by the snarling dogs, had never appealed to them.

Threading their way back the way they had come they gradually made their way towards their cart. There were more people than before crowding the lanes, pushing and shoving, laughing and arguing as they enjoyed the festivities. Nearing the butcher's stall, the flies hovering close above the cuts of beef, a fistfight suddenly erupted into the noisy chatter.

Two young farmers, who had had too much ale, were rolling and punching in the space cleared by the yelling spectators. A young, bright-eyed girl was watching eagerly, a bunch of colorful ribbons clutched in one hand, and a locket in the other.

"Fightin' over a woman." Sabrina heard someone say as the two men grunted in the dirt at the crowd's feet.

"Come on, Richard," Sabrina said nervously. "The crowd's growing restless."

Someone pushed a brawny boy, who turned and slugged a bespectacled clergyman whose friend tackled the offender in outrage and in the process fell into a pie-woman whose pies slid into the dust as she shrieked in rage. Fists began to fly and feet up-ended as people were knocked down in the scuffle. The butcher grabbed a cleaver should anyone come too near his display, and stood watching the tumbling bodies with glee.

Sabrina grasped Mary's arm, and pulling Richard between them they tried to press their way out of the mass of sweating bodies that surged forward at the sound of a fight.

Mary tripped, crying out as she began to fall to her knees, disappearing under the countless heads and shoulders surrounding them. Sabrina tried to reach out over Richard's head, holding onto him as he was pulled off balance as Mary fell, then just as suddenly as she had disappeared, Mary reappeared, her blue silk bonnet knocked sideways and a scarlet arm encircling her shoulders as Colonel Fletcher cleared a path through the crowd. He moved before Sabrina and Richard, shielding them from wildly flailing elbows and fists that were spreading throughout the crowd as tempers flared in the crush.

"Hold onto my waist," he called over his shoulder. Sabrina gratefully grabbed his wide waist, hooking her fingers through his belt and holding Richard close under her other arm.

Colonel Fletcher's shiny boots stepped on toes and kicked up dust as he cleared an avenue of escape through the melee. Sabrina thought she heard the sound of a fist hitting a jaw once and a cry of pain before they quickly passed a crumpled form. Sabrina kicked out at unprotected shins as they passed, often making contact with satisfaction as she heard grunts of surprise. She took a deep breath of fresh air as they made the open, the colonel leading them clear of the battling foray behind.

"Thank you so much," Mary murmured faintly as the colonel looked down at her pale face. His arm tightened around her small waist protectively as he watched her with concerned eyes.

"Are you all right, Lady Mary?" he asked worriedly.

Sabrina glanced up sharply at his words. Since when had he been concerned about Mary's welfare? She watched them closely as Colonel Fletcher handled Mary like a piece of porcelain. He glanced up suddenly, encountering Sabrina's interested and slightly hostile gaze, and flushed.

"Where is your carriage?" he demanded.

"We came in a cart. Over there." Sabrina indicated their cart, and followed as Colonel Fletcher half carried Mary to it.

Richard jumped in and helped the colonel lift Mary in, although the way he held her so easily, Sabrina thought he'd need little assistance.

"You ladies should not have attended without proper escort," he told them angrily. "These fairs always degenerate into rowdyism and fisticuffs."

He turned from Mary, who had closed her eyes, and stared accusingly at Sabrina. "I could scarce believe my eyes when I spotted you in the thick of things. You forget, Lady Sabrina, or are you more comfortable being called Charlie, that your sister and young brother are not quite up to your escapades, nor used to a certain element that you must come into contact with often. I thought I would never get them safely out of that crowd of ruffians."

"We are most grateful, Colonel Fletcher, but I for one have had enough of your company for the day," Sabrina told him, stung by his accusation. "First you accuse me of being a highwayman, and now of mistreating my brother and sister. You go too far. Good day to you, sir."

"If you were under my command I would have had you whipped long ago," Colonel Fletcher said through gritted teeth as he struggled to hold on to his temper.

Sabrina smiled unpleasantly. "I have felt the lash, Colonel, and it only serves to strengthen my resolve not to be bullied by the likes of you."

The colonel looked surprised for a moment at the sudden blaze of wrath in her eyes that just as quickly died, but a tightness remained around her mouth that betrayed her deep feelings.

"I will escort you ladies home now," the colonel said, not waiting for the refusal he expected as he looked down at Sabrina's frown beneath the wide brim of her straw bonnet, daring her to contradict him.

Shrugging, she accepted his escort and climbed into the cart. They waited patiently while the colonel fetched his horse and left orders for his men.

"Are you going to arrest all of those people?" Richard asked in awe as the colonel rode alongside their cart.

"No, that would certainly cause a riot, they'll be suffering enough with sore jaws, so I think I'll let that be their punishment."

"How are you, Mary?" Sabrina asked softly, the colonel's criticism still stinging as she touched Mary's arm lightly.

Mary smiled tiredly. "Fine, Rina. I'm sorry I acted so silly, but all of those bodies pressing in on me—I just couldn't bear it any longer. Thank goodness Colonel Fletcher was there." She glanced up at him shyly as he rode alongside them, his back straight as a board as he sat easily in the saddle.

"Keep your attention to the road ahead, Richard," Sabrina

reprimanded him sharply as his eyes kept stealing up to the proud military figure in awestruck wonder, "or I shall think twice about letting you take the reins."

Richard turned back to the road ahead, his hands firm on the reins. "I'm watching, Rina," he reassured her. "But did you see the way he cleared a path through that crowd?"

Colonel Fletcher glanced down at Richard's words. "When you're my size, Richard, you'll be able to push your way through a crowd too."

"Richard, eyes forward." Sabrina fumed inwardly. The colonel was certainly on friendly terms with her family, addressing them so informally, acting the uncle with Richard.

"Sabrina is going to teach me how to shoot now that I can see really good," Richard boasted. "She can shoot a pistol better than anyone."

"I'm sure she can, Richard. But then you've had a lot of practice, haven't you, Lady Sabrina?" Colonel Fletcher replied conversationally.

Richard flushed, looking chagrined as he realized what he'd let slip out. He glanced up at Sabrina worriedly and received a reassuring smile, his frightened features relaxing.

They rode the rest of the way to Verrick House in an uncomfortable silence, and when they reached it the colonel followed them in uninvited as though he belonged there. Sabrina quickly excused herself and followed Richard upstairs. The colonel could just wait for that little talk he wanted.

"Please be seated," Mary told the colonel as they entered the salon.

"It would please me if you would call me Terence," he said softly, startling a blush across Mary's cheeks.

"R-really, Colonel, I know that I am grateful for your assistance at the fair, but before that you made some rather serious accusations against my sister which I really cannot forget, nor forgive," Mary spoke quickly, mixed emotions flickering on her usually serene face.

"I am sorry if I upset you, Mary," he said her name deliberately, "but I think it is about time that a man stepped in and took command of this household. Your sister has been running wild long enough. God knows it started that morning so long ago in the hills of Scotland with a loaded pistol in her hand. Can't you see that I want to help your family? You have no idea of the danger your sister is in each time she masquerades as Bonnie Charlie."

Mary bit her lips. "No one has admitted that Sabrina is Bonnie Charlie. It is ridiculous, Colonel," Mary refuted his statement.

"Is it really so ridiculous? An odd coincidence that you are from Scotland and the highwayman is Scots also. He is rather small and his two henchmen are exceptionally large, like those two large men talking in such a friendly fashion to your sister this afternoon, and then, Mary," the colonel added as his final proof, "they called her Charlie."

Mary remained silent. "You still have no positive proof, Colonel. No one would believe you, you will look the fool," she told him quietly, refusing to trust him.

"Do you really believe that I would turn your sister over to the authorities? I'm not quite that inhuman, but neither can I allow her to continue to rob and terrorize the countryside. She must be stopped."

Mary turned away from his penetrating stare and looked out of the window. What was she to do? How could they afford to make an enemy out of this man? If only they had a little more time, then all would be finished and he need never know the truth. He couldn't hurt them then.

"Mary," Colonel Fletcher spoke softly as he came up behind her stiff back, "don't fight me."

Mary jumped as she felt his large hand lightly touch her shoulder and curve around it. She turned her head up against his shoulder and tried to pull free. "Really, Colonel, you are far too bold. Please release me this instant."

"I intend to be far bolder, Mary," he answered audaciously, pressing her closer against the hard metal buttons of his uniform. "You present quite a challenge to an old soldier, and I find I am always at my best when on a campaign with a particular objective to take."

Mary's face flamed at his words. "Sir, I will not become the object of your maneuvers, nor, indeed, are these your barracks that you may come in here and issue orders as though we were under your command!"

Colonel Fletcher laughed. "I'd wondered if you'd a bit of your sister's defiance in you. I've yet to meet such a cocky wench as that one. It seems inconceivable that you are related. So different in every way," he murmured as he lifted a red curl from the back of her neck, "one demure and sweet, the other high-strung and meddlesome."

Mary stared into his eyes in growing panic as she felt his arm slip around her waist. "I thought men liked women with spirit?"

"Some men, yes, but as a soldier who has been involved in far too many battles I now seek a gentle woman, one I can be friends with and share a home with, not a battlefield. I am tired of skirmishes and only want tranquility. I pity the man who takes on your sister, for that is all he shall have—one fight after another. He'll never have a peaceful moment, for she shall keep him wondering what she is up to. No, that is not for me, no matter how beautiful she happens to be." He looked down into the gray eyes staring up at him, the small nose with the light sprinkling of freckles, the soft mouth, and spoke more to himself than to her. "I think I have found my stronghold at last."

His tanned face lowered to hers and his mouth touched hers briefly before crushing its softness beneath his in a long kiss. He turned her unresisting body around and held her close as her untutored lips clung to his.

"Mary, let me help you," he spoke against her ear, his lips lingering against the smoothness of her fiery cheek. "You're so sweet, I want to teach you so many things."

"Please, let me go," Mary pleaded. "Someone may enter." She struggled for a moment before Colonel Fletcher released her, but kept a firm hold on one of her hands. Mary tidied her hair with a shaking hand, straightening the lace at her breast carefully, while the colonel watched in amusement.

"You've never been kissed by a man before, have you?" he asked although he already knew the answer. "Are you going to let me help you?"

"I-I don't know what you are talking about?" Mary answered, flustered, wishing someone would come in and rescue her from this predicament.

"You can't avoid the issue forever," he told her seriously. "I have my duty to perform, and I am one of the king's men, Mary. I do not want to hurt you or your family, but I cannot allow your sister to continue."

"Continue what, Colonel?" Sabrina demanded as she entered the room, noticing with a start the clasped hands of Mary and the colonel as she came forward to stand before the tall, red-coated officer. "You do persist in this outrageous notion of yours, and now," she said meaningfully as she sent a mocking glance at their locked hands, "what stratagem are you using to gain information? Are you seducing my sister in order to get her to tell you all you think she knows? Well," Sabrina laughed, sending Mary a cautionary glance, "she is not fool enough to fall for your sweet words and honeyed phrases. She knows that it would all be lies, don't you, Mary?"

The colonel's lips thinned ominously as he stared in anger at Sabrina. He looked down at Mary's stricken face and felt white-hot with rage. "Very well done, Lady Sabrina, I compliment you on your tactics, although I am not sure whether you believe your own words or not. However, you are mistaken about my motives, at least concerning Mary, for I have not lied to her. Although thanks to you I doubt whether she will believe me now."

Mary avoided his eyes and pulled her hand free, walking over to the bellpull to ring for tea.

"I've already ordered it," Sabrina told her as she took a seat opposite Mary, her violet eyes questioning as she stared at her.

They remained silent while the tea service was set up by a footman, and then as Mary busied herself thankfully with the teacups, the colonel said in a stern voice, "You should be turned over someone's knee and soundly spanked, Lady Sabrina."

Mary muttered beneath her breath as she spilled the tea, concentrating on it rather than look up at Sabrina, whom she knew would be glaring angrily at Colonel Fletcher.

"And you think you are man enough to do that, Colonel?" Sabrina demanded contemptuously.

"I'm man enough, but not the right man to do it," he answered back obliquely, smiling unpityingly at the thought.

"The day some man tries will be his last day on earth." Sabrina smiled unpleasantly, her eyes telling the colonel that she wished he would be the one to try.

Colonel Fletcher shook his head. "You have ruled this roost far too long, Lady Sabrina. It is time a man stepped in and took the lot of you under his guidance."

"And who would you suggest? The marquis? I'm sure he would appreciate that, since he has hardly played the father figure before." Sabrina sat down, accepting her tea and sipping it nonchalantly. "Let me see," she continued ruminatively, "he saw his son and heir for the first time a little over a week ago. And when did he last see us? Ten years ago? Yes, he is definitely the hand to guide us. All he cares about is money to fill his pockets. You think you have a chance to court my sister Mary? Oh, yes, I know you have probably made advances to her, and assuming they are honorable, do you really imagine you've enough money to buy her?"

Colonel Fletcher winced at the remark.

"Yes, you may well flinch. But that is the distasteful state of affairs we exist in. We, my sister and I, are commodities to the marquis. Since having set eyes on us he regards us in the light of assets. He will find the richest husbands for us, and I don't really think that your officer's pay will qualify you, Colonel."

"So young to be so bitter. If I did not know more about you than most, then I would not understand, nor be able to feel pity for you."

"I don't want your pity," Sabrina replied, her voice trembling. "I don't need it. We don't need you. Why don't you leave us alone?"

"Rina," Mary cautioned anxiously.

"Don't tell me you've fallen for him? You can't have. We don't need him, Mary. He'll try to take you away."

"You can't live in this fairyland of yours any longer, Lady

Sabrina. Don't you realize how lucky you are that it is me you have to deal with? Don't try so hard to hate me. Trust me. I can help you, all of you," he tried to placate her.

Sabrina wanted to believe him, but all the years of mistrust and the memory of him at Culloden came flooding back to her, clouding her thoughts. And yet, maybe it was time to trust someone, maybe him. Sabrina stood up and taking a tentative step toward him she was about to speak, when the door was opened and Sims announced Lord Malton and Lord Newley.

They hurried in, expressions of excitement on their faces as they greeted Sabrina and Mary, hardly noticing the colonel.

"My dear, dear Lady Sabrina," Lord Malton beamed coyly, "you never let on, we had no idea that you and the duke, why, it is remarkable, and, my dear, you have taken us all by surprise, yes indeed. I am agog at the news, even Newley here is struck dumb. Never been so dazzled," Lord Malton babbled.

Sabrina felt the blood draining from her face as she exchanged looks with a stunned-looking Mary. Colonel Fletcher found his voice first, impatience in it at the ill-timed interruption.

"May I inquire as to what you are referring, Malton?"

Lord Malton chuckled. "The announcement of the upcoming marriage of Lady Sabrina Verrick, daughter of the Marquis of Wrainton, and the Duke of Camareigh, Lucien Dominick. The sly devil never said a word about it. In fact, I assumed he was to marry Lady Blanche Delande, but—" He cut himself off in mid-sentence looking apologetically at Sabrina. "I beg your pardon, Lady Sabrina. No sense in talking about past loves, eh? Very strange though, you must admit, the way she just disappeared. No one has seen her since and some even say she eloped with a penniless soldier," Lord Malton confided in a theatrical whisper.

Colonel Fletcher stared at Sabrina's pale face, her look of despair confirming the news. "It would seem that you were right about the marquis," he said grimly. "I've not had the pleasure of meeting him; however, I intend to make his acquaintance."

"Glad you're here, Fletcher. Been wanting to ask you what you intend doing about that rogue, Bonnie Charlie. Thought you'd have caught the blackguard by now. We won't stand for much more of this harassment by that Scots cur," Malton threatened, his good humor forgotten for the moment. "Right, Newley?"

But Lord Newley wasn't listening, he was staring morosely at Sabrina's heart-shaped face, his eyes watching every expression that crossed her lovely features.

"Guess Newley's got other things on his mind," Lord Malton commented snidely, winking broadly at Colonel Fletcher. "He won't be the only one sorry to have the Lady Sabrina wed. Hear she made a big sensation in London."

"I think you need not concern yourselves over the problem of Bonnie Charlie much longer," Colonel Fletcher said, changing the subject, "for I feel it will resolve itself very shortly."

Lord Malton puffed out his cheeks and stamped his cane on the floor. "You know something, eh? Good. About time we ridded ourselves of this wretched fellow. Expect to be informed of your movements, Fletcher. Want to be in on the kill, damned if I don't."

Colonel Fletcher barely concealed his expression of distaste. How easily the civilian talked of killing. He wondered how eager he would be if he saw over a thousand mangled and dead bodies in one afternoon's fighting.

"The ladies were just telling me how fatigued they were from the fair, and about an unfortunate scuffle that ensued on the grounds, so I think I'll bid them adieu," he suggested, glancing at the two lords expectantly, leaving them little choice but to follow suit.

"I had hoped to learn more about your engagement, Lady Sabrina," said Lord Malton. "When the wedding will occur, and if you'll be married in London? So much to tell, what with everyone so interested. I do know that the duke had only until this week to wed or he'd lose Camareigh. Wonder if that still applies." He looked to Sabrina for enlightenment, but on receiving no encouragement on her ashen features, shrugged good-naturedly. "Well, must be off then."

"If you'd be interested in learning about my plans for Bonnie Charlie, I suggest we make haste, I've an inspection to see to, gentlemen," Colonel Fletcher spoke authoritatively, hurrying them on their way. Before leaving the room behind them he added, "I will be back to continue our discussion, ladies."

Sabrina sat as though turned to stone, the only sound the monotonous ticking of the clock. She bent her head, hiding her face from view, her shoulders slumped in defeat. A muffled sob escaped from her and she slumped farther into herself as she huddled in the chair.

Mary quickly rushed over and knelt beside her, wrapping her arms around Sabrina's shaking shoulders. She let her cry, her sobs racking her slim body as she drained herself of pent-up emotion.

"What am I going to do? I thought I would have more time, and I never imagined that they would go ahead and announce it without my presence. Once again I've underestimated Lucien. I had forgotten how cunning he can be." Sabrina looked up tearfully. "Well, I will not do it. I will not be forced into marriage with him. I couldn't bear it, not after the humiliation he put me through. I must do something. He'll pay for this. He deserves to lose his estates and become the laughingstock when I leave him at the altar as his previous fiancée did," Sabrina threatened, her violet eyes glowing with anticipation of revenge.

Mary shook her head helplessly. "I don't think you can prevent him. How can you stop the marriage now that everyone knows about it? Why not go ahead and marry him, Rina? It would settle everything, especially now that Colonel Fletcher knows about us. How can you continue to get money with him watching everything we are doing? I can't see any way out of this."

"I will not accept it," Sabrina said stubbornly, her voice beginning to grow strong and hardening with resolution. "Mary, we have so much money already. If I can just get a little bit more, then I will personally take it to the marquis and he will leave us alone. Besides, if the duke cannot find me, then he has no bride to wed."

Mary sat back on her heels, staring at Sabrina's determined face. "I think Colonel Fletcher was right, we've been living in a make-believe world."

"Mary," Sabrina pleaded, her eyes mirroring hurt, "you can't desert me now. I thought we were a family?" She bit her lip nervously. She just couldn't lose Mary. "You aren't turning against me, are you?"

"Of course not, Rina, how could you think such a thing," Mary reassured her, worried by the almost feverish look in Sabrina's eyes.

"Good." Sabrina smiled, giving her a hug before rising to her feet. "We've got to make plans, Mary. Unless I am sorely deceived I would imagine we are in for a visit from either the marquis or Lucien, and I have no intention of being present when they do show up."

Mary laughed shakily. "So I am to be the welcoming committee? I do not look forward to it. The Duke has struck me as being a very forceful man, and we both know only too well how he exacts punishment against those who cross him. He will be outraged if you make him the laughingstock of London as you have predicted, and then cause him to lose his estate." Mary shuddered at the thought, touching her own soft cheek as she remembered his. "That scar makes him seem almost diabolical, it is quite dreadful."

Sabrina turned on her indignantly. "There is nothing wrong with his scar. How dare you imply that it is ugly, or loathsome?" Sabrina said sharply, surprising herself by her sudden, passionate defense of him.

Mary's gray eyes widened in surprise. "I'm sorry, I didn't mean it was repulsive at all. It just makes him look dangerous. That is all, Rina," Mary explained gently.

"I'm the one who's sorry. I've been such a trial to you, I know, but everything is on the edge of collapse, and I'm at my wits' end. I'm meeting Will and John this evening, and I will figure out a plan. I won't be able to stay here and still get out as Bonnie Charlie. They mustn't be able to stop me." She left the room, her stride purposeful and firm.

"'O tiger's heart wrapp'd in a woman's hide!'" a voice said softly.

Mary spun around at the sound. "Aunt Margaret! Have you been here all of the time?"

Aunt Margaret left her seat in the bow window where she'd sat unobserved behind the folds of a velvet hanging. She tiptoed into the room, glancing about for anyone lurking nearby.

"I do so hate crowds of people, don't you? Odd," she said, "Malty hasn't changed any since he was just a little boy, although he was always plump and always telling tales, too."

Mary smiled at Aunt Margaret's description of Lord Malton, then tried to explain to her the importance of not talking about the conversation she'd overheard.

"But, my dear, I keep the most divine secrets, really I do, besides, that is no secret," she scoffed at Mary's surprised face. She hugged her tapestry to her as she rocked to and fro, a complacent smile on her lips. "Now I know a real secret, but I mustn't tell you, dear, at least not yet."

Mary walked over to her and taking her by the shoulders held her wandering attention. "Now, Aunt Margaret, you will forget all that you heard between Sabrina and me, and you promise you won't repeat it?"

Aunt Margaret shook her head conspiratorially, a sly look entering her blue eyes as she whispered, "My lips are sealed, m'dear." She slipped from the room quietly, the spaniels a step behind and just as quiet. Mary closed her eyes. What more could happen?

She suddenly heard the sound of horse's hooves and wondered who was calling so late in the afternoon. Surely Lord Malton would not have returned to quench his thirst for gossip? She walked over to the window and glanced out to see a solitary rider approaching the house at a deliberate gait, the big red horse kicking up dust as he made his way up the drive. The rider became visible as he passed by the window, and Mary drew back in panic as she recognized that arrogant face marred by the scar.

Chapter 11

"SABRINA!" MARY CALLED OUT AS SHE HURRIED INTO SABRINA'S room. "He's here."

Sabrina glanced around curiously. "Who is here?" she asked, hiding a yawn behind her hand. She'd removed her gown and was lying in her petticoat and corset on the bed. She wriggled her stockinged feet lazily and stared at Mary's flushed face.

"The Duke, Rina," she told her clearly.

The drowsiness left Sabrina's eyes abruptly, alarm spreading across her features. "Here?" she demanded.

"Yes. I just saw him ride up the drive. He is probably in the house this very instant demanding to see you."

Sabrina swung her feet to the edge of the big bed and hopped down. "Well, he will not find me here."

"Oh, but he already has," a cool voice spoke from the door.

Mary gave a startled squeal and spun around like a hare caught in a trap. Sabrina turned slowly at the familiar voice. She was breathing rapidly, her breasts rising and falling beneath their thin covering of lace as she faced Lucien. She stiffened her back and, squaring her shoulders, said dismissively, "I think you mistake the room you are in, your grace. As you can see, I am dressing."

Mary became aware of Sabrina's dishabille and hurriedly fetched her a dressing gown, which Sabrina gratefully accepted and quickly slipped on. The dark purple velvet sleeves covered her bare arms while the fitted waist partially covered her lacey bodice. She'd released her hair from its knot and it now hung down her back and over her shoulder in a smooth dark cloud.

"No, I've made no mistake, Sabrina. Women often invite men into their bedchambers as they dress, and, after all, we are betrothed, aren't we?" he asked softly as he left the doorway and intruded farther into the room. He wore buckskin breeches molded to his muscular thighs and a double-breasted frock coat. High jackboots reached his knees and were covered in a light coating of fine dust.

"I do not think the circumstances apply here," Sabrina contradicted him, "and I have not invited you in, either."

Mary glanced between them, afraid to move or make a sound. Lucien tossed his cocked hat and gloves onto a chair and turned his attention to the two women standing uncertainly before him.

"I can plainly see by the fear in your eyes, Lady Mary, that you have been given the worst details concerning me and you are concerned about having such an ogre for a brother-in-law. Of course, considering the company your sister keeps, you might have done far worse, say with a highwayman or pickpocket?"

Mary licked her dry lips, but before she could find a suitable reply, Sabrina answered abruptly.

"You may taunt me, Lucien, but not Mary. She is not up to your subtle sarcasms or cruel witticisms, nor does she deserve them."

Lucien inclined his head slightly. "I bow to your greater knowledge of the lady, but as she is a relation of yours, as is the marquis, I doubt your wisdom to judge them. It would seem there are certain character traits that are unmistakable in this family."

"How dare you come into my home and insult us, and how dare you make that ridiculous announcement when you know that I will not marry you?"

Lucien's mouth tightened ominously and his eyes narrowed as he held up his hand for silence. "I do not think we need an audience to play to." He turned to Mary and indicated the door. "If you will be so kind, your sister and I have a few matters to discuss in private."

Sabrina's nostrils flared in anger. "You go too far, Lucien. How dare you—"

"I'll dare anything, and unless you want to further embarrass and distress your sister by what I shall say, then I suggest you agree to our privacy."

Sabrina glanced at Mary indecisively, unsure of what to do.

"I shall get Sims and the footmen, and have him thrown out!" Mary declared bravely.

Lucien laughed unpleasantly. "I doubt they would enjoy throwing a duke out of the door on his tail, assuming they could, of course. And also, as I have a letter of introduction from the marquis giving me complete authority over this household in his absence, I imagine they would think twice before executing such a plan."

"You've complete authority," Sabrina fumed. "You can take your authority to blazes for all the notice I'll take of it."

"Lady Mary," Lucien said softly, placing a gentle, yet firm hand on her arm as he guided her to the door.

"Rina," she began, looking over her shoulder in consternation.

"It's all right, Mary, I'll handle his grace. But don't have a guest room prepared, for he shall not be staying."

Lucien closed the door behind Mary and turned back to Sabrina, a glint in his sherry-colored eyes. "So, I will not be staying?"

"No, you will not," Sabrina replied firmly, despite his approaching figure and menacing expression.

He came to a halt less than a foot before her and stared down into her violet eyes. "I do not enjoy being made the fool, which you seem fond of doing, nor do I like having my plans changed. I do not like having to chase across the countryside like some besotted fool in pursuit of his ladylove. You have caused me a great deal of inconvenience, Sabrina."

Sabrina allowed a small smile of satisfaction to curve her lips. "Good, and no less the amount of trouble you have caused me, your grace," she said insolently.

They stood staring at each other silently for a minute, neither moving until Sabrina finally broke the silence. "I will not marry you, Lucien."

Lucien smiled cynically. "You think not? It has gone past what either of us desires. We will be wed, Sabrina, that I promise you."

Sabrina stamped her foot angrily. "Damn you, why the devil won't you leave me alone?"

"Careful, Sabrina, your highwayman's manners—or lack of them—are showing."

Sabrina raised her arm swiftly, and before he could react she had slapped him hard across his scarred cheek, the contact sounding like thunder in the stunned silence.

Without stopping to think, Lucien slapped her back, reacting in the heat of anger and an instant's uncontrollable rage. Sabrina's head jerked back with the force of his hand, and the imprinted outline of his fingers stained her white cheek vividly in angry red marks. Huge tears rolled down her face as she put the back of her hand to her trembling mouth, her eyes staring at him dazedly. With a cry she hurled herself onto the bed, hiding her mortified face in the soft, cool pillows, her velvet robe spreading out like a fan on the quilted coverlet as she lay shaking on the bed.

She felt the bed sag as Lucien sat down beside her, and the next instant he had her in his arms, his lips caressing the weals on her cheek soothingly.

"All I want to do is kiss you, and I end up hurting you. Forgive me. I've never raised my hand against a woman before," he whispered, passion and remorse intermingled in his voice. His mouth closed over hers, pressing against her lips until they parted and he kissed her deeply. She felt his lips move along the arch of her throat and shoulders, the scent of him filling her senses.

His body was heavy against hers as his hands twisted into the thick strands of her hair, holding her face next to his as he rubbed his scarred cheek against the cheek he'd slapped.

"I was furious when I first came into your room, but, God forgive me, that's no excuse for striking you, when all I want is to hold you close in my arms and kiss that sweet mouth," he murmured as he found her mouth again and kissed her hungrily, his hands sliding beneath the soft velvet of her robe and cupping her breasts.

Sabrina pulled her mouth free, trying to turn her face from his eager lips. "You cannot seduce me again, Lucien," she whispered, knowing she lied.

Lucien gave a low laugh. "You act so disdainful, but I think you cannot resist my kisses. You want me, Sabrina," he said confidently, pulling her warm body closer.

"No, I don't," Sabrina denied. "I do not blame you for believing that. I did try to seduce you that first night," Sabrina admitted, "but things have changed since then. It was one night only, Lucien. I know what you are and what you are like, and I do not love you. You are mean, cruel, and selfish, and I will not be your pawn in whatever games you intend to play."

Lucien stared down into her defiant face, her cheeks rosy and her eyes bright with tears. "Bravely spoken, little one, but quite useless. We will be wed, so why not make the best of it? You will have all the money your heart could desire, a grand home, and"—he paused, giving her a bold glance—"you will have an attentive husband, which is more than most women have. You will not be lonely, Sabrina, that I can promise you." He smiled and placed a light kiss on her reddened mouth.

"And how long will you desire me, Lucien? How long will I be able to amuse you, for that is all I am for you. A new diversion, something to play with for awhile. Then what happens when you tire of me?"

"I doubt that will happen anytime soon, but when we tire of one another you may feel free to take a lover, as long as you are discreet," Lucien allowed generously, thinking to placate her.

Sabrina gave a sob and pushed him from her frantically. "Leave me alone! You've destroyed everything, Lucien. I hate you!" she cried.

"No you don't, you—" Lucien began, pulling her back to him determinedly when they were startled by the loud report of a pistol. Lucien rolled on top of Sabrina to protect her and looked over his shoulder, only to see a figure flying at him. He caught it as it hurled itself at him, fists swinging as they tried to make contact with his face.

"Leave my sister alone! Richard cried as he took a swing that barely missed Lucien's nose.

Lucien caught the young firebrand's wrists with one hand and moving from Sabrina's huddled form, managed to capture the boy's kicking feet between his knees. The figure struggled ineffectively for a moment before quieting.

"Let me go!" a childish voice ordered.

Lucien grabbed a fistful of red hair and raised the hidden face into view off his chest. Two angry blue eyes behind round lenses glared up at him. The little boy's stock was crumpled and he'd lost a shoe in the scuffle as well as a stocking that was partially unrolled down his calf.

Lucien returned the young boy's stare grimly. "From his manners I would hazard a guess that this pup is a relation."

Sabrina pulled herself up from the tumbled bedclothes and looked in amazement at Richard locked between Lucien's legs, his face red with anger as he tried to worm his way free.

"Richard," Sabrina coaxed, trying to release him from Lucien's hold. "Let him go. He's my brother," Sabrina told Lucien as she pulled ineffectively at his wrist. Her dressing gown had fallen open and the lace at her breasts fluttered with her heavy breathing as she confronted the blazing sherry eyes above her. "If you've hurt him?"

"Hurt this little brawler?" Lucien demanded. "If he were not such a poor shot, your knight-errant here would have killed us both."

"I wouldn't hurt Rina," Richard explained. "You were being mean to her. You made her cry, I heard you, and she told you to leave her alone," Richard defended himself with childish logic. "I'd never hurt Rina," he repeated tearfully.

A scuffling of feet caused them to look up as Mary, followed by Sims and a couple of footmen, Hobbs with a poker and the cook with a rolling pin, all fell into the room, their faces mirroring astonishment and consternation as they stared at the three people in the bed.

Mary was the first to reach them, her voice trembling with fear. "What has happened?" Her face was white as the sheets as her gray eyes searched the bed for any sign of blood.

Sabrina pulled her robe together and pushing a thick wave of hair out of her eyes looked up at the dismayed faces surrounding the big bed. "Richard was showing Lucien his new pistol and it accidentally discharged. Fortunately no one was hurt." Sabrina smiled stiffly. "I appreciate your concern, but everything is fine, truly."

Taking this explanation as a dismissal, they shuffled out, their faces wearing expressions of mixed emotions at her words.

"I'll be polishing the silver in the hall, Lady Sabrina," Sims added as he left the room, a warning glint in his eye as he watched the duke, who by now had released the squirming Richard.

Mary stood silent, her face drained of emotion as Lucien's shoulders began to shake and he gave a deep rumble of laughter. Richard moved out of reach quickly and stared from the protection of Mary's arms at Lucien's grinning face, while Sabrina and Mary exchanged uneasy glances.

"I haven't laughed so hard in years. You certainly have a loyal staff," he laughed again, "and who was the buxom harridan with the rolling pin?" His chest shook with mirth. "God, what a household. I've never taken such abuse in my life. Assaulted first by a wild-eyed wench, spitting like a ruffled kitten, then a tadpole hardly out of swaddling clothes brandishing a loaded pistol, and now to top it off, the servants wielding pokers and rolling pins. Well, who's next? Some mangy mutt to snarl at my ankles? Not a very hospitable welcome for your husband-to-be."

Lucien climbed from the bed, and with a sweeping bow to them all he left the room, his deep laughter ringing in their ears.

"I don't like him," Richard said gruffly. "Who is he, and why is he here?" He looked into Sabrina's violet eyes, a bewildered frown on his childish features. "What did he mean, husband-to-be, Rina?" Richard asked trustingly as he left Mary's arms and climbed back onto the bed beside Sabrina.

Sabrina rested her chin on top of Richard's red head

thoughtfully. "I wish I could explain everything to you, Dickie, but I am so unsure of what I am doing."

"The Duke spells trouble, Rina. He won't be put off this time."

"The Duke! A real duke, Rina?" Richard gasped aloud, looking up at her in awe.

"Yes, he is very much the arrogant duke," Sabrina answered simply, "and he makes the most of his title."

"Are you going to marry him?"

Sabrina closed her eyes and took a deep breath. "No," she said softly, yet firmly.

Richard's mouth opened soundlessly and his eyes widened in fear. "But Rina, he'll beat you if you don't. Did you see that scar? He must be ever so mean." He straightened his shoulders manfully. "I'll protect you from him, Rina. I'll get rid of him if you don't want to marry him."

Sabrina hugged Richard to her tightly. "Thank you, love, but it won't be necessary. I hate abandoning you two to the mercies of the duke, but I must leave here if I'm to stay free and be able to get the rest of the money we need. Look, if you need me, leave a note in the church under our pew. You know the loose stone. Slip it in there and I'll check every so often, all right?"

"Where will you stay?" Mary asked worriedly, not caring for this plan. "Can't you stay with the Taylors and send Will or John for news?"

"Lucien might see them; he knows them well enough by now. Their size would make him suspicious, and I might be seen leaving the Taylors' cottage, either as myself or Bonnie Charlie, neither of which would go without comment," Sabrina explained practically. "We've a hut in the marsh and that will suffice. After all, I don't plan on an extended visit. Lucien is so arrogant that he cannot imagine that I will not fall in with his plans, and he doesn't have the time to waste searching the countryside for me; so it's just a matter of out-waiting him, and then we can return to normal. Just wait and see," Sabrina said with growing excitement, her eyes bright with unshed tears as she masked the hurt within her with pretended exuberance. "We'll go on picnics again, and this time Richard shall go riding with us, and we can have so much fun. We'll forget all of this soon. You'll see it'll all end soon."

Mary lowered her eyes, hiding her expression from Sabrina's sharp gaze, hiding the doubt and fears that she knew for a certainty would come true.

&

"I thought I might be ostracized at dinner this evening," Lucien said dryly as Mary entered the salon, the first of the family to appear since afternoon.

Mary curtsied and approached the duke, an earnest look on her face as she stood before him. "I would like to speak honestly with you, if I may?"

Lucien smiled cynically. "By all means, it would be a pleasure and like a breath of fresh air to hear the truth around here."

They sat down in facing chairs and Mary began haltingly, "You must have a very poor opinion indeed, your grace, of our family, but you see us in unusual circumstances." She nervously twisted her lace handkerchief as Lucien watched and listened while sipping a brandy, having made himself perfectly at home.

"You are privileged to know our family secret, but I wonder if you've fully realized the extent of it?" she asked timidly.

Lucien smiled. "Had I not personally discovered the secret of the highwayman's identity I would not believe it if told."

"Did you know that we fled Scotland for our lives one cold, very bleak and terrible day? We had no future, no real plans, just a memory of this house where we were born, but which we had not seen in over six or seven years. We'd lived since our mother's death with her father in Scotland."

Lucien's interest had been caught, and he commented, "Bonnie Charlie now makes more sense."

Mary nodded sadly. "Yes, we are part Scots, although Sabrina bears the most resemblance to our English side of the family, Richard and I obviously showing our Scots heritage. Sabrina was, however, influenced the most by our grandfather. Richard was too young, and I," she paused almost apologetically, "well, I had not the wild spirit of Rina. Grandfather and she were kindred spirits."

Lucien nodded. "Raised by a Highland chieftain, no wonder she's an unprincipled little wildcat."

Mary looked down at her hands in her lap. "Sabrina saw him die. I did too, but in my dreams. Rina was actually there at Culloden."

"Sabrina was witness to that battle? My God," Lucien breathed, "she must have only been a child."

"She still carries the scars. She has nightmares and will not to this day wear red."

"The nightmares, of course," Lucien remembered.

"Can you imagine what that was like? The killing, the blood? Grandfather died in her arms in a crofter's hut in the hills," Mary told him softly, her voice edged with tears. "I'll never forget her face when she came back to the castle. It was like porcelain. I thought at the time if I stretched my hand out my fingers would touch cold china. She had seemed to age a century in a couple of hours."

Mary looked up into Lucien's thoughtful eyes, then looking around the room she gestured, encompassing it all, including herself. "All that you see, both here and on the estate, is because of Rina. Do you think this house was as it is now when we arrived? The whole estate had gone to seed. Our tenants were starving, the commons had been eaten up by the larger landowners, especially Lords Malton and Newley who have bought up most of the land in this valley, including a great portion of ours. When we arrived here in England we were virtually penniless. How could we live? Taxes had increased exorbitantly and the marquis' solicitors were being forced into selling unless we came up with the money. The marquis was living in Europe and could not have cared less.

"We had no other choice but to get the money any way that we could. So we paid our taxes, and then fixed up Verrick

House and the estate so that we could begin to support ourselves, and gradually as our finances increased we began to help the villagers."

Mary stared at the duke unashamedly. "I'm not excusing our actions. I'm not saying we've had the right to steal, but it was from those who had cheated others out of what they'd earned and was rightfully theirs. And we would've stopped soon, but then you had to catch Rina, and then the marquis showed up and blackmailed us into trying to catch rich husbands. Everything started going wrong." She shook her head helplessly. "I know things are changing, but Sabrina will not admit it."

"She will not accept it, or me. Is that what you are trying to tell me?" Lucien asked. "Are you warning me?"

"I just wanted you to understand everything about us, so you would be kind to Rina. I thought if you knew why she has done what she has, then you would treat her differently. She isn't bad, but you've wounded her pride and she is not one to forgive that. If you intend to win her, your grace, you will have to get her to forgive you first."

"I already have won her," Lucien replied arrogantly, "but I'm glad that you confided in me, for it does explain many things to me, and I will act accordingly."

Mary shook her head. He was just as arrogant and stubborn as Sabrina. How could they ever work their problems out? Should she warn him that Sabrina was planning to escape him yet again? Wouldn't it be far better to end it all right now? The outcome would be the same whether today or next week; for Sabrina could no longer change things, regardless of how hard she tried. Mary realized that Sabrina would never forgive her for telling Lucien, but she was worried about her health, and would have to risk Sabrina's anger.

"She is leaving," she told him quietly.

Lucien looked startled. "When?" he demanded, getting to his feet quickly.

"Now, at least that is what she has planned, and she intends to stay away until she has enough money to buy you off or you run out of time."

"Buy me off, eh?" Lucien said angrily. "We'll see about that."

"I think you should not wait any longer than necessary to marry her. Take her away from here right now. Kidnap her if necessary, but get her away from here. I feel that it is urgent that you do," Mary pleaded with him.

"You needn't fear, Lady Mary, for I shall have Sabrina under hand soon enough," he promised as he strode purposefully from the room. Mary sat silently staring for a few minutes, looking up as Aunt Margaret entered, a vague smile on her face as she drifted to the settee.

"He will not find her," Aunt Margaret whispered, a conspiratorial smile on her lips as she sat down and began to separate her tapestry threads.

Lucien strode unceremoniously back into the room, his scar livid across his cheek. "Damn her, she's gone," he swore, then upon seeing Aunt Margaret sitting complacently in the corner, apologized, "My pardon, ladies."

"This is our aunt, Lady Margaret Verrick," Mary said, her eyes lingering on Lucien, "and this is the Duke of Camareigh, Aunt Margaret."

Aunt Margaret looked up, her faded violet-blue eyes dreamy as she stared at Lucien. "We know a secret, don't we, Mary? Did you know that I once had a lover who looked much as you do?" She paused, her eyes unfocused. "No, I think maybe his eyes were a different color." She looked up at Lucien expectantly for a moment, then returned to her sorting of colors.

Lucien frowned, eyeing the spaniels sitting like privileged princes on either side of Lady Margaret before turning back to Mary. "The little fool, I thought she would see sense by now. What can she hope to do?"

"Sabrina is very proud, and you have humiliated her. She will not forget that, your grace," Mary told him. "She intends to give all of the money she has acquired to the marquis."

Lucien swore beneath his breath. "The marquis is probably in France by now," he informed Mary, who looked up startled. "I paid the marquis and the contessa a considerable sum for the honor of marrying Sabrina. What she is doing now is

completely useless and putting her in unnecessary danger,"
Lucien spoke angrily as he came to stand before Mary, a glint
in his eyes. "Will you tell me, Lady Mary, where she is?"

"If I knew, I would," Mary told him honestly, "but she
has so many hiding places that you will not find her until she
desires it." Mary watched the duke uncertainly, then added
reluctantly, "I think we've another problem as well."

Lucien raised an eyebrow inquiringly. "Indeed? I wouldn't
have thought there could be anything else to complicate matters."

"There is a Colonel Fletcher who has been sent from
London especially to catch Bonnie Charlie."

Lucien shrugged in unconcern. "Surely that poses no threat
for little Sabrina? She has successfully eluded capture until
now. I doubt this colonel will have any more luck than his
fellow officers."

"I wish I could agree with you, but you see, he suspects
Sabrina of being Bonnie Charlie," Mary advised him bluntly,
noting the look of worry that crossed his aristocratic features
at her disclosure.

"Why should he suspect Sabrina? No one could believe
that Bonnie Charlie is a woman."

"Strange how coincidences can haunt you, but you see,
Colonel Fletcher was at Culloden and knows that we are from
Scotland. It's another coincidence that the highwayman is
Scots, too. The colonel is not a foolish man, your grace, and
by putting various incidents together he has discovered our
secret," Mary told him worriedly, "and I do not know if we
can trust him or not."

Lucien ran his finger along his scar. "He doesn't have
proof of his speculations, he only has suspicions?"

Mary nodded, and Lucien smiled. "I think we need not
worry about Colonel Fletcher, and should he get too interested in our affairs, I shall handle him," Lucien reassured her.
"But now it is vital that I find Sabrina before she embroils
herself deeper into this mess."

"I know she will stay away at least until next week when
you have to have wed her."

"But that no longer applies," Lucien informed her with

confidence. "I have been given a slight reprieve, which means I can outwait Sabrina." His face looked savage for an instant as he thought of her. "The little fool, why won't she admit defeat? She cannot win."

Mary shuddered as she stared at his face, for he would make a deadly enemy and a ruthless victor. Poor Sabrina. Why did her path have to cross the duke's? She didn't think Sabrina realized what she was up against with the duke—he would not give up until he had caught her. Mary debated with herself for an instant and then said softly, "We can get a message to her."

Lucien smiled. "I thought you might. How?" he demanded, his eyes glinting in anticipation.

Mary swallowed her guilt. "We are to leave a note at the church and she will pick it up, but not until Sunday, it would appear strange otherwise."

"You do realize that you've done the right thing? The sooner we have her, the safer she'll be. Why put off the inevitable? I'll have my way regardless of her efforts. A pity, however, that we must wait and you must suffer my presence as your guest," Lucien apologized dryly.

"I think a truce would not come amiss," Mary responded with a half-smile.

"Agreed upon, Lady Mary," Lucien quickly accepted, then added mockingly but with a definite warning in his sherry eyes as Richard entered the room slowly, "but I trust no more bullets will fly my way during my visit?"

Richard flushed red to the roots of his hair as he returned Lucien's direct gaze. "You are a guest, your grace, and will be treated accordingly," he answered solemnly, his eyes very serious behind his glasses.

Lucien smiled with genuine warmth. "I'll accept your word, Lord Faver, I believe that is your title. We weren't properly introduced, Richard, if I may, but as you are to become my brother-in-law, as indeed this whole family is soon to become my responsibility, I would prefer you to call me Lucien."

His smile encompassed them all, drawing them almost against their will under his influence as he set out to charm them and win them over to his point of view. Richard was caught and held by Lucien almost immediately. His young boy's ideals of manhood seemed to be epitomized by this arrogantly handsome and friendly Duke, and never having come in contact with a domineering and awe-inspiring man before, he experienced his first taste of idolization. He stared in fascination at Lucien, who was being his most persuasive, his quick wit and easy manners taking them off guard as he settled down for his wait at Verrick House.

◦◦◦

Sabrina entered the warm kitchen quietly, unheard by the woman whose back was turned as she filled a plate with a succulent stew.

"I could use some of that, Mrs. Taylor," she said softly from the door.

Mrs. Taylor jerked around, her face startled and the big wooden spoon raised threateningly. She pressed her hand to her pounding heart. "Lord, but you did give me a scare, Lady Sabrina. Put ten years on my life, you did." Her eyes took in Sabrina's boots and breeches and cocked hat. "I didn't know you had anything planned for this evening. Will and John are at the Faire Maiden. Expectin' them back shortly though for dinner."

"Nothing is planned," Sabrina told her in a strained voice.

Mrs. Taylor clucked her tongue. "Here now, sit down and let me give you some stew, you look close to collapsing." She pulled out a chair for Sabrina, who gratefully sank into it, and resting her elbows on the table watched as Mrs. Taylor prepared another plate and placed it before her with a large slice of bread beside it.

"I'm afraid it's not fancy, just leftovers. I really do apologize, Lady Sabrina," Mrs. Taylor said in embarrassment.

Sabrina had eaten several mouthfuls and looking up answered sincerely, "This tastes like nectar. I'm starved and no matter what it is, your cooking is superb. Please sit down and eat."

Mrs. Taylor beamed with pleasure and dipping her bread in the gravy on her plate began to enjoy her dinner. They ate in silence until they heard voices and the sound of feet, and jumping up Mrs. Taylor ladled two plates full of the hot stew as Will and John entered the kitchen. They halted in surprise as they saw Sabrina sitting at their table eating stew.

"Hello," Sabrina greeted them calmly.

"Charlie," Will began, "what are ye doing here?" He looked at her outfit and added in uncertainty, "Didn't think we had anything planned for tonight."

Sabrina shrugged in resignation. "I'm afraid it's a bit more complicated than that. I've been forced to flee my own home."

Will and John opened their mouths to speak, anger bristling in their faces.

"That father of yours ain't causin' trouble, is he? We'll teach him a lesson if he is."

"Aye, that we will," John agreed, doubling up his fists at the thought.

"Why don't you go ahead and eat while I tell you about it. There's no hurry, for I'm afraid he'll still be there when you've finished," Sabrina told them as they sat down. "It's not the marquis, but our old friend the duke, who has forced his way into my home," she paused uncomfortably, then rushed on, "and is forcing me into marriage with him."

"You're going to marry the duke?" Will sputtered, setting down his mug of ale with a thud as the three Taylors stared at Sabrina's flushed features in amazement.

"Yes. He's at the house now, with a letter of introduction and authority from the marquis. He is in control, and thoroughly enjoying himself," Sabrina told them bitterly.

"How is it he found you, Charlie?" Will asked, his plate of stew untouched.

"He saw me in London. I didn't tell you about meeting him because I didn't want to worry you, and only told you that we needed the money because the marquis was forcing Mary and me to marry for money—which is true. Only it's the duke they are forcing me to marry. The marquis will get a large settlement, and the duke needs a bride in order to inherit his estate—so they are both agreeable to the arrangement."

"The swine," John said murderously. "Shot me and hurt

you, locked up Will, and now forcing you to wed him." He cupped his chin in his big palm as he placed an elbow on the table and asked, "He tell the marquis about us? That how he's gettin' you to marry him? Blackmail?"

"Oh, Lord," Mrs. Taylor said and poured herself a mug of ale, taking a deep swallow gratefully.

Sabrina shook her head. "He didn't need to resort to that, although he would've if he'd had too. The marquis had already planned on forcing us into marriage with any rich suitors we might have attracted, threatening to take Richard from us and throw Aunt Margaret out of Verrick House. He had a suitable son-in-law lined up when the duke interfered and ruined our chances. Because of some foolish stipulation in a will the duke must wed to inherit. His fiancée ran away from him, and so he has decided that I will replace her."

"Well, I never," Mrs. Taylor said indignantly.

"I will not be forced into marriage against my will, especially with the Duke of Camareigh, not after what he has done to us. He has humiliated me for the last time, and now he can suffer," Sabrina vowed, gazing at the pitying faces around her. "That's why we must get the money. You see, if we buy off the marquis, then I won't have to marry Lucien."

Will and John looked at each other without speaking, then, nodding, began to eat their stew. "Don't you worry, Charlie, we'll help you. No one, even some fancy Duke, will force you to do something you don't want to."

Mrs. Taylor patted her hand comfortingly. "You'll stay here?"

Sabrina shook her head. "No, it's not safe, in fact there is hardly any place that is anymore, what with Colonel Fletcher causing trouble, too. I'll stay in the marsh until this blows over. It won't be long, the duke doesn't have much time."

"Oh, you mustn't, you'll get the fever. It isn't good, Lady Sabrina," Mrs. Taylor argued with motherly concern.

"I'll be all right, Mrs. Taylor, and I'll be inside the hut," she reassured her, touched by her concern.

"It won't be for long, Charlie, we'll see to that," Will told her. "Damn, wish we hadn't already bought the Faire Maiden, or we could've given you the money."

Sabrina shook her head. "I couldn't have accepted it, but I appreciate the offer. You really are my best friends." She stood up, sighing as she looked around the warm little kitchen. "If I could trouble you for a few things, I'll be off."

"Of course. It's a disgrace that you should have to sneak off into the night like a criminal, while some blackguard makes himself at home in Verrick House."

"We'll ride along with you, Charlie," Will stated firmly, expecting disagreement.

"No, we're a recognizable trio by now. I'll be less conspicuous alone," Sabrina said, turning them down regretfully.

Mrs. Taylor gathered together some food and wrapped it in a large cloth. "This won't last you long," she told Sabrina doubtfully as she handed it to her.

"Listen, I'll ride over after you and bring you some blankets, and a cooking pot so you can heat up some coffee. Gotta gather you some tinder, anyway," Will said stubbornly.

Sabrina smiled, giving in without regret. "Thanks, I'll appreciate the company."

She rode through the darkness, taking care to avoid the roads as she made her way to the marshy ground. Once at the hut she stabled her horse under the overhang, rubbing him down and placing hay that had been stacked nearby for him to feed on. Sitting in the hut listening to the night sounds off the water, the frogs croaking and splashing about, Sabrina huddled in her greatcoat, staring at the emptiness of the room. She bit her lip as she felt a rush of self-pity overwhelm her, but vowed she wouldn't give in to it. She'd cried enough and it hadn't helped any—tears couldn't wash away fears or hurts. She shuddered as she heard a scampering on the roof, and then her horse neighed and stirred as another horse could be heard splashing through the water.

Will brought two thick blankets, a coffeepot and more provisions. He quickly gathered wood, which he stacked in the corner, then started a fire in the little fireplace, which slowly began to cut through the dampness that had clung to the walls. After he left, Sabrina rolled up in one blanket and put the other under her head and drowsily stared at the flickering flames that were beginning to die. She slept fitfully, her sleep punctuated by returning nightmares that left her shaking in a sweat.

Once during the night she got up to banish the nightmare and stood staring out the small window. Suddenly she drew in her breath sharply as she saw a shadowy form pass behind the large willow, then sighed in relief and happiness when the moon reappeared out of the clouds and shone on the figure, revealing Will as he paced quietly beside the hut. Sabrina settled down after that to sleep peacefully for the first time.

⁓

Lucien punched his pillow and then, unsatisfied, doubled it beneath his head. He sighed deeply and rolled onto his back, locking his hands behind his head. The satin of the pillow-case was smooth against his hand, reminding him of another smooth softness under his hand. Damn her. She was the most irritating female he'd ever met, besides his grandmother. He couldn't fathom Sabrina's moods and he was beginning to tire of her games of hide and seek. She really should be thankful that he was even offering marriage to her. She could do a lot worse, considering the atmosphere she'd been living in these past few years. What a moonstruck family. A dreamy-eyed aunt who flitted to and fro with her spaniels, a bristling cub taking wild shots at him, and a sister with eyes that stared through you. Of course, their sire was hardly a pillar of society. He'd never seen his only son, he had left his children to fend for themselves, leaving his daughters unprotected and unchaperoned on a country estate. For that he deserved to be horse whipped. No, he really was not in the least bit surprised that Sabrina had turned out the way she had. An overbearing, obstinate little roughneck just asking for trouble—well, she had found it this time. She would have her hands full when he caught up with her, and he would eventually—it was just a matter of waiting for the right time. If he was not so pressed for time he might enjoy this battle of wits and nerves, but too much was at stake to waste time. In the back of his mind he was still troubled by the problem of Percy and Kate and the distasteful memory of having to tell Lady Staddon that he thought Blanche might have met with foul play. And yet how could he prove anything? His cousins had been so careful not to become personally implicated in their schemes that he had no evidence to tie them to the attempts on his life. And of course as there was no body, how could he prove that Blanche had indeed been murdered? He rolled over and closing his eyes tried to get to sleep, only to be haunted by a pair of violet eyes.

The next morning he was making his way down the stairs when a soft voice spoke hesitantly, and looking around he saw a young girl standing below him in the hall.

"Yes?"

The girl's eyes were drawn to his scar as she said breathlessly, "There be a person wantin' a word with yer grace in the orchard. I'm a kitchen maid and Sims'll have my head if'n he was to find me in here and a'talkin' to ye."

She curtsied swiftly and excused herself before Lucien could ask who'd sent the message. Shrugging, he made his way outside and around to the back of the garden. A wrought-iron gate led to the orchard beyond, and opening it he winced as it squeaked protestingly and noisily. He passed through and walked into the orchard, the limbs of the trees heavy with ripening fruit. He looked around curiously, the only sound coming from a bird perched above him in the boughs.

The quiet peacefulness of the orchard was disturbed by the sharp, staccato snapping of twigs, and turning toward the sound Lucien came to a halt as two familiar figures emerged from behind a couple of tree trunks.

Lucien grinned humorlessly as he faced the two giants. "Well done, gentlemen," he complimented them sarcastically as they approached him warily. "Have you brought me a message from Bonnie Charlie? Ah, yes, I see that you have," he added in resignation as he became aware of their bunched fists.

"You've become a bit of a problem, Duke, and we thought

we might be able to change your mind about staying where you're not wanted," Will answered.

"I see," Lucien spoke softly, taking a step forward and spreading his legs, his booted feet firmly planted in the soft soil. "I take it all parties concerned are agreeable to this action of yours?"

"If you be meanin' Charlie, then aye, she wants you gone as well. You been treatin' the little lady kinda rough and we owes you for my shoulder and for tying up my brother."

"Nice to see you again, Duke," Will greeted him with a broad smile.

"And you intend to scare me off, is that it, and maybe inflict a few bruises while about it?"

Will smiled wider, and winking at John nodded his head. "You be real smart, duke. Now, we're fair, don't believe in ganging up on a helpless town dandy, so I'll let my brother here have a go at you first, he owes it to you."

John came forward slowly, his big fists raised threateningly as he circled Lucien, who stood his ground despite the size of the approaching figure.

John suddenly charged like a mad bull, sending his great bulk into Lucien's slighter figure, but Lucien ducked and sent John tumbling over his shoulder to land with a thud on his back. Roaring like a bear, John rose and charged again, only to be tripped by Lucien's outstretched boot and as he fell forward received a punch in the stomach that left him breathless as he stumbled into the ground.

Lucien spun as Will's fist collided with his jaw, knocking him to the ground. He rolled quickly aside and caught Will's uplifted, booted foot and gave it a vicious twist, throwing him off balance. As he fell heavily to the ground Lucien followed on top of him and punched him in the eye, dodging the big fist that whizzed by his ear, and landed another of his own on the giant's nose. He heard the reviving moan of his other opponent and quickly jumped to his feet. Reaching into his coat pocket he withdrew a pistol, and waiting for the large brothers to slowly pick themselves up he stood pointing the barrel at the two men.

"Well, well, the mighty do fall hard," he commented

with a grin, and then, feeling his own sore jaw, grimaced. "You should have known, gentlemen, that I do not frighten easily, nor do I take kindly to threats from country bumpkins. You may count yourselves lucky that I did not shoot one of you dead when you first threatened me. And you may tell Sabrina that her plan has failed and I am now, more than ever, determined to have my way. Do I make myself clear, my big friends?"

Will and John slouched uncomfortably, a look of grudging respect for their would-be victim's prowess with his fists warring with chagrined anger on their faces as they mumbled an indistinct reply.

"Not quite so voluble now, are you? Tell Sabrina I'll exact my revenge very shortly. She may count on it."

He turned and walked off, ignoring Will's, "Hey, wait a minute, you've got it all wrong!"

They watched his figure disappear behind the trees, then looked at each other silently for a moment.

"We done it good this time."

"Yeah," Will answered, holding his sleeve to his bloodied nose. "Made a bit more mischief than we'd planned. Charlie ain't going to like this. He's really out to get her now."

"Should've left it alone, I guess."

"Come on, let's be off before he returns and decides to put a hole in our thick skulls."

They trudged off, their big shoulders slumped dejectedly.

"Never seen anyone punch like that."

"Oughta be wrestlin' at the fair, the way he moves."

"Knocked down by a London gent in lace. Never hear the end of it if anyone knew," John complained.

"Been thinkin' maybe we ought not to tell Charlie about this," Will suggested.

John shook his massive head in agreement. "Nope, don't think we oughta."

Sabrina greeted them happily when they showed up in the afternoon, but as they came closer and her eyes scanned their bruised faces, her grin faded.

"What happened?"

Will shrugged. "Breaking up a fight in the inn. Couple of locals got carried away in an argument."

"You're in more danger running the Faire Maiden than you were as highwaymen," she laughed, accepting Will's explanation.

Sabrina sat down on a fallen tree trunk, the sun shining down on her shoulders and warming them. Her face was pale and drawn, throwing the smudges beneath her violet eyes into prominence.

John scuffed his feet as he said hesitantly, "You look pretty tired, Charlie, I wish you'd come and stay at Mam's. This marsh ain't good."

"I'm all right, really I am. All I need is a little rest. Once this is all over, then I can relax." She smiled. "If you really want to help me, then tell me what you've heard. Is the duke still at Verrick House, and has the marquis shown up yet?"

"No, haven't heard a word about the marquis, and I know for certain the duke's still at Verrick House," Will replied sourly, despite John's warning look. "In fact, he's getting mighty close to your family."

Sabrina's eyes narrowed and a flush appeared on her thin cheeks. "What do you mean?"

"Well, heard tell he's takin' yer brother out shootin' and even ridin'."

Sabrina jumped to her feet angrily. "How dare he make friends with my family. He's up to something, I'm sure. If only I could be there to deal with him."

Will and John looked at each other over Sabrina's head, both having seen the feverish look in her eyes and the agitated movement of her hands, but Will shook his head helplessly as Sabrina's hands went to her hips and she took up her defiant stance, her booted legs spread and reminding him suddenly and ironically of the duke.

"They'll all be sorry. No one mocks me. Lucien is going to be sorry he ever came here."

"Guess we better be gettin' back, and we'll see you tonight. Things been awful quiet the last day or two, hope somebody's on the road tonight at least."

Sabrina sighed. "All right, I'll see you then, and if you hear anything about a party let me know then. If we could just rob a few big parties that would be all we'd need to finish this once and for all."

As they turned to leave Sabrina got up and followed, calling to them. Coming up close she took one of each of their big hands and gave them a little squeeze. "Thank you for keeping me company last night. I truly appreciate it, but it's not really necessary."

"Don't like you being out here alone," Will replied gruffly. "Wouldn't be able to sleep anyway, thinkin' about it."

"Well, then, be sure to bring enough for us both to eat tonight. I don't like eating alone," Sabrina ordered good-naturedly.

"Sure, Charlie, John'll be here this evening," Will told her, feeling relieved at her acceptance of their company.

Sabrina waved as they rode off, a smile on her face, but as they disappeared, so did her smile, If she did not feel so bad she would be bored senseless, sitting about this dilapidated hut worrying and wondering what was happening at Verrick House, unable to do anything except helplessly watch events move beyond her control.

She shivered with a chill and wrapping one of the blankets around her went outside again into the warm sunshine and leaned against the side of the hut, feeling the sun's rays beating down on her and soaking into her chilled bones. A muffled sneeze shook her body and closing her eyes against the brightness she slumped down, resting her aching head on her drawn-up knees.

By the next morning, after a long and unprofitable night waiting on the side of the road, she was congested and her throat was raw and hurt with every swallow. John hovered clumsily about trying to be helpful, but only succeeded in annoying her as she watched in suffering silence. When he left and Will returned in his stead, he was loaded down with salves and brews concocted to relieve her headache and sore throat.

"A bottle of rum would've done as well," Sabrina complained with a smile as Will unloaded his medicines and extra blankets.

"Mam said to brew these herbs and honey for you and to rub this on your—" he hesitated in embarrassment "—your chest."

"I think I can manage that much," Sabrina assured him in a husky whisper which ended in a painful cough. She gratefully accepted the hot brew, feeling its soothing qualities slide down her sore throat as she relaxed next to the fire Will had started.

"Brought some rum, too. Figure it's always helped me the most," Will chuckled as he placed the bottle on the table and winked conspiratorially.

He straddled a chair and rubbed his ear as he gave a deep sigh of regret. "Wouldn't you know, there's a big party going on at Lord Newley's tonight, but you're in no shape to go, Charlie."

Sabrina looked up at him from her cocoon of blankets, her small nose pink from sneezing. "I have no choice but to go. This could be the last time, Will," she said in growing excitement.

"I don't know, Charlie. You're mighty sick with the fever. Wouldn't do to pass out in the middle of Lord Newley's guests."

Sabrina sniffed, whether at the thought of passing out or with her cold, Will couldn't tell. "You don't need to worry about me, I'll get through this night if it kills me."

"That's what I'm afraid of," Will commented glumly.

"Who's supposed to be there? Is it really a big party?" A reluctant smile tugged at the corner of Will's mouth. "Well, that's the odd thing about it, Charlie, you see it's in honor of you and the duke. Sort of an engagement party you might call it."

Sabrina's eyes grew wide and she gave a weak laugh that turned into a cough. "Yes, it's appropriate that I should attend this party. I wouldn't miss it for the world," Sabrina chuckled, her feverish eyes glowing brighter in anticipation.

Late that evening Sabrina leaned against the table as she braided her thick hair with unsteady fingers and tucked it up under the wig. Her face felt on fire and her head ached until she thought it would burst. For the last time, she hoped fervently, would she be putting this mask over her face. She set the cocked hat firmly on her head and pulled on her greatcoat. She swayed dizzily as she stuck her pistol into her belt, and holding onto the edge of the table tightly, closed her eyes. She had to get through this night. It meant everything—just this one last time, she prayed. She must find the strength to see it through. She opened her eyes and the room had stopped spinning, and lifting her chin she pulled on her gloves determinedly and left the hut, the swagger returning to her walk as she strode across the soft ground to meet Will and John, the spurs on her jackboots jingling into the quiet night.

⤬

"A party?" Mary repeated in amazement. "Surely you jest?"

"No," Lucien answered seriously. "It would seem that Newley decided to give one in my honor, or I should say in Sabrina's and mine."

"And you intend that we shall go? I wouldn't think that you would care to? We should be here in case Sabrina should decide to return."

"That is exactly why I shall be at that party. Can you imagine Sabrina passing up the chance to appear at her own engagement party? I certainly cannot, and I intend to be there as well," Lucien said, "just to make sure some trigger-happy guest doesn't cheat me out of a bride."

"You're right, she will be there. I know her too well to believe that she would not show up," Mary agreed unhappily, her face pale.

Lucien glanced at her, about to comment, when she suddenly pressed her fingers to her temples, her eyes turning cloudy as she swayed as though about to faint. Lucien rushed forward and scooped her into his arms, an expression of concern on his hard features as he began to lower her into a chair.

He was bending over her, his arms still about her when Colonel Fletcher walked into the salon, his expression of anticipation changing to one of startled jealousy as he thought he saw Mary wrapped in some man's arms.

"What the devil?" he said roughly as he quickly came forward and pulled Lucien away from Mary.

Lucien turned swiftly to confront whoever had manhandled him, his look of anger changing to recognition as he saw a soldier facing him and realized that this must be the colonel.

Colonel Fletcher saw Lucien's eyes narrow and a look of derision curve his lips, and drew himself up stiffly, wondering who this scar-faced gentleman was. They stood glaring at each other until a moan from Mary drew their attention, then each made a move toward her. They stopped as her eyes opened and stared unseeingly past them, the gray turning silvery before their startled eyes.

A pulse was beating rapidly in her throat and her hands gripped the arms of her chair, her knuckles showing white. "I see... a mist and people... and cries... I see Sabrina there... and Bonnie Charlie. Oh, God, she's on the ground... and I see pistols... and the duke's scarred face. But it's so clouded. I can feel the cold... Rina needs help... the duke is fighting Bonnie Charlie... double... double faces... I'm so confused," she cried, "Sabrina!" Mary held out her hands to some invisible image before her.

Lucien felt a shiver crawl over him as he stared in disbelief at the haunted face before him. Colonel Fletcher bent down and taking hold of Mary's shoulders gave her a sharp shake. Her head rolled sideways and her eyelids fluttered before her head dropped to her chest. She was breathing heavily, perspiration beading her forehead.

Lucien poured a sherry and handed it to the colonel, who tipped back Mary's head and held it to her bluish-tinged lips. A small drop trickled into her mouth and down her throat as her blood once again circulated warmly and color began to return to her face.

Colonel Fletcher lifted Mary in his arms and without a glance at the duke carried her from the room. Lucien picked up the forgotten sherry and drained it easily as he sat down and prepared to wait impatiently for some answers.

Colonel Fletcher removed Mary's jacket-bodice and turning her over on the bed, loosened the laces of her corset. He settled her comfortably against the pillows and taking one of her cold hands began to massage it gently.

Taking a deep breath Mary opened her eyes and looked into the colonel's concerned face. He ran his warm hands up her bare arms, and Mary blushed in startled embarrassment as she became aware that only her thin chemise covered her breasts.

"Why you women insist upon tying yourselves up until you cannot breathe adequately is beyond me. No wonder you are so pale half the time," the colonel chastised her gently. "Besides, you do not need such devices. Your waist is already so tiny." He let his hands move from her shoulders over her breasts, lingering for a second before they slid around her waist and he lowered his head and took her trembling lips, demanding a kiss that left her breathless once again.

"Terence," Mary whispered. "This is not right." His lips continued to caress hers as she tried to resist him, but she let herself be kissed, feeling a thrill as his mouth pressed against the soft swell of her breasts above the lacy corset front. Pulling his head back to hers she found his mouth with her eager lips, surprising him with her first real response to him. Mary drew back suddenly and turned her head away. "Please, Terence."

Colonel Fletcher sat back reluctantly and allowed her to try and compose herself. "Will you tell me about it, Mary?" he asked, watching her carefully.

Mary nodded her red head dejectedly. "I want to confide in you, Terence, I want to trust you," she said softly, looking up at him with pleading gray eyes.

Terence reached out for her and held her comfortingly in his arms. "I would never hurt you, Mary. Trust me, let me help."

"You aren't just pretending to like me so you can trick me into revealing something?"

Colonel Fletcher put a hard hand beneath her chin and raising her face to his, looked earnestly down into her beseeching eyes. "I will not lie to you, Mary. Have you never met someone for the first time and known instinctively that this was to be a friend? Well, when I first set eyes on you I knew that I meant to make you my wife. Does that surprise you, Mary? No, I can see that it doesn't, because I think deep inside you felt the same, also. But I am a man of quick decisions. I've had to be to survive the battles I've been in. And I've decided I want you, Mary. I'm not going to wait for the marquis to pick some rich suitor for you as he has for your sister. I'm not some young, fresh-faced lad courting his first love. I'm an old bachelor, certainly not the ideal man you'd dreamed of marrying and raising children with. I'm over thirty, Mary. What are you, eighteen or nineteen? Maybe there are too many years between us, but damned if I won't make you a good husband. I'll care for you, protect you, and love you as best I can. I want a family, a settled home. I'm tired of camping out, feeling the cold in my bones at night. I want a woman to warm my bed and give me fine sons and daughters."

He touched his finger to Mary's lips, feeling their contour as he looked deeply into her eyes. "Are you woman enough for me, Mary? I think so, and I intend to ask for your hand in marriage. I shouldn't imagine your father would have any objections. I'm the younger son of an earl, and I've a comfortable estate I intend to retire to soon. You'll like it there, Mary, I promise you." His gray eyes glowed in memory of his home as he described the scene to her vividly.

"It's north of here in a valley of beautiful lakes that shimmer under the moonlight. It's a place for lovers, Mary. And I'm not so old that I have forgotten how to love my lady to her heart's desire. The house is small but comfortable, and I've added a wing that will be completed soon. In autumn the—"

"Oh, stop, please," Mary whispered. "Do not torture me so."

Colonel Fletcher stopped abruptly, his eyes narrowed. Mary looked away from his steady gaze, unable to bear the hurt expression in his eyes. Her hands found his and curled into them as she searched his face for answers to her doubts.

"You honor me, Terence, by your proposal, but I cannot wed you, nor anyone," she explained softly. "I am needed here. After what I have just seen, I know I shall be. I could not marry you and leave my family when they needed me."

Mary looked down at their locked hands and added, "I cannot ask you to wait, either, it wouldn't be fair."

Terence wiped a tear from her face and pressed his mouth against her lips softly. "I shall wait, Mary, for you are the only woman I want for my wife. And I understand your decision, even though I am not happy about it. But your sister is in a great deal of trouble," he told her seriously. "I would like to talk with her. Would you tell her that?"

Mary's lips trembled. "She is gone. She has run away from the duke and will not marry him. That is why she has masqueraded as Bonnie Charlie again. She had quit doing it, until now." Mary's hands tightened on the colonel's as she tried to make him understand. "You do see why she has done it? We had to live, we had no money. Sabrina only did it to save us. You do see?"

"Yes, I do. But why does she pursue this dangerous path? She could marry the duke and be done with it all."

Mary shook her head regretfully. "Sabrina is a very passionate person, and she hates the marquis and the duke passionately. They both made serious mistakes when they threatened her and humiliated her the way they have, and she'll never forgive either of them. But what is so tragic is that it's all so useless. The Duke has already paid off the marquis, who has left for Europe. Sabrina will have no one to hand over all of her ill-gotten gains to, she'll have endangered herself for nothing. I'm so worried about her. She is so close to falling apart. Having the duke here does not help matters at all, for I believe he is not one to concede defeat."

"No, he is not," Colonel Fletcher remarked, "for I've heard of him, and he has quite a reputation."

"One I live up to, Colonel," Lucien commented from the doorway.

Mary gave a small scream and huddled against Colonel Fletcher's broad chest as she stared at the scarred face of the duke. His eyes were stony as he surveyed the scene. "I gather congratulations are in order?"

"Yes, they are," Colonel Fletcher answered coolly, measuring up the duke, who was standing carelessly in the doorway.

"If I might intrude into the festivities for just a moment?" Lucien asked, his eyes flickering over Mary's revealing neckline meaningfully. "I would like to know just what the hell that scene was about downstairs? You have the Sight?"

Mary found her jacket and was fastening it over her corset as she answered. "Yes, but I never see enough to tell anyone much. That's the curse of it, I see just enough to cause me to worry. I'm not even sure now what I told you."

"It had to do with Sabrina and myself—and Bonnie Charlie. Is something going to happen to Sabrina?" Lucien demanded bluntly.

"Yes," Mary answered faintly, "but I can't tell you when."

"Well, I shall see that it doesn't happen this evening, and then when Sunday comes I shall have her," Lucien promised.

Colonel Fletcher got to his feet. "I didn't think anyone knew about Bonnie Charlie's true identity. I rather doubt that she told you?" the colonel asked, looking between the two silent people curiously.

"It is not important how I found out, Colonel," Lucien informed him brusquely, "but it is important that the future duchess of Camareigh, and your future sister-in-law, is not arrested or shot this evening." He looked at the colonel searchingly. "I trust we need not fear that happening?"

"I am not one to follow orders blindly, your grace," Colonel Fletcher reassured Lucien. "I shall be there this evening, also, just to assure that nothing unforeseen occurs, and I shall see that my men are elsewhere and clear of the vicinity."

"Thank you, Colonel. You will not regret it, for you'll not have Bonnie Charlie troubling you after Sunday," Lucien told him with arrogant self-confidence.

"I once told Lady Sabrina that she needed someone to guide her, and she informed me she'd not met the man who could, but I believe she has," the colonel said, giving the duke a curious look.

Lucien smiled slightly. "I think we see eye to eye on this matter, Colonel. The sooner Bonnie Charlie is put out of action, the better. However, I am worried about this vision Lady Mary has seen. Maybe it was to warn us about tonight? I do not want to try and take her, even though we could, when she is armed and her two big friends are likely to do something foolish and get us all killed. Any word from you before Sunday would be suspect, I'm afraid, so it will have to be then. I just hope nothing happens to her before then."

"I fear that you are right. As Bonnie Charlie, she has led me into bogs and brambles, and has so many hiding places that we could never find her. Nor would she be likely to believe a summons from Mary. We will just have to make sure nothing happens tonight. That's all that we can do," the colonel advised.

Mary looked between the two men, so different and yet so much alike, as they stood there deciding the future of Sabrina, and of all of the Verricks.

❧

Lucien sat quietly alert at the large banqueting table. This was where it all had begun. They had come full circle, he thought. A look of cynical amusement crossed his features as he stared at the velvet hangings so similar to those that she had first appeared out of. Would she dare come tonight—knowing full well that he would be here?

He ran a forefinger down his scar. Yes, she would. She knew he expected her to, and she was not one to turn down a challenge. Last time he had been surprised, an unsuspecting guest. Now he sat here, watching the others as before, yet knowing that at any moment those curtains would part and in would step Bonnie Charlie. He looked at the laughing Lord Malton, whose face was flushed from brandy, and couldn't control the slight smile that curved his mouth at the thought of that jovial lord's soon-to-be astonishment.

Colonel Fletcher caught his eye in a questioning look from across the table and Lucien shrugged his shoulders in reply. It was growing late, and soon the gentlemen would join the ladies in the salon. He thought with pity of Lady Mary having to sit through their chatter not knowing what was happening, and yet knowing that something would.

Lucien took a sip of brandy, looking down momentarily as a burst of laughter drowned out all other sounds, and when he looked up he couldn't control his start of surprise as he looked into Bonnie Charlie's masked face as she stood silently behind Newley's chair, her pistol pointed at the assembled guests.

Gradually the others became aware of the newcomer and abruptly quieted. Only Newley, whose back was to the pistol, still laughed until he slowly became aware of the silence in the room. He jumped and knocked over his glass as a voice said behind him and much too close to his ear for comfort:

"Very amusing, I must remember to tell that one to my friends some eve while we sip ale," she mocked.

Will and John moved into the room threateningly as Bonnie Charlie swaggered forward. "Well, well, I feel quite at home seeing all of my old friends here this evening. Reminds me of another profitable evening. I trust this one will turn out as well."

Lord Newley's face turned ruddy with suppressed rage, his eyes bulging as he spluttered, "This is an affront to all decency."

"Now gentlemen, you all know what I shall require, and I dislike having to repeat a warning," Bonnie Charlie said as she saw Lord Newley's fingers come in contact with a dinner knife. She smiled with approval as his fingers stiffened and he slowly removed his hand from the table, his shoulders hunched forward as he felt the barrel of the highwayman's pistol pressed against his back.

"Be gracious and generous, gentlemen, for this, I promise you, will be the last time I shall trouble you or be an uninvited guest in your homes."

A murmur of conjecture went around the table at the highwayman's words.

"I'm not a man to push my luck and as you've all shown such generosity, I find I can retire to my country estate and live the life of a gentleman. I may even sup with you gentlemen, or meet you over a hand of cards, but you'll never know that it is I, will you?" Bonnie Charlie taunted them, her voice a husky whisper.

"Preposterous!" Lord Malton exclaimed. "The only time we'll toast you is when you are hanging from the gallows."

Bonnie Charlie laughed. "Ah, well, I suppose it was too much to have asked. However, I shall demand something else of you gentlemen."

Will held his pistol aimed at the table as John circulated among them collecting all of the valuables while Bonnie Charlie kept them preoccupied with her insults. As he came to Lucien he hesitated, looking to Bonnie Charlie for guidance. With a smile she stepped forward, taking John's place.

"Allow me," she said mockingly. "After all, his grace is the guest of honor, is he not?"

She bent close to Lucien and for the first time since entering the room looked him directly in the eyes. Sabrina had prepared herself for his anger, but was still startled by its intensity as he glared back at her. Taking his hand in hers she withdrew the diamond ring from his finger and then slipped her hand inside his coat, removing his watch from his waistcoat pocket along with his purse of money. For an instant she returned his stare, and then amongst the surprised gasps of disbelief of the diners, ran her finger down the length of his scar.

"The game is well-played," Lucien whispered to her as she straightened, "but you hold the losing hand, Charlie."

Bonnie Charlie's eyes glittered as she turned from Lucien abruptly to face Colonel Fletcher, who sat watching silently farther down the table.

"Well, now, if it isn't the brave leader of the king's men? Look well and long, Colonel, for this is as close as you shall ever come to Bonnie Charlie," she said with a laugh that turned into a deep cough. As the colonel began to remove his ring she held up a detaining hand. "No, Colonel, I have stolen enough from you this evening. To be held up by Bonnie Charlie, the highwayman you so determinedly chase, is penalty enough."

With a husky laugh Bonnie Charlie turned and strode to the window, but before she could disappear through it, there was a scuffle behind her. Turning, her pistol raised instinctively, she saw Lucien wrestle a pistol from the gentleman beside him, knocking it harmlessly to the rug, where it went off with a deafening roar. Meeting Lucien's sherry eyes, her own wide with surprised fear at the narrowness of her escape, Bonnie Charlie fled, Will and John close behind. The hangings billowed behind them as they left the gentlemen in stupefied silence.

"What the devil?" cried the gentleman who'd drawn his pistol, only to have it taken from him by Lucien. He glared at the duke angrily. "Why in blazes did you do that? I could've killed the swine."

"Yes, what kind of fool stunt was that?" demanded Lord Newley, his voice coming faintly and almost inaudibly as armed footmen crowded into the room and women's voices raised in alarm could be heard in the hall.

Before Lucien could respond to the charges made, the colonel answered in an authoritative voice that cut through the noise effectively, bringing a sudden hush.

"It was a crackbrained stunt to pull that pistol on the highwaymen in the first place. With five pistols trained on you, you do not take a wild shot at one of them. Do you imagine they would have just stood there? Hardly, they would have gotten off four or five good shots into any number of us unfortunate enough to have been in the way. Would that have been worth it? To leave widows sitting in the salon because of a foolhardy act?" he scoffed. "If his grace had not acted quickly, I doubt whether Lord Newley here would be alive, or even Lord Malton, sitting in the direct line of fire as he was."

"Good God," Lord Malton swallowed nervously. "Never thought of that. Would've tried to get me first, eh? I owe you my life, your grace," he breathed heavily, fanning himself with a linen napkin.

Mary was the first of the ladies to enter the dining room. She looked around quickly, and then to Colonel Fletcher, who shook his head in answer to her silent question. With a sigh of relief she came and stood behind the colonel's chair, his hand finding hers comfortingly. She looked to the duke, and couldn't suppress a shudder as she saw his eyes blazing with fury as he stared at the opened window Bonnie Charlie had fled through moments before, barely escaping with her life. The scar on his cheek looked angry, casting a savage expression over his features.

Lucien stood up, looking the perfect gentleman in his cinnamon velvet coat and gold-embroidered waistcoat. Shaking the lacy cuffs of his shirt indolently before tossing off the last of his brandy, he looked to Mary and the colonel.

"I think we will take our leave of you, Newley. I fear the excitement has been too great for Lady Mary. If you'll forgive us?"

"Of course," Lord Newley answered quickly. "I am outraged by this act and cannot apologize enough for the indignity and dishonor this blackguard has brought to my house." Lord Newley looked at the duke, mystified. "It is certainly odd the way the highwayman seems to dislike you personally and almost delights, it would seem, in taunting you, your grace."

"No doubt he disliked the cut of my coat," Lucien replied shortly, his temper barely under control. "Goodnight, gentlemen," Lucien said as he followed Mary and the colonel from the room.

❧

Will and John pulled off their masks and dropped them onto the table without regret. They looked at each other silently as they stood awkwardly beside the table where Sabrina sat, her head bent in her hands as she rested her elbows on the rough wood. She shivered and a cough shook her shoulders. Will signaled with his chin and John quickly set about lighting a fire.

"Do you know," Sabrina spoke suddenly, her voice hardly above a whisper, "I wish that bullet had hit me."

"Charlie!" John exclaimed with alarm at the lackluster tone of her voice.

She raised her head and stared at them dejectedly. "Why shouldn't I wish that? It would end all of our troubles. Besides, do you think I liked what I became tonight? I really was Bonnie Charlie. I felt all of the defiance and hatred that he would have felt. When I heard that pistol go off, I nearly pulled the trigger and shot that fool. It was so instinctive, so unthinkingly done, that I think I really am turning into a highwayman."

"Come on, Charlie, everything will be all right. You're just feeling bad, that's all. Things will look better tomorrow." Will tried to comfort her.

"I'm glad it's over," Sabrina said tearfully. "I don't think I could do it anymore. I'm so tired."

"Sure, Charlie," Will said softly, signaling to John to leave. "You better get some rest. John's fixed something hot for you, and if you want something we'll be outside, so just give a yell."

Sabrina regretfully watched them go. She didn't want to be alone. She needed someone to hold her and comfort her. She felt miserable and cold and just wanted to go home to her own bed. Seeing Lucien tonight had stirred up memories she wanted to forget and dreams of what could have been between them. She stared into the flames of the small fire, feeling no warmth from it, and closing her eyes she huddled under the blankets trying to get warm. Tomorrow she would check the church for a note from Mary. Maybe Lucien would have given up. He would realize after tonight that she never would.

Everything was quiet and peaceful the next morning as Sabrina entered the old Norman church, walking through the arched doorway and making her way up the aisle past the box pews to her family's place in the church. Sliding along the smoothly worn seat, Sabrina reached down and feeling beneath the seat for the loose stone in the floor, kicked it loose with the toe of her boot.

She felt in the space and withdrew the folded piece of paper triumphantly. Resetting the stone in its natural place she sat up and unfolded the note, her face showing confusion as she stared down at the blank piece of paper.

"There is nothing there," a voice informed her from the end of the pew.

Sabrina jerked her head up in surprise. Lucien stood casually blocking her exit, a satisfied gleam in his eyes as he stared at her frustrated face. He stood arrogantly in his black velvet breeches so similar to her own, his frock coat opened to reveal his frilly shirt front, his hand negligently on a lean hip as he tapped his booted leg with a silver-headed malacca cane.

Sabrina wished she had kept her mask on to hide the emotions that must be playing across her face as she stared at him, her hands clenched at her sides. "A trick?" she asked shakily.

"I'm afraid so. The game is up, as I told you last night when you so very nearly got your fool head blown off."

"How did you know? Only Mary—" she began, her voice fading as the awful truth dawned on her suddenly. "Mary? Mary told you?"

Sabrina's face grew white as she looked to Lucien for confirmation, her violet eyes feverishly bright.

"Yes, she finally became sensible and acted wisely." Lucien's expression became intent as he began to notice her bright eyes and thin cheeks spotted with color. Her breathing was raspy and came in quick little breaths. "You're ill. Are you trying to kill yourself?" he demanded , infuriated at the poor sight she presented.

"It would be a blessing. My own sister turning traitor. How could she?" Sabrina repeated, forgetting Lucien's presence for the moment.

"She loves you and cares what happens to you. That is why she did the right thing and told me. Also, she knows that your escapade is useless, for the marquis has already left for Europe, with a large settlement from me," Lucien told her, delivering the final blow.

Sabrina crumpled the thin piece of paper into a wad and let it drop. "You," she laughed, "have brought me nothing but trouble."

"You brought the trouble on yourself, Sabrina. After the way you acted last night, I should've let that fool put a hole through you."

"Fine, that would've saved us all a lot of time and trouble," Sabrina replied in a choked voice, "only then you'd be put to the trouble of finding another unwilling bride, and time is running short."

"That's right. I need you, Sabrina, but I also want you at my mercy for awhile. You need to be schooled in polite manners and the proper deportment for well-bred young ladies. I shall enjoy teaching you a few things, little Sabrina," Lucien responded, reining in his temper as she continued to defy him.

"Indeed, your grace, I fear I am beyond learning new tricks to amuse you." As she spoke Sabrina allowed her hand to slowly move toward her pistol, keeping her body slightly turned from his view. But Lucien had anticipated her thoughts and lunged at her, knocking her arm away and quickly finding her pistol and sword and disarming her as he spun her around to him, easily resisting her weak efforts to struggle free.

"You never give up, do you? And would you have shot me? I wonder," he murmured doubtfully. "Or were you going to use it on yourself?" He pressed his hand against her forehead and said with growing concern, "You're burning up. If I ever get my hands on those two big, dim-witted friends of yours for letting you hide out heaven knows where, I'll have their hides."

Sabrina jerked her head back and looked up at him, her eyes blazing with emotion. Her body felt weighted down and she could hardly find the breath to speak.

"I hate you," she began, only to have her words cut off by a spasm of coughing.

"I've heard that too many times to take any notice of it, and I'm beginning to suspect you've a very limited vocabulary," he replied and picked her unprotesting form up in his arms and carried her from the church to his carriage waiting outside.

Lady Malton was leaving the vicarage and glanced across the churchyard inquisitively as she recognized the Duke of Camareigh's carriage sitting in front of the church. Her round face beneath her canary-yellow bonnet sharpened with interest as the duke came striding from the church with what looked to be a young gentleman clasped tightly in his arms. All Lady Malton could see were a pair of booted feet bobbing up and down and an eagle's feather peeping over the duke's shoulder. She squinted her eyes to see better, stepping quickly behind a bush when the duke glanced up, an ominous expression on his hard features.

How extraordinary, Lady Malton thought excitedly as the duke's carriage rumbled off, a riderless horse following behind. Something was very strange here. There was something so familiar about an eagle's feather. What was it? She gave a small gasp as she realized where she had seen an eagle's feather before, but what in the world would the Duke of Camareigh be doing carrying the notorious highwayman, Bonnie Charlie?

⤬

Sabrina knew little of the next couple of weeks as she burned with fever and shook with chills. Drinking herb teas and having evil-smelling salves rubbed on her chest was all she recalled when she finally recovered her senses.

She woke one morning exhausted and drained, yet wonderfully relaxed as she lay in her bed. The sheets were fresh and cool and smelled of lavender. One of the casement windows was open and a balmy, rose-scented breeze moved the pages of a book left open in a chair near the bed. She turned her head towards the door as she heard voices and then it opened as Mary came in carrying a tea tray. She crossed the room silently and placed the tray on the table beside the chair with the book in it. Moving the book she sat down and poured herself a cup of tea.

Sabrina frowned as she noticed the dark circles under Mary's eyes and the paleness of her cheeks. She was surprised by the carelessness of Mary's appearance. Her primrose gown was wrinkled and had a stain near the hem and was too loose around the waist, and her hair was untidy with stray curls hanging down her neck. She looked tired and worried as she sipped her tea. This wasn't at all like Mary.

"Mary," Sabrina spoke distinctly from the bed.

Mary looked up startled, her cup clattering precariously in the saucer as she stared at Sabrina's face, the violet eyes clear and lucid as they returned her stare.

"Rina!" she cried tearfully, the tea sloshing out of the cup into the saucer as she hurriedly set it on the table. "You're yourself again?"

She rushed over to the bed and placed her hand against Sabrina's cool cheek and then kissed both thankfully. Sabrina looked at her in bewilderment.

"What is wrong? You seem so distraught," she asked Mary, who was perched on the side of the bed watching her carefully. "And you don't look yourself, either. I've never seen you so rumpled before. You look as though you'd slept in your clothes," Sabrina teased.

Mary smiled with embarrassment. "As a matter of fact, I have."

At Sabrina's expression of disbelief she nodded. "Yes indeed, I've slept many a night in my clothes since you've been ill." She took one of Sabrina's thin hands in her own. "We thought you would surely die. You've been seriously ill."

Sabrina looked up at her incredulously. "Ill? Me? I don't believe it," she laughed.

Mary frowned as she heard the positive note in Sabrina's voice. "Don't you remember how you became ill?"

Sabrina shook her dark head, beginning to feel panicked as her thoughts came vaguely to her. "I remember a picnic we went on. You and Richard, Aunt Margaret and myself. We had roast chicken and pickled salmon, which I remember Aunt Margaret said was a bit too salty," she told Mary, wrinkling her brow as she tried to remember, not seeing the disquiet in Mary's eyes as she continued, "and that was yesterday, wasn't it?"

Sabrina looked up at Mary, her violet eyes troubled. "That's strange, I can't seem to remember anything but the picnic. Everything else seems hazy. I don't remember becoming ill. But I suppose I have, for I do feel weak," she told Mary, then smiled up at her ingenuously. "Do you suppose there are any gooseberry tarts left? I am starved to death," she laughed, looking like the Sabrina of long ago, her eyes twinkling as her dimple appeared.

"Oh, I think we might find something in the kitchen for you," Mary promised, her expression strained. She pulled the downy coverlet back over Sabrina's shoulders and smiled with an effort. "Now that you are well again we must see that you stay that way. You lie back now and I'll go get you a nice bowl of broth, and maybe a small dish of custard."

"With cinnamon," Sabrina added as she settled under the covers and stretched lazily.

"With cinnamon," Mary agreed as she forced herself to sedately leave the room. As soon as the door closed behind her she leaned against it, feeling her knees too weak to hold her. After a brief moment she hurried downstairs, running into the salon, her expression apprehensive..

"Lucien!" she cried out thankfully.

He got up abruptly from the chair he'd been sitting in at the desk, his correspondence forgotten as he saw the look on Mary's face. He clasped her shoulders, dread in his eyes as he stared down into her stricken face.

"She's dead?" he said tonelessly.

Mary swallowed, trying to find her voice, but could only shake her head in reply.

Lucien's grip tightened painfully. "My God, Mary, what has happened? Is Sabrina all right, then?" he demanded, a light entering his darkened eyes.

"The fever has broken, she's awake."

Lucien released her and sank down on the edge of the settee. 'Thank God."

Mary bit her lip, not knowing how to continue and stood there silently watching until Lucien looked up, sensing there was more. "What is it? You might as well tell me."

Mary sighed and pressed her fingers against her eyes wearily. "I've said I thought Sabrina was suffering from more than just a chest cold and marsh fever."

Lucien nodded. "I remember." He could remember everything of the last fortnight as vividly as a moment ago. How many times had he sat beside Sabrina's bed helplessly watching her toss and turn with nightmares, watching her burn with fever as he cooled her with cold compresses, only to have her shake uncontrollably the very next instant, watching her grow thinner and thinner before his eyes.

"I think she had brain fever as well," Mary's voice broke into his thoughts.

"What are you telling me?"

"She cannot remember anything before her illness." She held up her hand at his ejaculation of amazement. "Oh, she knows who she is, but she doesn't remember any of the traumatic events preceding her illness." She paused, then continued hesitantly, "In fact, I don't believe that she will remember you, Lucien, or even masquerading as Bonnie Charlie."

Lucien's scar seemed to throb and Mary looked away from the look on his face.

"It's as though she has blocked out all that was painful to her and all that had hurt her. She is completely untroubled—almost like a child."

Lucien hid his face in his hands as he sat with his elbows on his knees and stared at the pattern of the carpet beneath his boots. "Well," he laughed harshly, "she never did intend to marry me, and it would seem as though she will have her wish—at least for now—unless she never remembers me."

Lucien looked up, a cynical sneer curling his lips. "Or maybe she does, and this is just another of her damned masquerades to elude me. Is it? Is it another hoax concocted between you two? Is she still playing games, Mary?"

"No, I honestly believe she does not remember. I know her—why would she pretend to me? We both saw how ill she was, she hadn't the strength to fight you, Lucien," Mary said honestly. "She has truly forgotten. I believe her."

Mary shifted her position uncomfortably, a distressed look entering her gray eyes as she coughed nervously. "I'm afraid there is another problem. I did not mention it earlier because, well, frankly I did not believe that Sabrina would live, so it did not matter." Mary spoke softly, looking Lucien directly in the eye. "I have cared for Sabrina most of the time, except when you sat with her. We have always been very close, of course, and living here in the same house, well, I…" Mary stumbled over the words and looking out of the window took a deep breath and said quickly, "I think Sabrina is with child."

Mary's face burned painfully and she felt it must be as red as her hair as she watched the duke for his reaction. She cleared her throat. "It could of course be that her illness has affected her, but I really do not believe that is the reason. S-she talked a lot in her delirium, and so I wondered if it might be a possibility, her being with child, and whether it could possibly be yours? I don't believe it would be any other man's."

Mary felt a shiver of fear run through her body at the angry blaze in the duke's sherry-colored eyes as he stood up and took a step toward her. She unhesitantly took a step backward and continued to face him.

"Mine," he said arrogantly, "and no other man's."

Mary expelled her breath, her shoulders sagging. "I don't know what to do. If she doesn't remember you, and she is with child—how do I explain the baby?"

Lucien picked up his discarded coat from the back of the chair he'd been sitting in and slung it across his shoulder. "You don't."

"But I don't understand? She'll have to know."

"Of course, but any necessary explaining will be done by me. After all, I am her fiancé—and the father of her child. I think I know what needs to be done."

He walked to the door, his step light for the first time in several weeks.

"Which means?" Mary persisted, not caring for the look in the duke's eyes.

Lucien turned, a half-smile parting his lips. "If she has no memory of me, then she also has no memory of her feelings towards me, does she? When I present myself as her fiancé, she will naturally assume she loves me, won't she? She will not recall hating me, nor her objections to marrying me."

Mary stared at him open-mouthed, unable to comprehend exactly what he intended.

"Actually things have worked out quite nicely, for Sabrina and I shall be married before the end of the week—that is all of the time I have—and without the declaration of war it would have previously involved." He rubbed his scar, his eyes reflective. "You do realize that if what you suspect is true, how necessary it is now, more than ever, for Sabrina and me to wed?"

Mary nodded reluctantly. "Yes, of course, but I do not like to deceive her. It's not right and can only end in tragedy. You'll give her time, won't you?" Mary pleaded.

Lucien shrugged. "I don't have much time, but she will have time to recover a little of her strength—but not time to recover her memory."

With that unyielding remark he left the room, leaving Mary standing irresolutely in the center, a look of deep misgiving on her face.

It was late in the afternoon of the next day that Lucien entered Sabrina's room. She'd insisted upon having a sponge bath and Mary had shampooed her long hair, rinsing it with warm water from a pitcher and then toweling it dry and brushing it soothingly in long strokes from scalp to waist. In a clean, snowy white nightgown of soft lawn, Sabrina sat propped up in her bed humming an old ballad from her childhood, surprising herself that she could recall it at all, when a strange man entered and came boldly to her bed and stood staring down at her enigmatically.

He was very handsome despite the scar on his cheek, Sabrina thought as she pulled the coverlet up around her shoulders modestly. He was tall and lean in leather breeches that clung like a second skin to his thighs, and his partially unbuttoned leather waistcoat and ruffled shirt front revealed a triangle of golden hair on his chest. His hair was the same dark golden color and curled behind his ears in unruly waves.

"You'll pardon my dress, but I've been out riding and was just informed that you'd awakened and were having tea, so I thought I'd join you," he finally said, and without waiting for an invitation, sat down on the edge of the bed, one booted leg crossed over the other. "I even brought my own cup," he added with a smile as he filled his cup from the teapot sitting on a tray beside the bed.

"Who are you?" Sabrina demanded curiously. "Why are you here in my room?"

"I'm thirsty," he answered mischievously as he took a large swallow of the steaming brew. "And in answer to your first question, I am Lucien." He narrowed his eyes speculatively as he added purposefully, "I would've thought you'd have remembered me, little Sabrina?"

Sabrina placed her fingers to her temple as it throbbed suddenly, "I am sorry, but I've been ill, and I've forgotten a few things, but I'm sure I would have remembered you. I am sorry, are you sure we know one another?"

"Oh, very sure, Sabrina, you see I am your fiancé," he told her bluntly.

Sabrina gasped, her violet eyes widening. "It can't be! I am not betrothed. I would remember, I know I would. You are a stranger to me," she contradicted him, shaking her head in denial.

Lucien put his teacup down and, taking her clenched hands in his, held them comfortingly. "Not very much of a stranger since we are lovers and you carry my child within you."

Sabrina's face was flooded with color and she tried to pull her hands free. "No," she whispered desperately.

"Yes," he answered firmly, and slipping his hand beneath the covers, placed it possessively on her abdomen, the gesture shocking Sabrina into frozen silence. "Soon it will show."

"Is that why you were to wed me?" she asked , mortified.

"No, I would wed you regardless. The plans were made before I knew of this." His hand caressed her hips and slid behind her waist, pulling her close to him. "Trust me, Sabrina. Would you marry me if you did not love me? Would you have let me make love to you otherwise?"

Sabrina turned her head and faced him, her eyes guileless. as she tried to read his thoughts. Why would he lie? And if she were with his child, could she do anything else? She must love him—she would remember eventually, but until then she must believe him. And there was something so familiar in his sitting on the edge of her bed, it seemed so natural.

She smiled sweetly, her lips parting as she put her arms around his neck and looked up at him with trusting eyes. Lucien drew a deep breath, feeling desire stir as he felt her pliant body in his arms. Gone was the defiance and hatred he'd come to expect. The spitting wildcat had turned into a purring kitten.

He lowered his head and kissed her gently at first and then as she responded, more deeply, parting her lips with his and kissing her mouth passionately, straining her body close to him. His mouth clung to hers as she freed her lips to stare up into his warm eyes, a smile on her soft, pinkened lips as she said, "You do tell the truth, I think, for I do remember a kiss such as this somewhere in my mind."

A very merry, dancing, drinking,
Laughing, quaffing, and unthinking time.

—*John Dryden*

Chapter 12

"OH, LUCIEN, LOOK," SABRINA CALLED OUT AS SHE HURRIED to Lucien's side, her hands cupped around a nest of twigs and leaves. Nestled inside were three small chiff-chaff eggs, smooth and warm from the sun. "They've fallen from up there," she told him as she pointed to a tree some distance away.

Sabrina looked up at Lucien entreatingly, her eyes darkened by the floppy silk brim of her hat. A dimple peeped out as she smiled and, unable to resist her soft lips, Lucien stole a quick kiss.

"Now what do you want me to do with this?" he inquired lazily as she placed it in his hands confidently.

"Put it back."

"You want me to climb that tree?" he laughed. "I outgrew tree-climbing when I did short pants."

"I bet you were a sweet little boy, but probably a little devil when you did not get your own way," she teased as she led him to the tree.

"And you still are a naughty little girl," Lucien complained good-naturedly as he removed his coat and waistcoat and rolled up his sleeves above his elbows. He stood silently studying the tree and then placing the nest in a branch temporarily, gauged the distance and hefted himself up. He looked down from his perch above Sabrina's head and smiled in self-disgust.

"Climbing trees. What next will you have me doing, I wonder. Rescuing frogs from lily pads or a mouse from a cat's paw?"

He stared down bemusedly for a moment at Sabrina—his wife. They had been married last week in the small Norman church in a short service with only the family present, for Sabrina was still recuperating from her illness and tired easily. They had decided it would be best for her to regain her strength in her own home with her family around her rather than trying to adjust to new surroundings. There had been one outsider at the wedding, and that had been his grandmother's solicitor who had witnessed the ceremony and then turned over the deeds to Camareigh. He had finally succeeded in claiming his inheritance. Soon he would take Sabrina there, it was where she belonged. His expression hardened as he thought of Percy and Kate, how they must hate him. He would deal with them as soon as he had Sabrina settled at Camareigh. His eyes roved possessively over her heart-shaped face raised to his, the black curls framing it delicately. Her cheeks were rosy and had filled out in the last couple of weeks and her eyes were bright and loving as they met his. She looked like a flower in her white dress embroidered with purple violets, a cinnamon rose he'd snatched from a stone wall tucked into her bodice, the little pink bud no softer than her own skin it lay next to.

His hand tightened on the rough bark as he thought of the last few days and the new love that had grown between them. He had learned of a different side of himself. A gentle and tender side that was irrevocably in love with the beautiful young woman below him. And what of her? He had gotten to know the real Sabrina. The one who laughed and teased him, who flirted with him and begged for more kisses. She'd fallen in love with him. But if she ever remembered? If she ever became aware of his deceit, would she forget their newfound love and turn on him? How could he deny that he'd married her for personal gain? But then, how could he convince her that something he had not anticipated had happened... he had fallen in love with her?

He picked up the nest and climbed higher, safely resetting the fallen home amongst the boughs.

"Be careful, Lucien," Sabrina called, shading her eyes from

the sun as she watched nervously as Lucien made his way carefully along the swaying branch. He'd nearly reached the trunk when the branch he stood on cracked sharply and with a lurch Lucien's feet slipped and he made a grab for the branch nearest to him.

Sabrina screamed helplessly as he hung suspended for an instant of time and then dropped to the ground through the branches below. Sabrina ran to him where he lay still on the ground, the tall meadow grasses concealing him.

She knelt down beside him and with shaking hands rolled him over, only to find his arms wrapped around her, pulling her down on top of him. He grinned up at her worried frown, his teeth gleaming white in the sunlight.

Sabrina gave a sigh of exasperation, pushing at his chest ineffectively. Still peeved by his trick she lowered her smooth cheek to his, smiling with satisfaction as he yelped when her teeth bit playfully on the lobe of his ear.

"Vixen," he murmured softly before his lips found hers and he rolled her gently beneath him in the sweet-smelling grasses. His mouth touched the rosebud and followed the stem along the warm flesh, feeling the round smoothness of her breasts with his lips.

Sabrina gave a sigh of contentment as she felt his weight against her and caressing his neck and face she met his amorous gaze warmly.

"I am so much better, Lucien, that I think I need not dwell in that big bed by myself any longer," she said shyly.

Lucien hugged her tightly and kissed her long and hard until she drew back breathless. "Do you, perchance, find sleeping alone as unrewarding as I do?"

Sabrina blushed, to his delight, and with a devilish look in her violet eyes said casually, "I am not sure my memory serves me, for it has been so long since I've enjoyed your company in bed, that I fear I have forgotten."

Lucien chuckled, anticipation darkening his eyes as he interrupted her. "You will soon remember it to your heart's content. I shall see to it that you have more than memories to remind you of me."

"I have indeed more than memories," she reminded him impertinently, "to remind me of you."

Lucien placed a firm hand on her stomach, a smile in his eyes. "Shall we have a daughter or a son, I wonder."

Sabrina gave him a provocative look. "You wouldn't allow me to have anything but a son, so he can swagger along in your disreputable footsteps."

Lucien's chest rumbled with laughter as he returned her look archly. "Me, swagger? I have seldom seen a pair of female hips swagger so! Be careful or the child will become seasick."

Sabrina giggled happily and winding her arms tightly around Lucien's neck kissed him hungrily, surprising him by her ardor as she clung to him.

They wandered slowly back to the house, their hands clasped, fingers entwined as they walked through the garden and entered the hall. Sims beamed with approval when he saw them, forgiving the duke past offences now that the young mistress was so obviously happy.

"Tea is being served in the salon," he told them, and then added, "guests are also present."

Lucien nodded and led Sabrina into the room where Mary was pouring tea for Lord and Lady Malton and Lord Newley.

"Tea?" Mary asked with a sigh of relief when she saw Lucien.

"Yes, please," Sabrina answered promptly. "We're famished."

She sat down next to Mary on the settee, pulling off her hat and shaking free her curls, unaware of being the center of attention is she selected a cream-filled cake.

"Lady Malton was just telling me the most unbelievable story, Lucien," Mary said as she handed him a cup.

"Oh, really," Lucien remarked in boredom, his eyes on Sabrina as she licked a dab of cream from the corner of her mouth.

"Yes, it is quite ridiculous, really," Mary rushed on, "for she claims that she saw you carrying the notorious Bonnie Charlie in your arms."

If Lucien was surprised he kept it well hidden as he laughed. "I was carrying Bonnie Charlie in my arms?" he

repeated incredulously. "I have always preferred my lovers to
be in skirts."

Lady Malton choked and turned red in the face while Lord
Newley hid an appreciative grin behind his hand.

"Well, really, your grace, Lady Malton didn't mean that at
all," Lord Malton said huffily.

"Although I Told her she'd been out in the sun too long,"
Lord Malton added with a mouth full of rich cream. "Make a
fool of herself, I said."

"I know what I saw, and I was wearing a bonnet," Lady
Malton persisted stubbornly.

"I really do not have the slightest idea what you are talking
about, or indeed why you should concern yourself with my
affairs. However, you might have mistaken my brother-in-
law, Lord Faver, for this notorious bandit, for I did carry him
one day when he had twisted his ankle, but as for him being
Bonnie Charlie, I seriously doubt that, Lady Malton," Lucien
replied suavely.

"But I saw the eagle's feather and a glimpse of plaid as
you turned to climb into the coach," she argued, refusing to
believe she'd been mistaken.

"Plaid?" Sabrina asked curiously as she sat innocently
sipping tea. "Our grandfather's—" she began conversationally,
only to be interrupted by Lucien.

"My dear, don't you think you should rest a bit, it has
been a rather fatiguing day for you," he suggested, cutting
off her words effectively. "My wife's health is still fragile," he
explained to their guests as they all stared at Sabrina.

"Yes, as a matter of fact, I do have the devil of a headache, it must be from too much sun, so if you'll excuse
me," she apologized, feeling suddenly very tired as she rose
to her feet.

"Of course, your grace, of course. Mustn't tire ourselves,
eh?" Lord Malton exclaimed, full of understanding for the
lovely young bride, while Newley just stared, his desire
openly revealed in his eyes.

Lucien watched worriedly as Sabrina left the room, impatient for the Maltons and Newley to leave so he could go

to her. He accepted another cup of tea and sat through the desultory talk, contributing little to their chatter until finally, during an uncomfortable silence, they took their leave.

Mary closed her eyes in relief. "That was awful."

Lucien turned, stopping his pacing. "I had no idea that woman had seen me leave the church with Sabrina. But the ridiculousness of the situation saved us. However, I thought Sabrina would surely give the game away with whatever she was going to say about your grandfather. I wasn't sure how she would react when the name Bonnie Charlie was mentioned, but she didn't move a muscle. I've been worried about mentioning anything concerning the past to Sabrina, so I haven't. I just hope this hasn't upset her. No telling what talk of Bonnie Charlie could trigger in her memory."

"You're playing with fire, Lucien, and I'm afraid someone is going to get burnt."

Lucien looked at her, startled. "You haven't seen something have you?"

"No, but it's obvious that things have not gone as you planned, have they, Lucien? You've fallen in love with each other, and yet you've built that love on a very shaky foundation. If she should remember, Lucien?" Mary looked at him pityingly.

"It will not matter. She will be my wife, and there is nothing she can do then. If she does remember, well, she'll remember the love too," he said obstinately. "She is tied to me as my wife, and as the mother of our child. The bonds are too strong for her to break."

"She will feel anger, and betrayal first," Mary warned him, "and later she may admit her love for you, but it may be too late by then."

Lucien stared at her wise face silently, and then arrogantly raised his chin. "I'll not lose her, Mary. She is mine—and no one else's."

"I pray that it will all work out. She needs you, Lucien, but the circumstances under which she has found out she does are odd to say the least. She is very stubborn and hot-tempered.

When she finds out that she has been lied to, that you have deceived her, well, I just hope that she never remembers. It would be far better."

Lucien found Sabrina lying on her bed, a hand pressed to her temple as she rested. Hearing him enter she opened her eyes and smiled, holding out her arms to him as he came towards her. With an answering smile he sat down next to her and took her into his arms. She snuggled against him and pressed her cheek against his throat.

"Lucien," she said hesitantly, "I feel as though I am in a daydream half of the time."

"Lovers always walk around in the clouds," he answered carefully.

"But it is different from that," she persisted as she looked up at him. "I feel I should remember something. There is something nagging at the back of my mind that is important. I know it is. Oh, why can't I remember, Lucien?"

"You don't need to remember. I can tell you everything you need to know. The past isn't important, only our future," he told her roughly.

"But I feel so blank at times. You don't think that I am becoming like Aunt Margaret, do you?" she demanded worriedly, gripping Lucien's forearms.

He gave her a gentle admonishing shake. "Of course not. You've been ill, and have just forgotten a few inconsequential details," Lucien reassured her.

"Forgetting you? I would hardly call that inconsequential," Sabrina retorted tartly.

"It doesn't matter, since I am here now to give you new memories. You'll remember someday, but by then we'll be in our home with our children and our new life to keep your mind occupied, and the past will seem unimportant. Believe me, Sabrina."

"But it plagues me, Lucien. I want to remember and when I try I get such headaches."

"I said not to try," Lucien spoke angrily, his voice hard for the first time. "I forbid you to continue. You have our marriage to think about. Let that be your only concern."

"Lucien," Sabrina said reproachfully, "you've never spoken this way to me before."

"That is because you have never defied me before as you now persist in doing," Lucien answered autocratically. "Will you listen to me, and do as I suggest?" he asked persuasively as his hand slid under the lace of her dress and caressed her smooth shoulder while his mouth pressed kisses against her temple and he rubbed his cheek against her soft curls.

Sabrina wrapped her arms around his waist, hugging him tightly. "I trust you, Lucien, please don't be angry with me. I can't bear it, I love you so. Don't ever leave me," she cried, clinging to his warm body desperately. "Promise, Lucien?"

Lucien held her tight. "You'll never get rid of me, Sabrina, my love. In fact, you shall probably tire of seeing this scarred face of mine, but leave you, by God, no I never shall," he swore softly against her scented hair.

Sabrina struggled from his arms and balancing on her knees faced him, a glowing light in her eyes as she leaned forward and rubbed her creamy cheek against his scarred one, letting her lips trace its ragged length until they reached his mouth and lightly touched his lips.

Lucien slid his arms around her small waist and pulled her off balance and against his chest, feeling the flame of desire flicker through his veins as she lay against him, her fragrant softness sending his senses reeling as he felt like staring forever into the dark purple depths of her eyes that returned his gaze with matching desire.

Her lips parted slightly and accepting the invitation Lucien lowered his mouth to hers and passionately parted the tempting lips that moved enticingly against his. He kissed her long and deep, pulling her close to his heart, wanting her so desperately and possessively that he agonized of losing her, and was jealous of anything that threatened their happiness.

Sabrina dragged her throbbing lips free of his, the rise and fall of her breasts rapid as she took deep breaths of air. "Thank you for giving me your child, Lucien," she whispered softly, her face full of love for him.

Lucien sighed deeply. "If you were not already carrying

him, you soon would be, Sabrina, my love," he spoke huskily, very moved by her sweet confession. "But now I must leave you to rest," he said reluctantly, unable to resist one last kiss from her lips before he got off the bed.

Sabrina settled down in the pillows and gazed up at him with possessive admiration. "Are you sure that I can't persuade you to stay, my love?" she asked as she stretched provocatively, her dress riding up over a silk-stockinged calf.

"Soon enough you will no longer have a wistful expression, my alluring little Sabrina." He walked to the door and turning to gaze on her beauty added, "You play the coquette well, but remember, my pet, you are the seductress only for me, or you'll fan into flame my already too jealous nature where you are concerned."

Sabrina smiled enchantingly, hugging her arms together, her breasts swelling beneath the lace of her bodice. "Only for you, Lucien," she promised, closing her eyes sleepily.

Lucien smiled with satisfaction and left her. He could handle her, he thought with assurance. She wouldn't remember because she didn't want to. She was in love with him, and remembering would destroy that. And should she ultimately remember, it would do her no good, for she was wed to him and she could not escape him—nor would she want to, he thought arrogantly, banishing even the thought of losing her from his mind.

"Hey, Lucien!" Richard called out as Lucien passed the opened door of Richard's room. He stopped and retracing his steps entered the room. Books abounded, but now there was also the addition of riding boots, a shiny new gun hanging over the mantelpiece, and a fishing rod propped in a corner.

"Are we still going to try out my new pistols?" he asked eagerly as Lucien saw the flat box on the bed, the lid opened to reveal two beautifully wrought pistols.

"Of course, Richard, and if you are to learn how to shoot, then you'd better learn properly. I can't abide carelessness or trifling with firearms or weapons of any kind."

"I'll be real careful, Lucien. You will show me how, won't you?" He looked to the tall man hopefully, admiration written on his face as he watched the duke handle the weapons.

"Tomorrow," Lucien said and smiled as Richard gave a crow of delight.

He started to turn and leave the room when he felt a tug at his sleeve and glancing down saw a small, slightly grubby hand holding on to the fine fabric of his coat. He looked into the young, earnest face, the eyes blue-gray behind the glass of his spectacles.

"Lucien," Richard began shyly, his cheeks flushed as he searched for words. "Are you going to take Rina away soon?"

Lucien nodded. "Soon, after she has gotten some of her strength back. You did know that we would not live here?"

"Yes," Richard murmured quietly.

Lucien put a finger beneath his rounded chin and raised his face. "What is troubling you, son?"

"Well, I know the colonel is going to take Mary away soon, too. I've seen them holding hands and looking at each other in funny ways."

Lucien hid his smile at Richard's description. "And?" he encouraged.

"And, well, I like the colonel, but I like you better, Lucien," Richard admitted, looking up into Lucien's face with his heart in his eyes as he added hesitantly, "I don't want to be left here. May I go with you to your home, Lucien? I'd work real hard, and never get in your way, and I don't eat much. Please, Lucien, I don't want to leave Rina. I'd miss her something awful," he choked, turning his head away with embarrassment.

"I just thought I'd ask, and if you don't want me, it's all right, I won't bother you again."

Lucien looked down at the bent red head compassionately. "Now, you don't really think Rina would go off and leave you? Why, I've already picked out a horse for you at Camareigh, so you'll have to come. You've no other choice for I insist."

Richard raised his face, his eyes shining. "My very own horse?"

"Your very own. Of course you'll have to name him," Lucien warned, "and take good care of him."

"Oh, I would, truly I would," Richard breathed in awe. "You won't change your mind, will you? Even if I'm bad and don't study my lessons? Mr. Teesdale said I'd been lacka—, well, lazy, and he was going to tell you."

Lucien laughed. "I'll tell you a secret, between only you and me now," he whispered conspiratorially.

"I promise not to tell," Richard answered solemnly, crossing his heart to seal it.

"Well, I played hooky more than I care to remember when I should've been cracking the books, but who can resist a warm afternoon when the trout are big and jumping in the lake? But don't do it too often," he cautioned him.

"I won't, in fact I'll study extra hard," Richard promised, a wide smile on his face.

Lucien patted his small shoulder fondly. "Good lad, and remember, tomorrow I'll teach you a few pointers about those pistols of yours."

Richard impulsively hugged Lucien around the waist, pressing his hot face against the man's waistcoat. "Thank you, Lucien," he mumbled before turning away, flustered, to examine his pistols. Lucien stared at the boy for a moment before leaving the room, wondering why pleasing that little fellow should leave him feeling so pleased himself? The poor little man. That was exactly what he needed—a man to take him under his wing and teach him what all young boys should be enjoying. His own son would not be left to grow up without a father's guidance. His son—yes, he liked the sound of that. He wanted this child that Sabrina carried. She was hardly more than a child herself, and yet she would bear him a child—his heir. And what a child it would be, he thought proudly, as he saw her beauty and spirit.

❦

Sabrina awoke from her sleep feeling refreshed. The doubts that had caused her headache had vanished from her thoughts. She slid from the bed and opening wide the latticed window took a deep breath of the sun-warmed garden. Giving a sigh of satisfaction she spun around the room, coming to a halt before the mirror. She stared at her reflection in the mirror, noting the color in her cheeks and the brightness of her eyes, pleased that she was not nearly so thin anymore. Soon she would see Lucien's home, Camareigh, and she would live there with him. She would miss Verrick House, but Mary would wed her colonel soon, and of course this would one day be Richard's, but until then he would live with her. She would have to talk to Lucien about that, and, of course, there was dear Aunt Margaret, and Hobbs and the spaniels, but she doubted whether she would leave Verrick House, it had been her home for so long. Well, she would let Lucien handle everything, he did these things so well.

Smoothing her curls and tying a fresh apron of cream silk embroidered in colored silks around her waist, Sabrina made her way downstairs.

Colonel Fletcher was standing by the mantelpiece sipping a brandy as he talked with Lucien. They turned as Sabrina entered, abruptly halting their conversation and exchanging glances as she smiled up at them, her hand tucked into the crook of Lucien's arm.

"I'm not interrupting anything, am I?"

"Not at all, Sabrina," the colonel answered quickly, a smile of genuine warmth in his eyes as he stared down at her smiling face, and then at the gentle possessiveness on the duke's. He hoped all would work out for them—and maybe she would be fortunate enough to never remember her unlawful escapades. He'd seen men under the stress of battle completely break down, and some never remembering anything.

She was very fortunate that the duke had fallen in love with her, for he was definitely the right man for the child—and that is how he'd always picture her. Running away from that Scottish hut, a little girl with fear and hatred in those remarkable eyes. They were clear of all emotion now, except for love.

He looked up, his own eyes softening as he watched Mary enter, her face serene and her gray eyes gentle as she returned his smile. Sabrina caught the glance and with a teasing smile lurking in her eyes said to Lucien, "And I always thought that spring was the time for lovers?"

Colonel Fletcher flushed, momentarily caught off guard, then grinned as he looked into Mary's blushing face.

"Sabrina," she protested half-heartedly, although not displeased.

"They cannot resist imitating our fine example," Lucien commented mockingly while Colonel Fletcher laughed.

"You'd best watch your step, Lucien, or we'll put you to shame," he responded easily.

"And when might that day arrive?" Sabrina asked.

"I think next month, if Mary agrees?" Colonel Fletcher said hopefully.

Mary gave a shy laugh. "Once Sabrina has left, I see no reason why we shouldn't marry. I have wanted to be here to help, but when Sabrina is completely well—"

"Which I am," Sabrina informed them. "I think you should get married while we are still here, so I may help with the arrangements. Don't you think so, Lucien?"

"By all means, it will save us a trip as well, so I would marry soon if I were you."

"Well, we will see," Mary hesitated, ignoring Colonel Fletcher's startled look.

The next day a summer rain shower kept them indoors as the distant rumble of thunder rattled china and flashes of lightning played across the windows.

Aunt Margaret was busily embroidering while Mary and Sabrina sat close, heads together as they contemplated several lists before them. Lucien was teaching an absorbed Richard the proper care and maintenance of his pistols, and occasionally Sabrina would glance up as she caught a word or two.

"You really shouldn't be demonstrating the use of a pistol in the salon," Sabrina said as she got up, stretching aching shoulders as she came to stand beside Lucien.

"Oh, Rina," Richard said worriedly, lest he be cheated out of a lesson, "Lucien did promise."

Lucien nodded his head. "I can't break a promise, now can I?" He winked at Richard, who was lifting one of the pistols and pretending to aim it at a distant target.

"No, no, Richard," Sabrina spoke suddenly, and reaching out casually picked up the other pistol and aimed it steadily.

"You grasp the butt firmly, yet not tightly, and easily pull the trigger. Don't rush it. And be sure to hold the barrel—" she began knowledgeably, stopping abruptly as she realized what she said. Her face grew pale and the hand holding the gun so assuredly a moment before began to shake.

Richard was staring open-mouthed and Mary's eyes had grown wide with consternation. Lucien reached out and pried the pistol loose from Sabrina's fingers.

"Why, Lucien? Why did I know what to do? How could I possibly be so at ease with pistols? I don't remember ever having held one before," she said in dismay as she looked up at Lucien.

He put an arm around her shoulders comfortingly. "It's not unusual, love. Your grandfather must have taught you as a small child. It's nothing to become distressed over." He looked down into her upturned face. "Now smile, come on, no sour faces on a day like this, it's bad enough outside."

Sabrina smiled slightly, unable to resist the look in Lucien's warm eyes, but her doubts returned to her later that evening as she lay in bed unable to sleep.

"Sabrina?" A voice spoke softly from the door.

Sabrina sat up in her bed and stared through the darkness. "Lucien?"

"And who else could it possibly be?" he asked as he drew near the bed. "I thought you might be lonely?"

"Not any longer, Lucien," Sabrina said softly, her heart beating quickly as she felt the bed give under his weight. He drew back the covers and slid beneath, taking her in his arms as he lay down beside her. Sabrina buried her face in his neck, pressing close to his warm body.

"I couldn't go to sleep. I've been so worried about everything, and all I needed was you, Lucien," Sabrina whispered against his throat.

"I knew I should've made your bed mine long before now," Lucien murmured as he nibbled at her ear. "I'll not have you worrying your foolish head about that incident this afternoon. I thought it was time I gave you something else to think about."

Lucien's lips captured hers as he pulled her tightly against his chest, her eager mouth opening beneath the pressure of his. She rubbed her hands over his chest and up behind his neck and into the thick golden curls, feeling herself respond to his hands as they moved over her body knowingly.

"Make me forget everything, Lucien, everything except you," Sabrina pleaded as she moved wantonly against his body. "Lucien, love me."

"Sabrina, my love," Lucien replied, kissing his name from her lips as he made her forget everything but his lovemaking.

Here's the devil-and-all to pay.

—*Miguel de Cervantes*

Chapter 13

"WE GET THEM EXTRA BOTTLES OF RUM IN YET?" WILL ASKED John, who was polishing several knives and spoons.

"Came this afternoon," he replied without looking up from his chore. "You know, I kinda miss the excitement of riding with Charlie."

"Yeah, being respectable isn't very exciting," Will agreed, picking up a spoon, and breathing on it, rubbed it clean on the corner of his coat.

"Wonder how she's doing? She was mighty sick."

"Poor little Charlie. Think she really did forget all about us like the duke said?" Will speculated doubtfully.

"Sure, she would've been to see us if she hadn't. Really miss her, so does Mam."

"After that meeting with the duke, when he was threatening to string us up for allowing Charlie to stay in the marsh, I sort of respect him. He isn't really all that bad, and I figure he really does care for her."

"Think so?"

"Yeah, and what's more, I think Charlie is in love with him," he said thoughtfully, then chuckled. "She better be, after he made us give back all of Charlie's loot. Be madder'n hell if she knew."

"He sure can fight," John said with admiration.

"Just glad that we're on the same side now," Will commented thankfully, "and that he isn't one to hold grudges against a person."

"But what about the colonel? He's gotten mighty sweet on Lady Mary," John said jealously. "Think he knows about us? Or even about Charlie?"

Will shrugged. "If he did, he would've been here with a patrol to arrest us, and if he knew about Charlie, do you think he'd ruin his chances with the Lady Mary by hanging her sister? Besides, Charlie's a duchess now, and I wouldn't want to tell the duke you was planning on stringing up his wife." Will rubbed his chin reflectively. "Yeah, we're sitting real pretty, John, and I figure it's better to be bored than hanged."

John nodded and put a big hand to his thick neck protectively. He glanced around the largest, and nicest, of their private rooms. The oak-paneled walls and oak beams, combined with the fireplace and colorful landscape above it, created a very hospitable room. It was especially nice when the sun shining through the only stained glass window in the inn, and imported especially from London, created a rainbow of colors.

Will left John to his work and went out into the hall, stopping as he heard the sounds of a coach pulling up close to the door. Opening it he stood waiting, a smile of welcome on his broad face as he watched a man and a woman climb from the coach. "Welcome, I'm Will Taylor, the landlord and your host while you stay at the Faire Maiden Inn. Will you be requiring rooms, refreshments?" he inquired of the gentleman before him.

Percy Rathbourne gave a cursory glance at the big fellow as he escorted Kate into the hall.

"We shall require a couple of rooms and your best private dining room. You may now show us to our rooms. Oh, and I expect neat wine," he told Will imperiously.

Will flushed with anger as he answered steadily, "We never water our wines. We've a good and honest reputation. Air our beds, good food and fair prices."

Percy started to make a scathing retort when he was interrupted by a peevish voice. "Oh, do come along, Percy, I grow fatigued listening to you argue with this rustic."

Will led them silently to their rooms, and finding John in the kitchen downstairs, grumbled to him about the fancy highborns upstairs. "Oughta double-charge them and pepper the beef, but good. Like to see the gent in such a sneezing fit he'd shake the wig off his head."

John grinned as he sampled a slice of thick beef, and nodding said, "Could use a dash here, I think." With a sly grin he shook a liberal dose of pepper over the meat. Looking at the serving maid he pointed to the cut of beef and ordered, "Make sure this goes to the new arrivals, eh, Midge?"

"Right, John," she answered with a grin of relish, having already crossed paths with the fancy lady upstairs. "Maybe they won't be a'wantin' to stay so long after samplin' our food?" With a broad wink she lifted the tray and carried it from the room.

Will had returned to the hall when three men entered, and he quickly took their measure, not caring for their unkempt appearance as they loitered in the hall. "Can I be of service to you gents?" he asked doubtfully.

"I dunno, who be ye?" one of the three demanded belligerently.

"I'm the owner of the Faire Maiden, that's who, so if you're wantin' a room, then fine, although I doubt you can afford it. If not, then be off," Will answered in slightly less than a roar.

The man who'd spoken for the three earlier shifted his feet as he reassessed the big landlord who stood glowering at them. He spread his dirty hands pleadingly, a deprecating grin on his face as he cajoled, "Ah, come on, mate, I meant no harm. My bunkies and me, well, we needs a place to ride anchor, so to speak. Now, we can pay for a couple of nights bedding. If our money's good enough?"

Will shrugged with displeasure. "Money is money no matter whose pocket it comes out of, but you'll have to eat in the kitchen," he cautioned, hoping it would put them off. "We haven't got a common dining room."

But the spokesman for the three merely shrugged. "As long as the food'll fill our bellies and ye got somethin' to wet our whistle, we're happy."

Will frowned. "Just make sure you do your heavy drinking elsewhere. We, and I mean my brother and me when I say that," he grinned as John came up behind him to tower over the three smaller men, "don't deal lightly with drunks who feel like brawlin' on the premises."

The three men grinned feebly before the superior strength of the two brothers. "Sure, mate, as innocent as little lambs we'll be. Not a peep out o' us, eh?" he promised, sending a look to his two friends who promptly nodded their scruffy heads in agreement.

"What are you doing here? We don't have entertainment that'd keep you more than a day," John asked, his eyes narrowing suspiciously as the three exchanged secretive looks between them.

"Just restin' up before we ships out o' Dover. No harm in a bloke gettin' a little country air, now is there?" the trio's spokesman demanded truculently.

"As long as that's all you leave with, mate," Will warned them, and then with a jerk of his sturdy chin, motioned them to follow him upstairs to their room.

As they made their way along the hall behind Will's broad back, they passed Percy and Kate who were on their way downstairs to dine. With little more than a perfunctory glance at the three, Percy continued behind the swishing satin skirts of Kate.

"See those fellows we passed in the hall?" Percy asked after having seated Kate and quenched his thirst with a goblet of wine.

Kate looked up at him derisively. "Dear, dear Percy, I am above casting my eyes at every male I happen to pass. Besides," she added, "I hardly think there is anyone here worth my time and effort. Not quite up to my standards, dear."

Percy scowled at her. "You put yourself to the blush, my dear, for I was not questioning your amorous intentions, but merely drawing your attention to the fact that those three gentlemen we passed happened to be none other than Jeremy Pace and his hirelings," Percy emphasized derisively.

Kate smiled at the revelation. "Jeremy Pace. How

wonderful. He is the chap we hired to dispose of dear cousin Lucien. I'm sorry now I didn't take a closer look. They say you can always tell a murderer by his eyes."

Percy snorted. "More likely by the sharpness of his blade and jingle in his pockets."

Percy took a bite of beef and began to chew, only to turn bright red in the face as he gagged. Kate stared in alarm as Percy choked on the piece of meat until he finally managed to spit it out. "Merciful God, what in blazes are they serving here?" he croaked, tears streaming down his cheeks.

Kate prodded her piece of beef experimentally, an uncertain look on her face as she found nothing. Cutting a small piece from the edge, she nibbled at it carefully, then finding nothing amiss, swallowed.

"It tastes fine to me, Percy. You must've taken too large a bite."

"Too large a dash of pepper is closer to the truth," he complained, pushing his plate aside and swallowing his glass of wine to douse the fire in his throat. "I shall certainly complain to the landlord over this," he promised angrily.

"Do remember, Percy, that we aren't here to attract attention, in fact, I wonder at you dragging me down here as well," she demanded.

"For moral support, of course," Percy sneered at her. "Haven't you always said that you could handle things better than I could? Well, now is your chance to see me finally rid our lives of Lucien's presence."

"You hope," Kate commented as she pushed the food around on her plate idly. "We haven't succeeded yet, have we, dear?"

"This time we will," he vowed, his eyes full of malice. "Lucien's time is coming shortly to an end."

"And will he leave a grieving widow?" she asked meaningfully.

Percy smiled and laughed with abandon. "I fear not, alas, the poor duke and duchess are to be murdered while still celebrating their marriage. A pity, for the new duchess was so young and beautiful to die so tragically," Percy concluded sadly, his sherry eyes sparking with anticipation.

"I do believe I underestimated you at times, Percy. You are a cunning devil. What is the plan?" she asked, intrigued.

Percy shook his head. "Not yet, my dear. The manner of his demise, is of course, all planned, but as yet the time is not set. Our not-so-nice friends upstairs will watch his movements and then we will act. He is lost, my dear Kate. Completely lost."

He walked behind her and placing a gentle hand on each shoulder, massaged her skin persuasively. "I think now all we need worry about is how I am to spend my inheritance."

"*We*, darling, how *we* are to spend it, and never fear that I shall not be able to think of something," Kate corrected her twin, then advised him, "and do try to show a small degree of grief when you see the dowager duchess. After all, Lucien is her favorite grandson."

"I shall be the picture of wretchedness. Steeped to the lips in misery, heart-stricken by grief."

"All right, Percy, just don't overplay your part. It's common knowledge that you and Lucien don't get along. It would be a bit odd at this late date to be in tears."

"Not to worry. I know how to play the role well. It will be my finest performance," Percy boasted confidently.

Two mornings later they were still paying guests at the Faire Maiden, although most of the staff, including Will and John, would have preferred to have seen the back of them rather than continue to accept their money and the gripes and unreasonable demands that accompanied it.

"Playing cards all day long, they are. What are they doin' here anyway?" John grumbled as he came back with another bottle of rum from the cellars. "Here, you take it in to them. I'm not taking any more of their orders."

Will took the bottle with a grimace and, taking a cloth, wiped it clean of dust. "Startin' on the bottle a bit early, aren't they?" Will commented dryly.

"Jumpy as cats every time someone enters the room. Act like they're sitting on thorns, the two of them, especially pretty-boy in there. Always asking for a bowl of water to wash his hands as if they was dirty, or something. Gives me the creeps."

"Well, this'll help cushion them." Will grinned as he made his way down the hall. He came abreast of the door and spotting a bit of dust he'd missed, paused to wipe it off. The door to the room hadn't been closed completely, and through the crack Will could hear voices, not paying much attention until a name he knew well was mentioned.

"So, will you now tell me how scar-faced cousin Lucien is to meet his untimely death?" Kate demanded peevishly. "I am hardly going to gossip about it to anyone."

"The soon-to-be late Duke of Camareigh will meet with foul play on his regular early morning ride down a very shady path, overrun with an abundance of perfect hiding places for an ambush by brutal highwaymen," Percy explained cheerfully, a smug look of satisfaction on his face.

"As you know, this area has been rife with highwaymen, especially one known as Bonnie Charlie, and it would seem as though he is about to claim another victim this morning, my dear," Percy smirked. "It will be the last early morning ride of the duke and duchess."

Kate clapped her hands, her eyes full of admiration for Percy's well-thought-out plan. "Superb, Percy. Who would suspect the tragedy as actually being a well-planned murder?"

"Yes, we will never be suspect, and our three friends will be shipping out soon for a lengthy voyage to the colonies, so I think we need not worry about them. And the seas can be dangerous.'"

"When is it going to happen, Percy?" she asked, her eyes glowing with excitement.

"Why, I should imagine quite shortly." He took his pocket watch out and checked the time. "Yes, very soon, my dear, we shall be the sole heirs to the Camareigh estates."

A smile of anticipation curved Kate's lips, softening them, and her cheeks were flushed delicately with excitement. She looked like an angel in her silver gown, her hair a silvery-gold and her eyes icy blue, and as the sun shone through the stained-glass window her figure was patterned with rich color that bathed her in an aura of warmth that was an illusion.

Will stood as though turned to stone, his breathing heavy

as he stared at the rough surface of the door unseeingly as the overheard conversation sunk in. Schooling his face into an amicable grin he knocked firmly on the door and entered.

Percy glanced up, his conversation halted abruptly as the big landlord came blundering in, a bottle of rum on a tray. "Well?" Percy demanded insolently. "I thought I said we did not wish to be disturbed?"

"Your rum, my lord," Will said ingratiatingly. "Our very best for you and the lady."

"Well, put it down and be off then," Percy ordered him arrogantly, surprised by the sudden glint in the landlord's eyes as he bowed obsequiously and left the room.

As soon as the door closed firmly on the two guests, Will dropped his slowness and ran through the hall as fast as he could to find John. John was sitting in the kitchen joking with one of the serving wenches and about to make a suggestion to the buxom maid when Will charged into the room breathlessly. One glance at his brother's flushed face and angry eyes told John something was amiss, and with a regretful look at the eager maid he followed Will outside and into the yard.

"What's wrong, Will? Looks like your blood's boiling," John asked with concern.

"Them two inside is plannin' to do away with the duke and Charlie," he spluttered wrathfully. "I heard 'em talkin' about it myself."

"What the hell?" John roared. "What're we standing here for? Let's go in and get them," he declared.

"That won't do any good. They hired some cutthroats to do it. Remember them three that showed up a couple of days ago?" he asked meaningfully.

"Here, in our inn?" John bellowed. "We been puttin' up murderers?"

Will grasped John's rigid arm firmly. "They plan to kill the duke and little Charlie as they're out riding this morning," he told him, his face turning purple as he added with fury, "and the three of them are going to masquerade as Bonnie Charlie and his men, puttin' the blame on us for the murder."

John opened his mouth, speechless in disbelief, and finally

managed to find his tongue. "What are we going to do? We gotta stop them. Want to go in there and choke the truth out of them?" he asked hopefully, already feeling the fancy gent's neck between his hands.

"Assault a lord and lady, especially with a room full of soldiers next door?" Will shook his head regretfully. "We don't need to, we know close enough where the duke and Charlie ride, so we'll just have to find them first and protect them from those bogus highwaymen."

"Right. I'll get the horses, you get our pistols. If there's killing to be done, then by God, it'll be done by us, and not those three dogs."

~

Lucien turned from his contemplation of a vase full of roses on the oak table as he heard footsteps descending the stairs. He walked forward and held out his hand for Sabrina to take as she neared the bottom step. His glance took in the sapphire-blue riding habit, the full skirt, the jacket and waistcoat cut close along the lines of a man's and her lace-edged stock pinned with a gold brooch.

Sabrina reached up to straighten the three-cornered beaver hat and inquired brightly, "Shall we go?" She slid her gloved fingers into his hand and smiled lovingly up at him.

"Have I told you how beautiful you are?" he asked, guiding her outside to their horses.

"Not often enough to suit my desires," she replied, then added cheekily, "but you are improving, my love."

Lucien's eyes glinted as he mounted his horse, having already helped Sabrina to sit her horse, and leaning over, pinched her cheek playfully. "Come, and I'll tell you more secrets that will turn your little ears red with embarrassment," Lucien promised as they rode off down the narrowly twisting, hedged drive.

Sabrina sent her white-stockinged mare ahead, calling over her shoulder a dare, but Lucien's mount easily caught her up, and slowing her down, kept them at a steady pace.

"We're out for a leisurely ride, and I shouldn't have to

remind you to take care. I don't want to have to curtail your pleasures," Lucien warned.

Sabrina raised her chin, a sparkle in her eyes as she said, "You're no fun, Lucien, now that you are to become the proud papa."

Lucien frowned momentarily, not sure he liked the role he was being cast in, but then one look at her laughing violet eyes and tip-tilted nose, her smiling lips parted to reveal small white teeth, and he knew he'd do it all again if he had to, just to receive that loving smile from her.

Coming to a hollow, the boughs forming a latticework ceiling above their heads, they dismounted and leading their horses walked beneath it in companionable silence. Sabrina stared up at Lucien's profile, loving every arrogant line. "I love y——" Sabrina began to say when she suddenly screamed as three masked men charged down on them from the undercover of the trees.

She heard Lucien curse and reach for his rapier, pulling her behind him to shield her as the highwaymen closed in upon them. The horses bolted, running in panic as the highwaymen yelled wildly. Lucien backed towards the safety of the trees, but there were three of them, heavily armed with pistols. They hadn't a chance, and yet he got the feeling the highwaymen were playing with them, circling and moving in close only to withdraw before he could reach them with his sword. Why didn't they just shoot them?

Suddenly Lucien became conscious of the rigid figure behind him, and risking a look over his shoulder he was shocked by the face of frozen fear he saw. He followed her eyes to one of the riders and stared in disbelief at the rider's black frock coat and beneath at the tartan sash. An eagle's feather waved in his cocked hat as he swooped close, his face covered by a black mask.

They came to a halt before Lucien and the partially hidden figure of Sabrina. "Know who I am?" the one dressed as Bonnie Charlie demanded loudly. "I'm Bonnie Charlie, and I want your money and your jewels. Hand them over."

Lucien reached in his pocket and withdrew a couple of

coins. "We're out riding, we haven't much money or jewels on us," he told them as he watched them with increasing concern. There was something not right about this whole affair.

These men were not accustomed to riding, they could barely control their mounts and hold their pistols at the same time. And pretending to be Bonnie Charlie and holding up two riders out for a morning stroll wasn't the usual tactics for highwaymen. It was too risky and certain not to yield much return.

"Well, then I guess we'll just have to kill you and the lady for our trouble, eh mates?" the mock Bonnie Charlie laughed, and taking aim pulled the trigger. Lucien anticipated him and jerked Sabrina to the ground as the shot struck the back of the tree where his head had just been.

Before the others could get off a shot and the spokesman could pull his other pistol from his belt, Lucien had jumped up and grabbed the reins, jerking the horse's head and causing him to rear up and unseat his rider. The man fell with a yelp to the ground and Lucien pounced on top of him. They rolled over, shielding Lucien from the other men's weapons as they wrestled in the dirt. If he could only get the other pistol, then maybe these other swine would back off. But as they rolled over he saw the other two dismount. One roughly grabbed Sabrina where she knelt in a numbed daze by the tree, while the other kicked at his body as he fought with their friend. Lucien felt the fellow's booted toe strike his ribs and winced as he landed a blow on his opponent's face.

He heard Sabrina's cry as the man holding her twisted her arm behind her back and struck her across the face several times. "Give up, or I'll run the little lady through," the man yelled down at the writhing bodies.

Lucien broke free and raised himself to see a knife held to Sabrina's throat, blood trickling from her mouth as she stared at him as though seeing a ghost. Lucien doubled over as the false Bonnie Charlie managed to get to his feet and knee him in the groin.

They were dragging him to his feet when they heard the sound of horses' hooves, and glancing up the highwaymen paled as they saw the two Taylor brothers come riding down on them. Will leaped from the saddle and toppled over one of the highwaymen, his pistol going off wildly into the boughs overhead.

John ran his horse between Lucien and the masquerading Bonnie Charlie, knocking the man off his feet, and then jumped down on top of him. Lucien got to his feet and lunged at the man holding Sabrina. He saw the naked fury in Lucien's eyes and pushed her forward into his arms and fled after his horse in panic.

Lucien caught Sabrina as she fell across his path, hugging her close to him as he watched Will, having quickly dealt with his man, now giving chase to the fleeing would-be murderer. He caught him easily and knocked him cold with one powerful swing of his fist.

Lucien looked down at the still form he held so closely to him. Her hat blocked his view of her face, and almost reluctantly he cupped his hand beneath her chin and raised her face to his.

Sabrina stared up into Lucien's sherry eyes, the loving look of minutes before gone, and replaced by the old wariness and defiance. Her brow was knitted in confusion and one hand was pressed to her temple shakily as she looked around at the fallen bodies, and Will and John and the duke staring down at her anxiously.

Sabrina stiffened and struggled free of Lucien's arms. Her mind was a swirl of thought and images that made her tremble with doubts. As the past came flooding back to her, Sabrina faced Lucien, outraged fury darkening her eyes as his deceitful actions of the past weeks, tricking her into believing she had loved and trusted him, made her quiver with mortification.

Lucien fingered his scar, and had she not believed it impossible, Sabrina would've sworn he was nervous. "So, you've remembered," he stated flatly, then laughed without amusement. "I suppose it was that damned Bonnie Charlie who did it?"

"You didn't really think you'd get away with your lies and trickery? How opportune for you that I should lose my memory, and become the malleable little bride you so needed to claim your inheritance," she said scathingly.

Sabrina turned from him as though she couldn't bear the sight of his face. Blood trickled from the corner of her mouth and her cheeks still bore the imprint of her attacker's hand. She looked to Will and John, who'd stood silently watching the confrontation.

"Will," Sabrina whispered brokenly, swallowing back her tears. "A horse, please."

John hurriedly walked over and caught up the reins of her horse where it was grazing under the trees and led it back to her, his eyes glancing uncertainly, first at the duke and then at Sabrina.

Sabrina took a step forward only to be halted by Lucien's hard fingers wrapping around her arm. "We've things to discuss, Sabrina. Remember that you are my wife, and nothing you can do can change that. You are also with child, so don't do anything foolish just because you've remembered some old hates," Lucien cautioned her, his sherry eyes glinting. "I'll expect to find you at Verrick House when I've dealt with these imposters."

Sabrina glared up at him as she jerked her arm free and ran to her horse. John gave her a leg up, and without a glance at Lucien she turned her mount and rode back down the path they'd just traveled up so happily.

Lucien stared at her retreating back, so stiff with pride that it would take more than his words to heal the breach. His attention was drawn from her disappearing figure by a long, painful moan. He turned and looked at the man masquerading as Bonnie Charlie, and picking up his rapier walked over to stand in front of the sprawled figure. He pointed it at the groaning man, flexing it against the man's chest lightly but firmly.

John glanced at Will who coughed and mumbled, "Soldiers will hang 'em soon enough."

Lucien turned his head, his eyes bright, the scar ragged against the whiteness of his face. Will and John shifted uncomfortably under that deadly gaze.

"How is it you two gentlemen came to the rescue just at the right moment?" he asked quietly.

"Not soon enough from the looks of it when we arrived," Will answered in self-disgust. "We overheard the plan at the inn this morning, but by then they'd..." He paused, spitting on the ground as he gazed at the three just coming around. "...already gone, and you and Charlie were out riding."

"We figured where the best place to ambush someone around Verrick House would be, and we hot-footed it here, only to find you already involved in a fight with them," John explained.

Lucien looked at the three men pitilessly. "Did I thank you for saving Sabrina's and my lives?" He looked back at Will and John. "If there is ever anything I can do for you, just ask."

His attention was drawn back to the three men as they tried to rise. "First, I think you'd better explain about overhearing plans to ambush us. You overheard these three?" he questioned Will, while keeping a wary eye on the man at his feet. John had roughly pulled the other two close together, and now stood holding each by the back of their necks.

"No, it was the fancy gent at our inn that we overheard. He and the lady was talking about it this morning and when I heard her say something about the death of their scar-faced cousin, and then call him the Duke of Camareigh, well I knew it could be none other than you, yer grace."

Lucien listened intently, showing no surprise as he recognized the description of Percy and Kate. He looked down at the masked man and, reaching out, ripped the mask from his face. The man cowered on his knees before Lucien, turning pale as he stared into the scarred face.

"Is what he says the truth? Answer me if you value your life," he demanded ruthlessly.

"Yes," the man spat back, cringing before the murderous look that entered the sherry eyes.

"And?" Lucien said softly, inviting the man to continue.

"We was to kill ye and yer bride, and blame it on the highwayman," he confessed sullenly as Lucien's sword point threatened him.

"I'd like to wring yer scrawny neck," Will threatened, taking a step forward, causing the man to crouch down at Lucien's feet.

"Don't let him near me! I beg of ye, please," he cried.

Lucien grabbed him by his shirt front and shook him like a dog shaking a rat he'd caught. "You wouldn't also happen to know about a couple of cutthroats who attacked me in London, or a wagon that crushed my coach while I was conveniently held immobile, would you?" he asked dangerously.

"Oh, no, wasn't us, really, sir! I swear on my mother's honor," he whined.

"Never had any honor, most likely," John said doubtfully, tightening his hold on the two that squirmed in his grasp.

"And were you to return to the inn after completing your task to collect your pay?" Lucien inquired silkily.

"That's right, we was to be paid by his lordship, and me and me mates was shipping out for the colonies next week."

"Oh, you may still be shipping out for the colonies, but in irons," Lucien promised him, "unless you and your mates are hanged or rot in prison first. Turn these gentlemen," Lucien said sarcastically to John and Will, "over to Colonel Fletcher, who will be relieved, I'm sure, to inform the neighborhood of the capture of the notorious Bonnie Charlie."

"Hey, but I ain't him!" the highwayman yelled at Lucien's back as he sauntered to his horse.

Lucien turned and arrogantly looked at the man. "Really? Then why are you dressed as this notorious highwayman if you are not he? I doubt whether you will find anyone likely to believe your tales."

"But we was hired by that gent from London, Lord Feltham. He'll tell you so. We ain't never been here before. Find him and he'll tell you!" Jeremy Pace cried frantically, already feeling the noose tightening around his neck.

"Oh, I intend definitely to speak with your employer. Most definitely," Lucien assured him, his eyes narrowed in contemplation of the event. "And I seriously doubt he will be in any condition, or position, to help you, if he was of a mind to, which I doubt."

Lucien mounted his horse, his coat ripped out in the sleeve and stained with dirt. His face was braised and his lip was swelling rapidly.

Will jerked Jeremy Pace to his feet and pushed him toward his horse, only to halt him beside it. "I think we'll let these three hearties walk back to town, *eh*, John?" he called as he climbed on his horse.

"Right, Will. Give them time to think over the error of their ways," he chuckled.

"Mighty glad I'm not at the inn right now, nor sitting tight in his stiff-necked lordship's breeches. Him and his lady are in for some powerful trouble when the duke walks in alive and well, and madder'n blazes."

"Swine, imagine trying to kill their own cousin."

"And a little girl like Charlie."

"Come on," John urged the slowly shuffling feet of their reluctant prisoners. "We ain't got all day."

Lucien rode into the innyard and dismounted without a glance at the ostler who came running out to take his horse. His anger had simmered as he had ridden along, but now it reached its boiling point and he could feel his scar throbbing in his cheek, his temper flaring into a black rage as he entered the inn.

He opened the first door he came to only to find the room empty. In the next he surprised an elderly couple sipping tea, then Lucien smiled humorlessly as he opened the third door and heard Percy's familiar voice.

"Well, what is it now? I told you we were not to be disturbed," he complained sulkily without bothering to glance up at the intruder.

"Really," Lucien spoke clearly, closing the door behind him, "I would've thought you'd be very anxious to know the unfortunate outcome of your murderous plot."

Percy jumped to his feet, petrified by the unexpected voice behind him. Kate gave a scream of fright that turned into a whimper as she looked into Lucien's deadly cold eyes.

"Lucien," Percy whispered hoarsely, trying to come to his senses. "W-what are you doing here, and what in the world happened to you?" he bluffed desperately.

"You bastard," Lucien murmured beneath his breath as he began to close the distance between them.

Percy choked on his words, turning pale as he watched Lucien stalk him. He tried to smile, but his muscles felt frozen. "Now, Lucien," he warned as he took a backward step.

Lucien grabbed Percy by his casually knotted stock, relishing the sound of it tearing beneath his hands and then, bunching his fist, swung it back and smashed it into Percy's sniveling face.

Kate screamed and ran to the fallen Percy, blood spurting from his broken nose. She found a handkerchief and pressed it to his face shakily.

"Get up, Percy, or aren't you man enough to do your own dirty work for a change?" Lucien taunted him, his face mirroring the disgust he felt for his cousin as he stared down at his crumpled form.

Percy glared up at Lucien with unveiled hatred in his eyes. Holding the handkerchief to his nose he struggled to his feet, Kate lending him support as he swayed. "How I hate you, Lucien," he spat.

"So," Lucien spoke softly, "you finally come out in the open. A pity you did not sooner, it would have saved us both a lot of time. I underestimated you and Kate once too often."

"Always a glib retort. Never without the quick reply to put someone in their place. Well, I'm not sorry for what we've done!" he yelled, losing control. "I'm only sorry those hired assassins didn't succeed. How you managed to escape them I don't know, but you won't escape this time," he promised, reaching into his coat pocket and pulling out a pistol. Lucien lunged forward and made a grab for the pistol, but Percy was strong with rage, the adrenaline pumping through his blood and feeding him strength. Lucien struggled with him, barely retaining his hold on the pistol barrel by feel alone as the pistol disappeared between their twisting bodies.

Kate backed into a corner, breathlessly watching the death struggle going on before her eyes. "Kill him, Percy!" she screamed shrilly, her eyes glowing with excitement as she saw the barrel of the pistol pointed into Lucien's face. "Put a hole through him! Now. Percy, now!"

They twisted and stumbled, knocking into the table and sending the dishes crashing to the floor. A knife skidded across the wooden floor and came to a halt near Kate's feet. drawing her attention, then looking up at the two figures she reached down and picked it up, wrapping her fingers around the hilt the sharp blade pointed toward the broad back of the duke.

A roar cut through the heavy breathing and scraping of feet and left a silence suspended in the room as Lucien and Percy caught their breaths in surprise, each waiting for the other to fall. Lucien stared into Percy's eyes, so similar to his own, his breath hot against his face. He could see every pore in Percy's skin as their gazes locked.

The door opened behind them and two soldiers rushed in, their pistols drawn. They came to an abrupt stop as they stared at the two gentlemen locked together in the middle of the room. A high-pitched scream shattered their immobility as a serving maid who'd followed behind the soldiers managed to sneak a look into the room.

Lucien pushed Percy from him, the pistol dropping uselessly to the floor. Percy saw the look on Lucien's face and the others standing helplessly in the room and, following their horrified gazes, saw Kate. With a sob of disbelief Percy fell to his knees beside her on the floor. Her pale yellow gown was stained with blood that trickled from a jagged cut across her cheek. From chin to temple ran a deep, vicious-looking wound.

Kate opened her eyes and stared up at Percy's appalled face. Dazed with shock by the unexpectedness of the searing pain she could only stare in confusion.

"Percy?" she whispered as pain shot through her face. As the pain increased so did her consciousness as she slowly became aware of the pitying looks on the faces crowding around. She gave a moan of disbelief and looked into Percy's eyes, only to see her worst fears confirmed.

Her eyes widened with shock as she raised a shaking hand

to her cheek and quickly withdrew it covered with blood. She opened her mouth, giving a soundless scream that everyone heard as she realized her disfigurement.

Percy doubled over and shook with sobs as he pressed his head into her lap. Kate stared mutely at the knife still clenched in her other hand, the knife she would have driven deep into Lucien's back.

"Get a doctor, quick." Lucien ordered one of the soldiers, and as he still remained, a look of revulsion on his face, Lucien gave him an impatient shove. "Go, man, and the rest of you clear out, except you," he ordered, grabbing the serving maid as she tried to slip by. "Fetch water and bandages. And some brandy, lots of it."

"Kate, Kate," Percy cried, his voice muffled by the folds of her gown.

Her whole face felt as though it were on fire, the pain shooting up into her skull like a red-hot poker. Blearily she glanced around the room until she found Lucien. He stood quietly watching them, his face blank of expression.

Despite the pain Kate managed a crooked smile, the muscle severed by the bullet allowing her mouth to pull down in the corner and hang open, creating a travesty of her once flawless face.

"Ironic, isn't it, that I should reap the rewards of my past actions in so bizarre a style," she whispered painfully. "You win, Lucien, you always do. God, how I've hated you all these years. Do you know how I enjoyed scarring your face? But you got over it, didn't you, Lucien? You still have all the women you want. You have everything, even Camareigh now. We thought we had defeated you when Percy killed Blanche, but the duchess had to give her golden boy another couple of weeks, and you would manage to come up with another bride. Always a step ahead of us Lucien."

Lucien stared at her, pity and disgust showing in his eyes. Kate saw it and laughed contemptuously. "Don't pity me. I don't want it. We don't need it. Percy, look at me, it'll be all right. Percy?" she cajoled lovingly, caressing his neck.

Percy raised his head and stared through swollen eyes into

her face, unable to hide the revulsion he felt as he stared at her destroyed beauty. Kate sensed his withdrawal and felt as if a knife had gone into her heart, then closed her eyes and let her tears of pain and anguish mingle with her blood.

Lucien left them in the doctor's hands and made his way from the room. He sought no more punishment for them. They would have to live with what had happened for the rest of their lives. Percy had worshipped Kate's beauty as an extension of himself, and Kate herself had used her beauty from the first time she'd been aware of it. What would they do now?

Lucien shook himself free of that nightmare as he rode back to Verrick House. What, he wondered, would await him there. A pity Kate and Percy did not realize that their mischief had indeed done irreparable harm.

Sabrina had remembered. Remembered the hate and the old distrust she'd harbored against him—and the reason for their marriage. It was indeed a pity, for he had been allowed to see a side of her he'd not known before, and he had found he liked it and enjoyed having her play the adoring lover.

It was regrettable she had to remember, but it changed nothing as far as he was concerned.

❧

"Lies. All lies," Sabrina confronted Mary angrily. "And you, my own sister, turning against me. How could you, Mary?" she asked, her violet eyes showing deep hurt and disappointment.

Mary linked her fingers together tightly, her gray eyes wandering about the room rather than look into Sabrina's. "What would you have had me do? You'd forgotten everything, Rina. You didn't remember Lucien at all. You forgot all of the years of worry and danger. Why should I try and force you to remember? You were so young again—so free of all cares. And, the most important detail, the thing you've seemed to have forgotten once again, is that you are going to have Lucien's baby."

"Why do you have to remind me of that?" Sabrina asked despondently, pulling off her hat and shrugging out of her riding jacket.

"Because it will be all too evident before long," Mary stated calmly, then watching impatiently as Sabrina dabbed at her swollen lip, cried, "Well, aren't you going to tell me what has happened? I can't believe that Lucien would have hit you. Why have you remembered everything suddenly?" Mary demanded in confusion. "Lucien has been so kind these last few weeks. Was it only an act? I can't understand."

Sabrina turned from the mirror. "Are you just now finding out how ruthless Lucien really can be when he wants something? Of course he's been pleasant. He's had his way. I've been the acquiescent, loving bride. Lucien gets his inheritance and a lover all at once. To think that I believed him. He must have laughed at me each time I said I loved him. I'll never forgive him. Never! Do you hear?" Sabrina vowed, "I wish those highwaymen had killed him."

"Highwaymen? Someone attacked you and Lucien?" Mary asked incredulously.

Sabrina laughed, showing a flicker of amusement in her eyes as she explained. "You can imagine my surprise to see Bonnie Charlie riding down on us. Seeing that familiar figure was enough to jolt my memory, and everything came flooding back. Then they started fighting, and Will and John miraculously showed up, and then it was quite an exchange of blows."

Mary was suddenly reminded of the vision she'd had about Sabrina and Bonnie Charlie, and Lucien in danger. It had come true, then. "If the Taylors showed up, then I don't doubt the outcome of the fight," Mary commented.

"No doubt at all, although Lucien took a bit of a beating before Will and John showed up," Sabrina said without emotion.

"What happens now?" Mary asked, dreading the answer.

Sabrina raised her chin, looking every bit the duchess. "Nothing, absolutely nothing."

Mary regarded her suspiciously. "And what does 'absolutely nothing' imply?"

Sabrina smiled unpleasantly. 'The Duke wanted a wife, and he now has one, so I shall enjoy my reign as the Duchess of

Camareigh. And I shall live the part, Mary. After all, his grace is rich. I just hope he will be able to afford me, for as a duchess, I shall have a duchess's expensive tastes," she informed Mary with a vengeful gleam in her violet eyes.

Chapter 14

SABRINA STARED OUT OF THE WINDOW ACROSS THE PARKLAND to the medieval chapel protected by cedars on the far side of the lake, and wondered at the fate that had brought her here to become mistress of this grandeur. To visit Camareigh was an awe-inspiring experience, but to live here was to be humbled. Her first view of Camareigh had been from the coach window as they had traveled down the terraced avenue flanked by chestnuts, past formal lawns and wooded slopes until Camareigh, with its noble facade and stately lines, had appeared almost magically out of the mists. She had counted over sixty windows alone along the east wing. The warm, honey-colored stone blended into the countryside as though it had stood upon sacred ground from the beginning of time in an undisturbed magnificence.

Now, through no wish of her own, all of this was hers. She had the right to walk in the topiary gardens and through yew-hedged walks to sunken gardens with hidden pools full of colorful water lilies.

It was a perfect, and appropriate, setting for Lucien Dominick, Duke of Camareigh. She could understand now the reason why he was so desperate to inherit his home, but she still could not forgive him for using her as a means to an end. He had wanted Camareigh, and nothing could have stood in his way to hinder him.

Sabrina thought of the elegance of the gold and white drawing room and the long gallery hung with beautiful paintings and portraits of the Dominick family; the great staircase painted with murals, the tall pier-glasses reflecting the hand-painted wallpaper in the salons, the plastered ceilings and tapestry-hung walls. It was undeniably beautiful—but she missed Verrick House. She missed the old, oak-paneled rooms and low-beamed ceilings, the crumbling walls of the garden and orchard, and the casual untidiness of the flowers. Sometimes life at Verrick House seemed like a dream, something that had never really existed.

Aunt Margaret was the only one who still lived there with Hobbs as her companion, along with the spaniels.. Mary had wed Colonel Fletcher towards the end of the year. He was a civilian now, and enjoyed playing the country squire for a change and living a quiet life on his estate. Sabrina smiled as she thought of Richard, who had gone through the most startling changes during the past year. He had lost a lot of his shyness and sedateness and replaced them instead with a young boy's natural exuberance and proclivity for mischief. The only thing that bothered her was the constant tug-of-war on Richard's emotions as he tried to remain loyal to her and at the same time resist his idolatry for Lucien, who represented the first father figure he had ever known. Sabrina had tried not to influence him, but he could not help but become aware of the state of affairs that existed between Lucien and her. She supposed that she was to blame for it all. Her cursed pride had blinded her to the truth for so long, but as the months had passed it had become increasingly hard to find the words to heal their differences.

How angry she had been when she'd first regained her memory, lashing out at Lucien for tricking her and playing her for the fool, or so she had believed at the time. Now that she thought back on those days she could see all of the mistakes that she had made. The first time she had sat before this window staring out, Lucien had entered the room behind her and at his words she had begun her plan of action. How vivid the past became as she remembered that day.

"Plotting my demise?" Lucien had inquired as he'd found her sitting there with a frown marring her face.

"You are quite capable of doing that yourself," she retorted, not bothering to look at him as he came toward her.

"A pity you remembered."

Sabrina smiled, and looking up at him thought he was like a small boy who'd been denied his favorite toy to play with. "Isn't it enough that you have your estate safely in your grasp?"

"I suppose I can't have everything my way," he returned regretfully, "although as I've said, it is a shame you had to go and remember your dislike of me."

He bent down and let his lips touch the nape of her neck, lingering for a moment against its softness. "I've fond memories of you, Rina," he whispered, his warm breath tickling her ear.

Sabrina stood up, moving out of reach of his lips, her violet eyes cold as she glanced at him scornfully. "As you've said, a pity, but then you really can't have everything."

Lucien smiled. "I can try."

Sabrina's eyes widened in momentary fear at the implied threat in his words. "It won't be easy," she warned him.

"I never imagined marriage to you would be easy, Sabrina. I could have told you that the first time I saw you swaggering my way."

"You should have taken heed of your warning, Lucien, for you've taken on more then you bargained for."

"Quite, but then I've always enjoyed a good fight, Sabrina," Lucien answered smoothly, "which reminds me, we've an invitation to Berkeley Square. My grandmother wishes to meet my blushing bride, so we'll be leaving for London in the morning. Maybe it's just as well we're to be amongst people, or I might be tempted to teach you a few lessons."

A few days later in London, Sabrina met Lucien's grandmother, the dowager duchess. Sabrina dressed for the occasion with special care, wearing a midnight-blue sacque gown, the pleats in back flowing free and disguising her thickening waistline. It was embroidered across the bodice in gold, with three lacy white flounces below the tight sleeves that matched her petticoat. Wrapped in a matching blue velvet cloak, as the days were cooler now that autumn had arrived, Sabrina sat nervously in the salon waiting for the majordomo to announce them, glancing curiously at Lucien's unconcerned figure every so often, intrigued by the slight smile on his lips as he played with a deck of cards.

"I hardly think you've time for that," Sabrina commented as she watched him shuffle expertly.

Lucien looked up in boredom. "You think not?"

Twenty minutes later they still remained in the salon. Lucien glanced up in amusement as Sabrina sighed in annoyance. "You will become used to Grandmère's little games, Sabrina. You must learn patience."

Sabrina glowered at him. "You obviously take after her."

Lucien laughed. "Actually, I was just thinking how alike the two of you are. I think this shall be a very interesting meeting."

He was wrong, Sabrina thought later as she sat facing the dowager duchess. She was not the ogre she'd imagined, whose jeweled hands had held the reins on Lucien for so long, and who was still hesitant to release him.

"So, you are the new duchess of Camareigh? You seem a bit small to hold such a powerful and esteemed position, child," the dowager duchess commented.

"Have you not learned, your grace, that size is not indicative of strength?" Sabrina returned boldly, her violet eyes challenging the faded sherry eyes so like Lucien's.

The dowager duchess sat silently for a moment, then chuckled in satisfaction. "Indeed, child, and it would seem you make up for your lack of size with spirit."

She looked at the smiling Lucien archly. "How did you catch her, my boy? For unless my eyes are failing me, she's been looking daggers at you since you came in here."

"You left me little choice in the matter, Grandmère, so as I was short of time, I saw to it that her reputation was ruined, and no one but me to wed her," he explained audaciously, while Sabrina seethed inwardly at his mocking face.

"I do not know whether to believe you or not, but knowing your reputation I would not doubt it. However, it bodes ill for any future heirs if you are hardly on speaking terms."

"Oh, I do not think you need fear that, Grandmère, for we have not always been at each other's throats," he reassured her as Sabrina blushed scarlet and shot a murderous look at Lucien's cool profile.

The dowager duchess. looked between the two in amazement, her eyes glowing with pleasure. "I knew I could place my faith in you, Lucien. You may be obstinate, but you've never let me down." She gazed at Sabrina's set features with pleasure. "You will give us an heir, and so soon? I feared of dying before I saw Camareigh's future secured. How I've longed to be the dowager duchess once again."

"I could always have a daughter," Sabrina replied firmly.

Lucien laughed at his grandmother's surprised expression. "And she most probably shall. Never have I met such an obstinate chit as Sabrina."

"I can see you shall have your hands full managing your duchess, Lucien, for once she has defied you and gotten away with it, you will never have complete control of her again—unless she wishes it, of course," the dowager duchess advised with a glint in her eye.

"Defy me?" Lucien asked incredulously, giving Sabrina a sardonic glance. "She wouldn't think of doing such a thing, would you, Sabrina, my love?"

Sabrina clenched her hands beneath the folds of her gown. "Think of defying you, Lucien," she said with a sweet smile. "Why, I've never given it a thought—I just do it."

Lucien held up his hands in surrender. "You see, Grandmère, I haven't a chance."

The dowager duchess nodded her head wisely. "You may not believe it now, for obviously the angers are still burning hotly, but some day this will be a good marriage. You take my word for it. You both have spirit and passionate natures, but my only worry is that you will kill each other off first. Please don't, at least not until after the birth of my great-grandson."

"Never fear, Grandmère, Sabrina is a survivor. She may look delicate and demure, but don't let her refined demeanor fool you, she's as tough as leather beneath her velvet and lace."

The dowager duchess. smiled, thoroughly enjoying herself. "So, you will stay to tea, and then you may leave," she ordered as she rang for the majordomo.

Lucien leaned close to Sabrina. "You have been approved of and should feel complimented. Grandmère seldom if ever invites someone to stay for tea. Even I have been seldom honored with the privilege," Lucien murmured.

"That is because you have seldom pleased me," the dowager duchess retorted, catching his words, "but you have now, by making this little one your wife and making me a great-grandmother."

"It was my pleasure, Grandmère," Lucien said softly, his eyes lingering on Sabrina's parted mouth.

"'Tis strange, isn't it," the dowager duchess said, suddenly remembering the letter she had received yesterday, "about Percy and his family—and Kate—leaving London in the middle of the night like thieves and disappearing somewhere on the Continent? It's quite extraordinary." She looked to Lucien questioningly. "You wouldn't happen to know anything about it?"

Lucien rubbed his scar absently as he sought an answer. "No, Percy and I were never too close, Grandmère, so I really know nothing of his affairs, except that he has sold all of his holdings, including their London house. It would seem as though they intended a prolonged stay on the Continent."

"Most strange, indeed. However, I imagine when you inherited Camareigh and Percy and Kate knew there was no longer any hope of inheriting, they decided a change of scene would be best. I know they would find your good fortune hard to bear."

"I suppose you are right, Grandmère," Lucien replied.

The dowager duchess tapped her cane thoughtfully. "What really has me puzzled, however, is this letter that I received. It is from Percy's wife, Lady Anne, and it would seem as though she has taken command of the whole family. The little mouse has at last found her voice. She says that Kate is quite ill, and never leaves her room, and that Percy drinks himself to sleep each night. I am completely baffled by the whole situation," the dowager duchess confessed with a frown.

Lucien remained silent, sipping his tea and giving a prolonged study to the plate of cakes before selecting one. Sabrina saw the twitch of his scar and knew from past experience that he was disturbed by something, but he obviously preferred to keep it to himself, for when he glanced up his face was free of expression.

Other memories came flooding back to Sabrina as she thought of the time Lucien had entered her bedchamber while she was dressing, only to find it crowded with people. Chairs and tables had been crowded with bolts of colorful silks and velvets, partially unwound for her inspection by eager dressmakers, while her hairdresser combed her hair into curls, and musicians strummed a melancholy tune in the corner. Her dancing master was impatiently waiting his turn for her undivided attention. Several of her admirers had breakfasted with her and were now volunteering suggestions as to which gown would be most becoming to her dark coloring.

Sabrina had watched as Lucien had retreated from the noisy group, feeling somehow at a loss when his broad shoulders had disappeared through the door, leaving her surrounded by the gossiping ladies and beaux who had become her retinue. She didn't really like any of them. In fact, she rather despised the lot of them, and had only associated with their wild set to annoy Lucien. But he never seemed to become perturbed at anything she did. She sometimes thought that he mustn't care, and then she would catch a glint in the sherry eyes as he watched her at some antic, and would sense that he was keeping himself under control with an effort. Sometimes she almost wished that he would lose his temper. She wanted some reaction from him, and that was why she had been driven into acting the way she had and had received the reaction from Lucien she had sought—only she had not counted on it being quite so violent.

They had been invited to a masquerade ball and Sabrina had excitedly planned her costume as a Greek goddess, the draped material of her dress barely covering her, leaving her arms bare and clinging to her body with every movement. She had smiled with satisfaction when she had seen Lucien's expression as she had entered the salon, his eyes narrowing with anger as she stood boldly before him, her bare toes in their gold sandals peeking out at him.

"You might as well return to your room, madam, for you are not leaving this house dressed in that manner," he ordered her coldly.

"You think not?" Sabrina defied him, her violet eyes glowing.

"Yes, Sabrina, I do," Lucien answered softly, looking austere in his black velvet suit, preferring to wear only a domino as a disguise for the masquerade.

"You have never objected before, why now?" Sabrina demanded.

"Because you are my wife, the Duchess of Camareigh, and I will not have you disgrace your position," he answered haughtily.

Sabrina's cheeks flushed with anger. "Oh, yes, I must never forget the high position in society that I occupy, nor disgrace the Dominick name," she responded.

Lucien remained silent for an endless moment, seeming more ducal than ever before. "I will give you ten minutes to change into something else, Sabrina," he warned, and with that ultimatum turned his back on her.

Sabrina ran from the room tearfully and hurried up the grand staircase, slamming the door of her room behind her. She stood indecisively as she tried to calm down. Lucien would not ruin her evening, she decided with a devilish glint in her eye as a sudden thought struck her, and she searched through her drawers until she found what she was looking for.

Fifteen minutes later Sabrina raced into the salon afraid that Lucien would have left. He was gazing into the fire when she entered. "Shall we go?" she asked breathlessly.

Lucien looked up at the sound of her voice, catching his breath as he stared at Sabrina's masked face. "So, Bonnie Charlie has decided on one last appearance?" he commented smoothly, a gleam of reluctant appreciation in his eyes as he took in her breeches and boots and the sword hanging from her waist. "Very well, Sabrina, you will go to the masquerade in breeches. You will, no doubt, be the darling of the evening.

I just hope none of your victims happen to be in attendance
as well."

He had been right, of course, for she had caused a sensation that evening when it had been revealed that the small
gentleman in velvet breeches was the Duchess of Camareigh.

Soon, however, the partying and excitement of London
began to bore her, and as she advanced in her pregnancy, her
social activities were brought to a close. Sabrina left London
without regret to return to the tranquility of Camareigh to
await the birth of her child. She had been surprised and hurt,
although she did not show it, when Lucien allowed her to
return to the country alone.

"I'm certain, as my presence seems to annoy and distress
you, that you will be relieved to learn that I will not be
accompanying you to Camareigh," Lucien had told her,
his sherry eyes narrowed as he watched her reaction to his
sudden decision.

But Sabrina was well used to hiding her true feelings and
managed a nonchalant shrug. "As you wish, and I appreciate
your consideration. For once you seem to be aware of my
feelings," she had responded, appearing to be relieved.

She had tried to assure herself that she truly was glad that
Lucien would not be at Camareigh, but on the long coach
ride she couldn't stop wondering what he was doing in
London. She sighed in self-disgust, not knowing what she
wanted. Her pride and anger still blocked her desires, for each
time she looked at Lucien she felt her pulse quicken and had
to admit that he still attracted her.

En route to Camareigh she had stopped at Verrick House
to pick up the anxiously waiting Richard, whose new home
would be with Sabrina, and also to attend Mary's wedding.
Sabrina had felt a stab of envy as she had watched Mary,
looking exquisitely lovely in a gown of silver tissue with a
train six yards long that Sabrina had had created especially for
her in London, walk down the aisle with orange blossoms in
her red hair, her gray eyes glowing mistily with love as she
stared up at Terence Fletcher. Lucien had appeared suddenly
the morning of the wedding saying he had stopped only

to wish them well, and left just as abruptly following the ceremony without explanation or farewell.

While at Verrick House Sabrina had paid a visit to Mrs. Taylor, leaving her a basket of oranges and lemons from the orangery at Camareigh. It saddened her to sit in the little cottage and remember all of the other times she'd talked and laughed with Mrs. Taylor—only now it was different. She could feel Mrs. Taylor's nervousness as she tried to entertain her, but conscious of Sabrina's title she could not relax. John and Will hadn't changed though, they were still the same joking friends as always, eager to see her and hear her news of London.

When she and Richard rode away from Verrick House she swallowed painfully, holding back the tears as her memories came flooding back to her.

The next months were spent quietly at Camareigh. The winter was cold and her figure that became rounder and heavier as the child grew within her kept them confined to the house. Lucien seldom visited, and when he did he seemed to Sabrina to spend all of his time with Richard hardly ever sparing a glance for her, and she supposed he must be repulsed by her misshapen form.

When Christmas arrived Mary and Terence did too, bringing Aunt Margaret, Hobbs, and the spaniels with them. Sabrina was amazed as she watched Lucien play the genial host, turning on the famous Dominick charm as he made their guests feel completely at home.

Sabrina caught herself thinking sometimes how their lives might have been had not all of the misunderstandings stood in the way. To have Lucien truly love her and care for her as he had when she had lost her memory. Only then it had just been a game with him, and now that he had what he wanted, both estate and heir, he was no longer interested in her.

Finally, as the long winter came to an end and the skies began to clear and show patches of blue, Sabrina knew that her time was near. She had felt for some time the amazing movements of the baby. She had given a startled gasp of surprise the first time it had happened, and placing a tender hand on her abdomen she had experienced it again. She had looked up, her eyes glowing, only to surprise a look of longing on Lucien's face as he'd watched her. It had been quickly masked as he looked at her inquiringly.

Rhea Claire Dominick was born early in the morning, her lusty cry of surprise as she entered the world bringing a grateful smile of relief to Mary as she placed the child in Sabrina's arms.

"So," Lucien had said softly as he'd stared down at his wife and daughter, "you are defiant as ever, Sabrina."

Sabrina looked up with exhausted eyes, the glow in his giving her strength to reply. "I always shall be."

By May Sabrina was back to her normal activities, but she had no desire to return to London and the life she had been leading before the birth of Rhea.

The dowager duchess had made a rare visit to Camareigh to see her great-granddaughter despite her attitude of disappointment that it had not been a boy. She had showered gifts on the child and even held the tiny infant in her arms, her disapproving frown fading as Rhea chuckled up at her with her violet eyes. The dowager duchess had left, but with the admonition, "Next time I shall expect a boy."

Sabrina had smiled slightly, avoiding Lucien's eyes, unwilling to tell her that there would not be a next time.

It had not been of her own doing that the final break between them occurred. In honor of his daughter's birth Lucien decided to have a ball, the first at Camareigh in many years. Guests arrived throughout the day and crowded into the salons and gardens under the warm sunshine. Many were her friends from London, but most were Lucien's. Sabrina found she liked Sir Jeremy Winters and his wife, and a few others, but the majority were of a rakish set and she resented their presence at Camareigh. She wanted to spend her time with Rhea and with Lucien, who since Rhea's birth had spent a great deal of time at Camareigh.

Sabrina had been surprised to see the Duke of Granston amongst the guests, but she supposed it would've been an insult to him not to have invited him. She was thankful now that Lucien had ruined her chances of marriage to him. He was quite as repulsive as ever, and surprised her by lingering at her side throughout the evening. Every so often she caught his pale eyes following her and shivered at the lecherous expression in them that he did not bother to conceal. The Duke of Granston had drunk too much as usual, becoming unruly shortly after two, and had to be led away by two sturdy footmen, so Sabrina had been surprised the following morning to find him beside her as she entered a belt of woodland on the estate. She slowed her horse as he crowded close, cutting across her path, his horse barring the way.

"Good morning," Sabrina greeted him steadily, ignoring the lecherous smile on his fleshy face. "Is there something I can do for you?" she asked doubtfully.

"Now, now, Sabrina," he cajoled, moving his horse closer. "You don't mind if I call you that? After all, we could very easily have become man and wife, only Lucien was a step ahead of me as usual. Or should I say, a kiss ahead?" he laughed, his eyes on her lips suggestively.

"If you will excuse me, your grace, I do have other guests to see to," Sabrina responded, her chin lifted haughtily.

"Now, now, Sabrina, you have plenty of time for me. I am one of your most prestigious guests. You should be nice to me, I don't care to be rebuffed."

"You will be more than rebuffed if you do not clear a path for me immediately," Sabrina warned him icily. "My husband would not take kindly to your bothering me, your grace."

The Duke of Granston laughed rudely. "Lucien? He's too busy elsewhere to care about your whereabouts. The Lady Sarah has him fully occupied, believe me. I saw them not fifteen minutes ago in the gardens. So," he whispered with a wink, "we have this little greenwood to ourselves, don't we, Sabrina? I was always regretful that we never formed a closer friendship, and then when you wed Lucien, I despaired. However, when Lucien returned to London alone, leaving you here at Camareigh, and returned to his old pursuits, well, my dear, I was given new hope that we might come to an agreement after all."

Sabrina had never felt so humiliated and insulted in her life. "Get out of my way," she said hoarsely, her violet eyes blazing furiously.

"You're beautiful. Never have I seen such beauty," the Duke of Granston murmured and urged his horse closer, wedging Sabrina's mount against a tree. Sabrina tried to back her horse away but before she could move out of reach the duke had made a grab for her, jerking her body into his arms. She tried to resist him as he lowered his hot mouth to hers attempting to kiss her, then felt a shudder of revulsion as his slobbering lips touched hers. With anger lending her strength she shoved against him, her brief surge of power catching him by surprise, and overbalanced, he fell from his saddle to land with a howl of pain in a patch of thorny brambles. Sabrina urged her horse through the bushes and clear of the woods, the echoes of the Duke of Granston's enraged curses following her across the fields.

When Sabrina returned to the house she found Lucien laughing with Lady Sarah in the salon while she acted the hostess and poured tea to a small group of people. Without a word Sabrina turned and made her way upstairs.

As Lucien caught sight of Sabrina's disheveled hat and blazing eyes he excused himself, despite Lady Sarah's pout, and followed Sabrina from the room.

Sabrina had pulled her hat from her head and thrown it down angrily on the bed, and was removing her jacket when Lucien walked into the room.

"What the devil was that all about?" he demanded as he watched her throw the jacket carelessly to the bed and missing, it fell to the floor. "You come storming into the salon like the hounds of hell were on your heels and then with a murderous look at me, stomp out."

Sabrina turned to face him, her lips trembling. "I have just been insulted in my own home, and then I walk in to find your mistress and you laughing your fool heads off. It is because of you that I've been placed in the position that I am, every man thinking I'm free for some dalliance just because you so obviously carry on your affairs under your wife's very nose."

Lucien's lips tightened angrily. "I do not know what in blazes you are ranting about. Nor do I entertain my mistresses under the same roof as my wife," he added silkily, "I usually buy them a house."

Sabrina's face whitened. "Then why not go to one of them, it is where you would obviously prefer to be!"

Lucien stared at Sabrina's angry face. "I thought time would change things between us. That maybe with the birth of our child you might soften a little, but no, you're just as obstinate as ever, aren't you, Sabrina? I'm beginning to think it really isn't worth it. I doubt you'll ever grow up."

Sabrina stared at his back as he walked to the door, wanting to call out for him to stop, when he turned and said, "I believe I will take your advice. A change of scene would do me good. I begin to grow bored of your frowning face and sulking moods. I want a woman, not a little girl."

Sabrina stared at the closed door feeling bereft and heart-broken, for she had never heard Lucien's voice so cold and implacable before. With a sob she sank down to her knees feeling completely lost.

That had been over a week ago, and now she was alone at Camareigh, Lucien having kept to his word and left for London along with all of the guests. Sabrina looked down lovingly at Rhea sucking at her breast and pressed her lips against the downy-soft head, loving the feel of the child against her breast, the little hands wrapped around a thick curl of her hair as it hung over her shoulder.

"Sabrina," Aunt Margaret whispered as she tiptoed into the room, the lads, having accompanied her from Verrick House, padding close at her heels.

Sabrina glanced up in surprise, her reminiscences of the past year having drowned out everything else. "Aunt Margaret, you're up early today. I would have thought you'd sleep late after your journey yesterday. I know how you hate to travel."

"I had to come. I've finished it," she said, watching Rhea expectantly, "and now is the time to tell you."

"The time to tell me what?" Sabrina asked politely but uncuriously, as she bent over Rhea.

"The secret, of course," Aunt Margaret exclaimed, "and you will learn it now, my dear. I can show you."

Sabrina looked up at Aunt Margaret's excited face in amazement. She had never seen her so animated before. "What can you tell me now?"

"Oh, but I must tell you in private, dear," she explained firmly, glancing meaningfully at the nursing baby. "No one must be able to overhear."

Sabrina frowned as she watched Aunt Margaret nervously twist her hands, violet-blue eyes shining with suppressed excitement. Sabrina looked down at Rhea, who'd fallen off to sleep, a little half-smile on her chubby face.

"Let me put Rhea to bed, and then we'll talk, Aunt Margaret," Sabrina told her gently. "I'll only be a minute," she assured her as she saw the flicker of impatience cross Aunt Margaret's usually serene features.

When Sabrina returned to the salon, Aunt Margaret was sitting on the edge of a chair hugging a thick piece of tapestry to her breast, her face flushed with anticipation. "You took so long, my dear, an hour must have passed," Aunt Margaret reproved her, although only fifteen minutes at the most had passed since Sabrina had left the room.

"I'm sorry, Aunt Margaret," Sabrina apologized. "Now what is the secret you wish to tell me?"

Aunt Margaret smiled slyly. "It is one I have known for the longest time, and never told. I could never speak of it. Angus made me promise, and I never break a promise," Aunt Margaret informed Sabrina primly.

Sabrina looked startled and sat down beside Aunt Margaret on the settee. "You mean, Grandfather told you a secret, Aunt Margaret?" Sabrina asked doubtfully.

"Oh, yes. He was very worried, although I can't seem to remember exactly why. I should ask him, but I never see him anymore," Aunt Margaret told her, looking confused. "I wonder where he went."

Sabrina patted her hand, impatient for her to return to the story, but knowing Aunt Margaret would never be rushed. "He is all right, Aunt Margaret, now do go on. What did he tell you?"

Aunt Margaret's eyes refocused as she hugged the tapestry, then looking around to make sure they were not being observed, she unfolded the heavy piece of canvas and spread it out across their laps.

Sabrina stared down in amazement at the colorful scene represented by the thousands of intricately worked stitches. "Oh, it is beautiful, Aunt Margaret," she breathed as she touched the exquisitely worked tapestry.

"Look at it, for there is more to see," Aunt Margaret advised her with a secretive smile.

Sabrina scanned the tapestry, her mouth opening in surprise as she recognized the scene sewn across it. "Why, it's the castle, and the loch. It's like a map of the Highlands," she said in amazement, then paused in astonishment as she looked at the little figures around the castle, and then at the same five figures shown in a boat on an expanse of blue silk stitches. Sabrina gasped. "You've chronicled our escape from Scotland." She studied the scene more closely, her eyes widening as each happening of that fateful day was depicted on the canvas. Suddenly Sabrina remembered the words spoken to her so desperately all of those years ago by her dying grandfather.

"Threads, golden threads," she murmured beneath her breath, jumping with a start when Aunt Margaret's bony finger pointed to the little church of white thread interwoven with gold.

The kirk, false, that is what he had said, Sabrina remembered now. And then as she continued to gaze at the picture she became aware of a trail of golden stitches that weaved through the edge of the loch and then through gray stitches of rock until it disappeared in an area of black, only to reappear as a solid gold chunk in the far corner.

"Oh, my God," Sabrina cried in rising excitement and disbelief. "It could be the buried treasure. Grandfather's gold, and all of the valuables from the castle and clan." Sabrina put her hands over her face, shaking her head in despairing regret. "All of this time. All of these years it was there. You knew all of those long years at Verrick House when I was forced to rob to keep us alive, and at your fingertips was the key to it all. Oh, Aunt Margaret, why couldn't you have told us?" Sabrina asked her, looking up only to find the chair empty. Aunt Margaret and the lads had slipped away. She had done what she had waited to do for over five years and now she was no longer interested.

The utter uselessness of it all, Sabrina thought in disgust. She couldn't blame Aunt Margaret, or be angry with her, for she had done what Grandfather had told her to. He had entrusted the secret to her capable fingers. He knew, should anything happen, that the secret would always be safe and not forgotten if sewn into a tapestry that would preserve it for generations.

And Aunt Margaret had interpreted his trust literally, not realizing how she could have helped them all of those years before. She must have had a map of the area drawn by Grandfather to guide her stitches.

Sabrina looked down at the revealing tapestry sadly. How different everything would have been if they'd discovered the secret of the tapestry. The colorful threads blurred before her as tears clouded her vision.

"Sabrina?" Richard questioned in concern as he came into the salon and found her crying silently on the settee, the tapestry held to her breasts. "What's wrong?"

He sat down next to her and put his arm awkwardly across her shoulders. "I thought Lucien had left?" he asked, assuming he was the cause of Sabrina's unhappiness.

Sabrina looked up at him, wiping her wet face with the back of her hand. "No, I'm just holding your inheritance. You are probably very rich," she told him with a nervous laugh.

"Me, rich?" Richard asked incredulously. "Is that why you're crying?"

"No, the past just caught up with me for a minute, and I let it have the upper hand."

"Isn't that Aunt Margaret's tapestry?" he asked suddenly as he noticed what Sabrina held clutched in her hands, her tears having dampened a spot.

"Yes, it is," Sabrina answered as she folded it carefully into a square.

"She'll be angry, Sabrina, if she finds out you've looked at it. You know she never allows anyone to touch it," Richard warned.

"Aunt Margaret has finished with it, Richard, and I doubt by now she even remembers it. She has kept it in trust for you all these years. It's your inheritance, Dickie," Sabrina told him.

Richard frowned. "A tapestry?" He looked at the piece of cloth dispassionately. "Why would anyone give me a tapestry? What would I do with it?"

"It is only part of your inheritance, the most important part, actually," Sabrina explained carefully, "for it is the key to the buried treasure of Grandfather's. He left it all to you, as his only male heir, and to keep it safe from the English he buried it in the hills. It is all here, woven into the canvas by Aunt Margaret's careful fingers."

Richard's eyes grew wide. "Mine? Grandfather left the treasure for me? I never believed it really existed. I always thought it was a story you'd made up."

Richard jumped up in excitement. "Oh, Sabrina I'm rich!"

"Richard, come here, please," Sabrina called to him as he hopped around the room. "I don't want to disappoint you," she said gently as he sat back down beside her, "but it may not be true. It could just be a figment of Aunt Margaret's imagination. You know how she is. You do understand that you mustn't count on it being there. Besides, after all of these years, someone may have discovered it, and the English were pretty thorough in their plundering."

Richard couldn't hide his disappointment, then raising his chin in imitation of Sabrina, he said confidently, "I know it's there, I just know it. It's mine, Sabrina. With it we can go back to Verrick House and live just like before. Everything will be like it was before Lucien came and spoiled things. He won't be able to make you unhappy again, I'll see that he doesn't. You won't have to live with him, or even see him again, Rina," Richard told her excitedly. "You and I and little Rhea will leave here. We can have a lot of fun like before."

Sabrina hugged him to her, touched deeply by his loyalty.

"Oh, Richard, I wish that too, but it's too late, far too late for our dreams, but I love you for thinking of Rhea and me."

"It's not too late, Rina," Richard persisted stubbornly.

"Someday soon we'll go to Scotland and look for your treasure, but I'm afraid we can't really depend on it, love."

Richard stared down at the tapestry folded neatly in Sabrina's lap, a determined look entering his blue eyes.

The next morning Sabrina was breakfasting when the butler entered the dining room and coughed uncomfortably as he stood beside her. Sabrina looked up curiously. "Yes, Mason?"

"I hesitate to disturb your grace, but one of the grooms has some rather urgent news."

"Urgent?" Sabrina inquired. "By all means, show him in, Mason."

"At once, your grace," he answered in relief and disappeared to fetch the groom.

Sabrina sipped her tea uneasily, wondering what could be so urgent that the very proper Mason would actually interrupt her breakfast and suggest he bring the groom in to see her. She looked up as Mason escorted the uncomfortable man into the room, his face flushed with embarrassment as he faced her. Sabrina recognized him as one of the head grooms and smiled at him encouragingly. "Please, won't you tell me what is troubling you?" she asked.

Mason nudged the silent man with his elbow. The groom looked up from his contemplation of his boots and cleared his throat nervously. "Well, yer grace, I'm not one fer tellin' tales, but I don't rightly think I be doin' wrong this time in tellin' yer grace about the young lord."

Sabrina's gaze sharpened at the reference to Richard. "Yes, do go on, what has Lord Faver been up to? He hasn't filled your boots with water again, or used your hat as target practice, has he?"

The groom shifted uneasily. "No, yer grace, he sneaked out before dawn and rode off on one of the horses, real quiet like. I only saw him 'cause I was, well—" He turned pink as he mumbled, "I was coming in kinda late."

"I see. Well, he usually doesn't leave without telling me

where he's off to but he must've wanted an early start. He is probably across the lake fishing or in the woods somewhere hunting," Sabrina explained, wondering why this should be so urgent.

"Well, yer grace, I would've thought that too, and not come a'runnin' to you about it, except a groom from the Flying Horse Inn brought young Richard's horse back later this morning."

"What?" Sabrina asked in surprise. "Was Richard thrown? Is he hurt?" She got to her feet hurriedly, fear in her eyes.

"No, he was ordered by the young gentleman to bring it back here, seein' how Lord Faver wouldn't be needin' it any longer."

"Why on earth not? And what was he doing at the Flying Horse Inn?" Sabrina demanded, feeling a sudden chill as the groom answered.

"'Cause he was leavin' on the coach headin' north, yer grace. Figured maybe you didn't know about the young gentleman's plans, and I oughta tell you," he concluded lamely, feeling a flicker of unease as he watched her face whiten.

"Oh, Richard," Sabrina breathed, knowing without having to look that the tapestry she had placed in the chest in her room would be missing. Richard was going to claim his treasure.

"Thank you," Sabrina told the groom gratefully, "you did the right thing in telling me so soon. And now will you prepare a carriage, for I shall be travelling within the hour."

⥊

Mary snuggled down beneath the covers, curling her toes as she felt the coolness of the sheets. She looked regretfully at the empty place beside her and wished Terence would hurry up and come to bed so she could warm herself against him. She had left him working on the accounts in the library, his eyes strained as he struggled to reacquaint himself with the running of his estate. Now that he was no longer an officer he was devoting all of his energies into reorganizing his tenants and holdings. He'd let them slide under the easy management of his estate agent in his long absences, but now

he was taking over like a commanding officer bringing order
to unruly troops.

Mary smiled happily and contentedly as she thought of
her life. Eight months as Terence's bride she had lived at
Green Willows, and now she could hardly wait until the
birth of their child. She secretly hoped for a son in the
image of his father, but Terence admitted that he would like
a little girl, claiming he couldn't resist anything in skirts. A
little girl like Rhea, Mary thought, then shook her head.
Never could there be another child as beautiful as she was,
with her golden curls and violet eyes and disposition sweet
as a flower. If only she could also have brought happiness to
her parents. Mary despaired at times of Sabrina and Lucien
ever finding happiness. They had drifted so far apart since
they'd married. How unlike her own marriage—but then
neither she nor Terence were like Lucien and Sabrina. They
were so proud and arrogant, neither one willing to give an
inch to make amends. It was so tragic when Mary knew
that they must love one another. But if they didn't find a
way to mend their differences, then it would be too late.
They would not be able to recapture their love because of
the bitter memories, and lately Mary had even heard rumors
from London. She didn't want to believe them, and yet was
it so impossible that Lucien would seek love from willing
arms; but she would not believe that Sabrina had a lover,
too. Those had to be lies.

Mary rolled over onto her back and forced her mind onto
other thoughts. Aunt Margaret would be paying them a visit
soon. She was staying with Sabrina now, but had planned
to arrive next week. Mary compared Green Willows with
Camareigh as she thought of the differences between their
homes, and how small Green Willows would seem after
the grandeur of Camareigh. Her home might not have the
grand staircases and painted ceilings, nor the state rooms
of Camareigh, but the red brick, mullioned windows,
and gables created a pleasing effect at the end of the yew-
hedged drive. They had a lovely, carved staircase and an
oak-paneled dining room besides the salons and drawing

rooms decorated in her favorite yellows and blues. She had just finished redoing the nurseries, placing toy soldiers confidently in a toy chest. With a satisfied smile she drifted off to sleep, dreaming of the day she would hold her son in her arms.

It was the sound of the big clock in the hall striking twelve that wakened her. She sat up with a start and was surprised to find her nightgown soaking with perspiration. Her face felt clammy and with a cry of terror Mary tumbled out of bed and ran from the room, nearly falling as she stumbled down the stairs in panic.

Terence was bent over the papers on his desk, his quill scratching across the surface as he wrote, when he was startled by Mary breathlessly running into the library. He looked up in surprise, muttering an oath beneath his breath as he saw her pale face and hurried to her.

"What in God's name has happened?" he demanded worriedly as he half-lifted Mary to a chair. "It's not the child?" he asked suddenly, fear on his face.

Mary shook her head, and with a deep sigh of relief he left her to pour a glass of brandy, wrapping her cold fingers around the glass and guiding it to her bluish-tinged lips. He took her hands when she had finished it and rubbed them vigorously, hoping to return the circulation to them. "Mary," he pleaded. "You must tell me what has happened. Something has terrified you. Now tell me, what is it?"

Mary looked at him with enormous gray eyes darkened almost to onyx. The bones of her face showed sharply under the grayish tinge of her skin, reminding him of a bleached skull.

"I had let my mind drift. I'd been so worried about Sabrina that I tried to put her out of my mind," Mary explained shakily.

Terence nodded. "There is nothing you can do for them, Mary. They must find the solution themselves, but they are so damned stubborn. I don't want you worrying yourself—"

"Oh, Terence, it isn't that," Mary broke in desperately, grabbing his hands in a surprisingly strong grip. "I feel death closer than ever before. As though a breath of cold air from the grave had caressed my cheek."

"Mary," Terence murmured, "this has got to stop. You'll make yourself ill."

Mary stared through him, looking a stranger to his eyes. "I heard pipes, and saw the moon shining across the loch. It was so sad, so bleak and still, as though time had stood still. And then I saw people, but the faces weren't clear at first, until the mists lifted and I saw a boat floating through it."

Mary's eyes refocused and she looked at Terence's reassuring face imploringly. "It was Sabrina in the boat, and Richard beside her, and I could feel something was wrong."

"Now, Mary," Terence patted her hand, a placating note in his voice. "You've admitted to yourself that you've been worried. It was a dream, that is all."

Mary pulled her hands free angrily. "Do not patronize me, Terence. This was no dream. It was a vision of something horrible that is going to happen. And," she whispered, swallowing back her tears, "it is going to happen to Sabrina. Oh, Terence, trust me. I've lived with these feelings all of my life, and I know when to believe them. It is something I cannot ignore. Please believe that what I am telling you is true."

Terence stared at her clenched hands and wide eyes, still doubtful. "What do you want me to do?" he asked. "I don't know anything except some vague images you've told me about."

Mary leaned forward, the color returning to her cheeks as the brandy warmed her. "We must go to Camareigh. We must make sure that Sabrina and Richard don't go to Scotland."

"Scotland! You think they would travel all the way up there? Why, for heaven's sake? Mary, listen to me, it doesn't make sense. Sabrina would not leave Rhea and go running off to Scotland, much less with Richard trailing along." Terence raised his voice, trying to make her see reason.

"You don't understand at all. If it's not in print before your eyes you refuse to believe it," Mary accused him, feeling in that moment the first impatient anger she had ever had toward Terence. "I know, and believe, with every breath in me that my vision will come true unless we do something to stop it."

Mary stood up, her rounded figure revealed clearly by her thin nightgown, and facing Terence, said with determination, "I will not have this tragedy on my conscience. I intend to drive to Camareigh and warn Sabrina—unless it is already too late." She turned stiffly and made to move past Terence.

"Mary," Terence whispered and taking her in his arms held her tightly against him. "My Mary, never be angry with me. I'm a selfish fool wanting only to keep you safe and with me, and you are right, I am slow to believe what I cannot see." He lifted her face and smiled into her gray eyes. "We will go, Mary. Now dry your eyes, and have the maids pack your clothes, and plenty of warm ones. I'll not have you catching a chill."

Mary beamed up at him, her eyes trusting, as she pressed a kiss on his mouth and then quickly slipped from his embrace as his arms tightened to hold her closer.

They traveled through the night and early morning, stopping only once for a change of horses and a quick breakfast, Mary refusing to eat, but gratefully accepting a cup of tea. At her insistent urging they continued on within minutes. Mary stared out the windows as dawn lightened the skies and revealed the countryside passing by, her eyes unseeing as she stared into her own mind, trying to see more.

It was mid-morning when they finally drove by the gatehouse of Camareigh. Entering the large hall unannounced, Mary headed for the stairs, but was halted by the butler who was descending them, his face showing surprise as he saw her swiftly climbing toward him, her husband close behind.

"Lady Mary," he stuttered. "I'm afraid—"

"Where is Sabrina? She is here, isn't she?" Mary interrupted him frantically.

Mason drew himself up with dignity. "I believe her grace has left Camareigh."

"Oh, God," Mary whispered faintly. Terence quickly put a supporting arm about her waist as she swayed. "Come on, dear, you'd better sit down. You get some tea and toast," he barked the order at the butler, who after a stunned look followed his instructions.

Leaning back against the damask chair Mary took a deep breath and tried to calm herself. Terence hovered nearby and as the door opened to admit the butler and a footman carrying a tea tray she demanded, "Where is the duke? Please tell him we are here and must see him immediately."

"I am afraid that his grace is not in residence at the moment."

Mary glanced to Terence helplessly, her fears evident on her face. "Is Lord Faver gone too?" she asked hesitantly, dreading the answer.

"Well, as a matter of fact, yes, he is," he confided, the distress on Lady Mary's face finally breaking through his reserve. After all, she was her grace's sister. "It is most peculiar. The young lord disappeared yesterday and upon discovering this, her grace seemed greatly disturbed and ordered her carriage. Apparently Lord Faver took a public coach north, but where I cannot tell you, although her grace seemed to have an idea of his destination," he informed them helpfully. "To be frank, if I may, we were in quite a quandary on what course of action to pursue as her grace left no instructions for us to follow," he concluded, a look of relief on his face as he disclosed his burden to someone of authority.

"What of Rhea?" Mary asked suddenly as she remembered the child.

The butler permitted himself a smile. "The young lady is quite safe in the nursery with a wet nurse and nanny in attendance."

"Thank God. I'll just go up and see her," Mary told Terence as she got slowly to her feet, her tiredness beginning to show.

"All right, dear, and why don't you see if you can get a little rest. There is nothing more we can do right now," Terence advised, then turning to the butler requested paper and pen. "I wish to send a message. The duke is in London, is he not?"

"Yes, I believe so," Mason answered, worry beginning to show on his stern features.

Mary entered the nursery quietly. The nanny was sewing while she sat close to the cradle. At sight of Mary she smiled in relief as she recognized her grace's sister. Coming close to the cradle Mary gazed down on the small, sleeping baby.

Golden curls covered the little head and her cheeks were pink and healthy. Mary put out a forefinger and touched the child's tiny, perfectly formed finger with its miniature nail.

"So beautifully fragile and perfect," she murmured.

"I've never seen such a pretty little mite in all of my days of caring for little ones," the nanny confessed.

Mary looked at her penetratingly, liking what she saw in the friendly face. "She is precious. Look after her carefully, for she means everything to Sabrina."

"Her grace was in here yesterday morning, her eyes red from crying and I knew she hated to leave little Rhea," the nanny said sadly.

"Did she give you any idea how long she'd be gone?" Mary asked quickly.

But the nanny shook her head. "She just tells me to take good care of her little girl, that's all."

Mary sighed, and with a last glance at the sleeping child leaned over and kissed her soft cheek lightly.

She found Terence eating hungrily from a tray when she returned, and accepted a cup of freshly steaming tea.

"You saw the child?" he asked, knowing the answer by the soft look in her eyes.

"Yes, and Terence, she is the sweetest thing in the world. She looks like a little angel. I shall be a very doting aunt."

"I look forward to our child, Mary," Terence spoke quietly.

Mary smiled, basking in his love. "I know, so do I, and our child shall be the most precious to us, to me," she told him, "because he is yours."

Taking her hand he held it enclosed in his while they waited, neither saying much until he felt Mary's head fall against his shoulder and heard her deep, even breathing. With a contented smile he rested his chin on the top of her red curls and closed his own eyes—just for a moment to rest them, he reassured himself.

❧

Lucien hadn't arrived by evening, even though the letter Terence had written and sent earlier in the day would have reached London by afternoon. Terence persuaded Mary to go to bed, and finally as he heard the clock chime twelve times he gave up his vigil and retired to their bedchamber.

It was still dark when Terence was rudely awakened by voices. Being a light sleeper he had lit a candle and was sitting up in bed when the door of their bedchamber was thrown open and the Duke of Camareigh came stalking in, his face lined with worry and fatigue as he stared down at Terence and a sleepy-eyed Mary, no apology on his face for his abrupt entrance.

"What the devil is this?" he demanded angrily as he withdrew Terence's letter from his waistcoat pocket and waved it in front of them. "And what in blazes is going on around here? I've been to Sabrina's room, but it's empty. Where is she? I can't believe she would go off and leave Rhea."

Mary stared in amazement at the duke's haggard appearance. His golden hair looked as though he'd raked his hands through it numerous times, and his face was thinner and had a strained look to it causing his scar to stand out vividly.

"Sabrina is in danger," Mary blurted out, unable to control herself despite Terence's look of warning. "She and Richard have left Camareigh and gone to Scotland."

"Scotland?" Lucien repeated, his eyes dazed-looking as he sat down on the edge of the bed, his shoulders slumped. "Why?"

Mary shrugged her shoulders. "I don't know why, I only know that they are in horrible danger."

Lucien looked at her silently, then at Terence, and getting to his feet came to a decision. "Thank you for telling me. I will of course go after them."

"Listen, you don't even know where to look. I do," Terence offered, climbing from bed. "I'll go with you, Lucien, you will need me," he told him abruptly.

Lucien nodded his head. "Thanks, Terence, you might as well be in on the final scene with Sabrina, since you were there at the beginning. Maybe she will listen to you," Lucien said with a cynical twist to his lips. "I'll have my best horses saddled and we will get an early start in the morning. It will be quicker traveling on horseback than by coach, and as an old campaigner you shouldn't mind a couple of nights under the stars, or a few hours in the saddle."

Lucien strode to the door, but before he left the room he turned. "My apologies for disturbing you," he said and with a casual nod of his head left the room.

Terence stared at the closed door thoughtfully, and lying back down he took Mary in his arms and murmured, "There goes a very troubled man."

What beck'ning ghost, along the moonlight shade
Invites my steps, and points to yonder glade?

—*Alexander Pope*

Chapter 15

SABRINA OVERTOOK RICHARD JUST INSIDE THE SCOTTISH BORDER when her coach pulled into an inn courtyard and found the big black, nail-studded stagecoach just unloading its half a dozen or more passengers. She watched, disappointment marring her features as the passengers left the coach and Richard was not among the group, and was about to turn away when she suddenly caught a movement on the top of the coach and saw a red head appear amongst the stack of luggage piled high. Richard scampered across the top and was given a hand down by the guard who'd ridden beside the coachman on the narrow boot.

Sabrina left her coach and followed Richard into the inn, looking around the large room of milling people until she spotted his short figure in the corner. He was standing forlornly by himself, his eyes lingering on the food being served the paying customers at a long table before a crackling fire.

He shoved a hand in his pocket and pulled out a couple of coins as a tray loaded with roast duck, meat pies, eggs, and tarts passed in front of him, the mouth-watering aroma drifting tantalizingly under his nose. He hunched his shoulders in dejection as he counted the small pile of coins and put them regretfully back into his pocket.

Sabrina moved into the room and quietly approached Richard, the busy chatter of the dining guests drowning out any sound the rustle of her skirts made. "Richard," Sabrina spoke softly.

Richard's red head jerked around and his eyes grew round behind his eyeglasses as he stared up at Sabrina as if seeing a ghost. "Rina?" he gasped, then hugged her tightly as he read the relieved smile in her eyes. "Oh, Rina, you always show up when I need you. I was wishing so badly you were here with me," he admitted chokingly, his face pressed against her shoulder thankfully.

"Are you hungry?" she asked as he drew back and bravely controlled the trembling of his lower lip.

"I could eat a coach full of that baked pudding," he answered eagerly, his dejection forgotten now that Sabrina was there to take charge.

She hired a private room and watched in amusement as Richard helped himself to a third portion of apple and orange pudding, his eyes bright as he complacently spooned the dessert into his mouth. Sabrina pushed her plate aside and took a sip of wine as she decided what to say. She had been so relieved to find Richard that she'd hesitated in voicing the anger that had been caused by her fear for him.

"You pulled a very foolish act by running off without a word to me. How do you think I felt, Richard, when one of the grooms told me you'd sneaked off in the night and then caught a coach for Scotland?" Sabrina asked him quietly, yet with a firm note of displeasure in her voice. "Didn't you stop to think how worried I'd be? You knew I would not allow you to go, so you defied me by running away instead."

Richard hung his head as she reprimanded him, his cheeks fiery with chagrin. He finally raised his head as two big tears rolled down his face. "I really didn't think, Rina. I was only doing it for us. Don't be mad at me, please," he begged, getting up and coming to stand beside her chair, his fingers pulling nervously at the lace of her sleeve.

Sabrina put an arm around his waist and gave him a squeeze. "I'm sorry I had to scold you, but you had to know what I felt like when you disappeared. You have to think of other people too, Dickie."

"But I was, Rina. I was going to get the treasure for us," he explained hopefully, then gave her a confused look as he said, "You never treat Lucien very nicely, Rina, and yet he's your husband."

Sabrina felt a wave of heat flush her face uncomfortably as she replied, "That's different."

"I don't see how. I wish sometimes you'd be friends again like before, and we could all be happy together. I wish you wouldn't hurt each other the way you do," he told her, a wistful look in his blue eyes as he stared at her, trying to understand adults.

Sabrina bit her lip. "I wish we could too, but Lucien doesn't want it that way, Dickie, and I didn't either."

"But you do now?" he asked hopefully.

Sabrina smiled sadly. "I don't really know what I want. And even if I did, well, I don't think it would be possible. Now," she said briskly, changing the subject, "we will stay here tonight, and then go back to Camareigh in the morning."

Richard pulled away from her abruptly, bristling like a growling puppy. "No! I won't go, Rina. We're so close, can't we go on and look for the treasure? Please. If we find it then we'll be rich and can leave Camareigh."

And she would not have to be dependent on a man who did not love her, Sabrina thought. She would not have to ask Lucien for anything when she left him. And she would take Rhea as well. She wasn't a male heir for him, so why should he care, although she had to admit that he'd shown a great deal of attention to her. Why not continue on and look for Grandfather's treasure? It was Richard's inheritance, after all, and he should be independent and not have to worry about the marquis coming back and threatening him. She disliked leaving Rhea for any length of time, but they would not be gone for long and she was safe and well cared for at Camareigh.

"All right, Richard, we'll continue," she told him, her voice drowned out by Richard's shout of joy.

❧

They were tired and homesick when they finally reached the Highlands of Scotland almost a fortnight later. The narrow, sometimes impassable roads often washed away completely by flooding slowed them down and made their journey almost a nightmare. The optimistic excitement that had been so evident on Richard's face when they'd begun the journey had now faded as the time dragged on and he was forced to sit quietly in the confines of the swaying coach day after day.

Sabrina watched the countryside pass in silence. Never had she believed that one day she would feel like a stranger in the Highlands—but she did. She no longer belonged here, and it was completely foreign to Richard, for he'd been far too young to remember them clearly.

They entered the small village of Timere and put up at the only inn, a small establishment that offered a few rooms and no private dining room. The landlord welcomed them suspiciously, having little liking for the English, but more for their gold. Sabrina would have been concerned about the coachman and grooms abandoning them in this inhospitable area, their grumbles of dissatisfaction not having gone unnoticed by her, but they were in the employ of the Duke of Camareigh and valued their positions—along with a healthy fear of reprisal from him should they abandon the duchess.

As they settled in their room for the evening, Sabrina tried to rally Richard's drooping spirits. "Tomorrow we'll leave early and ride into the hills. The castle is in a glen north of here and sits on a small finger of land that juts out into the loch. Let's draw a smaller map of the area from the tapestry so it will be easier to carry and refer to," she suggested practically, glad that it also would give them something to do.

"I can hardly wait, Rina," Richard said happily, a dreamy look in his eyes as he thought of tomorrow's adventure.

If the landlord was curious as he rented them their Shetland ponies, he managed to contain himself as he stood curiously watching Sabrina and Richard ride off on the small shaggy ponies towards the pines dotting the slope in the distance.

From the top of the rise they stared in silence across the dead brown heather of Culloden Moor, and at the snow-capped mountains against the Moray Firth and Great Glen that cut through the heart of the Highlands. Sabrina urged her horse away from the moor, her eyes filling with tears of memory as she avoided the bog with its treacherous holes, the land marshy and crisscrossed with small brooks feeding moisture into its spongy surface. Richard kept his pony close behind Sabrina as they entered the narrow passage to the glen. They rode through wooded areas and their attention was constantly drawn to the sound of waterfalls cascading from the crags, the outcropping of rocks that had been carved by nature out of the side of the valley. Sabrina felt a shiver as they traveled deeper into the wooded glen, her eyes lingering worriedly on the mists that clung to the mountain peaks. It could sweep low into the valley without a warning, entrapping the unwary in a sea of impenetrable fog.

Every so often Sabrina would halt her pony and, straining her ears, try to catch the elusive sound that drifted through the glen.

"What's that noise, Rina?" Richard asked as she stopped the second time and he stopped to listen, too.

Sabrina gave a nervous chuckle. "I must be crazed, I thought it was a bagpipe."

"I thought those had been outlawed, Rina?"

"I know, so did I."

The sun was blocked out as they rode through the forest of pine and oak and Sabrina felt the chill enter her bones, thankful that she had been wise enough to wear her velvet cloak with a hood covering her hair and partially concealing her face.

"It's creepy, Rina," Richard said uneasily.

Sabrina glanced back at him over her shoulder with a reassuring smile. His small body was snugly wrapped in a duffle surcoat, the coarse woolen cloth keeping him warm against the cool breeze off the snowy peaks.

"Are you sure, Sabrina, that this is the right valley?" Richard called to her above the roar from a stream boiling against the rocks beside the narrow and twisting path.

Sabrina hid any doubts she might feel as she called back. "Come on, we're almost there. Just a little farther, I hope," she added beneath her breath.

The path suddenly rounded an outcropping of rock and Sabrina and Richard came to an abrupt halt. Before them, glinting silvery, was the loch, and on its shore the ruins of the castle.

"Oh, Rina," Richard breathed in awe mingled with disappointment, "it's been destroyed. Do you think they found the gold, too?"

Sabrina urged her pony down the rocky descent to the shore of the lake, her eyes unblinkingly focused on the ruined castle, not even hearing Richard's question.

"Why would they do this? Why destroy it?" she asked as they rode along the lake toward the castle, the waves lapping gently on the shore. Sabrina dismounted and walked toward the crumbling walls, large stones of what had once been a watchtower now strewn across the old courtyard. Only a skeleton structure remained of the stone stairwell, and the roof had long ago fallen in on the great hall. Sabrina looked around her in dismay, holding Richard's hand tightly as he slipped it into hers. "It was another lifetime, Richard," she said sadly, hearing the sound of her grandfather's voice echoing through the ruins.

"I remember the day we left here and hurried down those stairs," Richard said disbelieving, as he stared around the hall overgrown with weeds and overrun by nesting gulls raucously crying out at their trespass in the castle.

He pulled out the map they'd made and stared at it. "I think the cave is over there," he said, pointing vaguely towards the far shore, "but how do we get there? The path isn't marked."

Sabrina looked down at the map and then at the far shore. "The path is hard to find. Come," she urged, feeling suddenly strange as they stood exposed in the center of the ruins. "We want to get back before the mist moves down the mountain."

Richard followed Sabrina's sure steps along the shoreline and then up through the big boulders that edged the loch in large clumps. They walked along the uneven path, clear of weeds as though the feet of the clan still trod upon it.

Sabrina stopped abruptly as the path disappeared into the

lake, and cried out in disappointment. "I had forgotten that this path only goes halfway around the lake. I don't think we'll be able to get across, Dickie. We don't have a boat."

They were silently staring at their reflections in the water, when Richard gasped, his mouth opening soundlessly as a third image was reflected in the water behind them. Sabrina swallowed hard and turned, her eyes widening as she stared at the specter that had quietly sneaked up behind them. Richard gave a small whimper and pressed close to Sabrina's side.

The figure stepped closer and stared at them, his eyes wild in a face with a full beard, his hair hanging in matted clumps over his shoulders, and in his bonnet a single eagle's feather.

Sabrina stared at his tartan and leather sporran hanging from his waist. His calves were covered to the knee in tartan hose and he wore heavy brogues on his feet. His tartan was slung over his shoulder and in one hand he held a claymore and in the other a dag, the blade glinting evilly.

Sabrina hugged Richard close and tried to control her trembling as they faced the outlaw. He wore a kilt, was armed, and had a bagpipe slung over his shoulder. Sabrina was surprised, for such dress was forbidden by law, as was the playing of bagpipes—but it must have been he who'd been playing earlier.

"Sabrina," Richard whispered, his frightened grasp painfully squeezing her fingers.

The outlaw's eyes left Sabrina's cloaked figure and took in Richard standing nervously beside her, a frown settling between his eyes as he narrowed them to see better in the dim light as the mists rolled into the valley. Drops of moisture clung to Richard's red hair, and the odd light reflected from his glasses gave his eyes a grayish tint as he stared back at the outlaw.

The Highlander took a hesitant step forward, his frightening face suddenly breaking into a broad smile of excitement. "Angus?" he said in disbelief. "I dinna ken for sure it 'twas ye? I hae been waitin' fer ye tae return. I dinna know wha' tae do when they took ye awa' frae the castle? Ye heard me pipes,

Angus?" he asked hopefully. "I been wanderin' aboot the glen playin' fer ye."

Sabrina gave a sigh of relief and breathed easier as she finally recognized the outlaw. He'd changed so much in the last six years that he could have been another man. "Ewan, Ewan MacElden, it is you, isn't it?" she asked hesitantly.

He turned his eyes from Richard's face and stared penetratingly at Sabrina, a puzzled look on his bearded face.

"I'm the laird's granddaughter," she said, her words an echo of those she'd spoken so many years before.

Ewan MacElden's eyes lit up. "The wee lass?"

"Yes. You remember me?" Sabrina asked eagerly. "And this is my brother Richard, the laird's grandson."

The Highlander came closer, a doubtful look in his eyes. "Grandson?" he asked with tears in his eyes. "Nae the laird, he's deid, isn't he? I thocht he wae a ghost comin' frae the grave fer me. I promised I would play me pipes every nicht," he mumbled, his eyes drifting back to Richard's face.

Sabrina smiled uneasily as she looked around at the thickening mist. "We've got to go, Ewan, or we'll get trapped by the mist. We'll be back tomorrow," Sabrina told him, urging Richard to move.

But Ewan stepped in their path, blocking their way. "Ye wouldna get far frae here in this," he told them as the mist swirled around them.

At their worried expressions he reassured them. "Dinna fret, I ken wheer ye be safe. Come," he directed, signaling for them to follow him.

"But what of our shelties?" Richard asked. "They're at the castle."

Ewan shrugged. "The gillies? Ach, they're be all richt."

They followed the Highlander blindly through the mist along the craggy hillside until he stopped and they could hear the murmur of the lake beside them again.

"We'll hae tae take the skiff across the loch, now," he said as he dragged the small boat from cover and across the pebbly beach, the hull scraping noisily in the muffled silence.

Sabrina looked around her doubtfully. "I don't think we

should. I'd rather not stray too far from the castle. When the mists lift I'd like to be able to get down the glen and back to Timere by dusk."

Ewan glanced around, too. "Ye've little choice, lass. Ye've no place tae go. Theer's none tha' escape the mists," he told them and stood aside for them to climb into the little boat.

Sabrina looked at Richard's pale face and, shrugging, climbed into the boat. Ewan pushed them off and they floated through the mists in an eerie silence, their faces becoming soaked by the fine drizzle floating down.

"How do you know where you are going?" Sabrina asked the Highlander as they continued through the thick, concealing bank of mist.

"Nae need tae fear, I ken full weel wheer I'm goin', lass."

Sabrina accepted his word for they scraped bottom and were suddenly surrounded by large, slippery boulders on the water's edge. He led them confidently along a steeply climbing path until they came to an opening in the hillside, then he made his way deeper into the darkness of a tunnel until they came out in an enormous cavern lighted by torches fastened on the wall and giving off a spicy piney-woodscent.

Sabrina and Richard stared around them in awe. Hanging by their heels were the carcasses of a sheep and a cow, and furs were stretched on the walls and spread on the floor where also there was a pallet covered by plaids and blankets. Sabrina lowered the hood of her cloak, feeling the warmth in the cave as she and Richard hovered over the wood fire burning in the center.

Ewan MacElden bustled around the cave gathering together blankets and stacked them near the fire. "Sit doon, an' I'll fix ye somethin' to warm ye oop," he said to them and Sabrina smiled her thanks, pulling Richard down beside her.

Richard huddled in his coat and watched the kilted figure carefully. "I don't like it here, Sabrina," he whispered as he glanced around at the smoke-blackened walls of the cave and the shadowy corners.

Sabrina bit her lip and forcing a smile said confidently, "We'll be all right, Richard. This is better than being lost in the mist, and Ewan is an old friend of Grandfather's, we can trust him."

"He looks at me strange, Rina."

"That's because you look a lot like Grandfather. He had red hair too, and I think your nose will eventually become beaky like his, but you'll have to grow into it," she said, trying to get a smile from Richard's serious face, giving a sigh as he grinned slightly.

Ewan acted the perfect host, making them believe he was entertaining them in the great hall of the castle rather than in a cave on the hillside as he conscientiously saw to their every need. He served them a strong, steaming soup in wooden bowls accompanied by barley bread and then fresh trout caught from the loch.

"That was delicious, Ewan," Sabrina complimented him as she set aside her empty plate, feeling relaxed and warm in front of the fire.

The Highlander's eyes glowed with pleasure. "Ach, weel, I'm afraid I've become a bit like a cailliach. It's nae a mon's place tae cook, but I've naebody tae do it for me."

"Well, no old woman could have done as well," Sabrina said and gave Richard a nudge.

"Thank you very much, sir. I enjoyed it," he told their host politely.

Ewan straightened his short figure proudly. "I'm yer mon, Angus. I'm here tae serve ye," he said humbly.

Richard looked at Sabrina, his eyes wide and troubled. "But I'm n—"

"He is very pleased, Ewan," Sabrina cut into Richard's denial, smiling at the wild-looking man.

"Guid, now ye'll take those blankets and sleep the nicht by the fire," he said as he busily cleaned the dishes and spread out their blankets on a thick pile of leaves and dried flowers he'd quickly spread on the floor.

Richard looked at Sabrina, his eyes pleading that they leave.

"The mist must have lifted by now. We really should leave, but we thank you for your hospitality," Sabrina began.

Ewan turned with his arms full of logs for the fire, his face showing surprise. "Dinna be fulish, lass, it hasna lifted. Ye'll be stayin' here," he said firmly, his kilted figure challenging them to argue.

Sabrina looked at Richard and, shrugging, accepted his offer, knowing that without him they could not find their way back to the castle, or even out of the glen in this mist. They settled down for the night, finding their pallets of leaves and blankets quite comfortable, Sabrina felt Richard snuggle close to her and wrapped her arm around his shoulders comfortingly.

"Who is he, Sabrina?" Richard asked.

Sabrina watched the flickering flames against the stone walls and answered softly, "He was the piper of the clan, and I owe my life to him. He showed me the way to escape from the English, and if it hadn't been for him, I probably would be dead now. That is why I don't want to hurt him, Dickie. We owe him our kindness. He's stayed up in the glen all of these years alone. No wonder he gets confused at times. I feel sorry for him."

Richard was silent for a moment, then asked barely above a whisper, "Do you think he knows about the treasure?"

Sabrina shook her head in the darkness. "I don't know, he might. He was very close to Grandfather."

"Should we tell him, do you think, about the map?" Richard asked. "He might know where the cave is. Maybe it's near this one?" he guessed with growing excitement.

"It might be. I suppose we could ask him tomorrow. Now go to sleep. We'll need to be rested if we're to find that hidden treasure."

Sabrina buried her face in her arm as she fought off the wave of longing to be at Camareigh. She missed Rhea so badly, and wanted her soft, warm body cuddled against her breast. She had forgotten how isolated and ancient the Highlands were. She could be on the other side of the world from Camareigh, so cut off were they. She sniffed back the tears that were gathering behind her eyes, blinking rapidly to keep them from falling. She wanted to go home. She wanted to be back at Camareigh holding her child, and even fighting with Lucien.

She didn't know why this morbid feeling of dread was hanging over her, but she suddenly felt as if she would never leave the Highlands and never see Camareigh and Rhea again.

Lucien must know by now that she was gone. Would he be worried, or wonder what had happened to them. She wondered where he was now, and what he was doing.

&

Lucien urged his horse through the stream that crossed their path, splashing water against the dusty blackness of his jackboots and turning their surface into rivulets of mud. He glared up at the gray skies overhead and then at the man riding silently beside him. "Does the sun never shine in this cursed land?" he asked with a mocking glance.

Terence Fletcher laughed tiredly. "Never while I was assigned here. They do tell me there have been sunny days, although I've yet to meet anyone who has seen one."

Lucien flexed his shoulders slowly. "You think they've gone to the castle?"

"I'm not sure, but I would wager that they have," Terence speculated gravely. "I hope to God I am right."

"What made Richard run off to Scotland?" Lucien asked for the hundredth time, and still came up with no answer.

"It must have something to do with the castle. We have traced your coach from various inns this far. It must be heading to Timere. The castle is up in the hills above it. It must be where they've gone. We can only be a day behind them at the most. If we hadn't gotten caught in those floods we would've been here before them. We must've lost three days," Terence complained in disgust. "I must be getting old, because these miles seem to get longer, the hills higher, and my back stiffer."

Lucien grinned sympathetically. "An afternoon's romp in Hyde Park doesn't prepare you for hundreds of miles of hard riding, I assure you."

Most nights they had managed to find an inn to stay at, but tonight they were in a secluded and uninhabited valley and were forced into sleeping under the cloudy skies. Lucien ate his share of rations hungrily, if not with relish, and was grateful for the ex-colonel's experience in camping out, as he planned their meals and routes as he would have a campaign.

"I've always felt strangely out of place up here," Terence commented suddenly from his side of the fire. "I can remember how relieved I was to receive orders sending me back to England. I've always felt as though I were entering another age when I travel through the Highlands. Even the language is different."

"Tell me about the first time you met Sabrina," Lucien asked as he pulled a blanket over his shoulders for protection against the cold night air.

"The coincidences of life never fail to amaze me. Little did I imagine then that years later I would be married to that little girl's sister and coming back up here to find, or rescue, her from some unknown danger."

"Mary said Sabrina witnessed the battle at Culloden," Lucien said.

"I suppose I'll always see her as that little girl. Her violet eyes blazing with fury, her cheeks flushed pink and her lips trembling," Terence said softly as he remembered. "She even took a shot at me with a pistol almost as heavy as she was."

"Sounds like the Sabrina of today. She has changed very little," Lucien commented dryly.

"She never will be completely docile, Lucien. She's a high-strung little filly and will always rebel," Terence warned him. "But then, that is why you love her, isn't it?" he asked, unable to see the duke's face in the darkness, but hearing his indrawn breath at the suddenness of the remark. "You do, don't you? You've just been too stubborn to admit it."

"Not too stubborn, Terence, just too unsure of myself. I fell in love with that little vixen long ago, but by the time I realized it, I'd already committed the mistake of my life— I married Sabrina under false pretences. Can you imagine she'd believe me if I'd told her after she remembered that I'd married her to inherit Camareigh that I'd suddenly found out that I really loved her? I think not. She was so full of anger and hurt pride, thinking she'd been made a fool of, that she wouldn't have listened to anyone, least of all me," Lucien said bitterly.

"But she is in love with you. I saw you two together many times when you were first married and you were very happy."

"That was because we were starting fresh, with none of the misunderstandings or hurtful memories of the past to ruin our relationship. And that is when I truly fell in love with Sabrina. I had desired her before—but that changed to something stronger and deeper," Lucien admitted softly. "It was something totally new for me, and I suppose in my inexperience I handled Sabrina wrong."

"Why, for heaven's sake, have you let a year pass and never told Sabrina the truth? You are barely civil to her, and leaving her to her own devices was bound to lead her into trouble."

"I wanted to give her time to cool off and let her wounded pride heal. I hoped she would forget the old hurts, and once Rhea was born I thought we might be able to start over again. Only as the months passed so did the chances to change anything. I've never been a coward about anything—at least not until then. I found I couldn't face Sabrina. I couldn't risk turning her completely against me. And then under the strain I lost my temper and stormed out, and so I wasn't there when she needed me."

"You can't blame yourself, Lucien. No one could've guessed something like this would happen."

"Mary did," Lucien reminded him.

"And it still has happened," Terence replied. "I just wish we knew more about it."

The next morning they had been traveling for about three hours when they saw a small village ahead. "Timere," Terence told Lucien, his eyes bright with anticipation. In the distance they could see a mountain range and the shimmering of water.

Terence looked to Lucien, noting the tightened lips and determined set of his shoulders. He had lost weight, and had a lean and hungry look about him as he rode down the lane to the village.

They both saw the duke's coach at the same time and the grooms busily scrubbing it clean of mud from the long journey. As they heard the sound of horses' hooves they looked up from their work, and upon recognizing the duke they gave a yell of surprised pleasure and ran forward to greet him, taking their horses as Lucien and Terence dismounted.

"Sure glad we are, to see yer grace," the coachman said, coming forward more sedately, but quickly, to greet the duke.

"George," Lucien greeted him, "you seem to have had quite a journey."

"That we have, and if I may say so, we'd not a bit o' trouble with the coach."

"Good, I expect her grace was relieved about that. See that our horses are well taken care of, we've ridden them hard, George," Lucien ordered as he made for the inn.

"Ah, yer grace," George called after Lucien, hurrying to catch up.

Lucien turned, looking at the coachman inquiringly. "Yes, what is it?"

"Well, it's about her grace," George blurted out.

Lucien frowned. "What is it? I take it she is in the inn? She isn't ill, is she?" he asked quickly.

"Well, to tell the truth, yer grace, she ain't in there."

Lucien looked at Terence, who was listening intently to the groom's explanation. George licked his lips nervously as Lucien asked, "Where is she?"

"She and the young gentleman rode out yesterday morning, and ain't come back yet. Must've gotten caught by the mist up there somewhere. I'm awfully sorry, yer grace. We offered to ride along but her grace refused and ordered us to stay here," he apologized. "We was out ridin' around the area earlier, but we ain't seen a sign of her or the boy."

"Thank you, George, you did what you could."

Lucien turned away abruptly and with firm steps headed for the inn, Terence close behind him. The landlord met them at the door, unable to conceal his surprise at finding, within a day, two more guests on his doorstep when he usually had one or two a year.

"You've the Duchess of Camareigh staying here. I wish to see her room, and prepare two more for myself and my friend," Lucien ordered as he faced the surly looking landlord.

"Maybe I canna dae that," he replied. "An who be ye fer me tae let ye in the lady's room?"

"I am her husband, and the Duke of Camareigh. That gives me the right."

The landlord shifted uneasily before the steely gaze of the scar-faced man. "Guid enough fer me. Ye'll be wantin' two rooms, and anything tae eat?"

"Whatever you have available," Lucien replied. "Which room is her grace's?"

"Tae yer richt, first door."

Terence followed Lucien down the narrow hall to the first door, and on entering they looked around curiously. At the end of the bed was a trunk which Lucien recognized as Sabrina's, and next to it a smaller one which must be Richard's. The room was neat and clean, the bed made, but no items identifiable as Sabrina's were sitting out.

Lucien gave a sigh of exasperation. "I don't know what I expected to find. As soon as our horses are rested we'll ride out again. We've got to find them. Maybe the landlord will know where the castle is?"

"You can forget about the horses. In this terrain, once we've left the main road, they are useless and dangerous to ride. What we need are a couple of shelties to carry us," Terence advised from experience, and glancing around the room said thoughtfully, "I think we should look in their trunks. They'd hardly leave anything important lying about."

Lucien knelt down by Sabrina's trunk, trying the lid, but it wouldn't open.

"Here," Terence said, handing him a knife.

Lucien slid the blade into the lock and moved it around, applying pressure until he heard a snap and with a triumphant sigh pried open the lock and lifted the lid. He stared down silently for a moment as he recognized Sabrina's dresses. His hands lingered on a delicate chemise as he felt down in the trunk, lifting various items from it, but coming across nothing that could possibly help them. He'd placed a couple of folded petticoats in a pile with some handkerchiefs while he went through the trunk and was about to put them back when Terence bent down and picked up a piece of tapestried cloth and unfolded it. "What is this, I wonder," he murmured, then blurted, "Good God."

Lucien looked up startled, and got to his feet quickly. "What the devil is it?"

"Look at this. Here is your answer to why Sabrina and Richard are here," Terence said in excitement, holding the tapestry spread before him.

Lucien gazed at it. "It looks like a map. There's a castle, and a lake, and a church—" He paused as his eyes narrowed, staring at the little figures and the trail of golden thread. "My God, a buried treasure map."

"Exactly. The old laird buried it six years ago to keep it safe from us. He was a wise old boy, for the army did plunder, and his castle was among the unfortunate ones, but we didn't find any gold. This is amazing. I wonder where it came from, and why now, six years later."

Lucien's hands gripped the tapestry, his knuckles showing white as he stared down at it. "Mary's vision, it had a lake and Richard and Sabrina in a boat, didn't it?" he asked in dread.

Terence nodded worriedly. "And they did not return yesterday. The castle is in ruins. I don't know where they would have spent the night?"

Lucien folded up the tapestry and tucked it under his arm. "I think we'd better have a word with this landlord and find out what he can tell us."

They found food had been set out, along with whiskey and ale on the long table in the dining room.

"If you will allow me to handle this, Lucien?" Terence suggested as they entered the room and sat down at the table. "If we rush things, he won't tell us anything, nor will threats help. Will you trust me?"

Lucien glanced at the landlord impatiently, then with a nod agreed. "Very well, but don't take too long," he warned, and pouring himself a whiskey took a large swallow without a grimace or shiver of revulsion as the strong stuff entered his throat. They ate in silence for a few minutes and Lucien was surprised that he could actually eat anything while he waited anxiously for Terence's move.

Terence called the landlord over as they finished, and to Lucien's surprise asked the man to join them for a drink. The landlord seemed momentarily surprised, although it was the custom to invite your host for a drink before you left the inn, but after a second's hesitation sat down and accepted a glass of whiskey. "I understand that the duchess and her brother did not return yesterday from their ride."

The landlord shrugged his shoulders uncommunicatively. "Canna be expected tae know wheer all o' my guests are."

Terence's lips tightened slightly and he sent a warning glance to Lucien, who was about to speak. "Did you rent them ponies?"

"Aye."

"Did you see which way they rode off?" Terence persisted, questioning him patiently.

"Canna say I did," he answered with a sly smile and made to rise, but Terence's next question stopped him.

"Did you know that the duchess is the old laird from the castle's granddaughter, and that the boy is his only grandson and heir?"

The landlord sat back down, a look of dawning dismay on his face. "Ach, wha' a fule I've been. I thought tha' lad had the look aboot hin. The red hair is of the clan. And now I remember them sayin' the granddaughter was different frae the other two. Dark as nicht, she weer, and just as wild."

"Did they go to the castle?" Terence asked, expecting a little more information now.

"Nae doot aboot it. They rode off fer the glen," he said, shaking his head. "I should hae warned them, ach, but I dinna ken who they weer."

"Why should you have warned them?" Lucien asked sharply, his patience wearing thin. "Because of the mist?"

The landlord shook his head. "The mists are bad, aye, but 'tis the ghost tha' haunts the glen tha' will get them."

Lucien and Terence exchanged surprised glances. "Ghost?" Terence said in disbelief.

"Aye. The English soldiers dinna believe, either, until they went in theer and only two came back, and they'd lost their wits. Naebody goes in theer and comes out alive, or not possessed by the devil."

⚜

"Guid mornin' tae ye," Ewan greeted Richard and Sabrina the next morning as he fussed over the fire cooking eggs. Then pouring a steaming herb tea into cups he handed one to each of them and beamed, "It's sweet frae the honeycomb. Ye wee folks like it sweet?" he asked.

Richard sipped his and nodded in approval. "It's quite good," he complimented the anxiously waiting figure.

"Guid."

"Has the mist cleared?" Sabrina asked hopefully.

"Nae, lass, it's still theer," he replied, keeping an eye on the eggs and not looking up.

"When do you expect it to?" Sabrina persisted.

"Dinna ken," the Highlander answered unhelpfully and spooned fluffy eggs onto their plates along with some cold mutton.

Richard ate his hungrily under the watchful eye of Ewan, but Sabrina just nibbled at hers. "You know the glen very well, don't you?" Sabrina commented.

"Aye, lived here ferever."

Sabrina nodded her head to Richard, who eagerly withdrew the map from a pocket of his jacket. "Ewan, do you know where this cave is?"

Ewan took the map and gazed down at it for a moment. "Wheer did ye get this, laddie?" he asked, his eyes going suspiciously between the two of them as they sat there watching him expectantly.

"Aunt Margaret made it. At least she made the tapestry of it and we copied it. She said Grandfather told her to make it, and then to give it to me and Sabrina. It's a map of the treasure," Richard confided with growing excitement. "Do you know where it's buried, Ewan?"

"Waur a secret, ye know," he said softly. "Naebody's tae know aboot it."

"As the laird's grandson, my brother has the right. Don't you agree?" Sabrina asked.

"Aye, he's the richt," Ewan said abruptly, and picking up his broadsword, held it casually in his hand. "Come, ye'll see the treasure, but ye'll nae tell anyone aboot it. I promised the laird to guard it with me life."

Sabrina and Richard got to their feet as he motioned them to follow him, but rather than leaving the cave he headed towards the back of it. He reached for one of the torches on the wall and holding it in front of him made for one of the dark corners of the cave, the light from the torch revealing a narrow passage they had not seen before. Following Ewan into it, Richard found Sabrina's cold hand, and they walked cautiously along the slippery stone path, moisture dripping from the walls as they headed deeper into the earth, the torch Ewan held before him making his kilted figure look grotesque as it cast huge, wavering shadows on the walls.

They came to the end of the passage and stopped, a large wooden door built across the opening barring their way. Ewan took a key from his sporran and fitted it easily into the lock, the noise as he turned it grating loudly in the close confines of the tunnel.

He pushed the door open and entered the darkness first, signaling for them to follow him. They moved carefully behind him as he made his way farther into the room, leading them to the distant corner. Suddenly Richard grabbed Sabrina's arm with his other hand and squealed in excitement. "Look!"

Sabrina followed his pointing finger and caught her breath as she stared at the big chests full of golden objects and coins revealed under the torch held above them by the Highlander. They looked just like a hidden treasure should, with the lid opened on the chest to reveal gold and jewels crowding inside and almost overflowing. Stacked around them were paintings in heavy gold frames, and vases and other objects d'art of priceless value.

Richard ran across and stared down into one of the chests, his hands finding a large gold goblet filled with golden guineas. He picked up a necklace of pearls and held it out to Sabrina, the large pearl drops gleaming ghostlike in the torchlight.

"The treasure, Rina, we've found the treasure!" he cried, jumping up and down as Sabrina came to stand beside him.

Ewan stuck the torch in the wall above the chests and moved away, lighting other torches around the room while Sabrina and Richard gazed in awe at the treasure. Richard stuffed as many coins as he could into his pockets as he gazed in rapture at the fortune that was his.

Ewan silently came up beside them and watched with a half-smile on his lips. Sabrina wished she could feel the excitement, but the look on the Highlander's face worried her as he stared almost hypnotically at them and the treasure.

As Sabrina remained subdued beside him, Richard turned around, his small face glowing with excitement as he said, "Come on, Rina. You can have wh—" He stopped what he was saying abruptly, the coins he had held in his hands dropping to the stone floor and rolling across it as he stared in stunned silence at the opposite wall of the cave that was not illuminated by torches.

Sabrina turned reluctantly to follow Richard's pointing finger, her startled cry echoing around the small chamber as she stared into the hollow-eyed skulls of skeletons hanging in chains from the wall. Richard buried his face against Sabrina's breast as she leaned weakly against him as they cowered in front of the treasure. They stood frozen in fear as the Highlander chuckled beside them.

"They waur fules. They shouldna come in tae the glen. They wae goin' tae steal the treasure. Naebody haed better try tae do that," Ewan said as he stood before them now, his feet planted firmly apart and his broadsword held carefully before him at an angle. He could easily lift his arm, bringing it down in a mighty swing that would split either of their heads wide open.

Sabrina held Richard rigidly still beside her, some instinct warning her should she move it would mean instant death.

The Highlander shook his head regretfully. "Ye shouldna hae come here, fer I canna allow ye tae leave knowin' the secret. Ye can stand watch over it like them on the wall," he told Sabrina and Richard with a sly grin, his crazed eyes glowing in the flickering light.

"You must not harm us," Sabrina told him shakily, "We are the laird's kin. He would be very angry with you."

Ewan frowned. "Angus wouldna be happy? I dinna ken what tae do? I'm supposed tae protect the treasure frae the English," he mumbled, then with a gleam in his eyes he looked at them. "I canna believe ye the laird's kin. He dinna like the English, and ye be English dogs, comin' tae steal our gold," he spat. "A real duinhe-wassel ye are, in yer fancy britches. Wheer is ye kilt, mon?" he asked Richard angrily.

Sabrina pulled up Richard's face, holding it to the light frantically. "Look good, Ewan MacElden," she cried "See the red hair, the nose, and eyes. He's Angus. Angus has come back from the grave to see you," she told him, urging Richard in front of her while she moved closer to the chest full of heavy gold goblets and plates, her hand searching for a weapon.

The Highlander peered down at Richard's face in doubt. "Come back frae the grave, the auld laird, just to see me, MacElden?" he whispered, his broadsword lowered for an instant.

Sabrina's fingers wrapped themselves around the thick stem of a heavy goblet and without warning or aim she swung with all of her might against the side of the Highlander's head. The goblet struck his skull with a thud, stunning him as he sunk to his knees.

Sabrina grabbed Richard's hand and ran from the room, the evilly grinning skulls dancing in the light behind them. They ran through the darkness of the narrow passageway, slipping on the rocks as they skidded down it. Richard missed his footing once, falling painfully to his knees, but Sabrina jerked him to his feet before he knew what had happened, her sense of urgency spurring them on faster. They breathed a sigh of relief as they came out into the lighted main cavern, and not stopping to rest, Sabrina urged Richard on through it, her heart jumping in terror as she heard the cry of rage echoing behind them. She remembered it from the battlefield, and knew the Highlander was out for their blood as he gave the war cry.

As they cleared the tunnel that opened into the hillside, Sabrina stopped in disbelief. Ewan had lied to them—the mists had lifted, she could see sky above them and in the distance through the trees the rim of the lake shimmering silver.

They ran down the hillside, fear quickening their steps as they scurried like rabbits through the pine trees and around outcroppings of rock until they reached the lake's edge.

"What do we do now?" Richard cried, looking back over his shoulder fearfully, expecting to see the crazed Highlander come charging down on them any second.

"Help me, Dickie," Sabrina called as she struggled to pull the small boat across the beach. Richard grunted as he pulled and pulled along with Sabrina until they finally managed to get the boat in the water. Jumping in, they slowly floated away from the shore, but not before Sabrina saw the glinting of Ewan MacElden's broadsword through the trees, and a spot of plaid near the shore.

They paddled wildly as they tried to move the boat across the lake, the water splashing noisily as they struggled. Sabrina looked up startled as Richard cried out a warning, looking over her shoulder to see another boat leave the shore with a kilted figure rowing smoothly through the water in pursuit of them.

"Together, Richard, together," Sabrina cried, tears of frustration and fear streaking her face as they moved jerkily through the water. But suddenly the little boat began to move steadily and faster toward the opposite shore where they could see the familiar ruins of the castle.

"We're in the current!" Sabrina called out, new hope surging through her as she saw the distance lengthen between the two boats as they neared the shore. The boat scraped bottom suddenly, throwing them to the floor as it beached. Richard scrambled out, giving Sabrina a helping hand as they stumbled over the rocky shore toward the concealment of the ruins of the castle. They ran along the narrow path they had traveled on only the day before and breathlessly fell into the castle grounds. They would never have made the cover of the trees along the shore or have made it back up into the glen.

Sabrina tried to catch her breath as she stared between two large blocks of granite at the empty lake. She could see the two boats bobbing on the shore, but there was no sign of Ewan MacElden.

Richard pressed against her as they hid under the overhanging stairwell and waited. Sabrina cursed beneath her breath at the cries of the gulls protesting their presence and certain to give their hiding place away.

"Rina," Richard whispered, "I'm sorry." Tears trickled from his eyes as he hunched beside her, his face white as a sheet.

Sabrina put her arm over his shaking shoulders protectively. "It's all right, Dickie, I don't blame you, love."

Richard sniffed, taking deep gulps of air as he tried to control his sobs. Sabrina rocked his body back and forth trying to calm him, when suddenly she stilled as she heard the sound of a foot striking stone. She could feel Richard's uncontrollable shaking as they crouched together.

The terrible scream directly behind them frightened Sabrina until all she could hear was the pounding of her blood in her ears, and looking up she screamed in pure terror as she saw the Highlander swinging his broadsword from the top of the crumbling wall above them, his eyes blazing with bloodlust as he screamed and jumped down behind them. He raised his claymore and began to run toward them. Sabrina pulled Richard behind her, shielding his body with hers and prepared to feel the cold blade cut into her body. But before he reached them a loud shot rang out, and with a stunned look on his face, Ewan MacElden fell to his knees, his broadsword clanging against the broken stones of the castle as he fell forward onto the ground, his plaid spread out across his arm and claymore.

Sabrina stared at the dead man in disbelief, not hearing the running footsteps that came up quickly to where she and Richard still knelt against the ruins.

"Sabrina, my love," Lucien said hoarsely as he pulled her up into his arms and held her body to his tightly, as if making sure she really existed.

Sabrina looked up into his scarred face, her violet eyes full of shock and disbelief. "Lucien?" she whispered, her hands holding on to him desperately. "You are here?" she asked in confusion as she managed to drag her eyes away from his face and saw Terence holding Richard against his chest comfortingly.

She looked back up at Lucien, her eyes taking in every detail of his beloved face. "You came, you came when I needed you. Oh, Lucien, I don't ever want to leave you again. Never let me go, please," she pleaded tearfully as she buried her face against his shoulder, blocking out the chilling sight of poor Ewan MacElden, once, long ago, piper of the clan.

❧

Sabrina smiled shyly at Lucien as he sat down on the edge of the bed in her room at the inn in Timere. Richard was asleep in the other room, his little face drained of emotion as he mechanically ate his dinner and then without argument allowed Lucien and Terence to put him to bed. Sabrina sighed as she remembered this morning, pain darkening her eyes to purple.

"Try not to think about it, Sabrina," Lucien advised as he took the tea tray off her lap and placed it on a table nearby. "The Highlander must have gone mad years ago, and now he's no longer suffering."

"I keep remembering how he saved my life so long ago, only now to try and take it," Sabrina said sadly. "Do you know, I won't be sorry to leave here. Once I would've given anything to have been able to return to the Highlands, but now all I want is to return to Camareigh and Rhea."

"And me?" Lucien asked softly. "Would you want to return to me?"

Sabrina looked up into his sherry eyes, humbled for the first time in her life. "I would *like* to return to you, if you want me. I know you do not love me, but," Sabrina hesitated, swallowing painfully, "it does not matter as long as I can be with you, Lucien."

"Oh, Sabrina, little love," Lucien spoke against her ear as he pulled her into his arms and held her against his breast. "I have loved you since we kissed in the fields at Verrick House."

At her start of surprise he laughed. "I was all kinds of a fool, and I knew in your anger you would never believe that I would've married you even if my inheritance had not depended upon it."

Sabrina's violet eyes were wide with astonishment as she stared at him.

"I decided not to pressure you, to give you time to learn to love me all over again, only your stubbornness and pride stood in the way, as well as my temper." He put his hand under her chin and held her face to his. "I love you, Sabrina, and I will not live without you. Do you think you can find it in your heart to forgive me?" he asked gravely, his eyes clinging to hers, waiting for an answer.

Sabrina clasped her hands around his neck and looked deeply into his eyes, her violet eyes mirroring her deepest feelings. "I missed you desperately, Lucien, and I longed for you to come to me. I thought if ever I got back to Camareigh I would do anything to try and make you love me. My pride be damned, life isn't worth living without you, Lucien," Sabrina confessed, then touching her lips to his softly, whispered, "I love you, and if you'll have me, this time I'll gladly give you a son."

Lucien laughed, holding her close to him, loving the feel of her soft body against his. "The sun is indeed shining in the Highlands today, for Richard has found his treasure, and I..." he paused, kissing Sabrina lingeringly. "I have found mine."

AN EXCERPT FROM

Devil's Desire

High in a cloud-laden afternoon sky, a free-spirited skylark soared gracefully; its spread-winged shadow traveling swiftly over the colorful autumnal countryside below. Its song pierced the primeval silence of the forest below as the cheerful cry carried through the chill air; the clear notes penetrating beneath the thick canopy of branches, and reaching the soft, loam-covered forest floor, the sound was absorbed by the bright carpet of fallen leaves.

The woods seemed to come to life, humming with the chirpings and chatterings of busy forest creatures contentedly gathering food for the oncoming winter, until another sound intruded into the aimless animal chatter and sent a hush over the clearing. An uneasy silence hung over it as the threatening sounds of baying hounds and pounding horses' hooves echoed in the distance.

The gossiping birds took wing and the bushy-tailed squirrels scurried into safe nests as a figure emerged from the trees, twigs snapping sharply as it moved into the clearing.

"Tally-ho!" Ribald laughter followed the cry of the hunt. "Where is that foxy wench? Damnation! Don't lose sight of her now, man!"

The excited voices drifted to a still figure, galvanizing it into action, and the raised voices became louder as the riders moved closer. Then the voices merged into one menacing sound as they intermingled with the snorting of their mounts.

As they came closer, Elysia could almost feel their hot breath against the back of her neck, as she held up her skirts and hurriedly climbed over a fallen tree. She stopped, pausing to catch her breath, panting heavily as she leaned against another tree for support. She could hear the raised voices of the men as they searched about the undergrowth, not far off, beating it back to find her hiding place. She shivered as she heard the throaty yelping of the dogs, and saw movement through the trees as the horsemen pressed on toward her; each passing second bringing them closer.

She stood still, frozen with fear, her eyes darting about like those of a trapped animal seeking safety. Suddenly, she noticed the hollowed out trunk of the fallen tree, the opening partially concealed by the full-fronded ferns and wild weeds that grew about the gaping mouth. She moved quickly into the cool, concealing darkness. Crawling past the thick ferns, she pulled them back into order as she stretched out full length on the rotted and damp bottom. She shivered as she felt the little crawling inhabitants of the decayed tree about her. Elysia's breath caught painfully in her throat as she heard the pounding of the horses' hooves coming straight towards her; shaking the earth beneath her body until she thought she would be trampled to death beneath them.

"Bloody fool! You've let her flee!" said a petulant voice, startling Elysia by its closeness.

"Damn it all, it's you who slowed me up—thought you saw her in a dozen different places," another voice complained.

"First decent bit o' muslin I've seen in this damned county, and what happens?" demanded the first voice, self-pityingly. "She gets away. Did you see that glorious hair! A real little fox she was—and those long legs! By God, I'll not be cheated out of my prize after going to the trouble of giving chase!"

Elysia heard the creaking of his saddle as the rider shifted impatiently, and the ominous snapping sound of a riding crop being tapped angrily against gloved hands.

"Where are those cursed hounds? We'd have had her flushed out by now if those hounds were on her scent. Could've sworn I saw something over here."

"Sounds like they've caught scent of something over that way," the other man spoke as the distant sound of raised voices and barking reached them.

"Damn! It'd better be the wench! I'll beat their hides off if they've cornered a bloody hare. I'm going to have that maid to warm my bed this eve. It's too damned cold in this blasted place to sleep alone." He sighed in exasperation. "We'd better find her soon, because I'm played out; too damned tired to even breathe, much less enjoy the wench. Wish I were back in London—don't have to hunt for my pleasures there. Plenty of high-steppers just begging for my favors," he boasted.

"You're getting soft, my friend. The hunt adds spice to the victory, but we'd best be off, or you'll only have your old housekeeper to warm your bones this eve," his friend snickered.

"I'll be warming myself against that red-haired wench. You can have my housekeeper, or one of the scullions—more your style," he said laughing loudly.

"You don't have her yet, and who knows, she might prefer me after she's caught a glimpse of you."

"Damned if she will!" he answered rising to the bait. "I'll wager my team of blacks she begs me to take her back to London before the night's out."

Elysia heard their laughter, and then trembled as she felt the fragile walls of her sanctuary shake as the riders urged their mounts over the fallen tree, and moved off into the trees toward the excited barking of the hounds.

Elysia waited, scarcely breathing as she listened to the retreating hoof beats. Breathlessly, she peered out between the lacy, interwoven fronds, seeing only emptiness in the clearing beyond. At last, they were gone.

Slowly, like a hunted animal, she crawled from the safety of her hole and paused, as if sniffing the air for the scent of an enemy, poised for flight at the first sign of danger. As she made her way through the trees Elysia felt tears of rage and fright well up in her eyes.

Her lips quivered as she thought of herself like some animal being hunted for pleasure. No wonder the villagers kept their young daughters close to their sides when the wild bloods, the fancy London gentlemen, paid their irregular visits to their estates in the country. Attired in their finely-cut coats and lacy cravats, jewels glittering from their long white fingers, they demanded, and expected, anything they wanted, causing havoc the few days they took up residence on their country estates. They abused their landlordly rights by browbeating their tenants, and seducing their daughters. From upstairs maid to milk maid—not one comely face was safe from their lust.

And now she, Elysia Demarice, daughter of aristocratic parents, was humiliated and reduced to cowering like a frightened beast afraid for her life. She had to suffer the indignity of being pursued by fun-seeking young bloods from London, out to satisfy their carnal desires. Were she still under the protection of her father's house, they would not dare to approach her; she was their equal—in name and position. Possessing beauty was a liability when one did not have the protection of one's family.

But a far greater outrage, Elysia thought, was her aunt's perfidy. She had sent her out here to the north end of the property, well aware that young Lord Tanner was visiting with a party of his disreputable friends. The possibility of their paths crossing while she innocently searched for acorns, had probably wriggled in the back of Aunt Agatha's mind like a worm in a rotting apple.

Aunt Agatha seemed to derive some sadistic pleasure in reducing her to the lowest level of human existence. What sin had she committed? What gods had she angered to deserve such a fate, Elysia wondered despondently? If only she could turn back the clock and return to happier days. The happier times, the innocence of her childhood—those were the things of which she dreamed.

Elysia slowed her pace, feeling safe as she skirted a field of dumbly grazing sheep, unaware of the burrs and mud clinging to the hem of her dress. She wandered down the stony path, her mind far too preoccupied by other thoughts to see the dark storm clouds gathering to the north, or to feel the wind gaining strength and threatening the colorful autumn leaves on the trees. The wind whipped the hair framing her face into curls of wild disorder and brought color to her pale white cheeks. Elysia clutched her shawl closer about her shoulders as it grew chillier and the cold penetrated her light woolen dress.

Jumping as agilely as a cat onto the wet and slippery stones bridging the gurgling brook, Elysia landed sure-footedly on the bank opposite. She looked towards the large house in the distance. A small copse of sturdy oak partially hid it from her view, but she knew by heart every line of its unwelcoming outline. She had memorized each ugly, gray stone in its walls, every shuttered window and locked door—each was indelibly imprinted upon her mind.

Elysia wished that she could travel on past the old house, passing without a glance of recognition at its unfriendly appearance; but she couldn't. She had lived at Graystone Manor, her aunt's house, since the death of her parents.

How different her life had been before that fateful day! She could never forget the image of her father's sleek new phaeton as it overturned on a sharp curve of the road near their home. The panicked horses raced wildly down the road, dragging the overturned carriage with her helpless parents trapped beneath it.

Their death had left Elysia alone in the world. Without a guardian she had been unable to deal with the affairs of their estate as the army of solicitors and tradesmen descended down upon her like vultures smelling death.

Her father, Charles Demarice, blithely unaware of his fate, had left no will. With his death went the last of the income they had been living on from day to day—money won in gambling. This, added to the inheritance left to her father by his grandmother, had allowed them to live comfortably, if not extravagantly. But now Elysia found, to her dismay, all that was left of that gradually depleted inheritance were the debts to be paid.

Her home would have to be sold, along with the furnishings, and their stable of horses. It would be difficult to leave Rose Arbor, the manor house she had known since she had been born; but the thought of parting with her treasured stallion Ariel was too much to bear.

She and her brother Ian had learned how to ride at an early age, and Elysia could mount and ride a horse with a skill few men could equal. She had been taught by her father and Gentle Jims, the family's groom, who seemed to read a horse's mind and had a hand as gentle as a baby's upon the reins. Riding was Elysia's existence, the breath of life to her and she rode like a wild and free spirit of the moors. Ariel was a pure Arabian stallion, sleek and white, his slender tapered legs barely touching the ground as he galloped through the misty mornings with Elysia joyously astride him.

Elysia had known that she had caused considerable talk among the villagers with her escapades. She had heard the gossiping about her, but it was of little concern to her; in fact it had amused her to hear what they had said, especially the self-appointed matriarch of the village, the Widow MacPherson.

"T'isn't natural the way her rides that horse. You wouldn't believe me if I was to tell ye that she talks to that beastie, aye, and by all that is Holy, if he don't understand her too!" she had raved. "I see dark clouds over the horizon. She be a heathen, that one." But Elysia had only laughed as she had listened to the Widow's rantings to a wide-eyed audience of avid listeners.

The Widow MacPherson had cautioned the villagers with this ominous prediction during the years that the Demarices had lived in their manor near the village. The villagers began to believe her prophesies when Elysia's brother, an officer in the British Navy, was lost at sea only a day after the tragic death of their parents. The villagers cowered behind closed doors as Elysia rode madly through the village at midnight after hearing the news, her long hair streaking behind her, Ariel a white flash of light against the darkness of the night.

That had been the last time Elysia had ridden Ariel. Within the week a relative she had never met arrived at Rose Arbor claiming to be her mother's stepsister. Elysia vaguely remembered her mother telling her that she had lived with a stepsister when she was a young girl. That was all she would tell her. What was in the past was best forgotten, her mother had said sadly, with a look of remembered pain darkening her blue eyes, and it had been the only time Elysia remembered seeing her so unhappy.

Agatha Penwick, a tall, thin woman in her fifties, had taken command of Rose Arbor and all business and financial matters with authoritative efficiency. Her plain, gaunt face, with its long, narrow nose and small, colorless eyes had a speculative, calculating look as she inspected the house; assessing the value of everything down to the last shilling.

"I am your mother's only living relative, and I believe your father had no one who could take on the responsibility of raising you now," she had said coldly, without a trace of warmth or commiseration in her voice for Elysia's loss. "The proceeds, if any are left after paying off your parents' debts, will serve as payment to me for taking you into a proper home."

Agatha had then proceeded to have auctioned off the family's possessions, pleasing the Demarices' creditors and solicitors. Everyone had been pleased with the results except Elysia, whose wishes had been ruthlessly dismissed as sentimental rubbish.

Elysia had been heartbroken as Agatha coldly dismissed all of the Demarices' faithful servants, most of them having served the family for over thirty years.

"They will have to find new employment. I have no use for them, and furthermore, they are past their prime. Do me no good," as she curtly answered Elysia's plea to take them with her to Graystone Manor.

Elysia had tried to reassure them; promising to find them all new positions as soon as she could. But she doubted whether the older servants could find new employers—or would want to. They were ready to retire—only having stayed with the Demarices out of loyalty and love.

The night before she had left Rose Arbor, Bridget, her old nanny, had sat brushing Elysia's long, silky hair as she had done each night since Elysia had been a little girl, a tearful smile on her wrinkled face as she tried to comfort her young charge. "You just take care, Miss Elysia, and don't you fret your pretty little head about me. If you need me—well, you know where I'll be, and even though my niece's place isn't very big, and it's way out in Wales, you'd still be welcomed. You just wait and see, we'll all be together again, little one, just like before, and someday I'll be burping your wee ones like I did you and Ian, God rest his soul."

Elysia had smiled, agreeing with her, but somehow she knew that nothing would ever be the same again.

Her eyes still filled with tears as she thought of Ariel. Her aunt had sent him to London to be sold at a higher price than they would have gotten in the Northern counties. Elysia had pleaded tearfully with her aunt to allow her to keep him, but she had brushed Elysia's pleas aside contemptuously, saying that she would have little time for riding or playing where she was going.

Elysia's only consolation had been that Gentle Jims had gone to London, where he would seek new employment, and would personally handle Ariel until he was sold. She knew Jims would take care of Ariel, who with the exception of herself and Jims, would allow no one else near him. Elysia had worried about this—afraid that as a one-master horse he would be useless to anyone else. She could only hope that whoever purchased him would be gentle with him and give him the chance to adjust to a new master. It was too much to hope for—that Jims might be able to stay with him and remain his trainer. But Elysia knew that she could never stop worrying about Ariel; nor would she ever be able to forget him.

Graystone Manor was as gloomy and gray as its name implied, Elysia thought, as they drove up the circular drive to the austere entrance of the house. She felt depressed and subdued after the day's journey in silence with her aunt.

That had been two years ago. Elysia's thoughts came back to the present as she stood again, staring up at the gray house that never seemed to change.

About the Author

Laurie McBain became a publishing phenomenon at age twenty-six with her first historical romance. She wrote seven romance novels during the 1970s and 80s, all of which were bestsellers, selling over eleven million copies. She is a winner of the Reviewer's Choice Award for Best Historical Romance Author. Laurie now resides in Northern California.